KU-151-341

Love on the Rocks

Also by Anne Christie

My Secret Gorilla
First Act
An Honest Woman
A Time to Weep
Growing Wings

Love on the Rocks

Anne Christie

'The Last Lauch' by Douglas Young is reprinted by kind permission of Douglas Young's estate and Penguin Books.

First published in Great Britain in 2003 by
Judy Piatkus (Publishers) Ltd of
5 Windmill Street, London W1T 2JA
email:info@piatkus.co.uk

The moral right of the author has been asserted

A catalogue record for this book is available from the British Library

ISBN 0 7499 0666 9

Set in Times by
Action Publishing Technology Ltd, Gloucester

Printed and bound in Great Britain by
Butler and Tanner, Frome

For David and Jennie Erdal: thanks for the Iona idylls

Chapter One

It took Maggie about five minutes to go up one side and down the other of the highest and craggiest rock on the beach near her house. She tried religiously to climb it every other day; there were always a few seconds of nervousness as she felt for footholds in the sandstone and tried not to look the fifty feet down to the incoming tide or the rocks below, but today she was at the top and the view was amazing. On the cliff path opposite, a young couple with a baby in a back pack waved to her as her mobile rang.

'Hello there, it's Niall. Just to say I should be with you between half-twelve and one tomorrow. How's the weather?'

'Great. Bring your swimmers!'

'No bloody fear, we've just been to Corfu.'

Thank you and goodbye for that, thought Maggie, and I'm sure Katy looks marvellous in a fairisle bathing dress.

'But I'll bring two dozen oysters.' Niall sounded remarkably cheery.

'I look forward to that.'

She locked the mobile and turned to scramble down the rock. On the beach she met a grey-haired man with a labrador.

He grinned at her 'What a beautiful braw day it is.'

'What a place, eh?' Maggie smiled back.

'It's marvellous!' he called out, euphoric, as the dog tugged him past.

Maggie rested for a few minutes on a grassy tussock above the beach, admiring the landscape with the blue pyramid of North Berwick Law and the chunky rocky Bass Rock (which had always looked to her like a giant elephant knee-deep in water) ten miles away across the Firth of Forth. Nearby, the village of Inverie with its red-roofed cottages and the old kirk, its conical spire set on a square stone tower, glittered in the brightness.

Euphoric, Maggie unscrewed her thermos and took a swig of coffee. She could barely believe that she had a whole year of this ahead of her; but it certainly made a change from crawling through London traffic-jams and screaming at her pupils in the Northolt Secondary Art Department three days a week. She'd taken early retirement and rented out her London flat till next summer to give her time to decide whether to live here in Scotland or to stay in London.

Often, when she looked at the view from here back towards the village, Maggie would have an image of her watchful mother, smoking, leaning on the sea wall of what was now her brother Donnie's place, or she would half remember herself and her brothers playing in the rock-pools, or running along the cliff path to the old ruined castle. Sometimes it was almost like seeing her own ghost; it was hard to believe it was all so long ago. As Niall used to mutter, 'Alas, it was in another country and they're all dead.'

Niall. What Maggie jokingly referred to as her married lover's 'seasonal visit' was tomorrow and she had things to do before he arrived. Opening her woven African bag, she eyed today's loot. Not bad pickings; she discarded two bits of wood for being too far gone and wormy even for her chicly distressed artistic creations, but there were a couple of good pieces of battered copper tubing and a pair of old pipe stems, which would be useful for making necklaces. For her year by the sea she had decided not to paint her usual exuberant landscapes, but to make assemblages from her beachcombings, and necklaces which looked like shaman's decorations, that she hoped to sell to a gallery in London where they'd already admired a couple she'd made for herself.

In her workroom at the top of the hill which overlooked the thirteenth-century church, Karin moved aside from the rug she was weaving to admire the day's perfection. Seeing her niece walking along the shore, she frowned. Maggie was wearing those purple shorts again, and Karin wished she wouldn't, she was too large for such an outfit, and it wasn't really dignified at her age – she was fifty-eight after all. Karin always worried about Maggie, the way she hurled herself at the rocks and insisted on climbing up to the top of the biggest ones. It was her form of exercise, Maggie would say cheerfully, much better than her London gym – a natural organic exercise instead of swimming in a yuppy-filled pool to piped music for fifty pounds a month. Maggie certainly seemed content to have come back here to live in the village for a year but it was early days; the winter grimness was still to come and inevitably she would find it physically harder than city life. Karin remembered how happy the young family had been when they first went to live down south almost thirty years ago.

'It's like living abroad, it's ten degrees warmer all the time. I could never live in Scotland again,' Maggie had said, and she'd even flirted, after her husband had died so tragically young, with going further south to live in France, where she'd spent several summers painting.

In Karin's kitchen a timer pinged, and she went through to stir the huge copper pot which steamed on the cooker. The dye she was making from local lichens needed to boil for longer. She put on the kettle and made real coffee which she drank at the studio window, gazing out at the view. The May Island, eight miles away, stood out clearly today. You could make out the steep cliffs and the white lighthouse and it was easy to imagine the thousands of birds – fulmars, puffins, gulls and terns – that lived on the mile-long island, whirling about in intersecting, but never colliding, circles. There were half a dozen fishing boats working offshore, which reminded her that she'd better collect the two crabs she had ordered from Bessie Fyall. She wanted to prepare them before going over to Patrick's.

The cauldron in the kitchen boiled over, filling the cooker top with deep blue colour. As the phone shrilled, Karin, with incredible speed for one of such dignified appearance, moved to answer it and simultaneously mopped and turned down the heat. It was Patrick. He sounded tired: it was his National Trust committee day, which inevitably either wearied or aerated him. He was just checking, what time to expect her, and did she really only want potatoes and salad prepared? Yes, Karin assured him, and she would bring the dressing this time. Patrick had become lazy since his wife's death and too often succumbed to only having tomato ketchup or Heinz mayonnaise in his kitchen, both of which Karin refused to eat. She didn't mind occasionally cooking for him, but liked to involve him too; it was good to get him going. A retired professor of architectural history, Patrick did little writing these days, instead, he spent a lot of time daydreaming, reading and rereading the *Scotsman*, and when alone he proudly survived almost entirely on boiled eggs, two of which he ate for every meal.

'I'll come before six,' she said, 'so we can eat and go to the concert in time.'

'Excellent, I've got a very lovely wine for us, cooling in the fridge. A white Burgundy. I'm looking forward to the partans, my dear.'

Karin put down the phone; and went back into the kitchen to test the strength of her blue dye, which had now reduced to a good strong colour. Pleased, she turned off the flame and looked at her watch, noting as she did, how ugly her hands looked, with their thickened, arthritic joints; but at least she could still manage her weaving, and the daily twenty-minute discipline of yoga certainly helped to keep the stiffness at bay.

Fife, the Scottish county which is shaped like the right-facing profile of a scottie dog's head facing the sea, is set between the estuaries of the rivers Forth and Tay, and can be reached from Edinburgh, Scotland's capital city, by crossing northwards on the Forth Road bridge. The East Neuk lies on Fife's north-east coast, where the River Forth begins to open out towards the North Sea. 'Neuk' is an old Lallans word for 'corner'. All the East Neuk villages – Earlsferry, Elie, Inverie, St Monans, Pittenweem, Anstruther, Cellardyke, Crail – and finally St Andrews – have ancient, well maintained stone-built harbours, and the houses which encircle the harbours are generally built of sandstone, often harled (pebble-dashed) and painted white, though that can vary, and typically have orange pantiled roofs with crowsteps on the gable ends. St Andrews is placed more or less where the scottie dog's eye would be, and Inverie by its mouth. Maggie was born in the East Neuk, just up the road in St Andrews, and sometimes she wondered if that was why she was so illogically attached to this rocky, unfriendly and often chilly corner of Scotland. From London it took a good eight or nine hours driving in her little French car. If you wanted to go into Edinburgh it could take an hour and a half. In the past she thought nothing of driving through to the Festival to see a show or two, and coming back late at night high on a culture jag, but these days she avoided the journey, preferring instead to walk along the foreshore or clamber on the rocks.

On the beach Maggie gathered up her bag of flotsam and jetsam and headed for home. Niall had said he'd arrive at lunchtime tomorrow, so there was no rush. This was how she wanted her life to be from now on: no more teaching, no more money worries. A peaceful life. The London place was rented out, and her son and daughter were pretty independent, happily living with people they loved, Sophie in

Edinburgh, Mark in Australia. For all their faults, Maggie and Fergal had at least given their children the legacy of love. Was it possible that she'd now at last reached a plateau, a proper, solid continuing plateau, and could truly relax, or was it all too good to be true? Last time she'd felt like this, Fergal had suddenly died of a heart attack and her mother had become terminally ill, since when Maggie had found it hard to have much faith in the future.

Back in her cottage, she picked up a towel and opened up a pack of hair dye. The red dye was a recent venture; last time she'd used it her London friend Felicity, a close friend since childhood, now a lapsing actress of great experience and talent, had unkindly declared that she looked like a Madame. The deed done, she put the timer on for twenty minutes and reluctantly heaved out the vacuum cleaner. She loathed housework, but it was worth the pain; the tiny cottage which was to be home for a whole year was heavenly when tidy.

Maggie coiled up the Hoover flex and put away the machine and went to wash off the red dye as the pinger pinged. She was startled when she peered in the mirror minutes later, to see that both her hair and the terracotta towel were exactly the same colour. Hopefully it would look better when she'd put a face on, a bit of lipstick and eyeliner. OK, so maybe she did look like a Madame, but a high-class one, surely? At least it covered the grey, but sadly, it didn't really make her look any younger or thinner.

She went outside again, and her neighbour, Gilbert Menstrie, who lived in the corner house next to the sea, muttered a greeting as he walked past, then did a double-take on her new appearance, which almost made him trip over. A tall, skinny man with thin, straight hair which he almost certainly Brylcreemed, Gilbert was not one of Maggie's favourites. He'd been born in that same house where he lived with his ancient mother, Effie, who still cooked for him and did all his washing. When Maggie and her brothers used to play on the beach, Gilbert, pale-faced with mean little eyes like raisins in a rock bun, used to watch them from the window. He'd always been a know-all, and would stand by when the other children made boats or caught crabs and advise them how to do it, or drive them mad by reeling off his encyclopaedic knowledge of instantly forgettable facts – the times and heights of the tides, the makes of buses or trains – or he'd ask deeply personal questions about their parents. How old was their Dad? Did their Danish mother speak German and what did she do in the war? One day he and Maggie's big brother Alistair had had a fight and Gilbert's glasses were broken (Alistair's were permanently held together with sticking plaster) and Mrs Menstrie and Maggie's mother, Astrid, had had a set-to. The battle had ended dramatically with Gilbert's mother shouting 'Your bairns are that wild and talk terrible nonsense. I am no letting my Gilbert anywhere near them!'

'I shall tell them that,' said Astrid calmly. 'They will be very pleased to hear it, and so am I.'

Mrs Menstrie had gasped at her rudeness, and slammed her door in Astrid's face. Maggie remembered finding her mother in the kitchen, pouring herself a sherry. She was shaking. 'I don't like to hate people,' she explained.

Poor Gilbert. Maggie watched his tall, skinny figure as he walked to his house. He was almost certainly still a virgin: the huge model train set in his spare bedroom was probably his only pleasure these days, and he'd soon have more time to play with it when he retired from his position as a local planning officer.

Was it not bliss, Maggie now mused smugly as her hair dried, to sit out here on her front step eating a bacon and egg roll, reading the paper and nodding occasionally to passers-by? Although there were few enough residents living opposite the old kirk, it was surprisingly busy throughout the day. There was always the postie, and nearly every day at least one of the houses had a visit from a workman of some sort – a joiner, plumber, painter, builder, gardener or window-cleaner, a parcel delivery, or a man in a van who'd come to examine the water main. And once a week the motley trio of rubbish men (one baldie, one tartan tammy, one flourescent baseball cap) would appear. When the churchyard was mown once a week in summer, Maggie nearly went daft with the noise. The air was often filled with the racket of diggers, tractors or seagulls, but the constant goings-on were also part of what she enjoyed about the place.

Tourists (nowadays often Spanish or Italian) were more frequent in this part of Scotland than they used to be, and all year round, oblivious to the weather, there were the walkers doing the Fife coastal walk. They'd march past, booted and haversacked, kitted out with binoculars, cameras and maps, and at least twice a day in summer, there were the motorists who would drive down the fifty meters of hill only to discover with annoyance that it petered out into the sea. Inevitably, they'd reverse back up the hill in disgust as fast as they could. Maggie was always tempted to shout at them that they had missed themselves and had, without realising, just passed by and rejected the East Neuk of Paradise.

There was a stone shelf in front of the cottage, about two feet wide, built originally for fisherman's tackle, where Maggie liked to lay shells, stones or bits of driftwood from the beach. They looked good against the pink walls, but she'd learned never to leave out anything that she liked, for the kids would always destroy it. Local children usually, they'd gleefully throw gravel from Gilbert Menstrie's immaculately joyless strip of grey stones, and shred Maggie's precious crabshells and scallops. Later, when they came out on the hunt for further mischief, if they saw her sitting out reading or eating supper, they'd smile and say with great innocence, of the few remnants they didn't wreck, 'I like all your crab shells, they're lovely.'

A particular quietness sometimes arrived at this time of

year (it was almost mid-summer); when the tide was full a breathless peace would settle, broken only by the chitterings of birds in the bushes and trees of the Burnside gardens and the louder screeches of seagulls. The little burn, which ran between Maggie's house and the church, added to the atmosphere with a constant tinkling.

What was now her brother Donnie's cottage, about seventy paces from where she was now sitting, had a twenty-foot-high stone wall rising straight up from the stony shore. In winter their mother used to put up wooden shutters against the worst storms, and more than once they'd found a rock as big as a coconut, hurled up by the sea, sitting on the storm-swept grass. When Maggie and the boys were young and spent their summer holidays at Inverie, the three of them used to sleep in a lean-to shed next to the sea wall. At night, the lighthouse signals flashed on and off and the deep notes of the foghorns on murky nights would reverberate through the children's sunburnt, sandy bodies. The shed had long since gone and been replaced with a huge picture window facing south. Standing there, with an unimpeded view of passing oil tankers, sailing boats, cargo ships, tall sailing ships, trawlers, the new big ferry bound for Germany, local fishing boats and small fishermen's craft, you could easily imagine yourself on the bridge of a ship. You could watch eider duck, gannets, herring gulls, an occasional porpoise or seal, a fulmar or a heron, still as a stone, always standing alone. And any day you could see the cormorants which posed almost comically with their wings splayed out to dry. Sometimes on the big white rock, which filled the right horizon, the birds huddled so thickly that you could mistake them from a distance for some surreal black vegetation.

All day long the dog-walkers passed by Maggie's cottage. She was gradually getting to know them by sight and say hello, to comment on the weather, the coldness or the beauty. Occasionally, a dog would stop inquiringly to sniff, or make to enter the house; others would disdain anything but the walk to come and bound towards the beach.

A few years ago, Maggie had inadvertently developed a relationship with a squat dog called Rambo, a bull terrier (crossed perhaps with a dachshund) who looked like a black leather barrel on four-inch legs. She'd often noticed the animal around the village where he ran wild, seemingly ownerless, but on this particular occasion she had been horrified to find him in her bedroom. Her brother Donnie had just got married for the second time, and he and his wife Morag had asked her to look after their amiable and generously proportioned golden retriever, Kellie, who happened to be on heat. 'On no account must she get preggers, Maggie,' the newly weds had warned as they drove off, tin cans clanking and confetti flying.

Maggie had gone for a walk with a friend to try and clear away the champagne fumes. Progress through the village would have been impossible with Kellie in season; inevitably she would have ended up looking like a canine version of one of those plump, jolly, half-naked Chinese gods of happiness who are almost smothered in babies (though in Kellie's case it would have been Jack Russell, Yorkie or Border terrier pups), so they'd left her locked up at home. But when they got back to the cottage, Maggie was dismayed to hear loud barking from inside. Running in, she was appalled to find Rambo (who would normally only have reached to Kellie's navel) lurching about on his back legs but obviously finding it hard to maintain his balance. The poor dog – demonstrably highly excited – was doing a sort of courtship *danse engorgée* as he leaped repeatedly, aiming for poor Kellie's trembling rear. Both creatures were barking hysterically and Maggie was livid. On no account must the honeymooning pair return to a litter of little black tubs. Rushing to the hallway, she picked up a giant welly boot with which she cruelly proceeded to belabour the barrel's rump while she shouted at him, threatening him with the extremes of violence until at last he desisted from his love leaps. Despite his look of disbelief at her cruelty, to assure him that enough was enough, Maggie belted him again several times as hard as she could with the welly boot and he retreated, sledging downstairs backwards, but on his front, which was fortunate for him considering his state of excitement. At the bottom of the stairs he turned to her with a last anguished look, before projecting himself through the cat flap in the closed front door – or such was his intention. In fact the white frame of the cat-flap came loose with the impact and he went racing off through the village sporting it like a square tutu. The funny thing was that after this, whenever Maggie met with Rambo in the village, or when his ageing owner took him for a bi-annual walk past her cottage, the burly black dog (long since free of the cat flap) would greet her like a long-lost lover. Barking excitedly, tail whirling, he'd bound up to his ex-torturer, exuding doggy friendship and devotion, and leap to lick her hands – which were almost too high for him to reach.

'He certainly seems to like you a lot,' his owner would mutter, impressed. Little did he know how the poor creature's psyche had been traumatised by the post-wedding experience in Maggie's bedroom. Maggie reckoned that the combination of black rubber, violence and procreative passion must have compounded to make the merest sniff or sight of her remind Rambo of the erotic excitement of her brother's wedding day. It was simple psychology really: was this not how neurotic behaviour in humans developed, when early experiences of sex, violence and affection become confused in the memory bank and create pathological and often conflicting impulses?

She loved the way the summers here were punctuated with calls as well as passers-by. 'Come and see, there's a seal in the bay! Look, dolphins! The eider ducks are back, the swans are here again. There's a puffin out there – I've never seen one so far from the May!' Or, exasperated,

'Ryan! Get out of that watter this minute I'm warnin' ye! I'm no tellin' you again!' or: 'Craig! Throw stones at the water, not AT PEOPLE!'

Today, her neighbour on the right had the electrician's van outside her front door. On the left, Gilbert Menstrie was supervising the installation of what looked like barbed wire on his garden wall. On her doorstep, Maggie, smiling, wiped yolk off her chin. She must remember to cook the egg for longer, next time. She watched as a red van drew up in front of her, and a tall, handsome plumber emerged, come to give her a price for plumbing in a washing machine.

'The East Neuk,' he said, grinning widely when she told him she'd come to live here for a year. 'It's an awfy place. Folk dinnae ken, they have nae idea. I tell you it's all wife-swapping and folk running away frae hame.'

Intrigued, Maggie decided to offer him a cup of herbal tea (the plumber's wife was a fully qualified aromatherapist and Reiki healer) in the hope that he would tell her more.

Chapter Two

A couple of miles away, in the rich Tuscan-red drawing-room of his sixteenth-century stone house, gracefully overlooking the wide sandy bay and harbour of Elie, Patrick Maitland (or Sir Patrick, as he had only recently become for services to architectural preservation) put down the phone. He was glad Karin was coming this evening; he hadn't seen her for several weeks since before her last trip to Denmark and he'd missed her – and if he were honest – her cooking, and all those little things she often so sweetly helped him with. She'd spent their last shared evening mending a couple of his favourite old shirts and darning his kilt stockings – and that was on top of hostessing a lunch party for six he'd felt bound to give in return for hospitalities received. She was a darling, always had been.

He tapped the barometer and smiled. It was going to keep fair; good fishing weather for tomorrow if his damned hip would allow him; it had been bad this week, but he dreaded having another replacement. Lord, this old age lark was certainly not for cissies, and it obviously wasn't going to get any easier. Maybe a wee nip would help, but he was already a trifle sleepy from the morning's meeting in Cupar, which had turned out to be an endless argument about plastic fascia, double glazing and planning permission for a huge new hypermarket on the outskirts of Upper Largo with that dreadful neighbour of Karin and Maggie's,

Gilbert Menstrie, who almost always made Patrick feel uncharacteristically apoplectic with his complete lack of aesthetic or common sense. A madness. Patrick was determined to oppose the hypermarket proposal till he expired, which – he smiled wryly – might not be so far distant, the way his old bones were feeling this afternoon.

His hand was already reaching for the bottle of malt. Maybe just a soupçon would help him relax before Karin arrived, and a little lie down would be more than acceptable, but first he must remember to set the table and prepare the salad. A power nap, that was the thing. He stood in the big window, small-paned, with stripped, polished pine shutters. There were quite a few boats out there today, and half a dozen windsurfers; he enjoyed watching the antics of the younger surfers and the jolly colours of their sails. Up to the bedroom with its subtle grey-blue walls and intricate plasterwork ceiling of twining leaves. Oh Lord, he'd left the place in a mess with that early start, with all those old *Scotsman* newspapers and underwear all over the place, and his pyjamas frankly looked a bit beyond repair, maybe not even Karin could salvage them. Perhaps he'd better throw them out; he could swear he'd had them even before Margot died and that was long enough ago.

Groaning, he harvested the clutter and sorted the papers into a presentable heap. He was delighted to find the book on Cistercian abbeys he thought he'd lost. And his pipe – that really pleased him, he was sure it had gone for good, fallen in the river or something. How about the sheets? He appraised them wearily; they weren't too good really, not exactly inviting. Had he the strength? He shook his head, no, he hadn't. He'd put on nice new pillowcases and shake the duvet, which should improve matters. Anyway, he didn't really imagine that it was going to happen at last, did he? Not after all this time, after all those years of yearning for her, when he was certain she'd felt the same way. They had after all both confessed it in Edinburgh that foggy night so long ago, when Andrew was away. Memories of that epiphany had secretly comforted Patrick for decades. How strange it was that now, half a lifetime later, when they were both 'free', with their mutual spouses both long gone, that they hadn't simply set up house with each other, but somehow it wasn't so simple. At times it seemed as though both their partners were still there. God knows he still missed his old friend Andrew almost as much as he did his wife, Margot, and he knew that Karin missed her friendship with Margot sometimes almost as much as she missed her husband. Their absence was a presence of sorts, but an inhibiting presence. It was bizarre. Still, he was longing to see the old girl.

Sighing, Patrick closed the heavy velvet curtains, knocked back his whisky, loosened his tweedy tie and slipped off his brogues. He supposed he'd better take the kilt off too, it didn't really do to sleep in it. And he must remember to do those pillowcases later – just in case.

Fifty years ago, when Maggie and her brothers used to spend their summer holidays in what was now her brother Donnie's house on the sea wall, the village had been very different. The fishing industry was still alive then and there had been a good forty fishing boats regularly using the harbour. There had also been at least four boatbuilding sheds. The one nearest to them was at the west end of the village hard by the harbour – their youthful paradise and playground – which was the very heart of the village. Best of all the things they occupied themselves with, Maggie loved to go fishing with her brothers. They'd set off laden with a net and fishing line each and a bucket. The boys also had both pocket and sheath knives as part of their artillery, which their sister greatly envied, but she had to wait several years before she was allowed to buy one for herself.

If they had any pocket money between them they'd stop off to buy crisps and lemonade from one of the two ancient sisters who ran the bakery opposite the pub. The sisters, tall, white-haired and bony, had pale blue eyes and ran their tiny shop in a converted front room, which had a window set with small square panes. The sisters' bakehouse was a separate sandstone building with a huge oven in the back garden, and the quiet-spoken old ladies wore white aprons and had their hair tied back in buns. The crisps were Smiths and had little blue paper screws of salt in them; sometimes you were given two screws and sometimes only one. Once, when Maggie had none, Alistair had demanded a payment of crisps in return for salt, which had made the wee girl sulk. In the end she was saved from this fraternal coercion by Donnie, the classic middle child, his loyalties always divided between his big brother and kid sister. Fortuitously, Donnie had three little blue parcels of salt that day, and was soft-hearted enough to give Maggie one of them. The three of them would always share the big bottle of lemonade, which grew steadily warmer during the day; they'd watch avidly when anyone had a slurp, marking exactly how far they were allowed to go down. If you stopped too suddenly, the lemonade bubbles would spurt up your nose and make the other two howl with outrage.

Once they'd stocked up at the bakery, they always paused at Reekie's boatyard, a big wooden shed hard by their end of the harbour, where they liked to talk to the men and watch them work. The harmony in the subtle lines and curves of the emergent boat was echoed in the skilful teamwork of the carpenters who worked on plank walkways, adzing, caulking, cutting, measuring, hammering, inserting planks of pine and oak. In those days, there was a constant background tympani of hammering, a noise that you were half-aware of – along with the calls of seabirds – whenever you went anywhere near the harbour. At nine, Maggie fell in love with a fair-haired boatbuilder called Andy Johnstone. She thought him clever, handsome and funny, and for days treasured a pan drop he'd given her till it grew sticky in her shorts pocket. To her dismay, when she tried to clean it up, carefully picking off its dusty accumulation of tiny fossils, string and shards of crabshell, and laid it reverently on the window sill by her bed, Alistair found it, and jeering, flung it over the sea wall in disgust.

Her brothers would conduct long technical discussions with the boatbuilders – who were always kind and joked with them – leaving Maggie to daydream, enthralled by the drama of the place. Lovestruck, she'd watch her hero Andy climb up ladders and walk perilously along the plank walkways which ran alongside the huge wooden ribs that made up the skeleton of the new fishing boat. The team had a concentration and alertness as they worked, a harmonious rhythm which, along with the strong, subtle curves of the wood, even as a child she found mesmerically beautiful. Under the raised belly of the majestic artefact the ground was soft, and Maggie could still remember the feel of the sawdust and woodshavings on her bare feet and the almost overwhelming smells of wood, tar and paint.

'Och, ye're an awfy lassie, have you no shoes to wear?' Andy would ask, which would make her giggle and look away, embarrassed.

On Saturday nights in summer if it was fine, there would usually be a 'Go As You Please' on the west quay of the harbour near the boathouse. People of all ages would come to dance and party. The children loved being allowed to stay up for these; there was always much laughter and singsong and for Maggie the thrill of seeing her brother and her hero play the accordian. Sometimes everybody sang along to Andy and Alistair's accordian-playing. Maggie was secretly proud of her entertaining big brother Alistair, redheaded, bespectacled, a hippy predestined, who even as a youngster managed to get people singing and jigging. The moon and stars and street lights danced, reflected on the black oily water of the harbour, and the silhouettes of the fishing boats creaked alongside the jetty, swaying up and down in the breathing of the tide. There was much communal singing; everybody joined in, young and old. 'Are ye no singing as well?' Andy would ask and Maggie would shake her head shyly. She didn't dare. Her brothers had too frequently and viciously declared her to be totally tone-deaf, though secretly she loved singing with other people more than almost anything. When she felt sleepy, she'd go and lie down, cradled on a heap of netting. Here she'd doze happily, aware of the beat of the music, tarry, fishy smells, and the rough comforting texture of the nets.

In the daytime, you could always find men and women sitting by the harbour on a bollard or a wooden fishbox, chatting, stolidly checking and repairing the heaped brown nets.

'Ye could walk across the harbour on boats when I was a youngster,' a retired fisherman had told Maggie some years ago. 'It was jam-packed, there was a big forest of masts.'

It sounded wonderful, but to herself and her brothers as children it was perfect as it was. Even now, half a century later, with most of the boats gone and the boatyards long since demolished or gauntly empty, she still found the harbour a place of beauty.

Before they started to fish they'd gather limpets for bait, knocking them off the rocks. 'Do it quietly and quickly,' Donnie would explain, 'otherwise they'll grip on too hard and won't budge.'

Alistair used to do an alarming comedy act with the limpets. He liked the big ones best. 'Look,' he'd announce, leering, and would display the flat fleshy interior of the conical shell. 'It's a lickle baby in a cradle.'

When he pushed in the limpet's flat muscular sucker (which to Maggie was obviously the baby's blanket) with his thumb, a little round head would appear, along with two swaying feelers that uncannily resembled a baby's bald head and uncoordinated hands. Maggie was simultaneously fascinated and repelled. A subliminal part of the fascination was that she'd once been Alistair's baby sister, and uneasily she sensed that his glee was somehow connected with this fact.

It was a long trek from the house to the far end of the harbour, and Maggie was always a little nervous of the last bit. To reach their fishing place on the far pier the children were forced to pass by an enormous black shed made of corrugated iron. This boatyard was an altogether bigger outfit than the one at their end of the village where the handsome Andy worked. It was much noisier, there were more men and larger projects so the joiners weren't always quite so chatty, but the wooden skeletons of the boats being built were just as fascinating. Immediately past this black barn was a bench where half a dozen retired fishermen always sat. They wore darned navy-blue jerseys, heavy black trousers, an occasional peaked cap, and most of them had white stubbly chins or tobacco-yellow moustaches and carried walking-sticks. To Maggie they all looked old and scary in a witchy sort of way, and their thick dialect was hard to understand, so she was never quite certain how to respond to their greetings, but what was really frightening was that nearly every one of the old men seemed to be missing some body part – an eye, a finger, an arm or a leg. The boys used to wonder why they were always out there, even in cold grey weather, and Alistair would imitate their wives shooing the men out with a broom, saying, 'Dinnae come back till yer dinner's ready, git oot the hoose and give me some peace and quiet for a change!'

He also had a funny story based on the old men sitting on the bench. One day, he told them, a pretty girl walked past three of them and the first old man said, 'Och, I'd like fine tae give her a kiss.' 'Aye, I'd like fine tae give her a cuddle', murmured old man number two (vividly enacted by Alistair, who would wink one eye horribly). After a long pause, the third old man would croak dubiously, 'And what was yon other thing we used tae do wi' them?'

At the end of this joke the boys would have wild hysterics and, desperate not to be excluded, Maggie would join in, but she had absolutely no idea what they were laughing at.

After running the gauntlet of the old men and along the big stone flagstones to the end of the pier, the boys would give Maggie a hand up and over the rusty iron rungs of a ladder set into the high wall at the end of the harbour. On the far pier the water never fully disappeared even with the lowest tide, so it was excellent for what Alistair called their piscatorial purposes.

Donnie showed Maggie how to gouge out the limpet flesh from its cradle and fit it on to a hook. Their mother was forever warning them to be careful with hooks; every week they seemed to meet some crying child whose finger had been caught on one. These accidents always uncomfortably reminded Maggie of the old one-eyed man. At last, her line baited, she would drop it, hook, line and round lead sinker, down the seaweedy stone wall, deep into the water, and patiently wait for the glorious tug which meant a catch. When she did hook a really big crab (she never once caught a fish) and manage to tease it up and out of the water on to the pier, Maggie was euphoric. They all cheered each other's catches, and then, fearful of the wicked nip she knew from bloody experience even a tiny crab could give, she would lift up the bubbling creature, carefully holding it behind its claws and put it into the communal bucket they'd furnished with salt water and an assortment of seaweed. The joy of the hunt was obsessive and exciting. Remembering, Maggie was reluctantly forced to acknowledge that never for a moment had she empathised with either the poor crabs or limpets.

Across the sea from the harbour they could see the octagonal stone spire of the old kirk and the house. When lunch or supper was ready, their mother would drape a white sheet over the sea wall to summon them. Maggie never actually caught her mother hanging out the sheet, but always felt oddly comforted by this personal family semaphore. One day, when they had stayed extra late, Mum was obviously exasperated, because two sheets were hung out, which made it seem like a shout rather than a friendly call.

The boys would proudly carry the bucket of crabs and little fish, and stagger home with half the water spilt. Usually they kept their prisoners overnight, or until their soft-hearted mother, unable to stand it any longer, would persuade them to let the poor creatures go. Freed, the crabs would teeter for a moment on the rock, blow a few bubbles, then skitter off sideways into the water and disappear. Maggie used to wonder what they'd tell their pals.

One night as she lay near the boys in the wooden shack by the sea wall, lit every minute or two by the regular beam of the May Island lighthouse, Maggie heard the boys talking about the village mottoes.

'In the church is carved *mare vivimus*,' said Donnie. 'What does it mean?'

'From the sea we live,' translated Alistair, adding that the meaning was obvious in this particular village.

Maggie wanted to know about the village's other, older motto, 'Grip hard'. 'Grip what hard?' she asked.

'It's what the sailors had to do, you clot,' said Alistair. 'Grip hard to survive. Grip hard to tiller, rope or hand, otherwise they'd be dead.'

She nodded sleepily and was reminded of the old sailor who only had one eye. Maybe he'd not gripped hard enough, or was his terrible cavity caused by a huge fish hook going astray?

It was a *coup de foudre*, seeing the little cottage for the first time ten years ago. Maggie had come up for a few days' holiday, and Morag, her future sister-in-law, knew that it was for sale and where to borrow the key, so they found themselves inside the place within the hour. It had changed since Jock the gravedigger – who had married Jemima when he was over eighty and she a mere lassie of fifty-two – had lived here.

'Jock's an awfy strong man. Awfy healthy,' Jemima had unexpectedly informed them one summer when Maggie and Morag stopped to admire her spouse's glowing dahlias and

giant leeks. Jemima had also proudly invited them to come inside to see her cottage and Maggie remembered that in the main room downstairs there had been some kind of a partition at the back of the room which was the original box bed. Box beds, once commonplace in the fishing villages, were wooden beds built in against a wall with one side open that was curtained off in winter for both privacy and warmth. They must have been very cosy. But when Maggie and Morag got inside this time the box bed had long gone. As for the exterior of the place, Maggie hated it. The cottage – one of three in a terrace – had a thick layer of concrete covering the original sandstone, which some tasteless builder had sculpted into pretend masonry which was now peeling badly. The front door too was nasty, with frosted glass so ugly that Maggie shivered. Worse still, its pea-green enamel paint was unhealthily blistered; it was definitely unliveable with. Both women shook their heads at the intimidating amount of work to be done.

Inside, the two-roomed cottage was painted white and the ancient beams which ran from the back to the front of the room, were uneven, badly woodwormed, but full of character. The downstairs room was a good size, almost four meters square, and had a small window with a kitchen sink underneath which looked across to the church. It was quite dark, and there was a hideous beige plastic sofa which seemed to fill the room – but she'd soon get rid of that. The doors were all faced with hardboard painted with slimy enamel white, alas, no lovely old pine delights. Morag went into the main room, lay back on the sofa, and Kellie, the golden retriever, tongue lolling, jumped up beside her. 'It's an awful mess, isn't it?' said Morag dubiously.

Maggie frowned in agreement and looked round the back of the room and then she saw it. There was a solid piece of rock – black whin that you found everywhere here – jutting up in the corner straight through the wooden floor. It was about two feet square and flat-topped, big enough to sit on, with the floorboards carefully cut to shape round it. It would be her very own, built-in portion of native land and here it was right inside the house. Bewitched, she went very quiet and climbed the wide, curving wooden stairs to explore upstairs. Kellie followed and barked when they peered into the bedroom which was unexpectedly huge, but very dark.

'Rooflights. I'd need to put rooflights in the coombe,' Maggie murmured. 'Then I'd have a work end, light enough for painting.'

Morag had managed to heave open the rusted window hinge and was hanging out. 'There's a really good view of the sea,' she called. Kellie barked again, and they gazed out together at the church, the rocks, the sea, the birds and one black fishing boat thrusting through the waves. It was sublime.

The bathroom was a decent size, and well lit, with the same view of the kirk, the kirkyard and the neighbour's gardens. The floor tiles were cracked and brittle and the wooden bath panels black and rotted. The lavatory worked OK, as did the various taps; she'd simply need to use some paint and find a decent wooden loo seat. Next door on the landing was a big cupboard with an ancient copper tank and a good set of hooks for hanging clothes.

Morag rolled her eyes, 'A built-in wardrobe. What more could a girl want?'

Maggie nodded. She'd already decided, but hardly dared voice her thoughts. 'Let's look at the garden.'

Like the house, the overgrown garden at the back was unexpectedly generous and faced west, slanting upwards to a twenty-five-foot-high wall of black rock like the one inside, and topped with a man-made sandstone wall which enclosed a neighbouring garden. From here they could even glimpse the sea. Maggie surged with excitement. Of course she had to have it.

Morag touched her arm. 'Maggie, are you OK?'

She nodded. 'If only I could find the money . . . when's the closing date?'

'Quite soon, I think, the end of the month.'

'I don't know what to do. I have absolutely no spare cash.'

'But you're definitely going to sell your London house and buy a smaller one soon, aren't you?'

By that time the London property boom was well under way and a year ago the London family house had increased by three times what Maggie and Fergal had paid for it only five years earlier. But the market was tricky; selling could take months, a year even.

'But you'll get a lot, won't you?'

'Eventually, but how to fill the gap? I already have a massive mortgage.'

They walked back to Donnie and Morag's place and Maggie stood by the sea wall imagining the wee cottage with her kelims and furniture in it. The bedroom would be fantastic with new windows in the roof. She didn't notice the seagulls screaming or the rain until she was quite soaked.

Morag was at her elbow with a mug of tea. 'Donnie's put some whisky in it. Come inside.'

Maggie wandered in and sat by the kitchen table, her gaze far away as she pulled up manky carpets, cleaned and painted, bringing light and love to Jock Anderson's cottage. She heard her brother's voice saying, 'Oh Gawd, she's got it bad. It must be love.'

He toasted her with his chunky glass of home-brewed beer. 'Liked it, did you?'

Maggie sniffed, gulped the tea (she'd forgotten about the whisky). Smiled.

'Magic, eh?' Donnie clinked again.

'Maggie,' Morag came and sat down. 'Can't you just borrow the money for a few months? It sounds like you're worth a lot down there.'

'I wouldn't dare. We lost three buyers with our last London house. I'd just be too scared. It's a different sort of market down there, much more brutal. I couldn't take the risk. As things are we can barely afford to live.'

'Did you not have any insurance when Fergal died?'

'Exactly enough to pay for the funeral.'

'And Ma's money?'

'It bought me the car. Apart from that I am perpetually skint.'

'Maybe better forget about it then,' advised her brother. 'There'll be others. There's always something for sale round here.'

'But that one's special.'

He shrugged as though she were stupid. 'The whole place is special. It's not going to go away.'

Maggie felt dismissed. Sometimes you'd think Donnie was still with his regiment. She'd never understood him since he became a professional soldier, any more than she understood his passions for golf and cricket. He'd retired from the army a good while ago, but had remained military to his core, obsessive about his garden, obstinate in his opinions. Maggie and he usually failed to see eye to eye on almost anything.

Morag looked at her sister-in-law. 'Shall we take the dog for a walk?' she suggested diplomatically.

Maggie nodded and stood up, feeling helpless, and the golden retriever lumbered after them, blond plume of a tail swishing optimistically.

They walked down the road, past glowing patches of sea pinks and vivid orange marigolds, crossing the burn by the stone slab bridge towards the church and down to the stony beach. Eight miles away, the May Island looked at though it had been gilded.

'You'd be just round the corner,' said Morag. 'It would be lovely.'

'Donnie might not like it so much.' Maggie bent down to pick up a smooth round stone, dark red with a white spider shape in its middle.

'Yes, he would. He adores you.'

Maggie sighed. 'But we still bicker like kids; sometimes

I even think he minds when you and I go off places together.' Morag and Maggie had been close friends from schooldays, but Morag's falling in love with Maggie's brother had inevitably changed things.

'Och,' Morag frowned. 'Not really. Not seriously.'

They walked along the beach, Kellie lumbering a little unwillingly after them. When they were well along towards the ruins of the old castle, Morag let the dog off the leash and the bitch suddenly became alive and rushed away, heading back towards the village. Morag swore, and shouted after her: 'Kellie, come here now! KELLIE!' but the dog was already almost out of sight.

Morag was flaming. 'She always does that.' She started running and Maggie joined her. 'I'm sorry, but we'll have to get her – she's a terrible scavenger, she upsets all the bloody rubbish bins.'

They were both running now, up the stone steps built by old Jock Anderson when he wasn't gravedigging, and planted all over with nasturtiums, which were still flowering. They found themselves up on the cliff path, which was easier underfoot than the stony beach.

Morag was speaking breathlessly as she ran. 'That flaming dog. I'll kill her! She runs away and goes to the house belonging to the old ladies who live at the bottom of the hill leading into the village. She knocks the lids off the rubbish bins and eats all their chicken bones and God knows what, then the old ladies all come out and say "Oh poor, wee Kellie she must be starving, poor, wee soul, they don't look after her properly . . ." and they take her inside and feed her a saucer of sweet tea and empty their biscuit tin and Kellie comes home and is sick on the carpet and farts enough to blow the roof off . . . I'll fucking kill her!'

The two of them kept on running, half-giggling, yelling for Kellie till they were hoarse. At the end of the path they took a short cut through the churchyard because the tide was coming in, and there, right in front of them, lit by the evening sun, its windows glinting like fool's gold, was the little cottage that Maggie wanted. If only she could lay her hands on the money to buy it; but she was leaving the day after tomorrow and with her present financial commitments and a new school term starting almost immediately, she couldn't see any way round it.

Chapter Three

Today's hair did look a bit red. Maggie peered anxiously in the mirror and tried on a different pair of earrings. Maybe she should pop up the hill and find out what Karin thought; her aunt would surely advise her honestly.

Karin, elegant as ever in grey-blue linen shirt, black jeans and clogs, was shelling crabs in the garden. Her yoga mat was rolled up on the bench beside her; she must have been doing her daily stint out in the fresh air. She looked up to see Maggie.

'Hello, darling. Lovely to see you. Goodness, I like your hair!'

'Not too bright?'

'No, I think it's lovely, it suits your colouring.'

'That's a relief.' Maggie sat on the bench beside her aunt and looked at the shellfish. 'Super crabs, what are you going to do with them?'

'Eat them straight with boiled new potatoes and garlic and lemon salad. I'm having supper with Patrick.'

'Nice. How is he?'

'I haven't seen him since I got back. He sounds well.'

'He came for lunch to me about a month ago when Sophie and Michel were over. We got the feeling he was a bit lonely.'

Karin sighed. 'I'm afraid he is, and he's not managing as well as he did. He's really getting quite wobbly. I do worry about him.'

'He'll never move out of the big house, will he?'
'Never.'
'It must be hell to heat. I remember going to icy winter parties there when we were young. Margot used to hand out hairy jerseys at the door to keep us warm.'
Karin chuckled. 'I know. All those poor girls in long white net dresses topped with Aran sweaters and fisherman's polo-necks. But no, he'll never leave. He now really only lives in the two rooms; he's got a microwave in the drawing room.'
'I wonder what Aunt Margot would have said to that?'
Karin shrugged. 'Margot was practical; she would have thought it sad but sensible. Anyway, Maggie, how are you feeling about spending the whole year here?'
'Excited. Delighted. Life feels like one long holiday at the moment.'
'How's the family?'
'All fine, I think. Mark's still working in Sydney.'
'Do you think he'll try to visit his Uncle Alistair?'
'He'd like to, but Alistair's such a hermit. He discourages visitors, and I gather his place is pretty inaccessible.'
'Does he write to you still?'
'Sometimes. Weird cannabissed letters, close-typed reams of almost unreadable jokes.'
'Do you think he's still drinking?'
'He claims not. It's impossible to know.'
'And how's your eldest?'
'Sophie? She still seems miraculously happy with Michel.'
Karin smiled. 'That's wonderful. How are they managing financially?'
'He's teaching French by day, doing music at night. He works hard, too hard, I sometimes think, and Sophie's been working part-time in a clothes shop in Edinburgh.'
'How does she like that?'
'Not as much as singing with Scottish Opera.'
'I'm sure not. She was always so gifted. I'm so sorry she doesn't have more vocal work.'

'So's she.' Maggie sighed. 'The arts, it's madness. You should be glad your three have sensible professions.'

'Maybe. I'm not sure that any of mine were very artistic, much as I would have liked it.' Karin stood up, the bowl of crab flesh in hand. 'I must put this into the shells and be off.' She bent to kiss Maggie and patted the ginger hair. 'You look like your big brother with that colour.'

'Like Alistair?'

Karin nodded almost tearfully. Maggie was surprised. None of them had seen her wild, big brother for almost forty years.

'Goodbye, darling,' called Karin as Maggie walked back down the hill. Smiling to herself, Maggie mused on how fond she was of her Danish aunt. Since her own mother, Astrid, Karin's younger sister, had died, Karin had really taken her place. Maggie always enjoyed her company and loved doing things with her. But she could all too clearly remember that time when she'd been so very angry with Karin.

It was that day ten years ago, after Maggie and Morag had first come to view the little cottage.

After Maggie and Morag had rescued Kellie from her elderly lady Samaritans (who informed them with wonder that she'd finished a whole tin of freshly baked shortbread), they'd gone back to Donnie and Morag's place, where Maggie gloomed alone on the sea wall, obsessively yearning for the little cottage. Her favourite aunt was coming to lunch, and she was looking forward to seeing her. Widowed in her late fifties, Karin had created a new life for herself teaching weaving in Edinburgh. Her aunt had wonderful taste, and always wore striking clothes; Maggie remembered in particular a duffel jacket, originally of arctic naval-issue white, which Karin had creatively dyed a deep orange. Slender and unfailingly elegant, she'd worn it for years with the sleeves rolled up, tight black jeans (just like today's) and a black beret on her grey-blonde hair.

Maggie remembered feeling pleased when Karin suggested they take a walk on the rocks while the others prepared lunch. Donnie was cooking a salmon and needed to be alone for the militaristic precision that this required. It would be good to have Karin to herself for a while. Since she and Fergal had moved their family to London she'd seen too little of her.

The tide was out and they could wander quite far out on the rocks.

'What a beautiful place this is.' As her aunt gazed westwards to the ruins of the castle and the Lady's Tower beyond the beach at Elie, her long bony face beautifully lit against the dramatic background, Maggie took a picture of her which she still treasured.

'It's wonderful to be here. You can't imagine the contrast after London.'

'But you have a good life there, don't you?'

'Yes, I have very good friends, I like the house. The children are OK, except for missing their Dad . . .'

Karin gripped Maggie's arm. 'But that would be the same anywhere. I still miss Andrew, and it's already more than twenty-five years since he died.' Karin's intensity was a huge part of her Scandinavian charm.

They sighed mutual widows' sighs and walked on, constantly picking up stones, searching for fossils.

'Morag and I went to look at that little cottage opposite the old church today. It's for sale,' said Maggie.

'So I heard.'

There was a clippedness to Karin's voice which surprised Maggie; her aunt was usually fascinated by the old properties and any interesting bits and pieces which she occasionally presented her with. When Maggie and Fergal had still lived in Edinburgh, Karin often used to come junk-hunting. Maggie remembered wheeling a pramful of babies, almost obscured by a dozen old blue and white soup plates Karin had insisted she must have. They walked on. Her aunt's head was down and Maggie was aware of a chill. 'The wee cottage is amazing,' she ventured at last.

'Is it?' Her aunts' voice could not have been more curt.

'I'd really love to buy it,' Maggie added feebly. 'But I don't quite see how I can find the money in time.'

Karin stopped by a big rock and gestured imperiously. 'Sit down, Maggie,' she commanded. Puzzled, Maggie obeyed.

'I have to talk to you about this, Maggie.'

'About what?'

'This cottage. This house you want to buy. I really don't think you should do it.'

'Do what?'

'Buy it.'

Maggie shrugged, confused. 'At the moment it doesn't really look as though I can anyway, but I definitely would if I could.'

Looking stern and even more aristocratic than usual, her aunt shook her head. 'I have to tell you I *really* think it's a bad idea.'

'A bad idea?' Now Maggie was bewildered. 'But why? I've wanted a place here for ages.'

'I have to tell you I don't think it's a good idea for you to buy a place right here.'

'Why on earth not?'

'Because of Donnie.'

Because of her brother? This was nordic madness. Frowning, Maggie thought of Munch's *Scream* painting, which expressed exactly what she was feeling. Half the niceness of being here would be that proximity to Donnie and Morag. Donnie and Maggie might often bicker, but they were basically fond of each other.

'Karin, I don't understand what this is about. Please tell me what you mean.'

It was Maggie's brother's territory now, the older woman explained. Before his divorce he'd been so unhappy for years and their mother had only left him the cottage so that he had somewhere to go, it was a bolthole for him. He'd feel invaded by his sister buying a place only three houses away. 'And . . .' here she looked at Maggie particularly beadily, 'he is a very, very sensitive person.'

'What about me?' Maggie wanted to yell. 'I'm a bloody widow! I'm alone, I need that little place to keep me sane. My kids need it, they've lost their father and their darling grandmother and her place here, all at the same time – and see me, I am a very, very, very, sensitive person too!' But she just stared at her, then looked away to the sea, speechless with hurt. This woman to whom she was devoted, her surrogate mother, her artistic mentor, her treasured wise woman, had suddenly declared herself an enemy of sorts. Not only was it unfair but it was also completely unexpected.

'I'm sorry.' Half-heartedly, Karin patted Maggie's shoulder. 'But I felt it was important to tell you.'

Tell her? Warn her off, more like. Donnie's territory? Dammit! Maggie's children had been tragedy-struck that their grandmother's house had been left to Donnie so that they no longer had a toehold in the village. They – Maggie, Fergal and the children – had practically lived in that house for all their school holidays and when they were still based in Scotland they'd even spent a whole year living in the village. The children had both gone to school there (Donnie had been with his regiment in Ireland at the time). Inverie was Maggie's territory quite as much as her brother's, and if she humanly could, she was going to find a way to buy that cottage and share it with her children. She stared at her aunt nonplussed.

'He needs to feel secure,' explained Karin firmly.

Maggie blinked. Fucking secure? What about her, Maggie's needs? Her poor, fatherless children's needs? At least her brother had a new partner, but Maggie was alone and now Karin too seemed to be abandoning her.

Of course she was unable to voice any of it. She had a momentary fantasy of whirling the aunt, duffel coat and beret, over the rocks and feeding her to the seals and gannets. Instead, finding her words with difficulty (a lump in her throat was almost choking her) she murmured something polite about appreciating what Karin had said but not feeling sure that she could agree with her.

Maggie still remembered, a little bitterly, how at that point Karin had smiled her most winning smile and hugged her. 'I understand that, I didn't expect you to, but I really felt I had to let you know what I think about it. I feel so sorry for Donnie, he's had such a hard time.'

Maggie refrained from pointing out that she considered she could easily upstage her older brother in the hard-time stakes, but suddenly she felt quite queasy as a rather nasty thought struck her. 'Has Donnie said anything negative to you about the possibility of my buying the cottage?' Surely her brother wasn't disloyal enough to have put Karin up to this?

'Absolutely not.' It was a very definite no. 'And please don't say anything to him about it. This is just between you and me.'

Maggie shivered. Her so sensitive brother (why did that make her feel jealous?) was probably about to give the salmon he had himself caught in the Highlands its three-minute, thirty-five-and-a-half-second cooking, standing strictly to attention as he did so. She stood up abruptly. 'We'd better go back,' she said.

Karin sighed and nodded. Maggie remembered how she'd walked silently, unable to think of anything even remotely pleasant to say. She felt incredibly weary and pained, but inside was more determined than ever to own her personal piece of East Neuk rock and sky, and not even the Valhalla wisdom of her aunt was going to stand in her way.

Maggie left for London almost immediately after the salmon lunch, which for her was rendered almost unswallowable by that same lump in her throat and the preprandial witch's warning. They didn't really speak much during the meal, they talked of other things, and when Morag did mention the cottage, yes, said Karin with a politely dismissive smile, it did sound sweet. Maggie decided not to mention her aunt's utterly unexpected negativity to either her brother or sister-in-law; she could barely cope with it as it was, and wanted to keep faith with her own instincts.

She told her friend Felicity about it when she got back to London. Felicity, just home from playing a rare walk-on part in a television soap, thought the wee house sounded lovely and advised her to have her London flat valued again. It was after all a year since the last valuation, so Maggie summoned three house agents, who gave surprisingly different assessments, but when she added them together and divided by three she realised with a shock that her house value had doubled again in the last year – which followed a tripling in six years. It was Monopoly time. She was rich on paper but still had no money. All three agents were eager to sell the property, but warned her that the market was jumpy, there were still gazumpings all over the place, which upset buying chains, and they didn't know how long it might take to find a definite buyer. People were tending to hold back, waiting nervously to see what happened next.

Maggie phoned Morag and told her what they'd said. Morag shrieked at the huge valuation, which was enough to buy at least fifteen little Inverie cottages. 'What are you waiting for, woman? You have got to do it!'

She was relieved that at least Morag didn't seem to think her proximity would harm her husband's sensitivity.

'I'm scared of borrowing and it might take a whole year before I have a firm buyer.'

'Maggie, the closing day is in three weeks. It's now or never.'

'I can't do anything, it's too difficult.' Maggie longed to tell Morag about Karin warning her off, but couldn't bring herself to; she felt too hurt and puzzled by her aunt. Miserable, she hung up. She remembered how ill and fraught her husband, Fergal, had got when they'd been selling their last house, and was haunted by what Karin had said on the beach; it would taint any happiness she and her family might hope for in the cottage. She simply didn't feel confident enough of things now to take any chances, so in the blackest of mental states she decided that she'd better forget about the whole thing.

The next evening, miserable, incredibly lonely, she slumped to watch the telly with an open bottle of wine.

At this point, so soon after Fergal's death, Maggie still had pets. The family dog Archy, a sandy-haired Irish mongrel, was worried; he whined and pawed Maggie's knee and the cat hissed at him from behind her. Impatient, she pushed both animals away, then jumped up in dismay as the wine glass toppled and spread an island of blood over the pale Berber carpet. Cursing, Maggie fetched salt and had frosted the stain with white when the phone rang.

'Hi, it's Morag.'

'Hi, I've just wrecked the sitting-room carpet. Hand me the bloody valium.'

'Maggie. Listen carefully.'

Maggie frowned. Had her aunt been nobbling Morag too, she wondered uneasily.

'Karin's here, and she and Donnie have been talking . . .'

Maggie's hackles rose. She could just imagine that conversation, the Keep Maggie Away one. 'And?'

'They've reached a decision.'

Shit. This sounded serious. Were they planning to ban her for life, because she'd gone to live in London?

'Donnie and I have been talking as well,' Morag was speaking now very deliberately and Maggie was visibly shaking.

'We decided this evening.'

Please come to the point, moaned Maggie to herself, then

I'll just quietly go and shoot myself.

'Here's Karin to speak to you now.'

Maggie frowned at the phone. She didn't feel like speaking to Karin, not ever again. 'I'd rather not . . .' she mumbled to Morag, but she was too late.

'Maggie darling,' Karin sounded her usual intense and friendly self. 'How are you all?'

'OK,' Maggie grunted unwillingly.

'Maggie, I've been thinking a lot ever since we last spoke.'

Join the club, thought Maggie bitterly.

'And I realise that I was wrong . . .'

Maggie tried to take a swig from her empty glass and managed to mumble 'Really?' very faintly and coldly, without even a hiccup.

'Yes, really. I've been talking to Morag and to Donnie, and Donnie specially really thinks it is important for you and the children to be able to come to Inverie and to have your own place . . .'

Maggie sat down and patted the dog, who was looking very worried.

'But . . .' That bloody lump seemed to have grown back in her throat and now felt twice as big as before, and she couldn't speak very well. 'I can't really raise the money at this point . . .' she managed to croak at last.

'That's why Donnie and I have been talking. He wants to speak to you now – and Maggie, I'm sorry, really sorry. I was interfering . . . just like my children always tell me not to do. Kerstin is furious with me.'

Maggie was reeling. Couldn't take all of this in. Kerstin, Karin's doctor daughter, was a great friend of Maggie's.

Donnie's voice was warm and cheerful. 'Hi there, sister, how're you doing?'

'Alive, confused . . . and you?'

'Never better. Did Karin tell you?'

'Tell me what?'

'That you've got to buy the cottage. Marching orders: phone your lawyer in the morning, first thing.'

'But I've got no money, Donnie. I'm mortgaged up to the hilt and what I earn barely covers it.'

'That is exactly why we – and by we, I mean Karin, Morag and myself, have decided that we will lend you the money so that you can buy the Anderson cottage.'

Maggie was amazed. She didn't think Donnie and Morag had any money either. 'How? I don't understand?'

'Here's your sister-in-law. Talk to her.'

Morag came back on the phone. 'Hi, Maggie, did she tell you?'

'Eeerrr ...'

'We'll lend you what the cottage costs, for a year if you want. Five percent, OK? Donnie and Karin got together over a bottle of whisky and decided to do it. Isn't it fabulous?'

The truth dawning, Maggie stared at the phone and laughed.

The dog read Maggie's body language and barked and barked. She shrieked and cried with joy. Donnie chuckled, and her contrary aunt, who did sound just a little pissed, spoke lovingly and said she was even thinking of trying to find a house in the village too.

It was all extremely perplexing, but at last, dazed, after mumbling her emotional acceptance of the loan, Maggie beamed at the phone open-mouthed, cheered and heard her brother's return shout.

Alarmed, the cat fled through the cat-flap and the kids appeared, Sophie with her flute, Mark in football kit.

'What's going on?'

Maggie gasped her thanks to her unexpected benefactors and said goodbye. Then, beaming, she held out her arms to the children. 'I'm going to buy the wee cottage. It'll be ours in three weeks if the lawyer can do his stuff fast.'

The dog was hysterical, dancing a Highland Fling. Mark

and Sophie were as excited as Maggie was. They'd have their own place again, to be happy, to walk, to swim, to eat crab, to hunt for stars in the stones. Amazingly, life could still after all be good without Fergal.

Chapter Four

At the concert in St Andrews, both Karin and Patrick were moved by the singing of the young German music student who was performing *Die Schöne Müllerin*. It stirred memories of love and longing in both their breasts and even gave Patrick the daring to hold Karin's hand for a moment. In return, she pressed hers against his, before delicately slipping her fingers away from his tentative clasp to lean them against her chin in a rapt listening gesture. Moments later, Patrick demonstrated that his hand too, was a perfectly free agent, and used it to hush a tiny clearing of his throat. When their eyes met after a few minutes, and Karin gave him a sunny smile, and whispered to him how fine she found the music, he relaxed and felt a little better.

In one of the musical pauses, the pianist accompanying the singer noticed the tall, craggily handsome man dressed in subtle mixtures of tweed and tartan and the fine-looking woman beside him and wondered who they were. They looked so distinguished, the pair of them, he wondered if he'd seen them on TV or in a magazine.

In the interval, Patrick fetched cups of coffee. 'Enjoying it?'

'Absolutely beautiful. I don't think I've ever heard it better performed.'

Patrick nodded. 'He certainly sings to wring your withers.'

'Patrick, my dear!' Suddenly a tall woman in emerald green intruded between them. 'Why didn't you tell me you were coming to this? Isn't that boy absolutely marvellous?'

'Oh, Jennifer, my dear, how nice.' Patrick was scarlet.

Karin watched as they kissed cheeks, and waited for her greeting. She and Lady Jennifer had met many times before over the last fifty years, but Jennifer Earlsferry somehow always failed to recognise her, and the slight had ceased to amuse her.

Patrick held Lady Jennifer's arm and turned to Karin. 'Jennifer, my dear, have you met Karin Maitland?'

'Ah . . . yes . . . I used to know your husband, Andrew.'

'So I believe.' Karin smiled stiffly. Years ago, her husband had told her that Jennifer Earlsferry as a young woman had tried (unsuccessfully) to deflower the shy sixteen-year-old Andrew at a Christmas dance at Earlsferry Hall. 'Traumatised me for years,' he used to say, laughing ruefully. 'Left me a cock virgin till I was over thirty.'

'I must go,' said Lady Jennifer. 'I haven't fed the poor dogs. I'll see you on Wednesday, Patrick. Looking forward to it.'

Patrick blushed and nodded. 'Ah . . . yes, of course. I'll see you then.'

'What's happening on Wednesday?' Karin asked innocently. She already knew that Lady Jennifer, who had blatantly admired Patrick for years, was now in the habit – on alternate Wednesdays – of bringing him a personalised gourmet lunch composed almost entirely of titbits from the Italian delicatessen in St Andrews (it was common knowledge that Lady J. was no great shakes as a cook). No doubt she fancied Patrick's historic house now too, because since her son had inherited Earlsferry House a couple of years ago, Lady Jennifer had been banished to live in a small cottage on the family estate, which was not at all what she had been used to.

Later, Karin parked outside Patrick's front door with its ornately carved stone lintel.

'Won't you come in for a wee nip, or a cup of tea?'

'I won't, thanks. I need to bottle my new dye before I go to bed.'

'Well, my dear . . .' He took both her hands this time. 'That was all splendid. The crabs were exquisite. I'm sorry I overcooked the potatoes.'

Karin smiled and kissed his cheek. 'And I'm sorry, but I must go. It was a marvellous concert, thank you.'

'Oh, my dear, you're the one to be thanked.'

'Don't be silly. Goodnight, Patrick.' She reached up and kissed his cheek.

He stood watching as she did a rather clumsy U-turn and screeched off up the hushed street.

It hadn't gone well. He didn't understand why, but Karin hadn't been her usual friendly self since her trip to Copenhagen. Before she'd set off for Denmark, he'd really thought she was almost ready to stay the night. Puzzled and a little dejected, he went into the house and rather wearily poured himself a consoling tumbler of Laphroaig.

Fifty years ago, Patrick, a young man at the time, had come unexpectedly to visit Karin in Edinburgh, who was alone with her three small children. Her husband, Andrew – Patrick's oldest friend – was away on an archaeological field trip, and Patrick's own wife Margot and young family were across the water in the old stone house he still inhabited today. That particular autumn evening, when he arrived at the door of Karin and Andrew's Edinburgh flat, the children were already asleep. Patrick had been on business in Edinburgh, and had three or four hours to kill before catching the night train south, and wanted to say hello. The two families were very close, Karin and Margot had become instant friends when Karin married Andrew.

It was a meeting neither Patrick nor Karin would ever forget, but which neither of them had ever referred to since, though sometimes it was as though Karin could still smell the aromas of Patrick's particular soap and pipe tobacco and relive her surprise and delight at seeing him that night. When, with almost connubial intimacy, they'd shared soup and bread and talked about their families and Karin and Astrid's ageing parents in Denmark, Karin's loneliness and homesickness for Denmark had moved Patrick, and he'd risen to comfort her. In moments, they were hugging and he found himself kissing her, muttering forbidden words, voicing secret longings. For a moment, choked with emotion, but brittle with loyalty to her absent husband, Karin had shown that she yearned to respond fully, to dive into the sensation of loving warmth that Patrick seemed to offer. In five years of combined family holidays, picnics and journeys, this was the first time she'd ever acknowledged that she shared such feelings with him. Since their first introduction, she'd secretly admired the tall young architect's scholarly but athletic good looks and intellectual quickness, but she'd met the duller Andrew first and had agreed to marry him long before encountering his best friend for the first time.

It was really only now, all these years later, that Karin could acknowledge to herself how frustrated she'd been at the time of that particular meeting. She was after all still a very young woman and she remembered wryly how three months of imposed celibacy had felt like a life sentence.

At last, reluctantly, Patrick had set off to catch his overnight sleeper in the foggy gloom of Waverley Station. As they parted, he held her to him, enfolding her in his long tweed coat, 'Don't give up hope. Remember I'll always love you, have always loved you, ever since the day I met you coming off the boat at Leith Docks.'

She'd tried to smile, to take it lightly, but before they managed to wrench themselves apart, Karin too had acknowledged her secret love, and for decades afterwards, there had remained a painful but unspoken awareness between the two of them of how things might have been.

Tonight, as she arrived home and went into her house, Karin felt uneasy. She was tired, and disturbed about Patrick. She knew he was lonely and longing for more, and she had to admit that for a very long time she had been drawn towards a closer relationship, but she just didn't feel the same any more. She'd noticed a big difference after her two months away; he was definitely more repetitive, a little vaguer – though he'd always had a tendency to be vague when it suited him. He was limping too, quite badly; she supposed his old hip must be playing up. She sighed, her feelings a mixture of guilt and tenderness, and went into the kitchen, where, before getting ready for bed, she sieved the blue dye mixture and carefully ladled it into a big jar which she labelled in her strong square writing using black ink. As the sitting-room grandfather clock – a Scandinavian heirloom, painted with blue and pink flowers – struck eleven, the phone rang; Karin flushed, and a little breathlessly, picked up the receiver and said 'Inverie two three one.'

When she heard the cheerful voice at the other end, she smiled with relief. It was the call she had been expecting.

The next morning, in the bedroom of the vast second-floor Edinburgh flat she shared with her boyfriend Michel, Maggie's daughter, Sophie, was just waking up. She turned to her sleeping man and shook him gently. 'Darling, it's nearly ten, we'd better get moving.'

There was a Gallic grunt as Michel pulled the duvet over his head and rolled away from her.

Michel never seemed to want to wake up these days. Sighing, Sophie climbed out of bed and went to pee and brush her teeth. As she peered blearily at herself in the mirror she groaned. Her hair, dark and curly like her lover's, looked like an electrocuted Afro. She filled the kettle and switched it on and went to shower. Minutes later, wrapped in a towel with a bright image of TinTin and Snowy, she carefully carried two mugs of tea back to the bedroom.

'Sweetheart, you've got to wake up. We're supposed to be at Garvald by twelve; it'll take a good while to get there and we've got to have a practice.'

They were booked to perform at a wedding in a village near Edinburgh, Sophie singing solo at the actual ceremony, Michel playing the violin with a small chamber group at the reception. Moaning, he rubbed his stubble. People were always asking if Michel was growing a beard.

'God, I am so tired, I could sleep till Christmas.'

'Ha! That'll pay the bills.'

Only a month ago, the scene had run thus:

'Can't you come back in for a little?'

'Michel, I have just showered. I need to rehearse.'

'Just a little, little cuddle . . .' And he'd lifted up the duvet cover, to which she'd responded with a giggle, saying something like: 'That doesn't look so little to me.'

'He'll make you sing better, I promise.'

Sophie remembered looking at the digital clock by the bed, relentlessly dripping their lives away, and declaring firmly, 'We haven't got time.'

She'd even stood up to go, only to find that Michel had grabbed her by the ankle and somehow managed to somersault her back into the bed.

'*Bonjour, ma petite*,' he'd whispered, and lightly kissed her nose, before exploring her further.

She'd tried glaring at him, saying, 'I thought you said you were exhausted,' but in fact she'd been more than pleased to see that he wasn't.

But today was different, and things had been different for a while now. Michel simply wasn't frisky any more.

Later, in the car on the road to Garvald, Sophie complained as she drove: 'My hair – it's wild – I look terrible.'

It was the look Michel had always adored, but today he didn't seem to notice. In fact today was the sixth anniversary of the day that they had met. It was her unruly hair that had originally attracted him, and the sad realisation of how different things had been for the last few weeks nearly made her swerve off the road.

The first meeting had been when Maggie's cottage in

Inverie was being reroofed and having new windows put in, so Maggie had asked Sophie to stay at the cottage and be in charge while Maggie was away teaching in France. Sophie, still hurting from a break-up with someone she'd been seeing for a couple of years, was too introverted at the time and too involved in the music she was learning, to take much more than a passing interest in the project, but she'd agreed to be there to let the workmen in and out.

She was expecting a couple of local men, and was really quite taken aback at eight o'clock the following Monday morning, when a man called Robert arrived with a Frenchman in tow instead of the legendary Pete Macfarlane, his usual carpenter.

'Pete's father's in hospital wi' a cracked skull, so he couldnae make it,' explained Robert. 'But I've brought young Michel instead, and he really knows his stuff. Pete'll be back later on to finish off of the interior wood bits.'

Still in her night clothes when they knocked, Sophie hastened to pull on jeans and sweater before letting them in. Michel, hairy-chested, in vivid pink vest, denim cut-offs and hefty boots, didn't speak much, but smiled shyly, nodded to Sophie and took a quick and thorough look at the roof, inside and out. In the bedroom, embarrassed by her unmade bed, she showed him where the new windows were to go.

'It all seems quite OK to do,' he said.

The men started on the outside, stripping off all the old tiles, which they laid in tidy heaps ready to be taken to the dump. They were a pleasure to watch, especially Michel, who was undeniably good-looking. His movements were as light and disciplined as a dancer's; you could see that he knew exactly what he was doing with every gesture. Both men were quick and efficient and worked harmoniously together, mostly without talking, but Robert whistled a slightly maddening gaelic-sounding melody almost constantly. It was very sunny and hot, and when Michel stripped off his top, he revealed a torso of such muscled elegance that it was exceedingly distracting to Sophie, who was trying to learn a long and difficult piece of music. But somehow she managed to continue working, stopping only if there was a question to answer or drinks to be made.

On the third day, Sophie took a coffee break with the men, and noticed that she and Michel both enjoyed Robert's chat in the same way. Their eyes met happily a couple of times as his boss talked.

They sat together outside, looking out to sea. 'It's very bonny here. Quiet,' said Robert appreciatively, then he looked at Sophie, smiling. 'Ye ken, I've never been down here before in my life.'

Both Michel and Sophie were amazed. 'But you were born and brought up in Pittenweem?' said Michel. 'It is not even one mile from here, surely?'

'True. But Pittenweemers and Inverie folk don't mix a lot. D'ye know what the Pittenweem folk call the Inverie folk?'

They both shook their heads and Robert grinned. 'They call them the Droners, because of the way they speak.'

'And what do the Inverie folk call the Pittenweemers?' Sophie asked.

Robert grinned again and looked at them slyly. 'Torn Arses.'

Michel guffawed.

They drank their coffee and Robert sighed. 'Aye, it's true, we don't really like travelling much.'

'But surely you 'ave travelled a bit?' murmured Michel.

Robert shrugged. 'Aye. I've been down to England once. I had a job delivering stuff down there, but we never like to be far from the village and certainly not from the sea. We're no happy if we're away from the sea for long.'

Sophie was puzzled. 'But what about holidays? Don't you ever travel abroad?'

'Oh aye, but that's different. That's holidays. My pal Pete and me have went to Spain a couple of times.'

'Did you enjoy it?'

Robert laughed. 'Aye, it was damn fine splendid, what I can remember of it.'

When all the tiles were off, the insulation and wood strapping of the old roof had to be removed. Sophie, who was working at the window end of the bedroom and had reached a particularly complicated piece of libretto that she didn't seem to be able to memorise, was amazed to have the outside world abruptly brought right into her room when the last bit of lathe and sarking was removed at the front of the house. Suddenly plaster dust was falling on to her head and work table from the ceiling; she went out to see what was happening and found Michel smiling down at her from the roof.

'I'm sorry, did I make you frightened?' he asked apologetically. 'I was just noting the line of the rafters between where the new windows need to go.'

'It's OK, I'll take a break.' Upset by her inability to concentrate, Sophie didn't really want to talk to anyone. Sometimes she wondered if there was any point in going on at all. Maybe she should forget the bloody singing and get herself a proper job.

Down on the shore, she gloomily watched some eider duck with their ducklings. The little ones were learning how to push their heads down into the water and dive; one of the babies was finding this new skill particularly difficult and she found herself giggling as he tried again and again, never quite managing to do it the right way. His mother swam round in him slow, anxious circles as he kept bobbing up instead of immersing himself, and far beyond, the bigger cormorants and seagulls wheeled and dived. You could see their splashes as they hit the water miles away.

When she went back to the house, Robert advised Sophie to clear her work stuff out of the upstairs room as they were about to cut away the plaster. She tried to carry on working downstairs at the kitchen table, but it was going very slowly, so she made them all some tea instead. The lads had laid a huge tarpaulin across the end of the bedroom to catch the dust and when she went up to give them their tea, she saw Michel's face looking down at her through a rectangular hole in the roof. He smiled shyly, and Sophie blushed as she remarked how light the room seemed already.

'It will be magnificent,' he assured her. Then he added 'You'll be able to lie in bed watching clouds and seagulls ...' and he too flushed.

Later that evening, Sophie had just washed and dried her hair and was reading the paper, when there was a knock on the door. She opened it and was surprised to see the handsome Michel standing there, looking a little awkward.

'Hello,' she said, 'What can I do for you?'

Hurriedly, he handed her a cassette with an almost illegible handwritten label. 'I just was passing and wondered if you'd like to listen to some music.'

'Won't you come in?' she asked.

Michel looked flustered. 'Thank you, but I have some things to do this evening.' And he fled, walking quickly up the hill.

Puzzled, she put the cassette on. It was a song in French, sung by a man in a high, pure tenor, with an accompaniment of violin, flute and piano. She didn't fully understand the words, which seemed to be half-lament, half-celebration, but it moved her deeply. She'd never heard anything quite like it; it was neither pop nor operatic, but had a completely modern feel. She was both thrilled and intrigued as to its origins.

The builders didn't come the next day as it was a Saturday. Late in the afternoon, restless, half-aware of missing their male presence, Sophie wandered over to the old kirk to practise the aria she'd been learning. The church was empty, and she didn't really expect there to be any visitors at this time of day, so she sang uninhibitedly. She loved the old building with its severe stone walls, bare of decoration except for two model ships which hung above the nave, one of a sailing boat, a well-rigged three-master, and the other of an old steamboat with both funnel and sail. The simplicity of the place always touched her and today she quickly felt calmer for being there.

She was warming up, singing a solo from Bach's St John Passion, loving the music, happy with the way her voice was performing, when she became aware of somebody sitting in one of the side pews looking at her. It was Michel.

'Please don't stop,' he implored. 'You have a most beautiful voice.'

'Oh . . .' Sophie fumbled for words. 'I . . . the music . . . the tape you lent me. I loved it. Who wrote it?'

'Your builder.'

'What do you mean?'

Michel stood up. He was wearing a red sweater and looked great. 'I am afraid to tell you it was me.'

'You're kidding?'

He shook his head.

'But it was extraordinary. What are you doing mending roofs?'

He shrugged. 'Earning some money to buy me time to compose. I was teaching French in Dundee but it's holidays now. D'you know how to sing *Dona nobis pacem* . . . This one . . .?' He sang a bar or two in a fine baritone.

Sophie laughed. 'Of course I do.'

'Shall we sing it together?'

They sang that and a dozen other songs, harmonising instinctively, and she sang the solo she'd worked on that day and he helped her to clarify and make the sound flow more freely. They were surprised when the kirk elder who was in charge of the keys appeared in front of them.

'I'm awfy sorry to disturb you. It sounds marvellous, but I'm afraid I need to lock up.'

They agreed that they were hungry and set off in Michel's car for the next village, picking up a bottle of wine on the way at the supermarket, which was open late. In Pittenweem, as they stood in the queue for fish suppers,

Michel whispered to Sophie 'D'you suppose they all have torn arses?' and they both got the giggles. They bought fish and chips and a white pudding (a sort of haggis sausage) which they ate sitting in the evening sun, down by the harbour, watched, to their delight, by the two resident seals.

'Will your mother be home tonight?' asked Michel.

'No, she's away in the south of France.'

'Where?'

'A place called Bonnieux.'

'Bonnieux? I don't believe it!'

'You know it?'

'Know it? Love it. Adore it. My parents live in the next village.'

'Seriously?'

'Seriously. The tape you liked, it was written there, and I performed it with a chamber group in the Avignon Festival. It's called *Chanson de Vaucluse*.'

'What a coincidence! But if you could be in Provence, why are you here? Surely Provence is nicer?'

'It is very different. But I adore Scotland. I learned my English in Edinburgh, and I'm now working here for a year.' He looked out over the harbour and sighed with pleasure. 'My God, I love this place. Look at those boats, the design and balance of them, the beauty ... they're like embodiments of music, the structure is so organic, so harmonious. Aah ... it must be fantastic to design such things.'

Sophie nodded, smiling at his enthusiasm. 'How did you learn to build houses?'

'In Provence. I made new the roof on my father's house; I love to do practical things. Would you like some more wine?' He offered her the bottle.

'No thanks, I've had enough. I'd better get back.'

'OK. Let's go.' Michel stood up and held out his hand.

She took it and he helped to pull her up and the next thing he was holding her very gently. 'Please, Sophie, may I come home with you?'

She smiled, aware of an all-engulfing blush. 'Well, I did presume you were going to drive me home,' she said shyly.

'Of course I will, but that is not what I meant.' He looked at her intently, smiling a little and she looked back, trying not to grin as he stroked her cheek. 'I love your hair,' he murmured.

There was a pause, and she felt his palm warm on her back.

'It's such a beautiful night,' said Sophie at last. 'What I'd really like to do, is walk home along the coastal path. It's light enough.'

A little thrown, Michel was silent for a moment. 'OK. I propose to you, Mademoiselle Sophie, that we'll walk home to Inverie together. That would be beautiful, and in the morning as it's Sunday and I'm not working we can walk back and collect my car. How about that?'

Sophie looked out over the harbour and up into the bright evening sky. Westwards towards Inverie and the sunset was the thin silver crescent of the new-born moon. For a long minute, she gazed towards the horizon, watched by Michel, his eyes glittering in the rosy light.

At last she turned to him, 'OK. That's a good plan. Let's go.'

Michel smiled and pulled her to him and they embraced for a long while, then, hand in hand, they moved towards the far end of the harbour which led to the coastal path and started walking back to Inverie at a good brisk pace.

And they'd been happy ever since. Up till now.

Chapter Five

On the other side of Scotland, just outside Oban, as Maggie's married lover, Niall Maclean, reversed his grey Mercedes out from the driveway of his stone-built house, his wife Katy peered after him out of the window. 'And good riddance to bad rubbish, at least we'll get a few days' peace now, won't we, Jocky?' she muttered, stroking the white West Highland terrier sitting half-asleep on her ample knees. She had plenty to do, and could get on with knitting that green jersey with the complicated pattern for herself. It was convenient for Niall that that Maggie woman's place was near enough to Cupar for his blooming book fair, but even if it hadn't been he'd no doubt have thought up some excuse.

'She's lonely, I feel sorry for her, I'll just pop by and see how she's doing, and maybe spend the night there. It'll save on a hotel,' he'd say.

Katy frowned at her four needles as she counted stitches. 'Aye, you go and stay the night, just like you always do, that'll no doubt please you both, and always has done. Please yourself, Niall, as if you ever did anything else.' He could stay as long as he liked really, she didn't miss him that much, to be honest. Those days were long since gone, and the truth of the matter was that she had little desire left for him any more. What they did have in that respect had been short-lived anyway, and on her part not greatly regretted. She'd always thought it an awful trauchle, and these days found it almost out of order. Her imminent hip-replacement did not of course help matters, in fact it was a relief to have that as an excuse. As long as he was back in time for the Scottish dancing night on Saturday, that was all that really mattered. She still enjoyed the chat, even if she hardly ever danced nowadays because of her hip, though strangely, on some nights she still managed fine. Katy was quite willing to acknowledge that she belonged to the Sex is Overrated school, though she'd enjoyed giving birth to Lachlan and breast-feeding him till he was almost walking and talking, but when he'd drowned aged seventeen, in a canoeing accident in the black waters of Loch Awe, any sexual spark that still existed in her had been extinguished too. So if Maggie (or that blonde woman down at the gym) wanted to pass the time with her randy pensioner of a husband, they were welcome, as long as he didn't rub Katy's nose in it and continued to live at home.

Katy had to admit that she was usually fairly pleased to see Niall back. He'd always be very affectionate, and inevitably (he wasn't mean and had very good taste) he'd bring her a nice present, and as well as having cheered himself up with one of his lady friends, he'd also have stocked up for the antiquarian book business and maybe have found himself an interesting first edition – a Dickens or a Scott – which was always something to talk about; at least he'd be satisfied with life for a while and they could get back to their normal moderately comfortable existence. Niall had taken her once to an exhibition where some of Maggie's paintings were on display in a gallery in Edinburgh. Not bad paintings, bright and cheery – a relief because you could see what they were meant to be – and Maggie herself had been quite friendly. She laughed a lot; maybe that was why Niall was attracted to her – she was so different to herself.

'Come on now, Jocky, let's go for a wee walkie.' The dog leapt from her arms and barked as she put on her (near bullet-proof) rain-proof jacket. She fancied picking up a prawn sandwich for lunch and maybe a few scallops for supper when the girls came round to play bridge. It would take Niall a good three hours to reach the East Neuk, and he'd probably phone her tonight before the pair of them got too pissed on that malt whisky she'd seen in the back of the Mercedes. What did it really matter? By the time he phoned, Katy and the girls would be having a grand game of cards and a good laugh, and that always made things seem much simpler.

Niall, meanwhile, was already driving along the banks of Loch Awe where the dark waters were narrow and deep and the mountain reached straight up to the sky. He'd always found it an eerie place, but since Lachlan's terrible accident he could hardly bear to drive along that bit of road where everything seemed to close in on you. Maybe he'd give Maggie a ring, tell her when to expect him.

In the little village church, after Sophie had sung Schubert's *Ave Maria* (which had gone beautifully, she was sure she'd seen the glitter of tears amongst the wedding congregation), she went to look for Michel and the other musicians who were rehearsing at the big house where the reception was to be held after the ceremony. To her surprise she only found the others.

'Where's Michel?' she asked.

Sylvia Mackintosh, pale, blonde, with huge eyes, green as gooseberries, put down her viola. 'He wasn't feeling well, he's gone for a wee walk.'

Anxious, Sophie went to search for him and found her beloved fast asleep in the car, wrapped, although it was a warm day, in their tattered tartan travelling rug. He came to when she tapped nervously on the car window, and wound it down unwillingly.

'Michel, what's wrong? Are you ill?'

He looked very pale, almost yellow. He'd been like that so much recently, and all too often in the last month he'd been tired and uncommunicative, which was very worrying.

Michel rubbed his face and smoothed his hair, which was tangled from sleep. 'I am just so fucking fatigued, and I don't want to play any more sweet Mozart for wedding parties, I'm fed up with it.'

'But you always used to like it . . .'

'Maybe I've changed,' he growled. 'Anyway, what time is it? God, I'd better go. I left the others to warm up by themselves. I shouldn't have done, but they said I looked awful, I'm certainly feeling awful.' He opened the door and painstakingly disengaged himself from the travelling rug. 'I'd better get going. Monsieur Mozart here we come.'

The others, relieved to see Michel walking and talking, played soothing music as the guests devoured the wedding feast. Afterwards, when the performers had also been fed and paid, they set off for home. Sophie and Michel were giving Sylvia a lift and Michel insisted on driving. The two girls sat in the back chatting and occasionally tried to make Michel join in, but he was rudely uncommunicative. A couple of times Sophie felt alarmed by his driving, but he'd been behaving so oddly that she stayed silent.

When they reached the flat, Sophie invited Sylvia up for coffee. Michel didn't want any and stomped off to bed without saying goodnight.

'What on earth's up with him?' asked Sylvia. 'I was scared stiff in that car; I've never seen him like that.'

'Me too. Absolutely terrified – he's usually so careful. He's been awfully touchy lately, overtired, I think. Sometimes he doesn't speak for hours – days even. He's even gone off sex.'

'Has he been doing more than usual?' (Michel's normal work output was twice that of most other people's.)

'He's been writing a piece of music for a play at the Traverse, teaching, playing with you lot, plus his own composing.'

'And the quartet's been really busy – it's good fun, but it's tiring.'

'He always used to love it, but everything seems a stress for him just now. We've not had a proper holiday for ages.'

'Why not?'

'We're saving every penny, hoping to get a deposit together to buy ourselves a place – the landlord wants us out of here next year.'

'Does Michel ever go home?'

'Home?'

'To France.'

Sophie was surprised. Michel had lived in Scotland for twelve years now, since he was eighteen. Scotland was his home.

'We did got to France a couple of years ago; we love it there – it's a paradise where his parents live – but we've been too busy and had no money. Anyway, we've got my mother's place in Fife to go to; she's got a wee studio in the village as well as her cottage, so we sleep there and that's lovely.'

Sylvia sighed, looked intently at her friend. 'Honestly, Sophie, I think your Michel's having a breakdown. Perhaps you should try to go there soon.'

'Maybe we should. We do both need a break.'

'You do. And try at the same time to get him to talk to your GP.'

Sophie nodded miserably. 'OK. I promise I will.'

At Inverie, restless, impatiently waiting for Niall's arrival, Maggie had a coffee with her brother; and the two of them stood in his garden, looking over the sea wall, admiring the view.

'There's some nice chunks of wood down there on the shore,' said Donnie with a grin. 'Shall we make a raft?'

The very first summer, fifty years ago, when the family spent their summer holidays in the village, Alistair was fourteen and Maggie only eight. Maggie hero-worshipped Donnie (who came exactly between them) for his fantastic throwing abilities: a soldier predestined, he'd pick his ammunition carefully, weighing each stone for smoothness and shape, then pause, aim and hurl as hard as he could. Sometimes the stones went so far and so fast Maggie thought they might hit the Bass Rock, miles away on the other side of the Forth. Even Alistair couldn't beat him. Mum used to love throwing skimmers. She and the boys would have intense competitions, shout at each throw, counting and arguing excitedly as to how many bounces the flat stones had made on the water's surface, but Maggie's skimmers never managed more than a couple of clumsy hops. Patiently, Donnie tried to teach her the skill, showing her how to choose her stone, stand and twist her body sideways before throwing, but she was never any good at it.

Alistair was determined to go to sea, so with Donnie as an apprentice, he set about making himself a raft from old oil drums and wood which he found on the beach and tied together with rope, and secured with nails the boatbuilders had given him. Gilbert Menstrie, a lonely only child, often used to watch them avidly through a pair of binoculars from his bedroom window, and Maggie would try to help the boys, standing at the ready to hand Alistair whatever he needed. Sometimes her menial status bored her, so instead she'd draw her brothers at work, which cheered her as she could already draw better than either of them. The raft was quite strong and floated well. The bow of the home-made vessel was pointed, and the back part consisted of a couple of wooden fishboxes turned upside-down, large enough for the boys to sit on and to contain the oil drums. At one point Alistair managed to construct a mast of sorts, with a cross-piece on which he tacked an opened-up pillowcase painted with a skull and crossbones. Sadly, the mast and sail collapsed and were lost on their first voyage, which took them from the comparative safety of their rocky bay, out and round the far rocks they called The Devil's Teeth, and along and into the harbour.

Maggie ran down to meet them there at full tide, and cheered as they came round the west pier and sailed triumphantly towards her. Alistair threw her up some money and instructed her to buy biscuits. She went barefooted and untidy into the big grocer's shop on the harbour front where she loved looking at the biscuit tins where many varieties of biscuit were displayed behind glass, flat and perfect, as in a museum, backed with silver paper, twelve or sixteen to a box. She also admired the enormous square slabs of cheese that sat on a marble slab on the counter which the brown-overalled grocer would painstakingly cut with a length of wire with wooden handles at either end, and the huge sacks of rice and lentils which sat on the wooden floor. On this visit, a couple of old ladies, dressed all in black, looked at the little girl and muttered darkly, 'Aye . . . she's an awfy tomboy. Awfy wild . . .'

Frowning, Maggie pretended to ignore them as she waited for her broken biscuits (which were much cheaper than whole ones) to be weighed out on the scales. 'That'll be saxpence,' said the grocer, and she paid him with sticky coins, thanked him shyly and ran back to her hungry brothers, carefully holding the paper bag bulging with sugary shards.

'D'you remember the canoe?' asked Donnie now, chuckling. 'That was really good fun. It's a wonder we didn't drown.'

The summer following the raft-making, Alistair was allowed to buy himself a canoe with saved-up pocket and birthday present money. Maggie remembered sitting on the grass in the garden drawing as the boys spread paint on its hull and keel, and quite a lot on themselves. After an impatient twenty-four-hour wait for the paint to dry, the three of them dragged the canoe down to launch it into the high tide. One of Alistair's finest stand-up comic turns was to imitate and exaggerate the Queen Mother's voice, which they'd all heard on the radio when she christened the ship Caronia. This outraged Gilbert Menstrie – who had crept out of his house to watch them – so much that he ran back in to tell his mother. Oblivious, Alistair declared in screeching countertenor, 'I name this ship The Astrid Copenhagen, may God bless her, and all who sail in her!' Then, to their own mother's dismay, although the boat was named after her, he gleefully smashed a half-bottle of fizzy lemonade on the newly painted bow (Mum was always gathering broken glass off the beach). Pushing the canoe out into the water, Alistair leapt into the seat and paddled away towards the far horizon as fast as he could, yahooing with delight. They waved and shouted as he kept on paddling and Maggie remembered wondering enviously if he'd reach the May Island and see seals and puffins, and later – when he seemed almost out of sight – daring to hope that he might never come back at all. Mum and Donnie were both yelling at him not to go out beyond the far rocks, but he was well out of hearing by then, glasses glinting manically as he waved his yellow and red striped paddle at them before disappearing round the biggest rock you could see from the house, which was as huge as a small hill.

They all ran along the clifftop path as he went, catching odd glimpses of him between seagull and rock. Near the castle, at the bottom of the cliff, lying between two jagged black skellies, lay the spine and ribs of a wooden ship which had been wrecked there years before. To Maggie the dead boat was alarming, because Alistair used to terrify her with stories of the drowned sailors whose ghosts wandered the shore. Their mother was justifiably worried about Alistair's madcap voyage, but eventually, breathless, even she stopped running. Alistair, they could just make out, was waving, and Astrid decided that the day was so calm and he so confident that she'd just have to trust him. Soon they saw that the canoe was heading speedily for the sandy bit of shore quite near them, and Donnie scrambled down on to the stony beach to wade out and get as close to the adventurer as he could.

Relieved that her firstborn hadn't disappeared over the horizon, Astrid relaxed and smoked a cigarette, smiling at her daughter as she picked posies of wild flowers.

Eventually the grinning Alistair, with Donnie paddling behind him, set off for home, and within half an hour they'd landed on the shingly beach under the house. They were both jubilant: to Maggie, Alistair's orange hair looked like flames and his freckles danced. The excitement and independence seemed to have made him grow in stature. 'It's a wizard canoe,' he gasped in his nearly broken voice. 'Absolutely wizard!'

On the sea wall today, Donnie drained his coffee mug. 'Aye, those were the days. The kids here don't make rafts like we used to, it's a shame.'

They looked at each other, startled, as a loud barking and howling as though from a giant dog sounded out from round the corner in the direction of Maggie's cottage.

Donnie frowned. 'What the hell's that?'

'Thanks for the coffee.' Maggie hurriedly handed him her empty mug. 'I think I'd better go,' she said, hiding a smile. 'I think my friend from Oban has arrived.'

'That was delicious.' Niall, his blond hair tousled, leaned back and beamed. Sitting at the cottage table, he and Maggie had eaten the dozen oysters and drunk a whole bottle of chilled Pinot Grigio.

'Great oysters, I've never seen such big ones.' Maggie drained the last drops of her wine and held the bottle upside-down. 'Oh dear, all gone.'

Niall stood up enthusiastically. 'Shall we have another one?'

'Let's not or you'll sleep all afternoon and I'll die of a headache. How about a walk to the old castle?'

He looked at her quizzically. 'Maybe later. I think perhaps we should go to bed . . .'

Maggie threw the used oyster shells into the rubbish bin and turned to him. He was standing right beside her, waiting. 'OK?' he smiled and clasped her.

'Sounds good to me.'

Grinning a little alcoholically, Niall started to undo his

shirt and the pair of them walked upstairs, arm in arm.

Later, when he was half-asleep and she flushed and cheerful, she murmured, 'You know Sophie's Frenchman?'

'Uhhmph, Michel?'

'Yes. Well, last time he was visiting here we had a walk along the clifftop together – Sophie was cooking and sent us away for half an hour. Michel asked me if I was still meeting up with you, and I said yes, every so often, when there's a book sale nearby.'

'My love,' Niall protested, 'that's a trifle cynical; you know I'd come to see you anyway.'

'That's not the point. Michel wanted to know . . .'

Niall chuckled. 'I bet he wanted to know if we were still doing it.'

Maggie laughed. 'Yes, he did. He actually dared to ask me. I didn't mind at all, I thought it was rather good that he was interested.'

'I hope you told him.'

'Of course I did.'

'I suppose he thought we were just too decrepit.'

'I guess so. He seemed very pleased to hear it.'

Niall grinned. 'The condescension of the young . . .' He kissed her and stroked her neck. 'My love, you are a splendid role model for a son-out-law. He probably sees us as dinosaurs all the same.'

'In some ways he probably does, but he'll be there himself sooner than he thinks.'

'Aye, he will. It's a good few years since we first played this game.'

'So it is.' She turned to kiss him, but Niall was fast asleep.

Chapter Six

Maggie left Niall to sleep. He'd had a long drive from Oban, and there were things she wanted to do, like unwrapping that wormy chair from its plastic bag. When at last she had come to claim the cottage for her own, she'd possessed almost no spare furniture except for one inherited pine chair, with sturdy turned front legs, which she'd brought up from London. The back legs were each made out of a single piece of wood which rose up in a gentle curve to become the back supports. Across these sat a simple curved shoulder rest about six inches deep. She'd always been fond of the chair, which had been in the family kitchen when she was young; it was a local design, and succeeded in being both rustic and elegant. She'd only ever seen ones like it in Fife, and was proud that she now had four of them. They all varied slightly, but made a pleasing set. The second one she'd found a decade ago in her first week of being an Inverier – as the Inverie folk describe themselves. She'd noticed it on the road to St Andrews, lying obviously cast aside beside a roofless cottage, and decided immediately that if it was still there the next day, it was her artistic duty to save it from the elements. After all, she argued to any conscience that dared to whisper its doubts, she was honouring the craftsman who had created the object in the first place. That particular one had quite bad woodworm, but she gave it a good dose of wormkiller and dried it out, then lovingly sanded and polished the wood till it shone like new. Two months later, walking along the beach in the middle of winter, she'd encountered a third chair, also a bit the worse for wear, and blackened by the sea. Somebody must have chucked it off their garden wall into a high tide, but when Maggie set it upright on the strand and examined it, to her primitive taste it appeared perfect. Euphoric, she raised it up and walked home with it on her head. Then to her amazement, all within the space of a couple of months, she found a fourth chair. This one, also abandoned, was sitting outside a farmhouse, next to the midden – also, coincidentally, on the road to St Andrews. She drove past once or twice a week for nearly a month, until she could stand it no longer, so at last she drove in and knocked on the door.

A suspicious young woman answered, bursting out from a multicoloured shambles of plastic toys and yelling kids.

'Are you . . . Do you . . . I was wondering about the old wooden chair in the front yard . . . Are you using it . . . or were you thinking of throwing it out?' Maggie blurted out awkwardly, but the woman couldn't hear above the Tellytubby din.

'Eh?'

Maggie repeated herself, feeling idiotic.

The young woman looked puzzled. 'What chair?'

She, three toddlers and an enormous dog followed Maggie out to the midden, where shyly she indicated the chair.

'Oh, that thing. Help yourself, it's had it, it's useless.'

Delighted, Maggie dragged it out of the mud and manure. She could see that the girl thought her completely mad, but even so she amiably helped Maggie to load it into her boot, before chasing her children and assorted livestock back into the house.

Back home, Maggie's serendipitous mania faded slightly as she realised that perhaps the young woman had been right. The chair was wormy, uneven-legged, and all of its joints were loose. It was also damp, smelly and stained, but it cleaned up well enough to become useable in emergency. The wood dried out in a few weeks, and she squeezed wood-glue into the loose joints, until after much sanding, scraping and sealing, the orphaned chair became almost respectable – if you didn't peer too closely or sit down too hard. Maggie felt pleased; it looked well with the other chairs, and as a house-warming present Morag made a set of tartan patchwork cushions which hid the majority of the ugly stains and faults on the flat wooden seats.

This poorest of her chairs did service for several years, until last summer when it had got the worm again, only this time it was really bad. Once more Maggie dosed it with killer, and then, as advised by a furniture restorer friend, shrouded it tightly in plastic (only he'd advised rubbish bags for a week, not for over a year as happened in this particular case). Strangely enough, Maggie had undone the black plastic bandages only last week and had stood the invalid seat out in the sun to try and decide if it was useable. It wobbled badly because one of its feet was quite destroyed, and she wondered a little sentimentally if she might carve a new shoe or splint for it. Worst of all, all the joints were really loose and as they'd been originally held in place with pegs, and she didn't have a drill here, she wasn't really sure what to do.

Over the lunchtime oysters, she'd explained all this to Niall and he'd sweetly offered to have a go later if she'd show him what tools she did have. This surprised and delighted Maggie – who had never seen Niall as a do-it-yourselfer. When at last he woke and wanted a cup of tea, she presented him with a paint-stained hammer and a Swiss Army knife and he set to work enthusiastically, inventively using a big rusty nail she'd found on the beach, to knock the dowels out. Maggie was impressed, as was her neighbour Wilma, who'd come out to watch the action. Refreshed from his sleep, Niall was being all man, hammering, pulling out rusty nail after rusty nail and efficiently and quickly knocking out the pegs. In the end the chair lay in pieces on the front step, looking like a Tate Modern installation: *Dispersal, Memory of Scottish Chair*. The rusty nails lay together in delicate curves, along with the pieces of peg, leg, cross spar, seat and backpiece, all artistically exhibited alongside Maggie's crab and scallop shells.

'What d'you reckon?' she asked nervously when Niall at last stopped his intense activity. Surgeon-like, he adjusted his half-specs and shook his head. 'You could put it back together, I suppose, but you'd need to replace at least a third of it. Feel this,' he held out the shoulder support, which almost collapsed as it passed from his hand to Maggie's.

Looking closely at the bits, she had to acknowledge that the chair wasn't really salvageable, any of it. Wilma shook her head. All three of them shook their heads, and sadly Maggie fetched a big black plastic bag to bin the remains.

Niall patted her sympathetically when the final bit of woodworm dust was swept up and the last nail bagged. 'Never mind,' he said. 'It's served you well. There will be others. You still have four.'

She nodded. It was true, she did have four. She'd cheated; she'd actually paid money for one not long after she'd scavenged the other three; it was a honey-gold, satin-polished, beeswax-perfect specimen which she'd found in an antique shop in Falkland.

'Thanks very much for trying.'

Niall grinned. 'A pleasure, I assure you. It was worth a try, but it makes a man have a terrible thirst . . . D'you think we should open the bottle of malt I brought with me?'

These days, it didn't hurt to say goodbye. Maggie and Niall didn't make love in the mornings any more – they hadn't for a year or two – not that she really minded. How different it was to those first years, when their meetings had been fiercely passionate. Maggie used to feel so unhappy after he left, she'd be thrown for days. Missing him; angry to have landed herself in a relationship with a married man in the first place. They'd be so close, so tender, so loving, so fucking domesticated. And then he'd go. Back to bloody Katy.

Agonisingly, Maggie had trained herself to treat him as a bonus. She smiled ironically to herself as she remembered how she'd wept when he retired from running the bookshop in London to live in his West Coast house with views of the Western Isles. She'd envied him and Katy, but nowadays it was different. She enjoyed his visits, liked the laughs and discussions, the meals cooked together, the wine and the sharing of a bed, but over the years as their hair grew grey, and the demands of sex became dramatically less imperative, that terrible yearning had disappeared. She seriously believed now that she could genuinely take or leave Niall; to be honest, the only mild upset she ever felt these days regarding her married lover was when he tactlessly described the joys of his foreign holidays with Katy (who Maggie imagined doggedly casting on and off her fairisle knitting as she and Niall viewed the majestic buildings of San Gimignano or the Taj Mahal), nor did Maggie enjoy when Niall and she went shopping together and Niall bought presents of aprons, sweaters, woolly hats and even jewellery for his absent wife. There should be basic ground rules for married people: do not buy gifts for your husband or wife when gallivanting with your lover, nor describe in tedious detail connubial trips abroad. It was plain bad manners. But – Maggie smiled ironically to herself – so was adultery, come to think of it.

And it had been kind of Niall to try to mend her chair, she acknowledged, as she put out the rubbish bag filled with oyster shell and chair detritus.

In the year after she and Niall had first met in London – almost ten years ago now, two years after Fergal died – their much more frequent liaisons used sometimes to leave her feeling twice as desolate as she'd been before he came, but the madwoman in her still thirsted for his warmth, his laughter – and most of all – his lovemaking. Their bodies yearned for each other. More than once Maggie had tried to avoid him, to finish the relationship, but somehow she always allowed him to slither back, cheerful as ever, bearing (usually consumable) gifts, and would allow herself to be temporarily distracted and pleasured by him. But when Niall drove off after they'd spent a night together, she used to feel utterly bereft.

That winter Maggie began to paint for her next exhibition. She'd managed to take a year's sabbatical from teaching so she could spend several months working in the newly bought Inverie cottage. When the first frosts came, she used to look out of her upstairs window on to the graveyard and think gloomily that she had picked just the spot for the sort of paintings that she was producing at that time – dark, textural works, with sad figures and collaged woodcuts incorporated with photos and drawings. She felt a need to make them, to somehow communicate the misery and loneliness she'd felt when Fergal died. One of them, a big drawing of a naked old woman, skinny and desperate, breast-feeding a cat, perfectly expressed the sense of abandonment that often engulfed her that winter; and too often she drank too much wine all by herself as she listened to the shrieks and moans of the winter gales.

When she learned from a couple of locals that the cottage had once been the village morgue, Maggie, who had a hangover, gave a hollow laugh. The information seemed perfectly suited to her state of mind at the time.

'It was for drowned sailors,' Morag informed her later. 'Your place is where the bodies were brought when they pulled them out of the sea.'

'Thanks very much, Cheery Jean,' Maggie smiled grimly. 'I'll remember that at three am.'

On Niall's last visit, she'd been insulted when they visited an art gallery in a nearby village. She'd recognised from the paintings on the wall that the man sitting in must be the person who'd once rented the cottage from her, so had introduced herself, saying that she believed he'd once been her tenant in Inverie.

His response threw her, because he looked at her coldly and grunted, with a charmless smile, 'Ah yes, the grave-digger's cellar.'

Maggie was too taken aback to answer. As they left the gallery, Niall said 'It's a pity we didn't enquire as to whether he was joking or merely being rude.'

Maggie was livid. 'The gravedigger's cellar! What a bloody cheek. OK, so what if it was once the gravedigger's house, but a cellar? How dare he? Even if it is a bit dark and has a rock sticking up in the corner. I love it all.'

Niall had hugged her. 'Of course you do. Dammit, it's virtually your geographical navel, and that's about as personal as you can get.'

Maggie's reverie following Niall's departure this time was interrupted by a knock on the door. It was Karin in gardening gloves; she'd brought some parsley and a delicious posy of pink carnations and wallflowers, surrounded by lambie's lugs, the soft silvery leaf that Sophie used to rub sensuously against her baby cheeks.

'Oh, I see you already have some,' said Karin, eyeing Niall's generous bouquet.

'These are beautiful, thank you. Would you like a coffee?'

'I'd love one.' Karin sat at the table and watched as Maggie busied herself finding a vase and making coffee.

'How was the concert?'

'Excellent.'

'How's Patrick?'

Karin shrugged. 'Fine.'

Maggie looked at her. 'Really?'

Karin looked away, her eyes sad.

'What is it, Karin?'

'I don't know. Old age perhaps. Creeping up.'

'But Patrick always seems so energetic, so full of projects.'

An even bigger sigh this time. 'Yes, he always used to be. He was extraordinary.'

'We . . .' Maggie decided to be daring. 'We've all been expecting you to end up living in Elie with him.'

'Have you really?' Karin laughed, her eyes desolate.

'You have seemed . . . er . . . very close.'

Karin fiddled with the tablecloth, where she seemed to be intent on counting the threads. 'Yes, we were. If I am honest, I think that's what Patrick would like.'

Maggie tried to lighten things. 'You could be Lady Karin.'

Karin groaned. 'I suppose I could. D'you know, Maggie, sometimes I think memory can be a terrible burden.'

Maggie recognised that one. 'God, yes. Sometimes I feel that my past is even more vivid than what's happening now, specially here in Inverie, with my own childhood, my children's childhoods and now me living here in the same place. It's weird. I wish we could somehow free ourselves from those old knots and ties, like wiping them off a computer; they can be so inhibiting.'

'Absolutely.' Karin's response was heartfelt. Sighing, she drank the coffee. 'I couldn't bear to hurt Patrick. He really needs somebody now.'

'We all need somebody,' said Maggie sadly.

'Yes, Maggie, we do, we really do!' This was emphatic. 'But I'm afraid that Patrick needs even more now than just that simple need.'

Maggie paused. 'To look after him, you mean?' she asked reluctantly.

Karin looked away, frowning. 'I suppose I do. Yes. Or he will do, soon.'

Maggie stood up at last and when she went to hug her, her aunt's body felt bony and fragile. 'Karin, please don't blame yourself. You're a wonderfully active woman, with lots of life left, I'm sure. If you don't want to look after Patrick, of course you mustn't feel guilty.'

Karin fumbled in her pocket for a handkerchief. 'Perhaps you're right.'

'I'm sure I'm right. First and foremost, you have to do what's right for you, not anybody else, otherwise you'll be miserable.'

'But I am miserable.' Karin laughed painfully and blew her nose.

Maggie went to fetch the whisky. Miraculously, Niall had left a couple of inches. He must be getting old, too.

'Let's have some of this, and I'll make us some lunch.'

'I don't want to be a burden.'

'Don't be daft. I also happen to have some delicious smoked lamb and salad. How does that sound?'

'I've never had smoked lamb. Are you sure?'

'I'm sure,' said Maggie, and blessed the absent Niall again, this time for his gift from the Oban smokery.

After lunch Maggie and Karin went for a drive. Before getting into the car, they stood for a moment to watch some holiday children who were playing on the beach.

Karin smiled. 'They remind me of you three.'

'Me too. That's the trouble with this place, there's a memory under every stone.'

By the time they'd driven to Pittenweem and back, her aunt seemed much more cheerful. They'd stopped to view a house that was for sale. Maggie, forever trying to decide on whether to retire to Scotland or to return to London next summer when her tenants would leave the flat, had taken to viewing anything that was larger than the cottage.

'There was an awful lot to do,' said Karin later.

Maggie nodded. 'At least you're not trying to put me off living here full-time. I thought you might.'

'Oh, Maggie. I'm so sorry for that time. I've so often regretted being so negative to you.'

Maggie smiled wryly. 'I was very upset, and then, only a year or two later, when you actually did go out and buy a house about two hundred yards away, I must say I felt not a little put out.'

Karin stopped in her stride. Covered her face with her hands. 'Oh . . . you must have been so bewildered. D'you know, Maggie, perhaps it wasn't really about you and Donnie, though I know you two have always seen things very differently, but I see now that it was more to do with my personal upset with my family. When Andrew died I wanted to stay on in the inherited family house, but my dear firstborn son – and you know how wilful he can be – was making my life hell. He wanted his inheritance and expected me to move out as soon as possible. I'm happy to say my girls had nothing to do with this – they were always kind, even while their brother was pressuring me when I was still newly widowed and hardly knew what to do with myself.'

'It must have been awful for you. I think I only began to understand that night after your house-warming, when we drank far too much wine and you explained it all to me.'

Karin groaned. 'I was drinking much too much at that time. That's why I started to do the yoga regularly.'

'But I forgave you completely when you took me to Gothland.'

Karin clutched her arm intensely. 'I'm glad. I felt so bad to have hurt you so soon after you were widowed.'

'Gothland was a good trip.'

'It was lovely. You should come to Scandinavia with me again – speaking of which . . .'

Maggie looked at her and was suddenly puzzled to see that her aunt was blushing deeply.

'What?'

'I . . .' Karin bit her lip. 'I'm actually going back to Denmark on Tuesday.'

'Tuesday? I don't understand – you've only been back for a week or so.'

'I have to go,' said Karin. 'It's a . . . er . . . a very good friend's birthday party.'

'But it's Patrick's big birthday next month. You aren't going to miss that, are you?'

'I don't know.'

Maggie, looked at her aunt. 'May I ask,' she said gently, 'is it . . . a man friend?'

Still scarlet, Karin brushed her hair out of her eyes. 'Well, yes it is,' she admitted. 'But I don't want you to talk about it. He's a very old friend, and it feels important to be there.'

Maggie nodded. Clearly her aunt, who suddenly had a lively, almost youthful look, wasn't telling her everything, which would surely explain all that guilt and upset about Patrick.

Chapter Seven

A couple of months after Niall's visit, on her way to St Andrews, an incredibly cheery Maggie was singing along to Bob Marley played very loud. She was pleased that Murdo had rung, although it had taken him long enough; she hadn't had a date with an unattached man for years. She and he had spoken a couple of times on the phone quite flirtatiously, but so long ago that Maggie had almost dismissed him as a possibility. When they'd last met properly, a year or two ago at a friend's barbecue in Edinburgh, Murdo had grown from a somewhat gangling and uncertain youth into a warm, attractive man. At the time he was still unhappily married, and for a fraction of a millisecond, Maggie had thought what a pity. Today as she drove, she imagined him clad in his black leather jacket and jeans, striding along the beach with her. Yesterday, to prepare for Murdo's coming, she'd felt impelled to move all the sitting-room furniture round and had even redecorated a wall in the bathroom, and a large part of today's trip to St Andrews was to buy a couple of new towels to enliven the place.

When her mobile (a parting present from her son Mark when he set off for Australia) rang, she was in a charity shop, halfway into a pair of tartan cotton trousers, her neck entwined by a billowing scarf of tie-dyed silk. She hadn't had the mobile for long and still felt a thrill from the independence it gave, but she disapproved of people who used their personal phones in public. When she located her own, trilling faintly at the bottom of her bag, she was embarrassed but pleased when she heard her daughter's voice.

'Hi, Ma. How are you doing?'

Maggie described the tartan trousers and felt disappointed when Sophie made only faintly enthusiastic noises. 'But, Ma, what I'm actually ringing about is that Michel and I would really like to come out to Inverie for a few days. Would that be OK?'

'That would be lovely. I'm not really using the studio much at the moment, the weather's been so good that mostly I sit out on the doorstep and make things, so you can sleep there and come to me for the odd meal – very odd, probably. I'm very lazy these days, addicted to bacon and egg rolls.'

'Sounds great. Mum – er – Michel's a bit – er – tired. He's been – pretty miserable.'

The maternal antennae immediately picked up that Michel wasn't the only one who was unhappy. 'Oh dear, has he been overdoing things?'

'As usual, yeah. He's really being a bit weird, Ma. Sometimes it's like living with a ninety-year-old Azerbaijani.'

'How do you mean?'

Sophie sighed. 'Well . . . like somebody very remote, who speaks no English – sort of hard to communicate with . . .'

'Doesn't sound like the Michel we know and love.'

'It's not. It's really not.'

Maggie's heart sank. Things sounded bad. 'Of course you must come, and for as long as you like. And remember, if you're here on Saturday week there's the big trip for Patrick's birthday. He's booked a boat to the May Island. I was going to ring you tonight anyway; he asked me to invite you.'

'What birthday is it?'

'It's the big eight-oh.'

Sophie gasped. 'Ma, you're joking? Patrick can't possibly be that ancient!'

'I'm afraid he is, but I can hardly believe it. I always think of him as being about fifty, but that's daft. The whole family's coming, William and Fanny, all the grandchildren, and Donnie and Morag, and Karin's lot, the grandchildren and all the cousins. It'll be fabulous if the weather keeps good.'

The curtain of the charity shop cubicle was suddenly violently rent asunder, and a woman who could easily have been Gilbert Menstrie's twin sister glared in at the half-dressed Maggie.

'Excuse me, madam, but there's people waiting. Could you kindly hold your conversation elsewhere.'

Maggie apologised profusely and hastily whispered goodbye to Sophie, adjusted her garments, apologised once more to the lady at the desk and emerged into the street, clutching a bag of nearly new delights.

On the way to the car she decided to stock up with wine. If Sophie and Michel were coming they'd get through quite a lot, and Murdo certainly always used to like a drink as a student.

Maybe Murdo's visit would improve matters. As Maggie's friends and daughter were always telling her, she deserved to have a proper partner, but to be honest, a companion was what she yearned for these days, more than a lover. How strange it was to be this age, with imperatives so different to those of even a few years earlier. Last time she'd seen Sophie, her daughter had really laid into her about Niall. 'He's a waste of your time, Ma. You're worth more. I know he's a sweet bloke and that you have a good time, but he's not ever there when you need him – it's always on his terms. His life always comes first, and I for one would like to see you coming first for a change.'

So would Maggie, but it was easier said than done. Besides, she did enjoy the old reprobate, and most other men she met weren't half as entertaining. Anyway, how many men wanted a Rubenesque widow of a certain age, however amusing and lively she might be? Judging from the lonely hearts ads they wanted slim dollies, and evidently many slender young women wanted the stability and maturity of older men – who, unlike women – could still happily breed in their fifties, sixties or seventies. Maggie's own great-grandfather, Old Chillianwallah, had fathered Great-uncle Ilbert at the age of seventy-four (and what a sad, lonely old man he'd turned out to be, with his patched denims, hens and fear of conflagration; he always kept dozens of buckets full of dusty water standing on the floor – just in case).

'Born a gentleman, surplus to requirements,' was Donnie's epitaph for Great-uncle Ilbert.

Maggie smiled grimly to herself as she loaded up the car boot. Maybe she was beyond being able to share her life with anybody any more. Too much had happened; she'd fought hard to become adept at living by herself, and she feared that she might now find it impossible to adapt to another person. Anyway, nobody was really knocking on her door, these days, except for the indelibly married Niall, and now Murdo, who was coming to visit tomorrow night, which was exactly why she needed to ring Sophie back pronto. She didn't want the youngsters to coincide with him – just in case his visit turned out to be a success.

Back at the cottage, Felicity, Maggie's London friend, phoned.

'Are you still overwhelmed with rural delight up there?' she asked, wheezing (foolishly, Felicity still smoked thirty a day. She swore that it gave her voice a gravelly quality which was useful professionally).

'I don't miss London much,' confessed Maggie. 'Except for you, of course, but you'll come to visit soon.'

'Of course I will. I must say you do sound happy.'

'I am. Where else can I find stars in my stones?'

Felicity phoned back later that evening. What exactly did Maggie mean by stars in her stones?

'I find them on the beach. Perfect five-pointed stars; they're in the middle of cylindrical fossils about an inch long, as thick as a small finger.'

'Extraordinary. What on earth are they?'

'Crinoids. Some people call them stone lilies. They're three hundred million years old.'

'How poetic.'

'I found my first one when I was a wee girl and ever since when I come here I search for them; you always think you're going to find the most perfect or beautiful one, it's a magical process – obsessive.'

Felicity chuckled. 'Extraordinary. A nice soothing occupation; it sounds like it might even keep you out of trouble.'

'The local fishermen call them crowpies. They used to keep one in their pocket for luck when they went out fishing.'

'Crowpies,' Felicity tasted the word. 'Lovely. You must take me on a star hunt one day. By the way, when's your visitor coming?'

'Which visitor?'

'The old flame.'

Maggie was indignant. 'He's not an old flame, he's just an old friend – a mate from school days – we're good pals, that's all.'

Felicity responded with a disbelieving, smoky giggle. 'Mmmmh . . . I believe you. It's not so very long since the other one was with you, is it?'

'Which other one?'

'You know. Your seasonal one.'

'Oh him. It's been ages, weeks and weeks.'

'Mmmmh. Too long. Being alone's very boring.'

Maggie was sitting down to supper when Sophie phoned again. 'I just wanted to check that tomorrow's OK to come, Ma.'

Maggie hesitated. 'Er . . . no, it isn't really, I'd much rather you came on Sunday.'

'Oh . . . Why?' It was almost a wail.

'I'm busy tomorrow night. I've got a friend staying.'

'Don't tell me Niall's coming again?' Her daughter sounded very stern.

'No, he's not.' Maggie snapped.

Sophie was intrigued. 'Who is it, then?'

'Just . . . an old friend . . . Nobody you know.'

'Mother, you sound secretive. Is it a fella?'

'Mind your own business.'

'But we could just have fish and chips and stay at the studio. I promise we won't bother you at all.'

'Sophie, I'm sorry, but I'd much rather you left it till Sunday. I want to show this friend some work in the studio.'

'Ah . . . Don't tell me – I bet it's the photographer – the one with the leather jacket . . .'

How the hell did she remember that?

'Ma?'

'What?'

'Is it him? I bet it is.'

'Mind your own business.'

'I hope it is. It's time you had some fun. OK, Ma, we'll come on Sunday.'

'I'll make supper if you like,' offered Maggie, automatically maternal.

'That would be lovely. And have a great time, Ma. Don't do anything I haven't done.'

Maggie put down the phone and wondered again how on earth Sophie guessed that it was Murdo coming. It was ages since Maggie had mentioned him, and even then she'd only said in passing that a photographer friend might come and visit, but Sophie had always been frighteningly intuitive.

She did feel just a tiny bit hopeful about Murdo. When he'd first rung to say it would be good to meet, he'd said he wanted to take her out for a meal, and Maggie, aware that it would be the opening night of the Pittenweem Arts Festival with its open studios, had suggested on impulse that he might like to stay the night.

She'd blurted it out without thought, and then she'd nervously added that she had a spare bed.

Murdo lived in Edinburgh, where he'd just retired from teaching photography, and they'd naturally want to drink wine at the open studios, and later with their meal, so he wouldn't be keen to drive home.

That afternoon, as she ironed her clothes and washed her hair, Maggie wondered if Murdo would find her orange hair too extreme? Unhappily, she examined herself in the mirror. Murdo, she knew, was in a state; it was only weeks since he split up from a twenty-year-younger woman; he'd insisted on the phone that he was fine now. 'I'm over it, I had eight sessions of therapy before it happened . . . I was really drunk every night for a week when she went, but I'm over it now, I'm quite relieved in fact . . .'

All in all, he'd been pretty unconvincing.

At school and later in their student years, Maggie had spent interminable hours sympathetically listening to Murdo's doleful stories and rambling poems of unrequited love for a fellow student. Although she was looking forward to his coming, she was also secretly a little apprehensive that this visit might turn out to be an action replay of those long-ago unpaid therapy sessions.

The previous night Maggie had slept badly; she had a runaway brain for half the night and was kept awake by a tentative enlivening of her body, which she tried in vain to ignore, that was at once optimistic and erotic. For much of the night the madwoman within was imagining the house by the harbour at Pittenweem (which she'd viewed several weeks earlier with Karin) with herself and Murdo (who'd had thick, dark curls when young), sunburnt and fit, building walls, creating a French window on to a huge garden with a view of the harbour with its fishing boats and seals. The fact that the actual house (whose wood-panelled walls were smothered by generations of dribbled enamel paint, whose patterned carpets verged on the obscene, and everywhere had hideous peeling wallpaper) had smelt of gas and stale urine, strangely didn't deter her from fantasising. The plusses were terrific: sea views, an outhouse which would make a perfect darkroom or studio, and two original box beds. The building had huge potential and the asking price was less than that of a grotty studio flat in London. If Maggie were to sell up in London she could buy it (and do it up, which would not be cheap) two or three times over. She often yearned for a last big project like that, before she became too old and lacking in strength. But not alone; it would be much too big a task. She'd definitely need somebody to share it with.

After lunch, Maggie lay down and tried to recoup some of her missing sleep. In moments, she found herself in the garden of the big house (at present abandoned and impenetrably but romantically overgrown with giant red roses and wild strawberries), where she imagined sweet peas twining upwards on a bamboo frame, and orange and red nasturtiums resonating against ochre sandstone walls. She was still half-asleep when she heard Murdo's knock on the door. Shocked, she scrambled up, whisked on lipstick and perfume, tidied her hair, and tried not to tumble downstairs as she aimed herself at the front door.

Murdo looked really good – she'd forgotten how tall he was. He was thinner, older, more dignified, than she remembered, but sadly his dark curls were completely white now, like a photographic negative of what they'd once been, and he was carrying a bouquet of roses – palest pink with red-edged petals – which he presented her with.

'You look lovely,' he told her twice, and they stood looking at each other, both moved, before he enfolded her in a long, loving hug. Maggie felt enormously cheered, confident it was going to be an excellent visit.

They sat together in the sun on woven cushions, eating raspberries and cream. Dogs walked by, pulling their owners towards the beach, and boys whizzed down the hill on bikes. Then to Maggie's dismay, Murdo almost immediately fixed her with his steely blue gaze and started retelling the story of his life up to date, beginning with the childhood horrors he'd all too often shared with her in the past. His mother had been an alcoholic and Murdo's father had run away when he was only five. He hadn't really changed; he still demanded her unwavering attention and failed to ask even a single question about Maggie. Her life down south, the family, Fergal's death, and her work past or present were all completely ignored.

He was a presentable-looking man. He'd taught in the same college for years, was practical, had built a darkroom studio in his garden, which he assured her was exquisite, and she was genuinely impressed to hear that he'd reroofed his Georgian house entirely by himself. But he was impossible. After only half an hour of his company, Maggie found herself thinking sympathetically of his ex-wife. How she'd managed to put up with Murdo's interminable solipsism for a quarter of a century was almost impossible to understand.

The open studios were enchanting; they bumped into a couple of mutual friends, and both Maggie and Murdo recognised several of the artists. The night was light and warm, and people wandered about the village, holding glasses of wine, going from studio to studio – the venues were everywhere, in old fisherman's cottages, garden sheds and outhouses. They were both excited by the paintings, prints and silverwork on show, and of course the alcohol they'd consumed. Briefly, the village appeared magical, and for all of twenty minutes Murdo even managed to stop talking about himself.

Years ago, Maggie had painted a canvas of a naked lover with a huge erection, a sideways, full-length figure, leaping hopefully, clasping a big bunch of blue cornflowers. Today, something in his manner – the relentless intensity of his communications and his heavy flirtatiousness – reminded her of that image. But very quickly, Maggie recognised sadly that Murdo was emotionally priapic with loss, with need, and understood that the painfully self-revelatory communication and the flirtations which accompanied it were not really inspired by her. Any presentable female would have done.

Late at night, back in the cottage, after a cup of tea for her and a huge dram for Murdo, Maggie stood up from the table and yawned.

'I'm sorry to be anti-social, but I'm really tired.'

She'd brushed her teeth and escaped to bed and was deep in her book, when suddenly the bedroom door swung open and Murdo, clad only in a bright red towelling dressing-gown, surrounded by an offensive miasma of after-shave, loomed in at her.

Startled, Maggie pulled her duvet round herself.

'Would ye not like a wee cuddle?' Murdo offered, bringing rather too much of himself into the room.

Appalled, Maggie couldn't help staring at his skinny white legs and crocodile toenails and noticing that his face was very flushed, though whether this was from alcohol, passion or embarrassment, she had no way of telling.

'Oh . . . Murdo . . . that's kind . . . but not tonight . . .' At which Murdo looked so downcast that she hastily stammered, 'I'm not saying no for ever . . . But we don't really . . . it's too soon . . .'

Noisily fingering his white unshaven chin, Murdo smiled in what he evidently hoped was a seductive way. 'D'you like my after-shave?' he asked huskily.

'It's lovely,' muttered Maggie nervously. 'Very vivid . . .'

'I was hoping it would turn you on.'

'It's very . . .' Maggie paused, 'unusual . . . but Murdo, I'm really zonked. I didn't sleep very well last night . . .'

'Join the club,' muttered Murdo. He came into the bedroom and closed the door firmly behind him. 'I was really nervous about seeing you again. But I was excited too.'

Maggie gulped, politely trying not to acknowledge the fact that he obviously still was.

'I'll just give ye a wee goodnight kiss,' persisted Murdo. 'Don't worry, I'm not going to rape you.'

Backing into her pile of pillows, Maggie watched in alarm as he bent down, sat heavily on the bed, and wildly clutched her to him. Uncomfortably reminded of teenage grapplings, she pulled away as he kissed her full on the lips and their teeth clashed.

'Just a wee hug, for old times sake?' pleaded Murdo. 'Or could we not just sleep together, non-sexually, just as friends? We both could do with a cuddle.'

Thanks a bunch, thought Maggie. That makes me feel really desirable.

'No, dearie,' she said resolutely, and pushed him away as firmly but neutrally as she could. Then, calculating nervously that her big black T-shirt nightie was not likely to further inflame him, she clambered out of bed, still holding up both hands to dissuade her hangdog suitor, who made one last lurching effort to clasp her to him.

'Goodnight, Murdo,' she said firmly and pecking him chastely on the cheek, shoved him gently but determinedly towards the door. 'Sleep well. I'll see you in the morning.'

'Goodnight,' muttered Murdo sadly, and exited backwards, his towelling garment held awkwardly across what she noted a little dismally was a pretty impressive bulge.

As Maggie closed the door behind him, a momentary memory of the dog Rambo and the reluctant Kellie in this same bedroom came to her, but at least she hadn't needed to belabour this particular rampant male with a welly boot. As for Maggie's own erotic preconceptions, it was now painfully obvious to her that they too had much more to do with her own needs and longings than with poor Murdo. Briefly, from the preliminary phone call to the first moments of their emotional reunion with flowers, they had existed as emblems of hope for each other – token male and female. If only life were so simple that they could fall into each other's arms and lives and stay there, attached both physically and metaphorically, contained with love, for ever, as still occasionally happens in films. Part of her did still truly believe that this was possible, just as you really could win the lottery, but it obviously wasn't going to happen this time. Disappointed, she wedged a chair under the door just in case, and frowning, returned chastely to her book and lonely bed.

In the morning, Murdo didn't even mention his unsolicited entry into her bedroom, but went straight back into his dronings of the night before: 'My daughter's been on heroin for the last five years, but she's doing re-hab. It's been terrible, I couldn't work for almost a year . . .'

Somehow, whatever the tragedy his family members had undergone, they always became Murdo's personalised dramas, his own special pain, which he obviously believed made him psychologically fascinating and complex.

At breakfast, in a brief and blessed pause from his mind-numbing reiterations of his own clevernesses and familial disasters, he instructed Maggie to admire his towelling dressing-gown, in which he evidently fancied himself (TK MAXX, only thirty quid, he informed her with painful honesty), a bargain surely acquired for her benefit along with the designer stubble and after-shave which now insulted every millimetre of the cottage.

His frankness was a further turn-off to Maggie. Women need a bit of mystery too, she decided; she certainly wasn't going to confess to her new knickers, new towels or the beautifying of self and house which had heralded his arrival. After enduring too much of Murdo's interminable self-obsession, Maggie had had enough, so she set about making coffee, and at last in desperation announced that she had a commission to finish. Murdo, obviously expecting they would spend the day together, looked crestfallen. To be honest, Maggie had hoped that they might do that too, but she couldn't now, not unless she knew for sure that he'd quit talking about himself, but that obviously wasn't going to happen.

An hour later, when Murdo had at last driven mournfully

away, an equally mournful Maggie went back into the cottage. She suddenly felt incredibly alone, and wondered if she should phone Michel and Sophie to summon them earlier after all, but decided to do some work instead.

In the living room, the bed which Murdo had feebly attempted to make was a shambles. The Indian bedcover and Morag's cherished patchwork cushions were strewn all over the floor; the bedlinen hung from the bed as though eviscerated; and as she later indignantly explained to the amused Felicity in London, the biggest turn-off of all was that her would-be lover had made the – for Maggie unforgivable – mistake of leaving the lavatory seat up.

This information made Felicity cough and laugh simultaneously. 'Oh dear,' she wheezed at last, 'I do feel sorry for poor Murdo, but you must tell him that it is very bad feng shui to do that. And he's old enough to know better. Leaving the loo seat up makes all the luck in the house go up the spout, or should I say down the pan?'

Chapter Eight

Rather bossy, young Jessica was becoming these days, mused Patrick as he sat in the window seat of his stone-flagged kitchen and watched his favourite granddaughter prepare leek quiches for his birthday picnic. Bossy but beautiful. She looked incredibly like her father at the same age – and her grandmother, come to think of it. Dear Margot, why did she have to go and die?

'How did you learn to be so damned efficient, my dear?' he asked benignly.

'Runs in the family, doesn't it, Grandad?' Jessica chopped and strained the leeks under the tap and put them on to boil. 'How many people are coming on this picnic anyway?'

'I'm not sure. Your mother and Maggie have been doing most of the organising. There's a list on the pinboard over there.'

Jessica went to look and smiled. 'It'll be great to see everybody. There are twenty-eight names here, but I don't see Aunt Karin's anywhere, isn't she coming? Her kids are all there, and her six grandchildren.'

'I don't know.' Patrick suddenly became very absorbed in cleaning out his pipe. 'She went back to Denmark about a month ago. It was all rather unexpected – some birthday celebration or other in Jutland, she wasn't at all sure if she'd be back in time or not.'

'But I thought she'd only just come back from there?'

'Yes, she had.' His voice was gruff.

'Oh . . . I'm really sorry. I love Karin. I was longing to see her. I've not seen her since last summer when you both came to see me in Oxford.'

Patrick grunted.

'You know, when you came to my end of term concert.'

'Yes, of course. It was a lovely concert, Jessica. We both enjoyed it, and we loved the trip in the punt.'

'I liked it best when Derek fell in.'

Patrick laughed. 'I felt sorry for the poor lad. How is he, these days?'

'He's fine. He's working in a good legal firm. Looking forward to your party.'

'I don't know why everybody's making such a fuss. It's only a birthday. I hate being so very ancient, hate being creaky.' He looked at her severely, 'Old age, you know . . .'

'Is not for cissies,' Jessica finished the sentence with him. 'Yes, Grandad, I know it's not, but you're not a cissy. Never will be. You look terrific, we all love you and you make me laugh more than anybody I know. Will you wear your tweed knickerbockers for me tomorrow?'

'You're very sweet, darling. Yes, I will. The kilt's not the best garment in a boat.'

'D'you have any nutmeg here?'

'There should be some in that little red tin, Karin usually keeps me well stocked.'

Jessica found a nutmeg and grated it into her white sauce.

'Smells good.' Patrick smiled over to her.

'I bet Karin'll turn up, Grandad. She wouldn't miss a tribal gathering like this – she's mad about the May Island – and she's pretty fond of you as well.'

Patrick shrugged. 'Doesn't make any odds to me, I see her often enough.'

The old lad didn't sound too convincing. Busy stirring,

Jessica didn't really know what to say.

Patrick stood up and peered out of the window. 'It's a beautiful night. I think I'll go and sit in the garden and have a pipe, if you don't mind.'

'OK. As soon as this is in the oven, I'll get some supper going and fetch you a glass of wine.'

The old man smiled. 'That's my girl. Bring one for yourself too.'

Sophie and Michel, walking through the village, carrying plastic bags from the supermarket, had stopped by the harbour to watch a fisherman unload his catch from a small boat when Sophie nudged Michel. 'He's got a lobster, and loads of prawns. How about it?'

Michel didn't answer.

'Michel,' Sophie persisted. 'What do you think?'

Michel started. 'About what?'

'The lobster, the prawns? We could take them to the picnic.'

'I don't know.' Michel shrugged.

Sophie shook her head. 'You never bloody know, these days. It's like talking to a zombie. Do you have any money left?'

Michel remained silent. He was peering out into the distance.

'Michel. Money. Do you have any?'

He frowned. 'Why are you shouting at me?'

'Because I don't want to have to ask you three times . . .'

'Why do you want money?'

'For the lobster and the prawns.'

'Why didn't you say so? Here.' He handed her some money.

Sophie glared and took it, and went over to the blond fisherman, who she'd once been to school with. 'Hiya, Kenny.'

'Hi there, Soph. I didnae see ye, I was busy unloading this lot. How're ye doing?'

'Good.' Sophie nodded. 'Any chance you'd sell us the shellfish?'

'Sure. I dinnae like lobsters. I've had that many of them, I'm fed up wi them, lobster sandwiches till they're coming out my ears. If they're too wee, we're not supposed to sell them. You can have that big one and all the other prawns and bits for a fiver, for old times' sake. Here, I'll just strap up its claws, and here's a bag for the prawns.'

Sophie watched enthralled as the young man expertly man-handled the enormous Prussian blue and orange lobster and swiftly secured the lethal-looking pincers (which could easily remove a man's finger) with twine.

Kenny eyed Michel, who was standing at the edge of the quay, staring sightlessly out to sea.

'Is that your French lad?'

Sophie nodded.

'I met him before, when he used to do building work with Robert Dougall in Pittenweem.'

'That's how we met.'

'Very good.' Kenny grinned. 'I'm married now. I've got two bairns,' he added proudly. 'My wife's a nurse, but she's not working just now.'

'We were just going to the pub,' said Sophie. 'D'you fancy a beer?'

Kenny grinned. 'Sounds good to me, but I'll need to make it a quick one, or I'll get told off.'

The pub was near the harbour and had a terrace looking out to sea.

'Let's sit outside, it's such a gorgeous night. I'll get us a table.' Sophie went out to the terrace which looked across the glittering sea. The evening was so clear and calm that you could almost see houses and cars miles away on the other side of the water. The mellow light made everything slightly pink.

She felt relieved that at least Michel had surfaced enough from his dream world to buy them all drinks.

'What a night, eh?' said Kenny. 'There can't be many

places this beautiful, not even in France, eh, Michel?'

Michel nodded. 'Yes. It is beautiful. It's even as beautiful as Provence.'

'We're going to the May Island tomorrow,' said Sophie. 'It's my uncle's eightieth birthday.'

'I know you are. I'm coming too.' Kenny grinned. 'He's chartered my uncle's boat and my uncle's asked me to help out.'

'Great.' Sophie grinned. 'Isn't that super, Michel?'

'What?'

Sophie leaned over to knock on his forehead with her knuckle clenched. 'Halloo . . . *bonjour* . . . is there anybody inside there?'

Michel frowned. 'I'm sorry. I was thinking about something, trying to work out something for the TV theme. Maybe I should leave you and go back to the studio.'

'Maybe you should. I'll go to Mum's place and cook the lobster – I'll need one of her big pots. Will you come to Ma's for supper?'

'I'm not very hungry.' Michel drained his glass, stood up and held out his hand to Kenny. 'Goodbye, nice to meet you. Please forgive me, but I need to do some work.'

'Thank you and goodbye,' murmured Sophie when he'd gone. 'You must excuse him, Kenny. He gets like that sometimes.'

'He's a composer, isn't he?'

Sophie nodded. 'Yes he is, and usually he's nice and sociable and loveable, not like this.'

'Artistic temperament, eh?'

'Something like that.' Sophie's face quivered and Kenny smiled sympathetically; then he looked beyond her and murmured, 'Who's this now? What a fine-looking giant of a man, eh?'

Sophie turned and found herself looking up at a man who was at least two meters tall, grey-haired and cheerful, smartly dressed in a subtle green, well-cut linen suit and shirt. He was walking out on to the terrace, carrying a bottle of red wine and three glasses, closely followed by a smiling Karin.

Delighted, Sophie jumped up and ran to hug her great-aunt. 'Karin! Hooray! You're here! We thought you weren't going to make it.'

Karin kissed her. 'I knew I couldn't miss Patrick's birthday, so we decided to come back today.' She turned to her tall companion, who was still holding the open bottle of wine. 'This is Sven Jacobsen, a very old friend of mine from Jutland.'

Sven put the tray down and held out his hand. 'We are very old friends indeed. Kindergarten friends from Copenhagen, so you had better not count up how long ago that was.'

Kenny was about to leave, but Sophie introduced him as her old friend from Inverie Primary School. 'He's just caught these,' she showed the Danes the shellfish. 'And he's taking us on the boat tomorrow.'

'Marvellous,' said Sven. 'Then please will you join us for a drink?'

'I really ought to get home . . .' said Kenny.

'Me too,' said Sophie. 'Ma'll be wondering if we've fallen into the harbour.'

'But Maggie's just coming,' said Karin. 'I rang to ask her to join us here, and Morag and Donnie.'

Sven grinned. 'Then I shall fetch some more glasses. You'll join us too, I hope?' he said to Kenny.

'Thanks but no. I'll get told off if I'm late. I promised to bath the kids tonight.' He stood up to go. 'Nice to meet you, and I'll see you tomorrow,' he said and left, at which point Maggie arrived.

'Heavens, it's a party. How lovely,' she said, and was introduced to the beaming Sven, who bowed sweetly and immediately had an intensely communicative exchange with her about the beauties of the village, Scotland, Denmark and Fife, and told her, as he shared out the bottle, that he'd been to school and university in Copenhagen with her mother. Tasting the wine, which was delicious, Sven nodded, pleased with his choice. 'I think I'll just go and see if they have another bottle,' he said, and disappeared back inside the pub.

'What a charmer,' Maggie whispered to Karin, who tried not to look flustered.

'He is. He's a scientist, still working on alternative forms of fuel. He has a laboratory in Aarhus, in a beautiful forest of tall oak trees overlooking the sea. It's a beautiful place, you can see sailing boats through the trees.'

'He seems quite a special man,' said Sophie.

'Yes.' Karin took a huge gulp of wine, and turned to smile, a little dizzily, at Sven, who was walking towards them, holding up a second bottle of Margaux. 'He's very special. He still windsurfs at his age.'

This impressed them all.

'Where's Michel?' Maggie whispered to Sophie as Sven leant over Karin to refill her glass and murmured something which made her blush.

'He wants to be alone,' Sophie muttered. 'He's worried about the TV job.'

'He's at the studio?'

'Yes. I think I'll leave him there tonight. He's just not well. May I sleep at the cottage with you?'

'Of course, darling.' Maggie patted her daughter's hand. She could see she was very fragile. 'Maybe he needs a bit of creative space.'

'Maybe. He's been very touchy all week.' Sophie nodded and smiled wanly as the regal old Viking refilled her glass.

'What's everybody giving Patrick?' asked Maggie. Then, turning to Sven, 'Have you met Patrick yet? I take it you'll be coming on this picnic?'

'I haven't met him, but I've brought him some smoked eel and some special Akvavit, which I hope will be acceptable. And yes, I'm very much looking forward to seeing the May Island.'

'I've made him a red cashmere rug,' said Karin. 'I wove

it just before I went away, it's very soft and warm.'

'Lovely,' murmured Sophie. 'Michel and I are giving him a tape of us both, Michel's songs mostly. We've just done the CD. And Ma, what have you got?'

'Just a wee painting of the old church, the view from my bedroom window with flowers in a vase.'

'It sounds beautiful,' said Sven. 'I wish it was my birthday again.'

Karin laughed. 'You did very well at your birthday. It was only ten days ago,' she explained. 'We went to Skaagen, all Sven's children and grandchildren . . .'

'And three great-grandchildren,' added Sven, beaming.

'There were thirty-five of us, and we swam in the sea and ate lots of fish.'

'Skaagen?' asked Sophie.

'It's the most northerly tip of Denmark,' explained Sven. 'A very dramatic place, where the Baltic Sea and the North Sea collide. You can walk on the sandy point right out to the very end of Denmark and see where the two seas meet. Sometimes it's quite amazing, both are so powerful. For us Danes it is a very special spot, a place of pilgrimage. People walk there with bare feet, sometimes they weep with national pride. Anyway . . .' Sven smiled. 'I think it will be a wonderful trip tomorrow if the weather is the same as today. I'm very happy to be in your beautiful East Neuk. *Skaal*, everybody. I am so glad to meet you all.'

Later that evening, as Gilbert Menstrie (returning from a convention of model railways enthusiasts in Kirkcaldy Town Hall) walked down the hill towards his house with a couple of fish suppers in his hand, he heard a yell from inside Maggie's house, and a moment later saw Maggie's wild-eyed daughter, who came out, shrieking 'I can't stand it! It's horrible!'

Gilbert wondered for a moment if he should help, but he was late and his mother would be wondering where both he and her supper had got, so he averted his sight and hurried past. He was intrigued all the same, because only minutes ago he'd stood in the fish and chip queue behind that long-haired boyfriend of Sophie's. Michel's hair which was usually tied back in a tail these days, was all over the place and he didn't look very well. When the girl in the chip van had asked him what he wanted he hadn't answered for ages; she'd had to ask twice. In the end he'd ordered a fish supper and then when she'd asked him if he wanted salt and vinegar, he hadn't answered at all.

The girl had rolled her eyes before decisively sprinkling a little of each on to his meal, parcelling it firmly up and saying very clearly, 'That will be three pounds and sixty pence, please.'

Michel had handed over the money and walked off heavily, with a worrying, old man's walk.

When Gilbert was walking home, he saw Michel, who was ahead of him, go into that wee place that Maggie had rented from the Hendersons – the two-roomed terraced cottage that old Jackie Henderson had grown up in, along with nine brothers and sisters and a couple of cats.

Outside his own house, where his ninety-year-old mother watched his arrival in the car mirror she kept at her kitchen window so that she could see who was coming down the brae, Gilbert paused and looked back. Sophie had obviously calmed down now, and was sitting on the doorstep, but she was looking very fed up. Gilbert frowned to himself as he let himself in to the house. There was definitely something up with Arty Maggie's family.

Maggie turned off the boiling cauldron and fished out the huge lobster. She wasn't surprised that Sophie had yelled, it was bloody murder; she hated killing the creature too, but tomorrow they'd eat the rich white flesh and exult. She knew Patrick would be pleased; he adored lobster.

'It's all done,' she called, and Sophie, very pale, came back in.

'I think I'll go along and see if Michel is OK,' she

said. 'I'll need my toothbrush and things if I'm sleeping here.'

'OK, darling. I'll be here, and if you don't come back I won't send out a search party. Maybe he just needs a real long sleep.'

'Maybe, yeah. See you, Ma.'

Sophie felt quite strange as she walked to the little studio. Up till now she and Michel had always been happy here, but today she was actually trembling when she tapped on the door.

At first there was no answer, so she tried again, a little louder this time. After what seemed ages, Michel, naked, wrapped in a blanket, opened the door. He looked at Sophie suspiciously as though she was a stranger. 'Yes?'

'I just wondered if you were OK . . .'

Michel shrugged.

'Maggie's made a lovely supper . . .'

'I've eaten.'

'. . . and if you still want to be alone?'

He nodded. 'I do.'

'Then I'll take my toothbrush. And what about the picnic – aren't you coming to it?'

He went to sit at the scrubbed wooden table without looking at her, and slowly finished his last fragments of chips, then he wrapped up the cardboard box and the greasy paper and put them into the wastepaper basket.

'No. I'm not able to be sociable.'

Sophie bit her lip. 'Shall I make us a hot drink?' she asked hopefully, when she'd gathered up her things.

He shook his head.

'Michel,' Sophie looked imploringly at him, trying not to feel alarmed by his awful pallor. 'Please can't you talk to me and try and tell me what's wrong? Are you worrying about the telly job, or is it something I've said or done? Just speak to me, please. Won't you go and see the doctor?'

'Why do you want me to be rational?' asked Michel at last, his eyes dull.

'Because you usually are. But for the last few weeks you've been weird, you don't talk to me, you don't answer me. I feel as though I don't really exist for you . . . that I've become invisible. Sylvia and the rest of the chamber group feel the same. And you've stopped doing things, helping with the house. Cooking, shopping. It's . . . it's almost as though you aren't there any more.'

It took ages for Michel to answer and when he did, listening to him, trying to understand, Sophie was shocked to see his eyes fill with tears.

'I feel as though you've been wanting me to love you for the last couple of weeks. Why? Why do keep trying to draw me into things?' he said at last.

'Surely that's a pretty basic human need? I am only human, I love you . . . I need you. I want to help you and be there for you,' she said, agonised.

Michel was silent for a long time, then he banged the table. 'I feel crazy! Yes, really mad. But . . .' He looked at Sophie with great passion and despair, 'I'm an artist, a composer, and surely it's reasonable to be like that sometimes. It's what can be expected of an artist, a good artist. And you seem to want me to be a happy artist, like somebody who composes jingles for muesli ads, and that would make me a terrible artist and an unhappy man.'

'No . . . I just want you to be the Michel you normally are. I miss you . . .'

He stood up and roared. 'But I'm crazy! Can't you understand?'

Sophie's tears came falling so fast she could hardly breathe. 'I'm trying to,' she said at last.

'Please, please,' said Michel, and he was crying fully now too. 'Just give me a little time. I just can't answer any questions about anything, not about milk or sugar, coffee or tea or do I love you. I just need to be here alone with my madness. I can't help it.'

Sophie looked over to the corner of the room where the calor gas heater stood.

'Aren't you frightened by how you are feeling?' she asked at last.

'Sometimes, yes. This afternoon at the harbour I was feeling pretty suicidal and that made me realise what a bad condition I was in, and that I needed some time by myself.'

Sophie put her bag down and tried to hug him but he flinched and drew away. The futon on the floor was a shambles. She looked at it. 'Shall I tidy up the bed?' she asked faintly.

'No!' Michel shouted. 'No! No! No! Just leave me alone, PLEASE.'

'OK. I'm going.' With what dignity she could summon, Sophie picked up her bag and went to the door. As she closed it behind her, she felt suddenly terrified, compelled to go back. Once more Michel opened the door and looked at her as though she were an unknown person. 'Is it anything special?' he asked.

No, she thought silently, despairingly, only our lives, our love, you, me, our everything, that's all.

'You won't do anything stupid, will you, please?' she managed to stammer.

Michel looked at her as though she was completely idiotic. Frowning, he said doubtfully that he didn't think so.

Sophie didn't feel ready to go back to her mother's. She felt like a refugee, deserted, with every security wrenched away from her. Only a few weeks ago, the pair of them had been blissfully happy and now it was as though that Michel had been a dream.

She truly didn't think she had done anything to make him like this: they loved each other, she knew they did. But now her beautiful, funny, partner had turned into this stranger who acted as though he didn't know, love or want her, and she had absolutely no idea how to help him.

She walked along the street, past the harbour and down to the shore, unhappily aware that every person she passed seemed to be one of a couple. Standing on the beach, she wondered, as she looked out at the sea, calm and inviting, rose-pink in the last rays of the sun, just how easy it would be to walk into the water and let go of everything, as the wife of a distant writer-cousin had done, long before she was born. It was a seductive thought. When is a breakdown not a breakdown? Was this to be the pattern for the future? Could Sophie stand it? Could Michel stand it? What on earth could she do to bring him back to himself?

She stood gazing at the sea for some time, and then slowly and very deliberately, walked into the water until it was well up over her knees. She stayed there for a few minutes, desolate, half yearning to immerse herself, but it was agonisingly cold. Eventually, she turned back and walked back up the beach and on to the road, her soaked jeans freezing on her legs, her shoes squelching. Not even when her father died had she felt so unhappy and abandoned.

Chapter Nine

Late next morning, at Anstruther harbour, Gilbert Menstrie, clutching bags of shopping, witnessed the gathering of the three families – Patrick's, Karin's and Maggie's – as they parked their cars and, laden with picnic hampers, rucksacks and clinking bottles, made their way to the boat which would take them to the May Island.

They were such a noisy lot, all speaking very yaw-yaw, with lots of hugging and kissing; it was too blooming theatrical for Gilbert's taste. And there was old Sir Patrick, who was well known to Gilbert through his work at the planning office, where they'd often clashed. The old boy must be eighty if he was a day, and my goodness was he dolled up to the nines today. Deerstalker, tweed knickerbockers, woollen stockings and red flashes, with a belted jacket, binoculars and a massive great cromach. Who on earth did the man think he was? And everybody was flurrying about, embracing him, handing over parcels, squealing at the top of their middle-class voices. Gilbert recognised a lot of them: he was sure the youngsters must be the grandchildren of that Danish weaver woman who lived up at the top. He recognised her two daughters and her son. He'd had more than one altercation with them on the beach when they were all young. But their mother had fairly kept her figure; she always looked swish, even in old jeans and jerseys, you could tell she was well bred. And who, he wondered, was that great telegraph pole of a man with her? He looked like an elderly Superman, and made her seem positively petite. She was introducing the big chap to Sir Patrick now, they were shaking hands, and it pleased Gilbert to see that even the tall Sir Patrick, who was well over six feet, had to look upwards to speak to him.

Despite his disapproval, Gilbert enjoyed the spectacle, and managed to take a very long time loading up his cherished Morris Minor shooting brake. After a while he saw his neighbour, Maggie, drive up and park. She emerged from the car looking a bit anxious, lugging a great big cool box all by herself. Her hair was a bright orange these days, which made his mother mutter in disgust, though Gilbert actually thought it quite suited her. She was wearing some sort of striped top – a cardigan of many colours – bright red gym shoes and jeans. She looked very attractive considering her age, he thought. Gilbert used to secretly fancy Maggie when he was a teenager, but she'd never even glanced in his direction, at least not in that way, but to be honest, nobody really ever had. There was no sign yet of young Sophie or the French lad. Curious, you'd have thought they'd come together. Maybe Sophie's shouting of the previous night had something to do with her absence. What on earth had all that been about?

When Sophie tapped on the studio door at a quarter past eleven, Michel, still naked and now unshaven, opened the door cautiously and peered out suspiciously. He looked awful.

'Yes?'

She could have been a brush salesman or a born-again Christian for all the warmth there was in his voice.

'Can I come in?'

Shrugging, he went inside and she followed, closing the door behind her. She watched as Michel went to the table and sat down to finish a mug of coffee.

'I made up some fresh fruit salad and muesli for you. Here.' She laid it in front of him.

'I ate some toast.' The studio only had an electric kettle and a historic toaster.

'Michel. It's Patrick's May Island picnic today. We've to meet in Anstruther in three quarters of an hour.'

'I'm not coming.' Michel shook his head and looked at the table top.

'But I thought you wanted to go. It should be lovely and relaxing, and everybody's going to be there – Jessica and her boyfriend, Derek, Karin and Ma and Karin's lot from Glasgow and William and Fanny and the kids – and she's got a lovely Danish friend staying who I know you'll like. I told Ma we were going to sing something for Paddy's birthday. Please come.'

'I said no.'

'But why?'

'Sophie, why do you want me to be rational?'

'I don't. I just want to try to understand what's happened. Please, Michel, if it's something I've done, tell me, because you seem to loathe seeing me.'

It didn't help. After a lengthy silence he sighed, and looking down at the table, said that he appreciated that it must be difficult for her to have a partner who suddenly went nuts, but that it really was nobody's fault. And when he'd finished speaking, he did look at her for a moment, and she felt icy with fear, his face was so white, his eyes so blackly remote.

'But . . . my love, if you're sick, surely you need help – a doctor or a therapist . . .'

'Yesterday afternoon I did think of becoming a voluntary patient somewhere, but decided against it.'

'But why didn't you tell me that?'

He ignored her, and as he kept on talking, all she could think of was how unwell he looked.

'It might be glandular, in which case drugs might help, but I'd refuse electric shock treatment, and I'd be scared of interfering with my creativity with drugs.'

'But . . .' said Sophie, 'I don't think they even do electric shock treatment much these days, but they do have really good anti-depressants.'

'I'm still very accident-prone.'

'Accident-prone?'

'Driving badly, like you said, and I've been clumsy, knocking things over.'

At least he was talking now, though he wasn't looking at her at all.

'And I have some very peculiar ideas.'

'Such as?'

He shrugged, and his eyes slid sideways, heavy lidded. 'I went to the harbour and realised that the boats were incredibly ugly, which was an interesting idea.'

At least, thought Sophie, he's rational enough to find his peculiar ideas interesting. But for Michel to say boats were ugly was really weird: he was always going on about how inspiring they were.

After a long silence, she dared to ask again if he wouldn't come.

'No.'

'Why?'

'I'm not ready for any responsibilities.'

'Nobody's asking you to be responsible. I'm asking you to come to a lovely trip with people you like, and to eat and drink good food and wine. It'll be really relaxing.'

'I'm not ready for any living in a social society.'

'It's only a picnic, Michel, but an important one! I'm only asking you to *be* there. You could be as quiet as you liked, you don't have to perform if you don't want to or even be particularly sociable, you can just come and enjoy it quietly – nobody's expecting anything of you.'

As he shook his head she thought how Rastalike his uncombed hair looked today.

'I don't even want the social responsibilities which that would entail,' he said at last.

Sophie couldn't speak.

'Anyway,' said Michel. 'I quite like it here. It's like being *en vacances*. I get up when I want, eat when I want.'

'But what about me?' wailed Sophie. 'What about us?'

'I'm sorry,' said Michel very quietly. 'But I can't help. Please, you go to the picnic.'

'I don't want to go without you. I'll miss you, it won't be the same, going alone. Anyway, what'll I say to everybody?'

'Tell them that Michel's brain has overheated like a car engine, that he just needs to cool down. He's been doing too much.'

'OK, I will, but if your brain's overheated, can we not find a way to help it to cool down?'

'No.'

It was no, no, no, all the way. Impasse.

'Please, darling,' she said at last. She was finding it hard to speak. 'I don't want to go alone. I won't enjoy it without you. I could stay with you if you like. Maybe we could go to the doctor?'

Michel shook his head. 'I need to be alone.'

He stood up at last without looking at her. 'I'm going to have a shower,' he announced in a cold, impersonal voice.

Her aching eyes on his impeccably muscled back and firmly elegant buttocks whose contours she had so often lovingly embraced, she watched speechless as he turned away from her and went into the next room, firmly closing the door behind him.

Sophie wanted to howl like a wild beast. She listened impotently to the sounds of water gushing. Then she saw a piece of paper with Michel's writing on the mantelpiece and went over to read it, nervously listening for the shower stopping. It was written in ink, quite neatly.

Why are all the boats in the harbour ugly, said the Madman.
Why are we all crying, said the Madman.

It was thoughtless of me to go mad, said the Madman.
Why can't I just sleep, said the Madman.
These Madmen think I talk sense, said the Madman.
I was under the mistaken notion that I was mad, said the Madman.

It didn't enlighten Sophie much. She wondered for a moment if he'd been on anything, but it was ages since he'd even had a joint. The strange poem alarmed her, and made her realise afresh that her man was in a mess, and she wished she knew if any of the Madmen were aspects of herself so she could find a way to help him.

She looked at her watch. If she was going to the picnic she'd better hurry. There seemed no point in her staying. Michel was taking ages in the shower, so she left a note for him telling him that she loved him and that she'd gone to join the others, and set off running up the hill to her car.

As she drove the few miles to Anstruther, Sophie could hardly see the road: she felt frightened, outraged and miserable in turn. Part of her wanted to scream and hurl rocks, or to drive into violent oblivion. How dare he behave as though he didn't really know or love her? She couldn't imagine life if things were to continue with him in this state. Today's Michel didn't seem remotely like her darling man; it was as though he'd had a personality transplant. It was his same beautiful body, only now it was a body that didn't want her; the Michel that she knew and loved simply didn't seem to be inside it any more.

But he did love her, she knew he did. Surely this madness would pass. She still felt absolutely certain that he loved her, and she loved him, but things couldn't continue like this. They'd have to get help.

She was lucky to find a parking space. Fortunately, Ma's neighbour and lifelong enemy, Ghastly Gilbert, was just pulling out from the kerb as she arrived, so she slipped into his place. She could see the boat over by the jetty, with her mother and one or two others waving like mad. They were just about to cast off, when, breathless, she ran up the gangway.

On the boat, there was much excitement as they sailed out of the harbour for the hour-long trip to the island. Patrick sat on the lower deck, beaming in the sunshine, bemused with all the loving attention. Jennifer Earlsferry, headscarfed, equipped with swirling tartan cape, walking boots and binoculars, managed to put herself next to him by aggressively squeezing her bulk in between young Jessica and her grandfather. His three children – Maggie's contemporaries, all in their fifties – and a handful of grandchildren, sat nearby.

William, a tall, good-looking man, obviously Patrick's son even if you hadn't been told – he had the same upsweeping eyebrows and generous mouth – stood up and announced that he wished to speak. It was hard to hear him, the wind and the sea whipped away his words, but everybody watched as ceremoniously he handed his father an elegant package wrapped in dark grey paper, tied with blue ribbon.

'It must be something he's made,' Karin whispered to Maggie. William was one of Scotland's most distinguished silversmiths.

Everybody smiled as Patrick carefully undid the wrappings, and Lady Jennifer took the pieces from him and stowed them away inside a voluminous National Trust shopping bag. The package contained a black box which opened to reveal a chunky, circular, slightly curved, beautifully made silver hip-flask with Patrick's initial and birthday date engraved on one corner.

He smiled up at his son as he fondled the smooth shining metal, savouring the shape.

'Made to measure. Beautiful. Thank you, William.'

William grinned. 'Please test the contents, Father.'

Patrick unscrewed the lid, sniffed and beamed. 'Now that, my son, is what I call a vintage malt.'

Everybody clapped enthusiastically as he tested the whisky.

'Marvellous. It's a truly perfect object. I am thrilled.'

Across from Patrick, Maggie could see from Sophie's white worried face that she was struggling. Everybody was naturally asking the two of them where Michel had got to, and they both said, as they had agreed to say, that he was working, had been overworking, and had an important TV commission.

'What's the commission for?' asked Sven, who was beside Sophie.

'It's a wildlife documentary about the Camargue, flamingoes and horses, stuff like that.'

'And mosquitoes?' queried Sven. 'There are very many of those too.'

'I don't know.' Sophie shrugged. 'But it's his first TV commission, so it's a big one for him. If it goes well it could lead to more. He's done wee bits, linking music and the odd little theme tune for radio, but nothing quite like this.'

'I wish him luck. I look forward to meeting him.'

Sophie smiled wanly. 'Me too.'

Anstruther, shrinking in the distance, looked like the most enticingly romantic village anybody could invent, and the company was filled with harmony as the boat moved towards the island. At last, there was a shout from one of the youngsters.

'A seal – over there on the right!'

Then somebody pointed out a couple of puffins and people chuckled as they watched the birds' whirring, clockwork flight.

Young Kenny was at the wheel, chatting to his uncle. The uncle, a sturdily built man with grey hair and lively blue eyes, looked slightly familiar to Maggie, she wasn't sure why.

'You'll not see so many puffins actually on the island today,' he told her. 'They're beginning to gather up for leaving. There were thousands of them yesterday, all sitting together in the water, at the ready.'

'Where do they go to?'

'Nobody's quite sure. They disappear at the end of August, all twenty-five thousand pairs of them. Somewhere out in the North Sea, they reckon.'

Karin and Sven joined them at the rail. The tall sheer cliffs of the Isle of May were standing out clearly as they drew nearer.

'How impressive it looks.'

'Aye.' The boatman nodded. 'It's a grand place. But I wouldn't like to be alone there in the winter.'

Karin turned to Sven, who smilingly took her arm. Maggie noticed her return the smile, but retreat delicately from his touch.

'Shall we go up on top?' he asked, and Karin nodded.

Patrick, woosy from the malt and the joys of patriarchy, watched a little glumly as they climbed the iron stairway. Karin was behind Sven, who turned to say something to her, and she laughed.

She was mad about him. It was obvious. She was glowing. It was a fait accompli, of that Patrick felt certain, and he didn't reckon there was anything he could do about it. Dammit.

Jennifer Earlsferry was on her feet, trying to haul him up to the rail. 'Oh, look, Patrick. There are lots of puffins over there – there must be hundreds of them. And seals. Oh, my goodness! What a huge one, lying on the rock here. Do look.'

She turned to him, gushing, teeth and eyes shining. 'Isn't it absolutely fantastic? And such perfect weather?'

Patrick heaved himself up and held on to the rail as he gazed at the sombre cliffs ahead, with clouds of wheeling screeching gulls whirling past.

'Very fine. We're extremely lucky,' he said gloomily and took a further swig from his new hip-flask, which fitted his hand like a sea-smoothed stone.

As the boat chugged nearer the island, they saw thousands of puffins, comical and adorable, and seals that stared at them curiously from the sea or flopped clumsily off the rocks. One seal came very close and gazed at them for ages and the children on board called to the creature and cackled with delight.

They landed in a rocky inlet with a strip of sand near the jetty. Kenny and his uncle tied up the boat and fixed the gangway and everybody gathered in a group, holding rugs, coats, bottles and baskets.

Silversmith William took charge and pointed up the hill.

'We're going to stop for our picnic up there, just beyond the monastery ruins. There's a lovely little natural amphitheatre, perfect for the job. Follow me, and bring everything with you that you'll need.' Everybody cheered. Maggie was relieved to see that even Sophie managed to raise a tiny smile.

At the end of the group heading for the picnic place, was Karin's thirteen-year-old granddaughter, Catriona, and her older brother, Callum. They were both giggling.

'I'm telling you, it's the honest truth,' insisted Catriona.

'It can't be,' snorted Callum. 'Granny Karin's even older than Patrick. I'm not sure if it's even physically possible at that age.'

'Well, I saw with my own eyes. I arrived an hour earlier than Karin was expecting me, because the people I was staying with were off to a gymkhana in Cupar and didn't want to be late. So I caught them completely unawares. They hadn't even started breakfast.'

'In flagrante?' Callum savoured the phrase.

'No. Not quite. Seven was wearing a dressing-gown, but I saw him come out of her bedroom, all rumpled and cheery. She nearly died of embarrassment, honestly.'

'Maybe he was just borrowing something?' reasoned Callum. 'Maybe *she* was sleeping in the spare room. He's very tall. Ordinary beds couldn't really fit him.'

'No, he wasn't. I peeked in the spare room, and it had

cardboard boxes of wool all over the beds, and books and things. No way did he sleep in the spare room.'

'Wow.' Callum looked up ahead to where the adults had stopped and Sven was helping his grandmother to lay out a tartan rug on the grass. 'Cool.'

Catriona nodded. 'We'd better not say anything. I don't think poor old Paddy's very happy.'

'Oh, shit. No. I never thought of that. Poor old Patrick.'

'D'you think she's two-timing?'

Callum grinned. 'I don't know, but whatever it is, it's certainly doing her good. She's mega cheery these days.'

Back in Inverie, Michel was heading slowly for the area of beach not far from Maggie's house. It was a flattish, raised beach, rocky and black, composed mainly of ancient lava, and if the tide wasn't too far in, and you walked across it towards the sea, avoiding fissures, rock pools and occasional black boulders, you met with the far rocks. The one Michel was heading for was Partan Rock, formed from white sandstone, which stretched for a couple of hundred metres out into the Forth. It resembled some huge prehistoric creature, and was peopled only by seabirds.

From her kitchen window, old Mrs Menstrie, leaning on her Zimmer, peered dubiously after him. 'There's yon French daftie,' she told Gilbert. 'Heading straight out for the rocks, and the tide's soon coming in. He must think he can walk on water.'

Michel clambered and even had to wade the last bit until he reached the furthermost area of rock, out of sight from the village. He found a place to park himself beside a pink clump of sea thrift, where with a sigh of relief, he shed his jacket and T-shirt. Then he sat down heavily and stared out at the water, the back of his head and his bare back leaning against a bluff, his eyes sombre.

The picnic party was well under way. There was lots of champagne, a huge supply of all kinds of seafood and home-made delicacies from many of the guests, who had arranged themselves in a circle, seated on tussocks of turf, rocks and tartan rugs. Patrick was on the highest flattest rock, a gold plastic champagne glass (supplied by Maggie from one of her Provençal trips) in hand. He finished scoffing yet another oyster (one of the guests had brought eighty, many of which the guest-of-honour had consumed) and wiped his chin. 'Delicious, absolutely delicious . . .'

'Speech!' shouted Catriona, followed by Callum and Jessica, then everybody was calling to him. At last, Patrick managed to stand up, and the handsome William handed him his cromach to help him keep his balance, and refilled his glass.

'My dears, I just want to welcome you all to this very special place on what is not only a gloriously sunny, but also for me a very special day. Both my parents died before they were fifty, and my poor dear Margot was only sixty-three, so I feel particularly grateful to have achieved this absolutely terrifying age in moderately decent health.'

This was greeted by huge cheers and great waving of glasses.

'I want to say how precious life is, how tenuous. I feel that we are only lent to each other for as long as life and love are granted. It's not something over which we have much control. But for myself, I can say that every new season that I am permitted to see, is a privilege and a delight. Life is the great miracle, the gift we are granted at birth, and as I grow every day older, so the world seems to me more beautiful and the people in it more precious . . .'

At this point, Patrick's newest family member, Rory, aged three and a quarter, wearing his first kilt and furry sporran, walked over to his great-grandfather, took his hand and smiled up at him, and everybody said Aaaah. Patrick handed William his glass, carefully lay down his cromach, and lifted up the little boy in his arms. William, watching, thought for an awful moment that his father might teeter and fall, but Patrick managed to maintain his chiefly stance.

'This,' he said, his voice vigorous and happy, 'this is what I mean. Life. The ongoing joyful unstoppable, and magnificently unpredictable miracle. Let's drink to it and all of us. To Life.'

He kissed little Rory and put the child down, grasped his glass again, and the boy stayed beside him, grinning.

'To Life. To all of us. To Patrick.' Everybody quaffed and toasted. But Patrick was by no means finished.

'I also want to thank you all for simply being, whether it is as part of my actual family, or simply for the sharing of friendship and for the good times and the hellish times we have variously endured or enjoyed together. I love you all, and cherish our subtle and varied connections.'

There were more cheers. Many of the group were moved, Karin perhaps most of all.

'You will all have noticed,' Patrick continued loudly, to quell his audience, 'that we have a Viking contingent with us today . . .'

Callum nudged Catriona and rolled his eyes at his sister as Patrick regally gestured towards Sven and Karin – Karin was now smiling a little anxiously.

'And I would like to bid today's Viking welcome.'

He looked towards Sven, who bowed regally in acknowledgement, smiled, and raised his glass to the speaker.

Patrick was getting into his stride now, but the little boy at his feet was engrossed by a ladybird on his knee, which he found much more interesting.

'What some of you may not know is that we had a visit from the Vikings here in much earlier times. In 800 AD, to be exact, and those Vikings managed to slaughter eight thousand people in the East Neuk alone, all in a very short space of time, which must have been quite a feat as I don't think the population can be much more than that these days.'

Glancing across, Maggie noted that Sven, still looking

friendly, was now also beginning to look a little puzzled. Karin, her eyes suspiciously moist, was definitely frowning, pretending to rub away a spot on her skirt.

'But I trust that today's Viking has come, not to rape and to pillage, but to briefly enjoy and share in what we have to offer, before he returns to his own beautiful country. *Skaal*, sir.'

Sven stood up, all two metres of him, and skaaled smilingly in return, and everybody clapped, relieved that things hadn't turned too pear-shaped after all.

A flurry of alarmed gulls and cormorants had greeted Michel's arrival on the tip of Partan Rock, but eventually, after he'd remained there a good long while, they returned one by one. At one point, when he'd already been sitting almost immobile for four and a half hours, a wild mink, eyes glittering, with a gleaming black coat, raised its head from a rock in the foam to peer at the strange man creature. In the end, the birds barely stirred when Michel stood up and kicked off his sandals. These were followed by his jeans, and moments later his grey Calvin Klein underpants.

At last he was standing naked. Michel looked up at the sky, round at the rocks and back to the top of the conical stone steeple of the old church – which was all he could see of the village, and appeared tiny in the distance – and he smiled. The cormorants and a heron, curious and alert, watched as the tall man stood there very still for a few moments, before walking purposefully towards the indigo water, now swollen to full tide, which gurgled at his feet. He understood now, knew for sure how he could resolve his problem.

Shaking his head, he sighed deeply, and moved to the very edge of the rock, where he squatted down and gazed into the sea for a while, still smiling to himself. Next, slowly and deliberately, with a huge gasp of relief, he slipped his slender body over the edge and immersed himself in the glaucous and chilly embrace of the dark water.

Chapter Ten

Maggie and Jessica had led the singing of 'Happy Birthday to You', the wine and food were finished and, gradually, the assembled company divided into small groups to explore the various bits of the island.

'What do you feel like doing, Patrick?' asked Karin. 'I though I might show Sven the lighthouses. Would you like to join us?'

'I feel like doing very little walking. I've got my collapsible leather stool with me, and I fully intend to sit on it on the clifftop up there, to watch the birds and admire the view. I shall be very content like that. I'd like everybody to go off and do their own thing.'

Karin swithered. 'Are you sure?'

'Absolutely. I shall be entirely blissful, surveying you all through my binoculars.'

'I would be very happy to stay with you, if I may,' suggested Jennifer Earlsferry. 'I do so want to bird-watch, there are thousands and thousands of nests up there on the cliffs.'

'Very well, my dear.' Patrick stood up and gallantly offered the beaming Lady Jennifer his arm. 'Let's go. See you all later, folks. Remember to be at the boat by four forty-five or we'll leave you behind!'

Karin, standing by Sven, had mixed feelings as she watched them set off up the tussocky hill. Part of her still felt responsible for – and fond of – Patrick, but Sven, at her side was looking very cheerful.

'Shall we go?' he asked, offering his arm, and delighted, she nodded.

'What d'you feel like doing, Sophie?' Maggie asked.

Sophie, whose mouth smiled clownlike in her white face – but whose eyes told the truth – whose every step, breath and heartbeat, tolled Michel's name, who for every second of the day, and much of the night, could think only of the man she loved, who, although she was bewildered by his apparent rejection of herself, wished now that she'd stayed near him, shrugged. 'I think I'll go up to the high cliffs,' she whispered. 'I like the view from there.'

Maggie moved to hug her, but Sophie drew away.

'I'm sure Michel'll be OK,' said Maggie. 'It's so unlike him. He'll be his old self soon, I bet you.'

Unconvinced, Sophie nodded, turned away, waved a half-hearted farewell and set off up the path which was outlined with blue-painted markers so you didn't wander off and disturb any of the puffin burrows which the birds shared with the island's numerous rabbits – left over from the rabbits the long-dead monks bred for food.

Maggie was relieved when William touched her arm. 'I think I'd better go up with her, do you think that might be a good idea?'

Maggie nodded, aching with anxiety. She felt so impotent, so full of longing to ease her daughter's – and of course Michel's – misery. William would help if anyone could, Sophie loved William, who'd in a way become her surrogate father since Fergal died.

Maggie pointed eastwards. 'I'm heading for that big rocky bay away down that end. Anyone want to come?'

'I don't think you're allowed down there,' said one of the cousins.

Maggie shrugged. 'I only want to gather some little pieces of driftwood, it's a particularly good beach. I don't really think anybody will mind. I promise I won't walk on any puffin burrows.'

'Can we come?' asked Catriona and Callum. They liked their artist aunt.

It took them fifteen minutes to walk to the rocky cove, where they found great square rocks covered in brilliant yellow lichen, and a beach of huge black cannonball stones. Whooping, the youngsters climbed the rocks, causing about forty cormorants to fly heavily away.

'This is cool,' puffed Callum, coming to rest beside Maggie and examine her gleanings: a pile of driftwood and tangled trawl. 'What will you make with them?'

'I don't know yet, I'll see what comes to me.'

On the clifftop not far from the one Patrick and Lady Jennifer had chosen for their bird-watching, William and Sophie lay side by side on a big tartan rug by the cliff edge and gazed down at the whirling, shrieking birds. In one swoop of the eye you could see people, flowers, insects, rabbits, dozens of species of gulls, puffins, terns, and far down below, in the Prussian-blue waters at the base of the precipitous cliffs, a seal who languished lazily, enjoying the calm weather, and even the occasional (perhaps imagined) glint of fish. It was a visual cornucopia.

Across the water lay the other islands of the Forth, and on the far side, on a day like this you could spot the distinctive shapes of the Edinburgh hills.

'Beautiful, isn't it?' said William softly.

Sophie nodded.

'Will we be seeing Michel at the party tonight?' There was a big party planned, back at Patrick's place.

'I don't know. I suspect not.'

'Tell me about your life, Sophie. I haven't seen you since Christmas, and things I know were very all-go then, but you did seem very happy, both of you.'

'We were. Michel is just a bit . . . well . . . strained at the moment, I think it's been the teaching that's done for him.

It's just too much along with his composing and our free-lancing. What with the chamber group and the gigs he and I do together, there's never a peaceful moment.'

William nodded. 'Sounds as though he's been spreading himself too thin. Did you know I had a terrible crisis about twenty years ago, when I was about thirty-two?'

'No, I didn't.' Sophie shook her head. 'Michel's thirty-one.'

'Well, we already had Gavin, and Jessica was well on the way. I was teaching almost full-time, and doing commissions at night and at weekends. Poor Fanny barely saw me. I'd come out of the workshop and collapse into bed exhausted at 3 am and behave like a zombie in the house.'

'Sounds a wee bit familiar ...' Frowning, Sophie chewed her lip, and looked at him reluctantly. 'So what happened?'

'I ran away from home. Drove up to the Highlands, stayed in a friend's cottage and walked for days, feeling completely insane. Drank a lot of whisky, cried and thought of feeding myself to the eagles.'

Sophie snorted embarrassedly. 'Sorry, I know it's not funny.'

'It is funny. Now it is. But it felt like the end of the world at the time. For all of us.'

'So what happened?'

'Fanny, dear, darling, pregnant Fanny, appeared completely unexpectedly one day – poor love, I hadn't even told her where I was going. She'd left Gavin at home with Ma and Patrick, and she brought lovely food and wine and we had twenty-four hours of talking, weeping, loving ...'

Sophie looked at her sensible, dependable uncle. 'It's hard to imagine you like that.'

'Sophie, it can happen to anybody. Freelancing's a bugger. It erodes people, wears them down, distresses them in every sense, but if you're a truly creative person, you have to make an act of faith upon yourself, otherwise probably nobody else will, unless you're exceptionally lucky. I had to make a choice, either to give up silversmithing or teaching. I couldn't continue doing both. So I stopped teaching.'

'And never looked back?'

William laughed. 'I often looked back. Even now, I sometimes do, but not for long, usually only to shudder at what life used to be like.'

Sophie nodded. 'Maybe you're right. It's not even as if Michel was teaching music, it's French – spelling, conjunctives and irregular verbs. He loathes it.'

'There you go, then.' William smiled at her, and pointed over the cliff edge where a black bird, elegant, with a black and white striped beak and a white front, sat. 'Look at that razorbill. What a perfect piece of design.'

Sophie nodded. Her heart was thumping, only now it wasn't so much of a repetitive dirge, it was more of an optimistic drumbeat. Michel must stop teaching. Yes, he must. That was the way to do it. If he stopped the teaching that would surely help to resolve the problem.

On their adjacent clifftop Lady Jennifer chortled, 'Oh, Patrick. Isn't it an absolutely splendid place? Oh, do look at those sweet, fluffy, little baby gulls trying to fly.'

'Mmmmhh. Splendid.' Patrick, unscrewing his son's present to take another swig, was disappointed to note that it was now empty. He showed her the silver hip-flask. 'A damned fine gift from young William, wasn't it?'

'Wonderful, my dear. I'm sure you'll have much good use of it.'

'I certainly hope so.' Patrick smiled confidently.

'Oh, Patrick. Do look there, just to your left – across the path. That's sorrel, isn't it? Can't you make soup with that?'

'Yes, you can. D'you want some?'

'Well, it might be fun to try.'

'If neither of us want it, I'm sure Karin or Maggie would find a use for it. It's delicious stuff. I'll pick some ...' Putting away the hip-flask, he heaved himself regally up off his leather shooting-stick and Lady Jennifer, watching, said, 'Oh, do be careful now, Patrick—'

Her admonition turned into a scream of horror as she saw him slowly cartwheel, head over heels, till he lay swearing with his head resting precisely on the small outcrop of sorrel he'd been aiming for, and his left foot resting at a decidedly odd angle to the rest of him.

Lady Jennifer rose abruptly to her feet and stood, hands and scarf flailing, shouting shrilly. 'Oh, my God, Patrick. What have you done? HELP! William, Sophie, somebody, HELP!'

In the stony bay, Catriona and Callum had run off to search for seals, but not before young Catriona asked, very meaningfully, what Maggie thought of their grandmother's new Danish friend.

'I think he's super,' said Maggie. 'Don't you?'

Both children giggled, and Catriona nodded. 'Yes, he's great. And we think Grandma's clicked.'

Maggie chuckled. 'Do you now? Well, I have nothing to say on the subject. I'm sure they're just good friends.'

At this, Callum grunted like a gorilla and suggestively scratched his chest, which made the two youngsters explode with giggles.

Catriona spluttered. 'He's actually her toy boy!'

'What?' Maggie couldn't help a smile.

'He is! Grandma Karin's eighty-two, but he's only eighty. She told us his birthday was only a few days ago.'

'I think that's enough,' said Maggie firmly. 'It's their business anyway, and if it's true, good luck to them. I can only hope that I'll be like that at their age. Now, I'm going to dump this stuff on the boat. I'll see you young reprobates later.'

'OK. Ma just went down that way, we'll follow her.'

Back at the boat, Kenny's grey-haired, good-looking uncle was relaxing with an anthology of Scottish poems, and

Kenny, half-asleep, was doing a crossword.

'Are you enjoying that?' Maggie asked the older man.

'Very much. I hardly ever read poetry, but my daughter, who's always trying to civilise me, gave me this for my birthday. There's a grand one here, listen to this one. It's called "Last Lauch".' And he started reading:

The Minister said it wad dee,
The cypress bush I plantit.
But the bush grew till tree,
naething dauntit.

Maggie smiled in recognition, and when the second verse came, she spoke it with him.

Hit's growin, stark and heich,
Derk and straucht and sinister,
Kirkyairdie-like and dreich.
But whaur's the Minister?[1]

Kenny, fully awake now, clapped them both.

'Now how on earth did you know that?' the uncle asked Maggie.

'I think it's probably the only poem in the world I do know by heart. I found it when I was a student, and it always made me laugh. It reminded me of a skinny old minister at Inverie, who really was dreich.'

'Well, I'm amazed. Would you like a cup of tea? That fairly deserves it.'

'I'd love one. I just came back to dump these things.'

As he set about making the tea in paper cups, Maggie suddenly looked at him. 'Do you walk your dog in Inverie sometimes?'

'Quite often. We've said hello once or twice. You in your purple shorts.'

[1] *Lauch* Laugh *dreich* grim *heich* high

The enthusiasm, the labrador. 'Of course, we met on the beach.'

'Aye. I live in Pittenweem, but I like Inverie. I used to work at the boatbuilding when I was first out of the school.'

'The boatbuilding? I used to go and watch them being built.'

He handed her the tea. 'Aye, I remember you. You and your two brothers, one of them had red hair and played the accordian, did he not?'

Maggie suddenly felt overwhelmed. 'What's your name?' she asked, looking closely at him.

'Andy.'

'Andy what?'

'Andy Johnstone.'

'I don't believe it!'

Andy grinned 'The very same, a wee bit older, but much the same. It's good to see you again, Maggie. *Slainte*. I'm sorry I've no sweeties for you today.' He knocked his cup of tea against hers.

Suddenly they were shocked by a shout from the hill. They looked up and there was Maggie's brother, Donnie, obviously distraught, running towards them, yelling something to them.

'Uh uh. Trouble.' Andy jumped off the boat and went to meet him.

Donnie was breathless. 'It's Patrick. He's had a fall and broken his ankle very badly.' He turned to Andy. 'Fortunately there's a doctor with him. How can we get help?'

'I'll phone the coastguard. We'll need the helicopter, it would be better than dragging him on to the boat, that would take too long.'

'Shall I go up there?' asked Maggie.

'Lady J's with him, gushing all over, and William and Kerstin are looking after him.' (Kerstin was Karin's doctor daughter.) 'Maybe you could take him some sweet tea? I'm sure he shouldn't have any more alcohol, he's obviously going to need surgery, his leg's a real mess. He's up on the cliff. Follow the blue path up to the right.'

Maggie filled two paper cups with tea and put lids on them. Andy was busy speaking to the coastguard. He nodded to her. 'The helicopter'll soon be coming. Leave him where he is, but keep him warm, he'll be very shocked. I have to stay on the boat in case I'm needed here.'

Did the birds send the message round the island? Within minutes, most of the party knew something was up and had gathered together on the clifftop by the ashen-faced Patrick, who lay cushioned and cocooned in woollen rugs, as William's wife, Fanny, helped him to sip the sweet warm tea.

'Lord, what an unearthly racket those birds make,' muttered Patrick feebly, but the noise wasn't only caused by the whirling screaming birds, it was the earth-shaking roar of the approaching helicopter which flew across them and landed a few hundred metres away, close to the lighthouses.

It was quite a business, lifting the agonised Patrick on to a stretcher, but the paramedics were efficient and kind, gave him morphine to relieve the pain, and managed to carry him along the narrow grassy path without stumbling.

'All he was doing,' wailed Lady Jennifer, who obviously felt responsible, 'was picking some sorrel for soup. And he went straight down into a burrow, he was only a tiny bit off the path . . .'

Lady Jennifer did her best to clamber on to the helicopter to accompany Patrick, but William and Dr Kerstin firmly but kindly insisted on going with him, and she gazed bleakly after them, her long chiffon scarf whirling in the maelstrom of air made by the big machine as it roared off.

Stricken and silent, the remainder of the group (only Sven and Karin were missing) straggled their way to the boat. A couple of the grandchildren were crying. Little Rory moaned over and over, 'I want my Grand Paddy,' and

Lady Jennifer, shocked and weepy, had to be given whisky and was half-carried, supported by Donnie and Morag, who discreetly grimaced their distaste to Maggie (none of them had taken to Lady Earlsferry). Maggie was laden with Patrick's and Lady Jennifer's binoculars and Lady Jennifer's rug and handbag. Young Jessica, at the end of the line, very upset, wore her grandfather's deerstalker and her boyfriend carried his cromach and the folding stool.

The boat was ready to cast off, when at last Karin and Sven came panting down the road; Karin's son, a slightly pompous Edinburgh lawyer, ran up to meet them and told them what had happened.

'That's terrible,' said Sven. 'We had no idea. We were looking at the mechanism of the wonderful lighthouse, we saw the helicopter but didn't realise why it had come.'

'We should have stayed with him. Perhaps it wouldn't have happened. I feel I'm to blame.' Karin was obviously very shocked.

'Don't be silly,' snapped her son. 'He simply fell down a burrow. He went off the path to pick some sorrel. It could have happened to anyone.'

The gathering that evening at Patrick's house was more like a wake than a party, but the food had been prepared and everybody came – except of course for Patrick, who was about to undergo a long operation with steel pins and plates to hold his shattered ankle together. Lady Jennifer was also missing. She had gone home in a state of collapse, and neither Sophie nor Michel appeared, which once again made everybody wonder what was going on with them.

Much of the talk was about how Patrick was going to manage, and who'd be able to help.

'We can come out at weekends,' said William, 'but we're both very busy during the week.'

'I can help a lot,' offered Karin.

'So can I, we can work out a relay system,' said Maggie.

Dr Kerstin was gloomy. 'It'll probably take months to

heal at his age, and I shudder to think what the fall will have done to his bad hip.'

Patrick's daughter, who lived in Oxford, nodded. 'Maybe he should come and stay with us?'

'A helluva long journey if he's in much pain,' said William. 'I'm sure he'd prefer to be here if it's possible.'

They all nodded. 'We'll just have to wait and see how things are, how mobile he is, but I'm not optimistic,' said Kerstin.

'What a horrible business,' Karin sighed. Sven, beside her, patted her shoulder and frowned sympathetically.

'Come on, everybody, cheer up,' said William, appearing with a newly opened bottle. 'There's absolutely nothing we can do about it tonight, so let's have some more wine.'

Maggie had been unhappy about leaving Sophie behind, but Sophie had urged her to go to the party. As soon as her mother had driven off with Karin and Sven in his big Volvo, she went anxiously to look for Michel, but found the studio empty, and the kettle cold. There was no sign of her beloved, except for another strange poem on the table, which she found chilling.

And they took him away
From his Para-do-ray
And they said 'if you can't like it here
You're a silly big oaf
Self-abuse of your loaf
Is a waste, man – and wipe off that tear.'
And he couldn't decide
And he said 'Please be kind, I'm not well.'
But they'd many more calls
So they kicked in his balls
And he screamed and they sent him to hell.

It was now almost seven hours since Sophie had last seen Michel. Quivering with unease, she went to the harbour and looked for him; she asked in the supermarket, the pub and the neighbouring houses beside and opposite the studio, but nobody had seen him. She decided to search along the shore up near Maggie's, where they usually walked. She even, hopelessly, looked in Maggie's house, just in case he'd let himself in to make some food, but he obviously hadn't been there. The place was exactly as she and Maggie had left it that morning.

Maybe he was in the church, she thought hopefully, but the building was cold and deserted. She walked right round the churchyard, remembering with an icy feeling that a young woman had been found there a couple of months earlier, dead from an overdose, but there was no still sign of Michel.

As she came slowly down the stone steps which led to the church, she saw Gilbert Menstrie in his garden. He was cutting his grass, watched intently from the kitchen window by his ancient mother, but he stopped in order to stare at Sophie. 'Are you looking for somebody?' he called after a while.

Sophie went across to him, trying not to recoil. 'It's just ... my boyfriend. I've been away all day, and I wondered ... if he'd ... er ... gone for a walk or something. Have you seen him by any chance?'

'I maybe did.'

'Maybe?'

'Well, I did see somebody away out on the big white rock, about as far out as you can go. It could have been him.'

'What time was this?'

'A good while ago. Mid-afternoon, maybe. It was about full tide, whenever that was.'

The tide was well out now, it must have been ages ago. 'You only thought it might be him?' asked Sophie. 'You weren't sure?'

'It was hard to tell,' said Gilbert slowly. 'It was somebody of his build with long dark hair ...'

Sophie nodded anxiously.

'Only,' Gibert's voice grew portentous. 'This particular young man didn't have any clothes on. He was bollock naked, if you'll excuse my language.'

Sophie swallowed. 'What was he doing?' she asked, as lightly as possible.

'Standing.'

'Nothing else?'

'No. He was just standing, and the next time I looked, he'd disappeared – to find his clothes, I sincerely hoped.'

Sophie felt very alarmed. 'OK. Thanks,' she stammered. 'I think I'll go and have a wee look,' she smiled nervously. 'See if I can find him.'

Gilbert watched the girl as she ran along the shore and out towards the far rocks. He was absolutely sure it had been Michel he saw. To be honest, he'd even been wondering if he should phone the police: after all, anyone could have seen him like that – it really wasn't good enough. But in the end he'd decided it wasn't actually any of his business.

Out on the rocks, calling his name hopelessly, Sophie's heart almost stopped when she found Michel's discarded shoes, and then his denim jacket. 'Oh God, what has he done?' she asked, looking all round, but there was no further sign of him.

On a far out, almost submerged crag, the huge cormorants, mournfully holding out their wings to dry, watched the weeping girl, half-collapsed on the hard ground. Beyond her, behind a rock, they saw the man they'd been aware of for much of the day, turn and listen, and slowly rise to his feet. He was dark from the sun, wearing jeans and T-shirt.

'Sophie? What's wrong?'

'Oh, my God! Michel! I thought I'd lost you. Where have you been?'

Michel, his expression pained, looked at her as she wept.

'I'm sorry,' he said. 'I didn't mean to frighten you. I've

been here all day. It was wonderful, I had a swim – it was freezing, but it made me feel a bit better, then I just sat out here for the whole tide. And I know now exactly how I must do the flamingoes . . .'

Sophie listened, bewildered.

Michel shook his head. 'I'm sorry,' he said sadly. 'But I just needed some space and silence.'

'Patrick's had a terrible accident . . . and I thought you were dead . . .' wailed Sophie, and told him what had happened.

He nodded, a little distractedly.

She looked at him anxiously. 'Are you still feeling weird?'

'I feel very tired. And a little strange – wobbly . . .' Michel bent and painstakingly put on his shoes.

'I really missed you . . .' said Sophie. 'Can we be together tonight? Please?'

Michel frowned and stood up. 'Maybe . . .'

Sophie nodded and moved closer to him. 'Michel, I've been thinking. You should quit teaching.'

Immediately Michel looked worried again. 'How can I? We need the money.'

Sophie frowned as she tried to remember what exactly it was that William had said.

'It's an act of faith we have to make on ourselves,' she said slowly. 'Otherwise nobody else will.'

Michel nodded and bent to pick up his jacket. 'You mean to stop the day job?'

'Yes.' She stood looking at him and he almost smiled. 'I suppose perhaps if I could really dare to . . . It would help.'

'There's some lovely food that Maggie said we could have,' ventured Sophie. 'And there's that bottle of wine we bought in Edinburgh, maybe we should have that too.'

'Maybe . . .' Michel paused doubtfully.

'Please . . .' She put out her hand to him. 'Please come with me,' she begged and moved to touch him, but Michel didn't respond.

Sophie eyed him. 'I'm really glad about the flamingoes . . .'

He nodded, looked at her almost sadly. 'I think I'll have to go to France to write the flamingo music.'

'Fair enough, as long as you promise to stop the teaching.'

As dusk fell, infusing the rocky shore with a luminous beauty, Gilbert Menstrie watched the young couple come back along the shore, walking slowly, side by side.

'All right?' he called awkwardly.

'All OK, thanks.' Sophie smiled faintly. Michel just looked weary.

Gilbert nodded. He felt quite relieved, really. It would have been an awful mess and to be honest, Gilbert would have felt just a wee bit guilty, if the French lad had gone and drowned himself or something.

Chapter Eleven

Dozing, Patrick heard whispers, and as his eyes fluttered open he became aware that his hospital bed was surrounded by family – William, his wife Fanny and Patrick's granddaughter Jessica.

'What's going on? You all look as though you're at a funeral,' he murmured. 'But I'm afraid I'm not dead yet.'

'How are you, Pa?' asked William softly, touching his father's arm.

'Pretty seedy, son. Pretty seedy. It's extremely painful, the old ankle, as is the hip which they tell me I've wrenched badly. Apparently I managed to break the ankle in three places and they want me to stay put here for quite a few days. Very boring. I was hoping to go fishing on Loch Tay next week.'

'We brought you some fruit,' said Jessica, busying herself unpacking grapes and a big ripe mango.

'Thank you, darling. I adore mangoes.'

Jessica nodded benignly. 'I know, it was you who first taught me how to eat them, cutting them up into squares, turning them inside out, and eating them in the bath.'

Patrick smiled at her and closed his eyes for a minute. Then he opened them again. 'I was mortified that the accident happened when it did; it must have wrecked the day for everybody; it was so stupid of me to fall like that.'

'Don't be silly, Grand Paddy.' His daughter-in-law

smiled. 'It was a heavenly day up until your accident, and the helicopter was as dramatic as you could get. We were all very impressed.'

William nodded. 'Some people will got to any length for attention. You're front page news in today's *Courier*, and you even made it to the evening news on Radio Scotland.'

Patrick gave a hollow laugh and winced. 'Well, it's not the way I would have chosen to enter my tenth decade, but thank you all for coming, it's a long trek to the hospital.'

'We stayed in your house, but we have to go back home today,' said Fanny, and looked at William.

'Dad, we've been thinking,' William's voice was serious. 'When you're allowed out of here – and the doctors say you won't really be mobile or independent for several weeks – you'll have crutches, but they don't reckon you'll be able to manage by yourself.'

Patrick frowned. 'I'm sure I'll be able to manage, with a bit of a look-in from friends and neighbours.'

William shook his head. 'No, Dad. We've spoken to Kerstin and the doctors here and they all say no way. You will need lots of help.'

Patrick shut his eyes and sighed. 'I can't even smoke my damned pipe in here.' He glared round at them. 'Or have a nip. It's very boring.'

'Patrick,' Fanny, an elegant woman of forty-five, with piles of dark hair pulled into a bun, sat down beside her father-in-law. 'William and I would like you please to come and stay with us for a few weeks, until you're able to manage by yourself. There's no way you could negotiate your stone stairwell and uneven floors by yourself. You really will have to bite the bullet and accept help. And . . .' she smiled. 'Of course you can smoke the pipe and have a dram when you come to us.'

Patrick nodded feebly and murmured. 'That's very kind, my dear, but I'm sure I'll think of something.' Then he closed his eyes and appeared to be asleep except for an occasional pained grimace.

William nodded to the others. 'Let's be off. I think he needs to rest. He'll come round. He'll have to.'

'I heard you, you scallywag,' Patrick opened his eyes. 'Let's wait and see how things are, shall we? But thanks for offering.'

Tenderly, they kissed him goodbye and he watched through hooded lids as they walked out of the ward. He didn't remember ever feeling so angry and frustrated with himself.

A young nurse who looked as though she ought to be in playschool pulled the curtains round him, cheerfully took his temperature, watched him swallow some painkillers and left him to doze.

Sophie glanced at Michel, white-faced and fast asleep in the passenger seat, as she drove back to Edinburgh. She'd felt so relieved and happy when she found him on the rocks, and when he'd agreed to come back to eat supper at Maggie's she'd presumed that things would soon get back to normal, but when they reached the cottage, he'd barely spoken and had hardly drunk any of the wine she'd opened because it gave him heartburn. She'd made him a milky drink at his request, trying as she did so to disguise her anxiety, Michel was sunburnt from being out all day, but under the tan he didn't look that good. It was worrying that he didn't want to eat, but he complained that he had a burning sensation with almost everything he swallowed.

He looked at her miserably. 'I don't really seem to be much further on.'

'But what about the flamingoes?' Sophie asked, desperately trying to disguise her trembling.

He nodded sadly. 'Yes, that's better. I do know how to write that music now, but I'm still feeling strange. I can see how awful you have been feeling about me, but all the time I have known that you were wrong to feel guilty about me. It is nobody's fault. It's simple really. The decision-making part of my brain has overheated and seized up.'

Eventually Michel asked if she thought it would be OK for him to have a bath. Knowing Maggie wouldn't mind, Sophie went to check if there was enough hot water. When she came back, he was asleep on the sofa. Eventually, still trying not to cry, she fetched a towel and woke him and Michel went groggily off to bathe himself.

As Sophie finished clearing up and had another glass of wine, she felt all her tenderness for him revive and at last some understanding crept in, instead of the earlier bitterness and uncomprehending misery. She could hardly believe he was here; they hadn't touched or kissed, she'd just brushed his shoulder once; he seemed like a delicate shell-less creature that needed to grow a new outer layer. She must expect nothing, she told herself, just keep quiet and hope, and suggest nothing, not yet anyway, only wait for it to come from him.

When he emerged, damp-haired and pink from the bath, she longed to embrace him, but didn't dare.

'I think I'll go to the studio,' he said dully.

Sophie's heart clunked. 'By yourself, you mean?'

Michel nodded. 'Can we go home tomorrow?'

'We have to, or I'll lose my job.'

'I know, and I'll go to the GP. I promise.'

'Right.'

'But I'll have to go to France to do this music.'

What about me? Sophie wanted to howl. I want to go to France too! We need a holiday, we need each other! But she didn't risk vocalising any of her internal cries, or she would have bawled; instead she just swallowed and nodded. Then she dared to ask, 'Shall I come with you to the studio?'

'I'd rather be alone, Sophie. I just want to sleep by myself. Please try to understand.'

I know, I know, don't tell me: *you are a machine, an overheated car engine*, thought Sophie miserably, only I'm not a machine. I just happen to be human and normal and averagely needy and longing for some straightforward love and affection.

She stood there, frightened to speak for fear of toppling her delicately nurtured invalid, and watched, helpless, as Michel walked across to give her a tiny childlike kiss, and left her, standing alone in her mother's house. After he'd left, all Sophie could think of was how her warm, funny, sweet, clever, loving man had turned into a stranger who didn't seem to want her at all.

Sophie didn't want to wait up for Maggie. She felt too fragile for her mother's anxious probings. Instead, she bandaged herself in the duvet, and pretended to be asleep when Maggie came home from Patrick's party.

For Patrick, it seemed only moments, but he could see from his watch that he'd been asleep for more than a couple of hours, when he looked up and saw Karin sitting beside his bed.

'Hello, Patrick. How is the poor ankle feeling?'

'Pretty bloody,' he admitted. 'It was rather a long and complicated op., I understand.'

'So they told me.'

'Kind of you to come,' he muttered. 'It's a bore to have to drive so far.'

'It doesn't take that long. It's a nice place they've put you in.'

Patrick grunted.

'I brought you some strawberries and cream. I've asked one of the nurses to put them in the fridge, she'll give you them for supper. And some flowers . . .'

Patrick watched as Karin fetched a jar and arranged her posy. She always did flowers beautifully; her impeccable aesthetic sense was one of the things he'd admired her for, right from the beginning. She was still a remarkably beautiful woman. Her dress suited her very well; he hadn't seen her wearing hyacinth before, it was lovely.

'Where's your Viking?' he enquired at last.

Karin blushed. 'Sven? He's gone to have a look around. He drove me here.'

'How long will he be staying?'

'Only a few more days. He's very busy in his lab at the moment. Doesn't like to be away from work for too long.'

'He seems a nice fellow.'

Karin nodded. 'He's an old friend.'

'Yes, I know.' It was almost a bark.

Karin looked at him, agonised.

'You're very fond of him, aren't you? I can tell.'

'He's . . . a good friend.'

Patrick nodded. 'Will you be going back to Denmark again soon?'

Karin was silent, looked at the flowers and adjusted a couple of leaves. Then she looked straight back at Patrick, who met her gaze steadily. 'I expect I will go back there quite soon. Yes.'

Patrick sighed. 'I was too slow off the mark, wasn't I? Simply left it too bloody late. Missed the boat.' He frowned, longed for some tobacco.

'I am so very fond of you, Patrick.' Karin took his hand.

'I know. And I am very fond of you, Madame. Always have been. Perhaps that was part of the problem. I'd grown used to your being unattainable, and couldn't quite accept that things were different. I don't know.'

'Your birthday speech, Patrick. It was so moving.'

'That seems a long time ago.' He chuckled. 'Little Rory had the gift of perfect timing on that occasion, didn't he?'

Karin nodded. Patrick stroked her hand. 'Please don't start crying. I really couldn't bear it. He's a lucky man, your Viking. I sincerely hope you'll be very happy, but you'd better get a move on. Time's winged chariot and all that . . . We're all on double if not triple borrowed time at our age.'

'I'd better go.' Karin stood up. 'I wanted to say . . . When you come out of here. Maggie and I have agreed that we'd like to look after you for a week or two. You could sleep in my spare room. It's on the ground floor and the bathroom's next door.'

Patrick shook his head. 'William and Fanny have offered me house room for a while. I think that's the best answer. Thank you, though. It'll probably only be for a few days, so I'll go to them, but I'm reluctant. I do so dread being a burden.'

Karin nodded, shivered. 'It's my greatest fear too. I hope you'll soon be on your feet.' She bent to kiss his cheek. 'I'll be back soon.'

'*You can go, but be back soon . . .*' sang Patrick croakily.

He waved feebly and watched as Karin walked down the ward to the exit, turning only once to smile at him before she disappeared. Patrick, his heart and ankle shattered, closed his eyes and lay back on his pillows.

Alone, alone, alone. What a fool he was, what an absolute blundering idiot. But she was lost and gone for ever, like bloody Clementine, and there was absolutely nothing he could do about it.

Michel had been asleep since they left Inverie. Glancing at him as they approached the Forth Road Bridge, Sophie sighed and reminded herself to think positively. '*I will be kind, I will be patient, I will be loving, and Michel will get better soon, and he'll stop teaching*,' she chanted to herself, over and over like a mantra, as she drove towards the familiar skyline of the city, and was cheered when for once she found a parking place immediately in front of their flat.

When she'd waved them off, Maggie hadn't liked the look of Michel at all. He'd barely allowed her to hug him, and had scarcely responded when she said she hoped he'd soon be feeling better. As she held him, she noticed that his breath was heavy and bitter. She could hardly believe it was the same young man who normally sang and laughed and drank wine and flirted with her. This Michel was an alien being. Sophie's face too, looked pinched and small, and Michel's eyes were almost unseeing as Maggie waved goodbye.

Alone again, worried about Michel and Sophie and upset about Patrick, she felt profoundly lonely, and couldn't even summon up the motivation to make a new necklace or construct anything from the new bits of driftwood she'd found on the island; it all seemed pointless and childish, so she decided to make some coffee. One of the things that also saddened her was what Kerstin had whispered to her at the party (late at night, after much wine had been consumed all round), 'I rather fear we might lose Ma after all this.'

'What d'you mean?' Maggie had asked, appalled.

'I have a very strong hunch that she's going to pull out of Scotland and go back to Denmark.'

'But what about all of you and the grandchildren? That would be awful. We'd all miss her too much. We need Karin here. She's our wise woman.'

Kerstin had shrugged, pointing discreetly to where Sven and her mother sat ensconced, talking intensely. It was obvious. You could see that the whole world was contained there for both Karin and Sven in the circle that they made together. Nothing else really existed for either of them.

'I see what you mean,' said Maggie, her heart icy. It was only ten years since her own mother had died and she wasn't ready to lose her second mother, not before time. She was glad to see Karin so obviously happy, but was also aware of a tiny illogical voice inside her screaming, 'Why not me? Why not me? I want love and new life too!' But she pushed away the voice for being undignified and idiotic, and poured yet another glass of wine for herself and her niece.

A couple of days later, Maggie was sitting outside on her doorstep with a cup of coffee, feeling even gloomier. It was the first week of September; autumn was definitely in the air. She really felt cold, perhaps from all the worry about Sophie and poor Michel, and was wearing a jersey for a change. Yesterday, Sophie had at least promised her that Michel would go and see a doctor, and now all Maggie could do was to wait nervously till she next heard from them. It was heartbreaking, but she must remember that it wasn't her business; the youngsters had to deal with it themselves. She sighed. Nobody really needed or desired Maggie any more, and this was hard to accept, sometimes.

She was woken from this dismal reverie by the unexpected, warm, wet prod of a labrador's snout in her crotch.

She yelped and spilt coffee as the owner shouted 'Dougie boy, stop that!'

Maggie jerked up in surprise and was delighted to find herself looking up at Andy Johnstone, the man from the boat.

'I'm really sorry,' said Andy. 'He's a daft dog, still young, needing a lot of discipline. He's not usually as bad-mannered as that. I just came by to ask how Sir Patrick was doing.'

Maggie stood up. 'He's had his op. Ankle broken in three places; he's in a lot of pain and it's going to be a long slow business. Now, would you like a cup of coffee? As you see, I am actually having one.'

'I'd love one. Milk, no sugar, please.'

'Let's go inside,' said Maggie. 'I find it a bit chilly out there.'

'Aye, it is. Time for the winter woollies, I'm afraid. A shame, it's been such a beautiful summer.'

Inside the cottage, Andy looked at the table, which was piled high with bits of brightly coloured nylon twine, knots of copper wire, stones with holes in them or strange markings, and all sorts of bits of sea-worn wood. 'What d'you do with all this stuff?'

'I'm an artist. I make things – objects, figures, jewellery even.' She showed him her favourite necklace.

'That's really beautiful, it's sort of primitive but sophisticated all at once.'

Maggie curtsied. 'That's me all over.'

'D'you drill out the holes in the things you put in the necklaces?'

'Up till now I've been terribly purist, trying only to use things that had holes in them, but yes, I do need to make holes. Look at these.' She showed him some fossils and a piece of melted and contorted aluminium. 'These could all do with drilling out. Two of them have holes but have got silted up and I've been trying to make a hole in this metal with my Swiss Army knife, but haven't been very successful.'

'That would be really easy to do. All you need's a wee drill.'

'I've been meaning to get one.'

'I've got one you could borrow. I'm not using it at present. I sometimes make model boats in the winter. It saves me from getting depressed.'

'I know the feeling.'

'I'll bring it round, if you like.'

'That would be great, if you're happy to be without it for a while.'

'No problem, and it's really easy to use. D'you make these for fun, or to sell?'

'A bit of both, really.'

'Sounds like a nice life.' He grinned.

'I took early retirement from teaching.'

'So did I.'

'I thought you built boats?'

'That was years ago, just after I left school at fifteen. I did my apprenticeship as a joiner in the boatshed, then I went to be a student.'

'Where did you go?'

He smiled. 'Liberton College for Knowledge. Brains for Weans. Nobody's ever heard of it, but I got my degree when I was thirty and taught history in a comprehensive school for quite a few years.'

'Sounds like a rich life.'

'It has been. I was in the Merchant Navy too for a while. Nowadays I've a share in the May Island boat with my brother, and Kenny and my son help out, so we share the work. It's never really a burden. I enjoy it.'

Dougie had run upstairs and was now sniffing all over the floor. 'Shall I give him some water?' asked Maggie.

Andy nodded. 'Please.'

They sat and talked and drank two cups of coffee each.

'When did you get divorced?' asked Andy.

'I didn't. I'm a widow, have been for over twelve years.'

'That's awful bad luck. Such a long time. You must have been a babby.'

'I was forty-five; so was Fergal, my husband. He died of a heart attack. Out of the blue. I felt very old at the time, but from this age it seems very young.'

'Aye, I know what you mean. But you've not been on your own for all that time? Surely not?'

'Yes, I have. I didn't want to be, or really expect to be. I've had other relationships, but I have never actually lived with anybody else. I've just never got lucky. Or . . .' she shrugged. 'Maybe I couldn't compromise.'

'What a waste, eh?' They both nodded.

'How about you?' asked Maggie. 'Are you married?'

'Same as you. Only my wife died five years ago from cancer; she was ill off and on for about four years.'

'I'm sorry,' said Maggie.

'So was I,' said Andy. 'She was a grand girl; she was five years younger than me, a nursing sister. She worked on and off right through her illness. I miss her a lot. I miss a good laugh, and I miss the cuddles. But you just have to get on with things, don't you? We have no choice but to carry on.'

Maggie had been trying to work out what age this very attractive man was. If he was working already when she was eight, he must be at least seven, maybe eight years older than her; but he certainly didn't look it; he was obviously in very good shape.

Her phone rang, and she frowned. 'I'll just leave it, unless it's something important.'

She listened as her own voice came on, then froze when she heard Niall's cheerful sing-song.

'Hi there, it's Niall. Missing your delectable body. It's been too long no see, and I wondered if I might please stay the night on Saturday next?'

Maggie closed her eyes, mortified. She didn't know what to say. She couldn't explain that Niall was a stop-gap, that he filled a hole (both phrases were too Freudian for words) that he was married, that her relationship with him had no substance, no future, that he was friend, her brother, her son. Anything but a lover.

When she opened her eyes again, Andy was looking at her, amused. 'Don't you want to ring him back? He sounds quite keen.'

He stood up. 'Anyway, I need to get on my way.' The dog, he added, was dying for a walk, and he'd promised he'd get back to Anstruther for the back of one as he was babysitting his grandchildren.

Numbly, Maggie said goodbye and gazed after him. What a lovely man he was. Damn bloody Niall. Had it never struck him that somebody might be listening, that she might have a life of her own? She was so annoyed that she shattered one of her favourite hand-painted mugs when she was washing up, and cut her finger quite badly.

Chapter Twelve

Young Callum and Catriona came running down the hill to Maggie's house, where, delighted to see them, she offered them shortbread and orange juice.

'Sven and Grandma Karin say they're going to do the Chain Walk tomorrow,' panted Catriona. 'It's the last day of our holidays. They want us all to go. We've come to ask you as well – we're taking a picnic lunch with us, to eat in the big stony bay.'

'Heavens,' said Maggie. 'Isn't that rather over-ambitious for two people of that age?'

'Don't be ageist, Maggie,' reprimanded Callum. 'Sven can do it, I'm sure, he's amazingly fit. He windsurfs all the time in Denmark.'

'I only hope I can do it,' muttered Maggie.

They laughed. 'Of course you can. You did it with us last year.'

'I was knackered for days afterwards and very sore. I thought I'd cracked a rib – I'm not joking.'

'Oh, come on, it'll be great. Mum's coming. She reckons they'll be OK.'

'Well, if we have a doctor with us, that's not quite so alarming.'

'And Uncle Donnie'll be there as well.'

'Oh good,' Maggie smiled. 'As long as he doesn't make us march in strict military fashion.'

'If Sven did collapse, we could never carry him home. He's far too big,' said Catriona pragmatically. 'He'd have to have a Viking burial in a boat right out there on Kincaid Point.'

'You're awful. Don't say things like that!' Callum thumped her.

'Maggie, are you really worried that Karin might not manage?' asked Catriona, after she'd punched her brother in return.

'Well, there's a lot of quite hard climbing up cliffs and hanging on to the chains, as I remember. Some of it's really tricky; I honestly find it pretty hard at my age, and I know that Karin's amazing and has been doing yoga for decades, but let's face it, your grandmother has reached the great age of eighty-two.'

'We'll help her,' said Callum. 'But she's absolutely determined. You couldn't stop her. Our Dad says she's a one-off ageless Amazon.'

Maggie nodded. 'Did I ever tell you about my trip to Gothland with her?'

They shook their heads.

'It was years ago, when you were wee. Karin and her friend Antje, an artist, were both about sixty, and I was forty. Fergal went camping with the kids to give me a break. The three of us, Karin, Antje and myself, went on holiday to Gothland, which is a beautiful island in the middle of the Baltic, with lots of lovely orchards full of fruit, and beaches with strange rock formations, and every day we'd go down to the sea where your grandmother and Antje would fling off all their clothes . . .'

'Sounds just like Grandma,' murmured Callum. 'Skinny dipping at sixty.'

'And in to the Baltic they would run and cavort and swim and shout, even if the day was freezing.

'And of course, I felt that I had to do the same. They were inspirational older women to me. So I flung off all my clothes and ran into the water and nearly froze. I could barely move for cold, and afterwards, for hours on end, I swear I was pale blue and half-paralysed, but the two of them were dancing about, rosy-cheeked, ready for anything.'

'Wow.' Catriona's eyes grew large.

Maggie was well into her stride now. 'And at night, there were hundreds of mosquitoes where we were sleeping – we shared a sort of wooden dormitory in the woods – and I'd be exhausted, ready to pull the sheets over my head and sleep, but Karin and Antje, in white nighties, would leap up, clutching huge fly swats, and they'd dance about, shouting in Danish, "Yes! Got him! That's twenty-seven! No . . . twenty-nine!" Splat! Squish! Until they'd killed all the mosquitoes and could safely go to bed.'

'Awesome,' said Callum.

'It's all true,' said Maggie. 'In the morning there were spots of blood all over the walls where they'd squashed them flat.'

'Yuck,' said Catriona. 'But you are coming with us, aren't you?'

Maggie beamed. 'I wouldn't miss it for worlds.'

The Chain Walk was only safe to do at low tide and, happily, the day they had chosen was fine. The seven of them, Karin, Sven, Maggie, her brother, Donnie, Callum and Catriona and their mother Kerstin, parked and set off towards the sea. First, they had to walk for about a mile along a wide sandy bay which ended in black rocks which rose up precipitously and disappeared round the point. Kerstin, walking behind with Maggie, frowned. 'I actually think this Chain Walk is a really silly idea, but the oldies were all set to do it by themselves. Ma's really quite creaky, despite the yoga. I know that her knee joints lock sometimes – and she quite often has days when she's just completely whacked, not fit for anything – though she hides it well. If I was her doctor I'd forbid it, but I'm only her daughter.'

Maggie nodded sympathetically. She didn't want to admit it, but she wasn't all that sure of her own strength to do the Walk. Sometimes her own knee or ankle joints would suddenly lock too, which was both alarming and uncomfortable; she'd woken this morning feeling exhausted and achy, and it had taken depressingly long for her body to defrost.

Now the little group stood together, looking up at the steep cliff, which had footsteps cut into the rock and a substantial chunk of chain hanging down for the climbers to grip.

'This looks good fun,' said Sven. 'How exciting.'

'It was rather too exciting before they renewed the chains,' said Kerstin. 'They'd all got very rusty and wobbly and had fallen apart in a couple of cases.'

'Heavenly weather for it,' murmured Karin, who had paused for a rest. 'It reminds me of The Last Rose of Summer.'

Kerstin and Maggie smiled and began to sing:

'*Twas the last rose of summer . . .*'

The children, Donnie – who had a rich deep bass voice – Sven and Karin all joined in, harmonising. Not everybody really knew the words, but it sounded good. When they stopped, Sven clapped and said, 'Fantastic.'

'*Fantastisk*,' Karin smiled at him.

'What's that noise?' said Catriona frowning.

They all listened. It sounded like dogs barking.

'D'you think there are some poor dogs marooned out there on the rocks?' asked Catriona, her eyes big. If there were, Catriona, a great animal lover, was obviously ready to swim out and save them.

Callum was peering through the binoculars. 'No, it's seals, a whole lot of them, a couple of really huge ones. Look.' He handed the glasses to his uncle.

'Amazing. So it is.'

As they clambered and gazed at the seals and the landscape and stopped to sip water, Maggie saw that Karin was managing remarkably well, but was sometimes grateful for a helping hand from Sven or Donnie. A couple of times she saw her pause, a little unhappily, until Callum or Catriona showed her where to put her feet. Twice, the children and their mother stopped off for a quick dip in the pale green water of a sandy cove, and the rest of them were relieved to stop and sit for a moment.

Halfway through the walk, they came to a spectacular, big bay with tall, hexagonal, black pillars of stone at one end and a cobbled beach composed entirely of rounded black stones graded neatly from small to large upwards from the water's edge.

'This is marvellous,' said Sven. 'Isn't it like your Fingal's cave, or the other place in Ireland?'

'The Giant's Causeway, yes. It's not as grand as either of them, but this place has its own beauty,' murmured Maggie, who was lying on the beach. 'And here you hardly ever see more than a couple of other people.'

Karin, sitting nearby, elegant in a floppy cotton sun hat that would have looked terrible on anybody else except a cricketer, said, 'I've done the Chain Walk every single year since I landed at Leith, except for the summer I had Kerstin.'

'Sorry, Mother,' murmured her daughter, half-asleep beside her.

The children, wet and starving, arrived, begging for lunch.

'OK,' said Kerstin sitting up. 'Let's have it now.' And she delved into her rucksack and handed round huge slices of quiche.

'This is brilliant,' said Callum. 'I'm really glad I'm Scottish.' And everyone laughed and toasted the Chain Walk in elderflower cordial.

When they'd eaten, the youngsters went off to explore by themselves, while the grown-ups rested. After a while, Kerstin sat up. 'Would anybody like some coffee?'

Everybody did, and as they sipped and savoured the

place and the day, Karin took Sven's hand and announced: 'We've got something we'd like to tell you.'

Sven smiled at her and put his arm round her shoulders.

'Shall we call Callum and Catriona?' asked Kerstin, who, Maggie noticed, was looking strained.

'No. Leave them just now. We can tell them in a minute.' Karin looked at Sven. 'Why don't you tell them?'

Sven looked at each of them. 'It's quite simple, really. Karin and I have decided that we would like to live together. We want to be married as soon as possible. I hope you will agree that I am a very lucky man.'

'And we're going to live in Denmark,' Karin spoke softly and earnestly. 'But I'll keep my house here and we'll come for long visits at least twice a year.'

'Nooooo!' Maggie hadn't noticed that Catriona had crept back and was standing near them, listening. 'NO, you can't – it's not fair – I don't want you to go away to Denmark, Grandma!'

Tears streamed down her freckles, and the adults watched, shocked, as she turned, howling and rushed back into the water, and set off swimming wildly straight out to sea.

'Catriona, come back here this minute!' shouted her mother, her face scarlet, and she started running. Donnie and Callum rushed after her, Donnie wading valiantly in khaki shorts and sandals.

'I'll get her!' Kirsten and Callum reached the water and dived in almost simultaneously.

Karen, Sven and Maggie stood and watched. In the middle of the drama, Maggie wished for a moment that she could show her own feelings as clearly as young Catriona had. She felt incredibly upset at the thought of Karin's departure. Life would feel utterly devalued without her.

Sven hugged Karin. 'She'll calm down,' he said. 'But of course she's sad that you're going.'

Karin bit her lips, nodded. She looked her age for once, hunched and vulnerable.

Catriona, who had swum dramatically out for about a hundred metres, now alarmingly disappeared behind a large black rock.

'Catriona, stop right there! Don't go any further!' bawled Donnie, thigh deep in water.

Callum and Kerstin weren't very far behind the girl now, and the watchers on shore heard the swimmers shout as they rounded the rock and also disappeared. A minute or two later, they were relieved to see Kerstin standing, waving from the rock. They waved back as Kerstin held up her thumb and gave them a large nod.

'Her mum will calm her down. She's just upset – she loves you, Karin,' said Donnie, wringing seawater from his shorts. 'She's a very emotional one, Catriona, but she'll come round. I must say I think it's wonderful that you two are taking such a brave step. Congratulations to you both.'

They waited, watching anxiously for some action from the rock. After nearly twenty minutes had passed, Maggie felt she must do something. 'D'you think I should swim out and join them?'

Donnie frowned. 'They shouldn't stay there too long or we'll be in trouble with the tide – oh look, here's Callum coming back – he'll tell us what's what.'

Callum, breathless and dripping, threw himself on the shingle and reported that Catriona was being a complete diss. She'd also scratched her leg on the rocks when she climbed out of the water and wouldn't stop crying.

'How bad is her leg?' asked Maggie.

'It's just a wee scratch from the barnacles, honest. She's just in a state.' Then he looked at his grandmother and Sven. 'I think it's great what you told us. Cool.' He grinned at them both, then asked Sven shyly, 'Will you be our new granddad?'

'I suppose I shall officially be your stepgrandfather,' replied Sven with great seriousness.

Maggie glanced at Karin. Her aunt was looking her most intense.

'Ah . . . Here they come at last,' shouted Donnie, who was back down by the water's edge.

Catriona and her mother came out of the water hand in hand. Catriona was very red and her face swollen, but she'd stopped crying. Karin walked down the beach to her granddaughter and knelt down beside her and Catriona showed her scratched leg and Karin mopped it with her hanky and Catriona blubbed again and they talked and then they hugged for ages.

'Oh Catriona – what a hopeless case you are,' groaned her big brother.

'That's enough,' said Kerstin. 'Leave her alone. She'll be OK.'

Eventually Catriona calmed down, and the three generations of females came over to join the others. Maggie hugged Catriona and asked if she was feeling better and she nodded a little tearfully.

'Good,' Donnie grinned. 'Now maybe you'd like some juice, while we all have a wee dram.' From his back pack he produced a small bottle of whisky and six little metal cups. 'I do think it's great news. And we'll miss Karin like hell,' he said, as he handed round the drinks, even giving a small one to Callum. 'I thought we might have need of a drop of whisky if the Chain Walk proved too hard physically, but I didn't know we would also have reason to toast Karin and Sven.'

'I want a dram too,' moaned Catriona.

'Here. You can have a tiny sip of mine,' said Maggie.

Catriona tried it and spat it out. 'Ugh! It's disgusting. How can you drink it?'

Karin, still upset, could hardly speak. She took Catriona's hand and made her sit down beside her. 'You'll come and stay with us,' she promised. 'And we'll often come to Scotland to see you.'

Catriona frowned. 'It won't be the same. I want you to be here all the time, same as you are now. I don't want you to go.' She wiped her nose on a tissue and looked imploringly at Sven. 'Please can't you stay here instead?'

'I wish it was possible,' said Sven. 'But I'm still working and my laboratory is in Denmark. And I have four children and twelve grandchildren and three great-grandchildren in Denmark.'

Catriona sobbed loudly at this information, and it seemed that nothing would calm her until at last Karin said, 'Maybe you could be a bridesmaid?' but even that had only a very small effect.

Eventually, Donnie stood up, rucksack in hand and looked at the little group. 'I have a suggestion,' he announced. 'How about, instead of doing the rest of the Walk – and I promise you, we have already done the best bit – how about going back the way we came, which will still give us good exercise but'll save us from the rather tiring and dreary walk back over the clifftop to the golf course?'

Sven and Karin glanced at each other and he nodded. Karin looked relieved, Maggie certainly was. She knew already that her legs would ache tomorrow.

'Shall I carry your bag, grandma?' asked Callum.

Karin looked surprised. 'Yes, Callum. That would be kind. Thank you.'

Glared at by his sister, he walked along beside his grandmother till they reached the next bit of cliff and chain, where they paused to work out how best to climb down.

'Karin,' said Callum. He sounded very grown-up.

'Yes, Callum?' Karin always liked it when the children used her name straight.

'I think it's great news. I feel proud of you.'

Pleased, his grandmother hugged him. 'I'm very proud of you too, Callum. You're a wonderful grandson to have.'

'When I come to visit you in Aarhus, could I maybe learn to windsurf?'

Sven, right behind them, chuckled. 'Of course you can, Callum. I will teach you myself, or one of my family will.'

'Great.' Callum grinned.

'Perhaps you'd like to do that too, Catriona?' asked Karin gently.

'No thanks,' said Catriona, and scowled. And Maggie, watching the interchange, realised from the pain in the small girl's face that she thought her brother Callum was a traitor.

In his walled garden in Pittenweem, which had a fine view through old apple and crab apple trees of the historic stone-steepled church, Andy Johnstone was dead-heading and pruning his roses. There were still a good few left, but the garden needed a tidy. He'd mown the lawn, and needed now to have a sit down. Dougie the labrador came to him and laid his head imploringly on his knee.

'Ah, you need a walk, son. I know. I'll take you in a minute. Maybe we can take that drill to Maggie that I said I'd lend her.'

He sighed as he thought about Maggie. He'd really liked meeting her. It had been a definite click on both sides, of that he was sure, but then that West Highland chap had phoned, who sounded as though his boots were well under her bed. It was a shame, Andy and she had seemed to be getting on so well. But at least he could look in on her and lend her the drill; maybe they could be friends, have the odd chat, or walk the dog. Even that would be better than the perpetual silence he and the dog seemed to inhabit at present.

He'd never seen Maggie with a bloke; she'd been very much on her own on the May Island trip, and if he saw her on the beach, she was usually by herself or with a woman friend. If she wanted the drill, he was happy to let her have it. He decided to put it in the back of the car when he next took the dog along to Inverie.

Almost a month after Patrick's birthday, in Edinburgh, Sophie, desolate, desperately trying to be brave, was seeing Michel off on the overnight bus to London. He still wasn't his old self; he was pale, always tired and uncommunicative, but at least he'd started to take the anti-depressants which Kerstin had advocated and his own GP had prescribed. It was a mild nervous breakdown, and he needed rest, the doctor had advised; he should take a break from work and try to keep down the stress levels.

And Michel had actually resigned from the teaching. Neither of them could quite believe it. The money aspect was scary, but they reckoned they would manage somehow.

'OK. I'll get on now. I want a window seat.' Michel put down his bag and they hugged for a long time.

'I'll miss you. Please come home soon.'

He nodded. Kissed her, picked up his bag and climbed on to the bus.

Sophie watched as he chose a seat and put his things up on the rack. A month he had asked for, a whole four weeks to himself. Almost thirty days in the wilderness. With probably no communication, was what he had stipulated.

Sophie had gasped. 'But I need to know where you are. A month will seem like a life sentence . . .'

'I'll phone you when I get there,' he had promised. 'Papa's going to meet me and take me home for a couple of days, before I go down to the coast.' He looked at her intensely. 'I will come back, Sophie, I promise you.'

When he was settled, Michel looked up, smiled faintly and blew her a kiss. After that he mouthed something and held up one finger. Was it 'one month' he was saying? Or 'I love you'? She mouthed 'I love you' and the palms of their hands met on the glass. *I mustn't cry*, Sophie told herself. Then Michel nodded, took away his and, waved an almost ghostly farewell and appeared to go to sleep.

Sophie stood there, hoping he'd wave again but his eyelids barely fluttered when the bus revved up, and she stood there watching till it was out of sight, wondering how on earth she was going to survive the coming weeks.

Maggie had agreed a little hesitantly to Niall's visit. He'd been persistent and persuasive, and she couldn't really invent a reason for him not to come. Nor did she see what she could do about getting to know the attractive Andy better now that Niall had blown it for her. She was fed up with him for calling as he did, though he, of course, was oblivious to that, but the wine would be good and his visits were always entertaining. Cooking supper together was usually quite fun; she knew she'd enjoy that. The short times they spent together usually felt uncannily comfortable and domestic.

Niall arrived mid-afternoon. In the old days it would have been knickers off and into bed long before a cup of tea was even suggested, but this time they did have a leisurely cup of tea before setting off on a sedate walk to the ruined castle.

'You seem depressed, my love,' said Niall, and took her hand. Limply, she allowed him to hold it. It was a relief to have somebody to touch her, hold her, eat and sleep with her, even for a few hours. You could almost forget for a while what it was like to be alone.

Maggie poured out to him about Patrick, miserable in hospital, aching for his lost love. 'To top it all,' she added, 'she – my eighty-two-year-old aunt – is in love with a younger man of eighty, and is flitting to Denmark to get married.'

'*Tristan and Isolde* for wrinklies . . .' Niall chuckled. 'I think it's wonderful. They're setting us all a fantastic example. I bet that's what you'll be like.'

At this, Maggie smiled feebly and passively allowed him to put his arm round her, at which exact moment they met with the cheerful Andy and his bounding labrador.

Maggie pulled away from Niall as the three of them almost collided and Dougie leapt ecstatically to greet her. Mortified, she momentarily imagined pushing her married lover off the cliff, or hurling herself into the sea. Instead, she was polite.

'Andy Johnstone, this is an old friend from Oban, Niall Maclean,' she murmured awkwardly.

The men nodded curtly and shook hands and Andy,

obviously embarrassed, went on his way, calling to the dog to follow.

'What's wrong?' asked Niall. 'Why so black?'

Maggie shrugged. What was there to say? Life with a capital F? 'Too much to explain,' she murmured.

'It'll be all right in the end, my love. You're an awful worrier. Let's *carpe* the *diem* and go home and open that bottle of Burgundy I brought.'

Chapter Thirteen

'There we go.' Gently, William pushed Patrick's wheelchair over the threshold, through the wide hallway and into the big kitchen-diner of his Edinburgh flat. Jessica, seated at a pine table reading the *Guardian*, looked up and grinned. 'Hi, Grandad, welcome,' she said, and rose to give the old man a hug. He looked ancient, and his skin felt papery to her touch.

Patrick nodded and smiled, a wintry smile to suit the day, which was icy outside, grim and grey.

'Lovely to be here, and how warm it is. Marvellous.'

'Shall I make some tea?' asked the girl.

William nodded. 'It took ages, there was a traffic jam before the bridge stretching back for miles.'

'Where are my crutches?'

'They're in the car, Dad, I'll just go and unload.'

Patrick nodded gloomily. 'Sorry to be a nuisance, hopefully it won't be for too long.'

If only he could believe it. At present, he could barely manage the trip to the lavatory unaided, it hurt so much to stand, much less walk. 'Where's Fanny?' he asked.

'Ma doesn't get home till half past five.'

Patrick nodded. 'And how's my Jessica, eh?'

'Fine. I'm only here because I came home for a job interview tomorrow. Here's some tea. Would you like a biscuit?'

'What I'd really like is a nip.'

William, coming back with a zipped travel bag and a pair of crutches, looked apologetic. 'I'll get you a drink, Dad. Sorry, I should have thought.'

'I've not had a drop of alcohol for weeks,' complained Patrick. 'It's not good for a chap. But I'm afraid I need a pee first of all.'

'Of course. D'you want these?'

Grunting, Patrick reached for the crutches. 'I'm not very good with these ones, they only changed them yesterday from the kind that went up to my armpits.'

They watched as he tried to heave himself up, and William went to help, but that only made his father angry.

'Don't fuss. It just needs patience. I can manage, thank you.' Grunting, he manipulated himself on to his feet and they could see him grimace when he put any weight on the bad ankle. Wincing, Jessica turned to her father when at last her grandfather had reached the bathroom door and closed it behind him.

'I can't bear it. He looks so old,' she whispered. 'He's completely different – he's a cripple. What's going to happen?'

William winced. 'I don't know, Jess. We'll just have to see. But it's going to take time. It's fortunate that I work at home.'

After what seemed ages, Patrick, with some help from William, managed to return and manoeuvre himself to a large armchair. Jessica brought him a handsome foot rest covered with an Afghan kelim and helped him put both legs up.

Ashen-faced, her grandfather sank back. 'That's more like it. Lord, am I glad to be out of that hospital.'

William handed him a glass of whisky. 'Here you are, Dad. Get this down you, it should do you good.'

But it didn't. It made him feel woozy after only a few sips. Patrick handed the half-empty glass to Jessica. 'I'm afraid I can't manage all of this. I think perhaps I'd better have a lie down.'

The two of them helped him to bed. Jessica put on the electric blanket and William helped him to undress and to heave himself on to the bed which they'd prepared for him.

'Bloody bodies . . .' muttered Patrick.

'You'll be stronger soon, Dad,' William assured him. 'It'll just take time.'

Patrick looked at him sadly. 'I wish I could believe you, son,' and closed his eyes.

They left him to rest, and went back to the kitchen. William picked up Patrick's unfinished whisky and knocked it back, glancing over at his daughter, who looked miserable. 'Don't worry, Jess; he's just tired from the journey and fed up that he can't go home to Elie yet.'

'But will he ever?' wailed Jessica. 'He can hardly walk. It's terrible to see him like that.'

William, who felt like joining in with her wail, stroked her hair. 'I think he'll get stronger. Remember back to the picnic, how wonderful he was and how well he was feeling. He's had an awful shock with the accident and the operation. It'll take time. Basically, he's an amazingly tough old man.'

'Who's going to tell him about Karin and Sven?'

'He knows. They both went to see him together a week before their engagement party in Fife, to tell him and to say goodbye.'

'What did he say?'

'I think he had a pretty good idea before they came. Karin had visited him a few times in the hospital, and Sven told me that Patrick shook him by the hand and said, "You're a better man than I am, Gunga Din."'

'What on earth does that mean?'

William smiled. 'That's exactly what Sven said. Let's have some of that tea if it's not too cold and I'll see if I've still got a copy of Kipling's poems.'

In Pittenweem, Andy Johnstone frowned at the greyness of the day as he laced up his walking boots. He hated this time of the year. The May Island trips had stopped for the season, so he had less to do, and inevitably it reminded him of when Nancy was dying. The darling girl; it was hard to believe that she'd have been sixty this year. Even when she had been so ill he'd thought of her as a lassie. They'd been married for thirty years when she went; they'd just had their thirtieth anniversary that last summer. Some mornings, even now, he'd wake up and think for a minute that she was still there, lying smiling beside him. Then he'd wake up properly and realise that it was just himself, alone in the big empty bed. It didn't really bear thinking about, but a good brisk walk to Inverie and back should change his mood. The dog, who was already barking with anticipation, running backwards and forwards to the door with the lead in his mouth, would love it. For a moment, as he set off, Andy wondered about Maggie and realised that he felt decidedly uncomfortable about taking his usual path past her house, so he decided to take the top way past the old kirk and walk through the fields as you were advised to do at high tide. That way, unless he was very unlucky, he'd probably avoid a meeting altogether. It was a pity, but his unease at the thought of seeing her made him feel awkward. And as for that Cocky Jock who was with her, he hadn't really liked the look of him at all, him with his purple shirt and buttonhole.

'Come on, son,' he called, and Dougie bounded out of the door in front of him. It really was a ghastly day; Andy pulled up the zip and hood of his hurricane jacket and set off westwards, hoping that the weather report which had said the rain would clear mid-morning had been right.

In Edinburgh, Sophie was shutting up the trendy clothes shop where she worked. She was feeling rotten, and couldn't wait to get home. Sylvia, her friend from the quartet, was coming over for supper, and for the life of her, Sophie couldn't imagine what they should eat. Even the idea of food made her feel slightly queasy. Maybe she should ring Sylvia and ask her not to come. She tried her on the mobile, but it was engaged, so she decided to let things be and hoped she'd feel better after a lie down.

She was asleep when her friend arrived. Sylvia worked part-time at a wine bar that also did excellent salads, and as she often did, had brought some leftovers. As she unpacked the food, Sylvia saw immediately how pale Sophie was.

'Are you still not right?'

Sophie shook her head glumly.

'Still no news of Michel?'

'He was due back on Tuesday.'

'Last Tuesday?'

Sophie nodded. 'Last Tuesday, ten days ago.' She sighed. 'I don't know where he is. I've tried his parents' number and his brother's in Avignon, but nobody was there, just the answerphone message which doesn't tell you anything. I know his parents and brother's family were all going off to Brittany together, but I don't have a number for them there.'

'That's rotten. Not like Michel, surely?'

Sophie shrugged. It seemed to her all too reminiscent of the recent Michel.

'What you need,' said Sylvia, standing up, 'is a drink and some food. You stay there and rest on the sofa and I'll get it ready.'

'I'm honestly not hungry.' Sophie closed her eyes, but opened them a minute or two later when Sylvia presented her with a glass of Baileys.

'Cheers, Hen.' Sylvia grinned. 'Here's to happy times. The Baileys was on offer at Tesco's. I thought it might cheer you up. D'you remember that time when we got legless on it?'

Sophie smiled faintly. 'When we were first-year students.'

Sylvia nodded, took a swig of the creamy drink and

smiled naughtily. 'It's a shame that spunk doesn't taste like this, isn't it?'

'Don't!' Sophie laughed painfully.

'I'm sure he'll be back soon, I'm sure. He's probably still communing with those bloody pink birds.' She peered at a flamingo postcard Michel had sent. 'Can I read this?'

'If you want.' Sophie swung her legs down to the floor and took a doubtful sip of her drink, but Sylvia didn't see her grimace.

'*Je t'aime, tu me manques beaucoup. La musique coule bien. Bisoux. XX Michel*,' read Sylvia thoughtfully. 'That's nice. Brief but positive. Don't worry, Soph. He'll be back and OK sooner than you think, I bet you.'

But Sophie didn't hear her because she was up and running for the bathroom.

Retching.

Sylvia stood by her, wiped her down, helped her back to the sofa.

Sophie closed her eyes, and only opened them again when Sylvia sat beside her and handed her a package.

'What's this?'

'Open it and see.'

Sophie peered in the paper bag. 'Oh God,' she groaned. 'I'm not sure . . .'

'Just do it, Soph,' urged her friend softly. 'I've been wondering for the last couple of weeks. It must surely have crossed your mind as well?'

'Yes, of course it has . . . but what on earth'll I do?'

'How late are you?'

'Three and a half weeks. We were hardly even doing it when he was so depressed . . .'

'You only have to do it once.'

Their eyes met.

'This only takes moments as well,' said Sylvia briskly. 'Do it now.'

In Inverie Maggie was miserable. Her London friend

Felicity was trying to persuade her to come back to the great metrollops, as she called it.

'It's obviously cold and gloomy up there, and you sound lonesome. There are some great shows on and about five films I'd like to see with you, and there's a new incredibly cheap Thai restaurant opened up just across the road. Your presence is required down here – people are complaining about your absence. You've had a lovely summer, why don't you just cut your losses and come home for the winter?'

'Because I've rented out my flat for a year,' wailed Maggie. 'There's nowhere for me to go, but it's just so empty without Karin here – I really miss her. I feel bereft – as though I'll never see her again.'

'I'm sure you do. But your brother and Morag are there, aren't they?'

'Yes, sure. But they're always playing golf or bridge, neither of which appeal – in fact, both repel – so I don't see that much of them. Everyone seems to be married; I always feel a bit awkward being on my own.'

'Sounds to me like you need a lover, honey-chile,' Felicity wheezed sympathetically.

'That's the last thing I want, believe me. I think I'm beyond such things anyway.'

'Well, your Danish aunt wasn't, or isn't, from what you've been telling me.'

'That's different,' snapped Maggie. 'She's rare – exceptional – and also just happens to be very bloody lucky.'

After the phone call, which made her feel restless, Maggie peered out at the weather and frowned. Living with this climate was like living with a manic depressive: one minute sunny with shining silver seas, and the next, windy, soaking wet and deathly grey. It was also freezing. Last night she'd needed an extra duvet and had been glad of a hot water bottle. She'd felt so happy and problem-free in the summer, but now things felt very bleak. The loss of her aunt – and Maggie could only think of it as a loss, much as she applauded and envied Karin and Sven – was a real sadness. The gap Karin left was enormous. Maggie missed their gossips, their walks and seeing the rugs and cloths her aunt wove being created, and she missed showing her what Maggie herself had made. There was nobody here now she could talk texture and colour with, or argue as to how to finish off a necklace, how to knot it or glue it or what to add or take away from it.

She even missed Karin's occasional contrariness, like when she'd warned Maggie off buying the cottage and had then gone out and bought herself one. Maggie felt positively nostalgic as she remembered her outrage and then bewilderment at her aunt's climb-down over this matter.

Sighing, she went to the fruit bowl to pick up a pear, and was horrified to find the fruit half-eaten and the bowl speckled with mouse droppings. She swore. She'd undergone an earlier invasion of field mice which had badly damaged an electric cable and gnawed at rice and soap, and wrecked her best Nepalese paper. The arrival of the mice proved that autumn was here with a vengeance. She could empathise with the poor little creatures: modern farming methods left them little to eat over the winter and any mouse worth his whiskers would certainly want to come in from the cold. But she certainly wasn't prepared to share her house with them, so it was out with the traps, which she loathed using.

Maggie was still feeling depressed and annoyed with everything – herself, the mice, her aunt, Sophie, Michel and the weather (it was still spitting) – when at last she ventured out. Cocooned in waterproof, fleeces and boots, she was well protected, but glad to see that it wasn't raining so much that she wouldn't be able to see when she went beachcombing; if it was raining heavily, it was impossible to see properly through her specs.

Most of all, she was annoyed with herself for feeling lonely. She hadn't felt this bad for a long while.

Fortunately, she wasn't quite back to the Old Lady Breast-Feeding-Cat level of loneliness, but it was definitely hovering. And bloody Niall, who had turned up at quite the wrong moment that day. It was such a shame; she'd really like to ring that Andy man, ask him over for a drink or remind him about the drill, but felt too embarrassed. Doggedly, she stomped along the path to a beach beyond the village, where she often found interesting pieces of metal, pottery shards, fossils or multi-coloured nests of plastic-covered wire that she could use later. It was harder in winter, because everywhere lay thick cables of slithery orange-brown kelp, which were piled up on the beach several feet deep, often completely obscuring her favourite hunting grounds. In the old days the locals used to harvest the seaweed for manure, and on some parts of the raised stone beach you could still see grooves worn by their cart wheels.

As she searched among the shards and pebbles, Maggie managed for a while to forget herself and her problems completely. She pocketed the occasional stone with a hole in it, or a ring of battered copper piping, which would metamorphose when she strung them together. The weather was lifting, too. Cheered, she looked across to the far side of the Firth, stranded with silver and grey, with the dark silhouettes of a tanker and a couple of fishing boats in front. Suddenly transformed, the view was sublimely beautiful. She must always remember that this was why she was here: the beauty. The beauty, the peace and the joyous serendipity of the objects she found every time she searched the foreshore for its treasures.

Today she was lucky. She cheered discreetly as she picked up a tiny white ceramic arm, complete with seaworn hand and chubby fingers. Magically, it was already pierced at the elbow (it must have come from an articulated Edwardian or Victorian doll) and was perfect for her purposes. 'Thank you,' she murmured, to what or whom she did not know. If it was only chance, she was thanking, that would suffice. Life was unpredictable and that was what was marvellous – and sometimes terrible – about it.

Andy, head down, walked vigorously, avoiding the muddiest bits of the path. Dougie, tongue lolling, ran ahead, sniffing excitedly at every interesting smell. There were no other walkers out today, the weather was too vile.

What was that Noel Coward song? *Mad dogs and Englishmen go out in the mid-day sun* . . . Here it would be, *Only the bereaved and lovesick go tramping through the storm* . . .

Bereaved, yes, that he obviously was, even now. But lovesick? That was a bit of a Freudian slip, surely?

'Come on, son, come here.' Smiling, he bent to put the dog's collar on as they were nearing the village. As he fixed the clasp, he noticed a huddled figure on the beach that seemed to be picking up stones and peering at them intently. A bit strange at this time of year. Whoever it was, was so wrapped up that it was hard to tell if it was a man or a woman, but for a moment he wondered what on earth he or she could be looking for in this gloomy weather. It was amazing what people found to entertain themselves with. Moments later, the sun blazed through the grey and lit up the whole sky.

Magic, thought Andy. Total bloody magic. Come wind, come rain, it was still stunningly beautiful here, and sometimes, like today, it was so lovely that it could make him greet like a bairn when it caught him unawares.

Then he realised with a start that the crouched figure on the beach was Maggie. He stared at her for a moment, and when she looked up, their eyes met.

'Oh – hello there,' she called shyly.

'Hi,' he called back, certain he was blushing. 'How's it going? Have you found any treasures?'

'One or two.' It was hard to shout him from such a distance.

He stood for a moment, feeling distinctly awkward.

'Well, let's hope it keeps dry for a while. We could do with a bit of decent weather.'

Maggie nodded, and watched as he waved briefly to her, called to the dog, and hurriedly went on his way. Why didn't she just call him back, she asked herself bitterly. She could explain to him that Niall was married and not really much use to her. But she was too shy, too unsure of herself. She grimaced as she watched him disappear, and felt more desolate than ever.

Sophie woke abruptly the next morning and remembered with terror that she was pregnant. The blue dye in the pregnancy test kit had declared it to be definite. In a way she'd known that she must be, but hadn't acknowledged it to herself, hadn't even wanted to consider it a possibility – not with things as they stood. Not without Michel, who seemed to have done a runner. His one postcard had come quite soon after his first phone call to say he had arrived in Provence and was OK, but that was ages back. A lifetime ago.

She shuffled into the kitchen to make tea and sat sipping it unhappily. Sylvia, who had a two-year-old and was planning to have a second child soon, had advised dry biscuits to help the sickness, so she unwrapped an oatcake and nibbled it gingerly.

She eyed the clock on the kitchen wall. It would be just after nine in France; they were an hour later than here; so she decided to try his parents' place again. She dialled the number and waited for the ringing tone, but after listening yet again to Michel's father's voice on the answerphone, she frowned and put down the receiver. She'd already left them a message. It was the same story with his brother's number. When, as a last resort, she dialled the number of a musician friend in Marseilles, the man's girlfriend answered and said yes, Michel had spent a few days with them, but it was almost three weeks ago and they supposed he'd returned to Scotland long since.

It was no good. Sophie looked down at her tummy, which sat there all innocent and normal-looking. It wasn't the right time. She knew with a deep conviction that she didn't want to have a baby and bring it up all by herself. If Michel wasn't coming back – and that was certainly how things seemed – this baby must not be born.

'I simply couldn't cope,' she said aloud, but the option of abortion did seem horrific, though several good friends had undergone at least one termination and hadn't seemed much the worse for it. Mind you, Jackie, who already had three kids and had got rid of what would have been number four, had told her once when she'd had a lot to drink, that she cried every year on the anniversary of what would have been that fourth child's birthday.

Sophie shivered, and found herself suddenly angry. 'Damn you, Michel. Damn you for doing this to me. I hope the flamingoes chew your flaming balls off!'

Slamming her mug down in the sink, she went to run herself a bath. While the water flowed, she leafed through the Edinburgh telephone directory and looked up the family planning place in Stockbridge. Writing down the number in her diary, she closed it carefully. She'd phone tomorrow morning during her coffee break at the shop.

Chapter Fourteen

In the warm cottage, Maggie frowned at the perfect little body of a field mouse which lay dead in her trap. Its eyes looked so alert it could still be alive, and she felt momentarily guilty when she put it into her waste bin. If she were a Buddhist she supposed she would have to devise a humane trap so she could catch the creature and let it loose in the fields, 'So that it could come straight back in and eat my fruit, I suppose,' she muttered, as she several times tried to reset the trap – which kept snapping on her fingers – with a new bit of cheese. The trip-wire balanced at last, she sat down to phone her daughter, who should be home from work by now. Maggie wanted to firm up their plans to meet later in the week. Maybe they could have a meal out and Maggie could stay overnight. As she dialled, she wondered if the wandering Michel was back yet; it was surely time he was.

'Hi, darling,' she said when Sophie answered at last. 'How's things? I was wondering if you fancied an Indian meal on Thursday?'

There was a strange noise at the other end of the line, a sort of lurching gasp followed by silence.

'Sophie? Are you there?'

More gasps.

Maggie felt cold. Sophie was obviously crying. Her 'Darling, what's wrong?' was greeted by a full-blooded incomprehensible wail.

'Sophie, what on earth is it? Are you ill? Has something awful happened?'

A long pause. 'Sort of.'

'Sort of what?'

A long pause.

'I'm pregnant, Mum.'

'Oh my goodness . . . Uh . . . that's real big news . . . Er . . . does Michel know?'

'No. I can't get hold of him. He wanted a month with no communication.'

'And how long is it now?'

'It's nearly six weeks . . .' The last word was drowned in weeping.

'Have you phoned him?'

'Answerphones all round.' More sobs, big hiccoughey ones. 'Ma?'

'Yes, darling?'

'I can't have a baby all by myself.'

'I . . .' Maggie didn't know how to respond to this.

'I really can't, Ma. I've decided. I've made an appointment.'

'For?'

'To have an abortion.'

'Oh my God.'

'Please say something better than that, Ma. After all, you're not even religious.'

Maggie's car key was in her hand. 'Sophie, darling. I'm coming over. Stay where you are, please. Don't worry, you're going to be OK . . .'

She wished as she said the words that she could believe them. 'An hour and a half should do it. It'll be rush hour on the bridge, but I'll come as quickly as I can.'

'OK.' Sophie sounded just like the frail child she'd been when her dad had his last heart attack. 'Wee Soph. O Lord,' moaned Maggie as she set off, 'tell me this isn't really happening . . .'

She grabbed from her fridge a chicken and a bottle of

wine. When at last she stood in Sophie and Michel's flat and hugged her daughter, almost her first question was, 'Have you eaten anything today?'

Sophie shook her head, eyes brimming. 'Thanks for coming, Ma. I just feel so miserable, I miss him, I can't stand it without him . . .'

Maggie scrabbled in the kitchen drawer to find a corkscrew. 'Here,' she poured her daughter a glass of wine.

'Thanks,' Sophie took a sip, then grimaced. 'Shit! I can't even drink. It tastes weird.'

Maggie tested hers. It was delicious; she took a huge gulp. 'It's your sensible body telling you what's what. I couldn't drink at all when I was pregnant.'

Sophie nearly smiled. 'Knowing you, it's a miracle you decided to have more than one, then.'

Maggie hugged her. 'It didn't seem to matter at the time; wine or any sort of alcohol simply tasted awful.'

This time Sophie did smile. 'Well, you've certainly made up for it since.' Then she burst into tears. 'Oh Ma, what am I going to do?'

'Whatever you decide, you must tell Michel. It's his baby too.'

'We always wanted children; we thought we might go for it soon – it was just a matter of time – and money. I do love him, Ma. I just . . . miss him.'

'Of course you do. He's a lovely man. I'm sure he'll come back.' Maggie stroked her daughter's back, handed out tissues. 'Listen, why don't you go and have a lovely long bath. Have you got some nice oils?'

'Uhuh,' Sophie nodded wanly.

'And some candles?'

'Yes.'

'I'll cook us supper. You're not off chicken, I hope?'

Sophie shook her head, then looked at her anxiously. 'I've got an appointment for an assessment at the clinic tomorrow morning . . .'

'Bath.' Maggie pointed imperiously. Sophie nodded, wiped her face and disappeared into the bathroom and Maggie, trembling, poured herself a generous second glass of wine. She felt very perturbed, angry with Michel, and worried for both him and her daughter.

She searched through the CDs in the kitchen and chose a late Haydn quartet, which played as she prepared the food and tried to be strong. Ever since she was little, Sophie had been a lover of long baths, so Maggie reckoned she'd take an hour at least. She put the chicken in the oven with fresh ginger and some coconut milk. Then, the Haydn finished, she listened to *The Archers*, which she was annoyed with herself for finding strangely comforting.

Sophie luxuriating in the bath, half-asleep, listened to Berlioz's *Nuits d'été* in a haze of rosemary, lavender and geranium, with two candles glowing beside her. For a moment or two she felt almost cheerful, but then the misery engulfed her and her salt tears rained into the perfumed bathwater.

The chicken was smelling delicious already. Maggie was glad that she could do this for her daughter; a good meal nearly always helped in a difficult situation, even if it only made you feel better while you were eating it. She made a salad dressing, and prepared a salad with a flicker of toasted pinenuts on top. It looked good enough to cheer up a corpse.

Ready at last, she went to sit on the sofa, where she sighed as she acknowledged to herself how completely worn out she felt. She'd almost dozed off when she heard the doorbell ring.

Sophie was standing in the sitting-room doorway, pink and lovely, wrapped in a towel, hairdryer in hand.

'It's probably a neighbour. I don't want to see anybody,' she hissed, and retreated towards the bedroom.

'D'you want me to go?' Maggie rose from the sofa.

Sophie nodded. 'Yeah, please. But I'm not here, OK?' And she disappeared into the bedroom and shut the door.

Maggie wondered who on earth could be ringing the bell at this hour. As she cautiously went to pull the front door open, she heard the whine of the hairdryer start up.

It was Michel. He looked beautiful – sunburnt, with a travel bag, a bottle of champagne, flowers – and very short hair.

'Oh, my God. Michel! Is it really you?'

He nodded sheepishly. 'Ma-out-law ... *Bonsoir* ... Am I allowed to come in?'

'I don't know – Where have you been? She's been trying to contact you for days, but there was never anybody there ...'

'My brother was in Paris, and my parents were in Brittany. Did she not get my card to say I was going to the mountains for a few days? To follow some of the Compostella pilgrims' walk ...'

Maggie shook her head.

'I posted it almost two weeks ago.'

Maggie realised that they were whispering. 'Why on earth didn't you phone her, Michel? She's been desperate.' She was shocked to see Michel's agonised response.

'After I'd been so crazy ... I was afraid that she would tell me to piss off.'

'She's just had a bath – she's drying her hair,' said Maggie. They looked at each other as they listened to the dryer, for a moment, then it stopped.

'Maggie. I love your daughter. I can't survive without her.'

Maggie could hardly speak. 'Please ... Tell this to Sophie, not to me, but Michel, dearie, darling, I'm awfully glad to see you back.'

'Who is it?' Sophie suddenly called.

Silence.

Michel swallowed, eyed Maggie briefly, and still laden, bravely entered the house. 'It's me,' he called.

Sophie came into the big hallway, wrapped in a huge green towel, hair stupendous.

Michel stared at her.

'Oh fuck.'

'I'm off,' muttered Maggie to the air.

Michel set down his bag and the bottle, and he and Sophie hugged wordlessly, the flowers still clutched in one of Michel's hands.

Neither of them noticed Sophie's mother crouched in the kitchen, turning down the chicken and the boiling rice, nor did they see her tactful exit.

Half an hour later, Maggie was halfway across the Forth Road Bridge when her mobile rang. Her hand was trembling violently when she lifted it to her ear.

It was Sophie. Happy.

'Ma, it's me. Thank you for being there, I love you and I'm fine. Michel has something to say to you.'

'Ma-out-law. We want to tell you, you are going to be a grandmother – and we are so joyful!'

Maggie, suddenly finding it very hard to see where she was going, started to drive very slowly, causing one or two other drivers to hoot furiously.

'That's fantastic, Michel ...' She was also finding it hard to speak – her heart seemed somehow to be blocking her throat. 'Absolutely fantastic. Congratulations.'

Sophie again: 'Thank you, Ma. Thank you for everything. I'll phone you tomorrow.'

Michel came back on and she heard them both giggle. 'And Maggie, your chicken is absolutely delicious, fantastic. Thank you ... We love you ...'

Somehow, Maggie managed to switch off the phone and pull into a lay-by, where she sat quietly for a moment before she began to weep. She was thrilled about the child, glad that Michel was back and that they both sounded so happy. There were so many emotions surging inside her, she hardly knew why she was weeping.

Unexpected, piercing memories of early love and her first pregnancy reeled before her, and she remembered her darling, dead Fergal, who would never see this grandchild.

How he would have loved to hold his children's children; it would have been the crowning of his life and love, as perhaps it would be hers. But for the moment, alone in the dark and wet, insulated in her car, strongest of all the feelings that made her weep, was the overwhelming sense of being utterly alone in the world. Orphaned from love.

Chapter Fifteen

In Oban, Katy Maclean peered sourly at her sleeping husband, who lay sprawled on the sofa in front of the television, his right leg supported on a large cushion. It was almost time for Niall to go to the GP's surgery and she resented the fact that she'd have to chauffeur him: she had a lot of things to get ready with her sister coming to stay the next day, and she was also anxious that Niall wouldn't now be going away for the week as planned. If his toe continued to be as agonising as it was now, there was obviously no way he'd manage. Flora and Niall had never liked each other much, and as the two sisters had a full schedule planned – meeting up with old school friends, a patchwork lecture and a couple of good meals out – Katy could only hope the doctor would have some magic potion to make the pain go away as quickly as it had come. You'd think he'd broken the toe, the fuss he was making, but he swore that he hadn't fallen or knocked it at all.

'Time to wake up, Niall,' she muttered, shaking him. Dear God, he did look an awful old man when he slept like that, with his mouth open and the dribble coming out.

Niall groaned, wincing as he stretched. 'What's the time? Oh dear, we'd better hit the road.'

'Can you put your shoes on OK?'

'No, I'll need my slippers, and a walking stick.' He shook his head gloomily. 'Lord, I feel awful.'

'Here.' Sternly, Katy handed him his slippers. Niall tried to fit one on and yelped. 'It's no good. I'll just have to put one shoe on my good foot and hop in my stocking sole with the bad one. It's too bloody sore. D'you mind getting me my jacket?'

'I'm standing here with it.'

Blearily, Niall took the garment, pulled it on, grimacing.

'Don't forget this.' Katy handed him his hill-walking stick, a present from their long-gone son. 'Come on, now. We'd better get a move on, or we'll be late for your appointment.'

'I hope to God she knows what it is and can do something about it quickly. I need to be fit to drive to Edinburgh tomorrow.'

'I hope so too,' murmured Katy. If he didn't go to Edinburgh the week would be ruined – she'd invited all the girls for Wednesday night. If Niall was still here it just wouldn't be the same.

What would he do if he was stuck here with Katy and her bloody sister, wondered Niall. A whole week of the judgmental and pious Flora was a nightmare prospect; what's more, he'd got tickets for that concert in St Andrews and had arranged to take Maggie; he was damned if he was going to miss that.

In Denmark, Karin and Sven were saying goodbye to the last of their wedding guests.

'Goodbye, little one.' Karin hugged Catriona. 'Thank you for being my bridesmaid.

'She was nice,' said Catriona.

'Who?'

'Your priestess, the one who married you.'

'Ah, the woman priest. Yes, she was fine, wasn't she? I hope you've had a good time and that you will soon come back to Denmark. It's so lovely to swim here in the summer – there are so few people and long sandy beaches. We'd love to see you, and now you know some of Sven's family too.'

Catriona nodded, and as Karin hugged her granddaughter tightly, she saw her lip quiver. 'Please don't cry, darling, we must all be brave, I promise that we'll be back for a long visit in the summer.'

'Ma, we'd better get going.' Kerstin came up to them. 'Come on, Catriona, we have to leave now, or we'll miss the plane.'

The next day, on the shores of the Limfiord, which glittered like silver in the early winter sun, the newly married pair walked and searched for the fossils of ancient sea urchins. The church where they had been married, which was painted white and had a containing wall of huge granite boulders, was well known to both of them through family connections. They'd chosen to have a quiet ceremony, with only a couple of dozen close friends and family present, and the wedding feast had been held in the Kirsten Kjaersmuseum, a remarkable sort of arts centre which two male doctors, old friends of Sven – one Danish, the other English, who'd lived together happily for thirty five years – had miraculously created in the wilderness of Jutland.

Karin, fur-hatted and clad in sheepskin, bent to pick up a perfect stone sea urchin, rounded, pale grey, with delicate markings on its top. 'This is a really beautiful one. I wish Maggie could see it. I think she was sorry we didn't ask her to come.'

Sven admired the fossil. 'But we didn't want any more people than we had, it would have been too much. Why don't we send her this?'

'Good idea.' Karin stood and looked out across the fiord to the other side, where a thin layer of snow lay on the hills and fields. Beyond, pine woods stood out dramatically, black against the landscape.

'I love this place. At any time of year, the landscape's extraordinary.'

Sven put his arm round her. 'It's one of the most beautiful places I know.' He pointed up the hill behind them. 'Do you know the Viking burial mounds up there?'

Karin nodded. 'Of course. They're the ones with one of the best views in Jutland; they chose well where to be buried, didn't they? Do you know whose graves they are?'

'No. Only that they must have been important kings or warriors, they're so impressive.'

'A wonderful place to lie for eternity.'

Smiling, Sven pulled her to him.

Karin looked up. 'It's starting to snow. We'd better go back to Langvad.'

'Harald said he was cooking a leg of lamb tonight, one of his own animals.'

'Maybe it's the one whose fleece he gave us,' Karin smiled.

'Very possible. Come.' Sven held out his hand and she took it and they walked slowly back up the hill to where their car was parked.

'Do you mind that I have to go back to work tomorrow?' he asked at last.

'Not at all. I'll enjoy doing things in the house, setting up my loom and seeing people. And we need to put down that new wooden floor.'

'We'll lay that floor together,' promised Sven. 'And I swear to you that we'll have a real honeymoon in Scotland in May. That's only six months away.'

'May is my favourite time of year there.'

'And we'll spend time with all your children and visit the islands, then come back to Fife and stay in your house for at least a month.'

Karin looked at him happily.

'And maybe . . .' added Sven thoughtfully, 'maybe we will even attempt to do the Chain Walk once more.'

Karin frowned.

'We can compromise,' he said later, 'and perhaps just walk a quarter of the way this time.'

This time Karin nodded, and Sven hugged her again.

As they walked entwined, they were watched by a large hare, who quivered with curiosity and stood transfixed for some moments before elegantly loping away towards the woods, unnoticed by the newly weds.

November in Inverie: Maggie was preparing supper for Michel and Sophie, who were coming out to her immediately following the first hospital check-up for the baby. Maggie was relieved that the pair of them sounded so full of plans, excited about the pregnancy, and reassuringly, Michel was much calmer and happier, and being careful not to overwork. The anti-depressants were obviously doing their job.

She was also quite looking forward to Niall's next visit, to the good eating and drinking they always shared and to the Michael Marra concert. And even the sex, though she was surprised how rarely she gave it a thought these days. The time before last, when they'd actually come together, even Niall, she knew, had been pleased. He never said much, really, but it had been a vintage fuck. 'It's just sex, you daft besom,' he'd say, grinning, if she ever got too emotional. But it was nice to know they were still capable of it, even if she had got cramp in her leg in the middle of it all.

She felt festive as she cooked, and set the table with candles, flowers and a treasured linen cloth woven by Karin.

The youngsters both looked good. Michel had a shine to him, with his new short haircut, a sweater of multi-coloured stripes and an unusual new black jacket with big sleeves. He reminded Maggie of a troubadour.

Pink-cheeked and grinning, Sophie handed her mother a small envelope. 'We've brought you a very special picture.'

Maggie opened the envelope and peered, puzzled, at what looked like a photographic negative.

'You have to hold it up to the light,' Michel showed her. 'Like this. Now you can see your grandchild.'

Entranced, they all peered at the image of the embryo.

'Feet, fingers even ... it's amazing.' Maggie was

thrilled. 'It's wonderful; looks like he or she has quite a big nose, too.'

'Of course.' Proudly, Michel displayed his profile.

'They offered to tell us what sex, but we said we'd rather wait and see. Imagine if they said it was a girl and it turned out to be a boy with a teeny weeny willy.' Sophie was so unrecognisably different to the unhappy, frightened girl of only six weeks ago. Maggie surged with optimism.

'Sit,' she urged. 'Have a drink,' and poured bubbly into glasses.

'No wine for us two,' said Sophie patting her tum.

Michel laughed. 'I can drink for two. Sophie can eat for two. We have a perfect balance.'

'So what's the good news?'

'It's the TV people . . .' began Sophie.

'They were very pleased with my Camargue music and they've commissioned me to do the music for another nature programme about the Isle of Skye, with quite a lot of money and a good time schedule.' Michel gulped the bubbly. 'I can hardly believe it, and they are lovely to work with, gentle but exacting in a good way. It feels more than OK to do it.'

'No compromising of your artistic integrity?'

He shook his head. 'Sometimes nearly, but I fight it – it's interesting to do, political, artistic – I like it. But the best thing is that I really have stopped the teaching. I was hating it so much; it's a huge relief.'

'Marvellous, it's all great news, so double *Skaal: Skaal* to the Babby, and *Skaal* to the TV!' Maggie clashed glasses.

Michel really did seem to be his old self again: hopefully Sophie's ninety-year-old Azerbaijani had disappeared for good.

Hours later, when the young couple had left, headed for a night in the studio, Maggie unplugged her cordless phone and cleaned the points to check that it was working. Blooming Niall hadn't rung her as promised, which was very unlike him. She certainly wasn't going to phone him and be forced to talk to Katy, but what on earth could have happened to the man?

In Oban, Niall was shouting: 'Katy, could you fetch me something, please?'

'In a minute, I'm in the middle of something.' Katy, in the kitchen, was beating up a cake mixture.

Niall sighed and flicked the television zapper. Oprah again, this time about married men who had affairs. A couple were confronting each other: 'How could you do that to me?' the woman was asking over and over again, as the man shrugged sheepishly, sitting awkwardly between mistress and wife, Niall watched for a moment, then yelled in agony when Jocky, the West Highland terrier, unexpectedly leapt up and tried to settle on his legs.

Exasperated, Katy's head appeared in the kitchen doorway. 'What on earth's wrong?'

Niall grimaced, and the quivering dog – always over the top emotionally, in Niall's opinion – lay on its back, trembling, begging for absolution.

Hastily, he zapped to a gardening programme as Katy came in, wiping her hands. 'That bloody animal landed right on my bad foot.'

'Poor wee Jocky, poor wee soul,' she picked up the dog, who responded to her comforting with breathless, near orgasmic licks.

Niall watched them glumly; there was obviously to be no such comfort for him. Katy openly considered Niall's malady to be entirely self-inflicted – a well-deserved punishment for decades of over-indulgence.

'Here you are, darling, let's find you a wee bikkie,' soothed Katy, kissing Jocky's hairy snout.

'I need to write some letters.' Niall's voice was gruff, almost apologetic. 'Could you possibly fetch me some paper and envelopes.'

'How many envelopes?'

'A couple will do. Thanks.' Niall sighed, wincing as he moved up the sofa. Bloody gout. He could just imagine Maggie's peal of laughter. It was such a demeaning illness to have. Too much uric acid in your toe joints; it was a joke, and no alcohol or rich food for a good couple of weeks. He'd much rather have broken his leg climbing a hill like his friend Colin did last month; at least that would have had some street cred compared to this cringe-making ailment.

'Why don't you do them on the computer?' asked Katy.

No fear. That way she'd almost certainly see what was being printed; she liked to keep an eye on things, did Katy.

'It's not worth the bother. It's just a wee note about what I want Robert to bid for on Saturday.'

'Why don't you phone him?'

'It's more businesslike on paper.'

Katy muttered something about the oven and returned to the kitchen and Niall, frowning, set about writing as fast as he could. He was sealing an envelope when his wife brought him a cup of tea and a lone cracked Jaffa cake.

'Thanks. I need this to catch the five o'clock post, it's quite urgent.'

'What's the hurry? The auction's not for over a week. I've got my cake in the oven, I need to watch it.'

'It would only take you five minutes,' Niall pleaded. 'Please . . .'

'Give it here.' Obviously not pleased, Katy pulled on her winter coat and hat, called to the euphoric and noisy Jocky, and took the stamped envelope from her husband. 'Where's the other one?'

'Which other one?'

'The other envelope. You said you needed two.'

'Oh . . . it's er . . . enclosed. I couldn't remember an address in Glasgow, but Robert'll know.'

Frowning, Katy and the dog exited, and Niall lay back in relief. He wondered for a moment if he dared telephone Maggie, but decided not to because Katy's newly arrived sister was clattering about upstairs, taking possession of the spare room, and would be bound to hear.

In Inverie, in the little studio, Sophie lay resplendent on the double futon with Michel spreadeagled across her, his hands spread out as he listened intently to what was happening in her bulging stomach.

'Can you hear anything?'

'A big heartbeat, yes, but I can't hear a wee one.' Michel's voice was muffled. 'Lots of gurgles and bubbles, it sounds like you're fermenting.'

Sophie laughed. 'Ouch! That was a seriously big kick. Surely you felt that one?'

'I did. It must be a boxer in there. He could give his father a black eye at this rate.'

'It might be a girl boxer.'

'Sure it might.' He smiled and kissed the bump all over. '*Bonjour* Boxer. This is your father speaking, can you hear me?'

Sophie sighed contentedly. 'It's so strange, isn't it?'

'What?'

She gestured to her belly. 'This whole business, it's so surreal. To think that there's an actual person ripening in there, waiting to come out and live with us. It's amazing.'

'It's almost impossible to imagine.'

She stroked his hair, twisting the short dark tendrils in her fingers. 'D'you find it scary?'

Michel thought about it, his eyes sombre. 'A little. It's a huge responsibility. A new human being and we must guide him or her and try to be loving and giving and not one little bit selfish for the rest of our lives. Yes, I'm scared. I wonder sometimes if I'll be any good at being a parent. What if I get crazy again?'

'We'd know quicker how to deal with it if you did. Anyway, I don't think you will. You'll be a fantastic father, I know you will. But . . .' her words petered out.

'What is it?'

'It was terrible . . .'

'When I was ill, you mean?'

'Yeah.'

Michel nodded, frowning, bit his lips, eyes anxious.

'I was really frightened; it was as though you weren't there. Your body was there, you were walking and talking, but you yourself weren't actually present. I honestly was scared stiff.'

Michel closed his eyes and grimaced. 'It was horrible for me too; I wasn't present for myself – not just for you – and because I wasn't present for myself, I didn't know I wasn't there. Terrifying.'

They were silent, then he tickled her. 'But before I wasn't present for anybody, I was wise enough to choose you.'

'Cheek! I chose you!'

'We chose each other, or maybe the little flamingo in there made us choose each other.'

'Flamingo. Hey . . .' She tasted the word. 'That's a great name.'

Michel sat up. Grinned, hugged her. 'I like it. Flamingo . . . Flamingoooo . . .' he sang the word several times and Sophie harmonised with him, up and down the scale. Sometimes Michel crooned falsetto, sometimes a deep bass. Pleased with themselves, they finished the improvisation.

'Great!' Sophie was pink with delight. 'Let's call the baby that for now.'

Michel stood up. 'Yes . . . I really like it, and it would do for a boy or a girl.' He paused. 'But how would you shorten it?'

'Flam, Flammie?' Sophie frowned.

'*Flamme*'s OK. The flamingoes look like flames when they fly sometimes.'

'In French, yes, but in Scotland they'd probably shorten it to Phlegmmie, and that would be awful, or they might call him or her Mingie, which means smelly in Scots – that wouldn't be too great either . . .'

'Just Flamingo, then. For the moment. Agreed?' Michel patted her tum and whispered 'Can you hear us there, little one? You've got a working title ... *Bonjour* little fermenting Flamingo, *c'est ton papa ici.*'

They smiled at each other.

'I would like to do a little work.' Michel took her hand. 'Is it OK if I go for a small walk by myself? I promise I'll not disappear again. You look like you could do with a sleep.'

Comfortable in the bed, Sophie nodded. 'Don't be too long, sweetheart. It's chilly out there.'

Michel put on his jacket and a dramatically patterned hat and wrapped a striped scarf several times round his neck. 'Bye bye, I'll see you later.' He leaned over her and they embraced and he went out, shutting the door gently behind him, leaving Sophie to snuggle down under the duvet.

And while she dozed, half-aware of her embryo's butterfly dancings, dreaming of a baby born with bright pink hair and wings, her lover paced by the harbour, humming softly to himself, and composed *un petit chanson pour Flamingo.*

Chapter Sixteen

In a second-hand bookshop near St Andrews West Port, so dark and cluttered with cardboxes and dusty books as to seem subterranean, a small, bearded man with half-moon specs, his bald head dimly illuminated by a forty-watt light bulb, was opening his mail. Frowning, he slit open a hand-addressed envelope postmarked Oban and withdrew a letter and a second folded envelope, which was stamped and addressed to a woman in Inverie unknown to him, and marked *please forward* in its top left-hand corner. He chuckled when he read the accompanying note and learned the nature of Niall's malady, and noted that Niall had listed certain books he wanted as well as asking him, as a favour, to post on the enclosed letter. *Will explain when I see you*, Niall had added as a PS beneath his usual flamboyant signature.

The bookseller knew Niall of old, having shared digs with him when they were students in Glasgow. Womanising again, no doubt, he presumed. Niall would never change, though he wondered a little enviously – as he'd always done – where his friend managed to find the energy. He had to go to the post anyway, so it was no skin off his nose to oblige his randy old pal.

Well wrapped up against the cold in a navy-blue woollen helmet with a pom-pom, and a grey home-knitted scarf,

Gilbert Menstrie, bony nose scarlet with cold, was lovingly restoring the wooden body parts of his cherished Morris Minor shooting brake when Maggie walked past him. He nodded to her and muttered a greeting, but if she replied he didn't hear it. Gilbert, not usually much aware of other people and how they felt, was struck today by his neighbour's demeanour. He wondered what was up with her. She was looking older, beat. Downright bloody miserable in fact.

Gilbert was right, Maggie's mood was black. The oddly brief note from Niall had nonplussed her. The envelope postmarked St Andrews had a *please forward* note on the front which somebody had crossed out in red biro.

In haste, imprisoned by gout, inconsolable. Can't make it this time, tickets enclosed. Enjoy. Will make up for this, I promise. Love and kisses, I miss you. Niall.

Maggie had smiled to hear of the gout. She knew it could be agonising, but it was undeniably one of those comic illnesses, certainly not a dignified complaint; poor Niall would need to keep off the booze, which he certainly wouldn't like, but her amusement didn't last long, for in spite of everything she'd been looking forward to seeing the old reprobate, and now there seemed little else to look forward to. Since the Murdo débâcle, she'd been feeling so alone that she was even thinking of getting herself a cat or dog. At least it would be company of sorts. The imminent grandchild was definitely an excitement but it was obviously the flip side of her own ageing, and she had to acknowledge that she'd simply been feeling lonely. Karin wasn't up the road any more; the London friends were 450 miles away and when she shivered alone in her bed at night and the wind howled and the sea roared, she sometimes felt utterly bereft.

Neither Morag nor Donnie were free to go to the concert

with her (Donnie tended to favour brass bands or bagpipes anyway), Sophie was still working, and Michel busy with his TV commission. She'd also tried a couple of friends in the village and one in St Andrews but it was too short notice. She'd even rung Patrick, who was back living in the castle with a lot of domestic help; he'd been charming, but he couldn't come because he was having dinner with Jennifer Earlsferry. Bitterly, Maggie walked along the muddy path on the way to the ruined castle. The sun was beginning to set and there were streaks of red and yellow above the sea, which was an improvement after the day's relentless grey, but today not even the stark beauty of the landscape touched her. It just seemed gloomy and uncomfortable and she wondered why she'd ever been deranged enough to claim she loved this place. Angry with herself for her negative state, she walked as energetically as she could, but it was muddy and slippery underfoot so she didn't make very good progress. The summer had been such a happy time, with a great sense of renewal, that to find herself stuck back in this familiar bleakness was a most unwelcome misery. Maybe the concert would cheer her up, though she hated going to such things by herself.

Sighing, she put her head down against the wind and plunged her hands into her pockets. Walking was supposed to cheer you up, so why the hell didn't it?

The concert, in a hotel in St Andrews, was extraordinarily badly attended: there were only a few people sitting at scattered tables to hear music made by a man who ought to be cherished as a national treasure. Maggie ordered herself a plate of food and a glass of wine and took her place at a huge round table with a couple of women sitting on the far side, who eyed her briefly then ignored her. She ate her meal gloomily, hoping the place would fill up a bit, but it was still only a third full when the concert started. As the lights went down she was startled to recognise Andy Johnstone, obviously also by himself, sitting on the far side of the hall. Their eyes met and he raised his glass to her with what she felt sure was an ironic little smile. Maggie drained her wine and frowned as she remembered Niall.

One of the first items was a young fiddler, red-haired and thin, who played fantastic whirling Scottish rhythms – one of the tunes made her almost breathless with delight – and the tiny audience clapped like mad. The star of the night, Michael Marra, was a small man with intense dark eyes. She'd heard him before and played his tapes many times. The songs, which he composed, were all local, Dundee-based, sad, funny, loving. His voice was gravelly and his timing impeccable. It was marvellous. Alone or not, gradually Maggie thawed and began to really enjoy herself. To hell with it; she wasn't the only single soul in the world.

At the interval, she slipped out to the Ladies and renewed her lipstick. When she came back and went to the bar she found Andy standing with a beer in his hand.

He grinned openly. 'Hello there. Can I buy you a drink?'

'Thanks. I'll have a red wine, please.'

'Are you enjoying it?'

'It's wonderful. We're privileged to be here. I can't believe there aren't more people.'

'It's not been advertised properly. He's a grand singer, I've always liked him – and the ginger-headed laddie was fantastic.'

'Wasn't he just?'

'How's your necklace-making going?'

'Slowly. I've been a bit preoccupied, thinking too much, doing too little. This weather gets me down.'

Andy nodded. 'I know what you mean.'

'How about you?'

He shrugged. 'There's not so much to do in the winter. The garden's a no-go area; the boat's in dock. I do a bit of work on that – painting and carpentry, basic maintenance – it keeps me busy enough, but I get a bit fed up as well.'

'D'you see much of your family?'

'Oh aye, but they've got their own lives. I have my grandweans for the night sometimes and that's chaos, but I enjoy it. I honestly don't know what I'd do without them.'

'My Sophie's expecting her first baby in May.'

'That's damn fine splendid. *Slainte.*' He clinked glasses. 'You'll enjoy that.'

'Promise?'

'Aye, I promise. It's maybe the best thing that ever happened to me – barring my marriage, I suppose – but it's all part of the same thing, the love, the family . . . you know what I mean?' Suddenly, Andy looked embarrassed.

'I do know what you mean and I'm looking forward to it, but at the same time I feel a wee bit sad about it.'

He looked at her keenly. 'You mean . . .?'

'Well . . . Because there's nobody to share it with. I miss my husband, I suppose, though I should have got used to it by now.' She drained her glass, and saw that people were going back to their seats.

The lights were starting to go out. Andy put his glass down. 'It's the same for me, lass, but we just have to make the best of it.' He looked a little puzzled. 'But I thought you had somebody?' he said. Then he took her arm gently. 'Incidentally, would you like to sit together for the second half?'

'Why not?' Maggie nodded and followed him back to her table, laughing emptily. As they sat down she leaned over to him and whispered on impulse, 'You had every reason to think that, but my West Highland friend is long married and ever more shall be so.'

'Oh Lord . . .' Andy groaned sympathetically. 'One of those, eh? I had a married woman friend in Cupar for a couple of years and it nearly did for me.' He sat down. 'I tell you, masochism, that's what it was; it was like bashing my head against a brick wall.'

'Too bloody right.' Maggie sighed sympathetically.

When Michael Marra returned to the platform to enormous applause, he announced, smiling, that Sheena, who had already bowed to the audience as being the person responsible for bringing the young fiddler and a group of local country dancers to perform, was going to sing for them.

Maggie felt momentarily disappointed; she wanted more Marra, not somebody she'd never heard of, who didn't look particularly like an artiste. Sheena Wellington, who was a well-built woman of about Maggie's own age, wearing a businesslike trouser suit, smiled and walked towards the rostrum, where the star of the show was holding out his hand to her.

Maggie turned to whisper her disappointment to Andy, but he was clapping enthusiastically. He turned to Maggie, obviously delighted. 'Just you listen to this.'

And it really was something special. The big woman stood silent for a moment, then began to sing Robert Burns' 'My Luve's Like a Red Red Rose', to a tune even more subtle and haunting than the one Maggie already knew. It was beautiful, pure emotion – the original Niall Gow version, the singer told them afterwards.

'She sang "A Man's a Man for a' That" at the opening of the Scottish Parliament,' whispered Andy.

'This is getting to be a class gig, isn't it?' announced Michael Marra shyly as he thanked the singer.

Maggie felt so moved by the music that she just nodded when Andy asked if she had enjoyed that. She was sure she wasn't the only speechless member of the audience.

The show ended at last, with the audience reluctant to let their wee man go. Still clapping, Andy stood up. 'Have you got transport?'

Maggie nodded and they went out, stopping to buy a CD each on the way.

'That was wonderful, by world standards wonderful.'

'Aye, I'm sure it was as good as you could find anywhere.'

Outside, it was cold and dark. 'Where are you parked?' asked Andy.

'Just up the road.'

'So am I.' They walked for fifty yards or so in silence,

aware of the two single journeys ahead. Andy stopped first. 'Well, this is me.' He turned to her. 'It was nice meeting up with you. Maybe see you one of these days.'

Maggie wrapped her scarf round her. 'That would be nice.'

'Are you – er – still wanting to borrow an electric drill?'

'Yes. That might actually inspire me to do some work. I'd love that.'

'I'll maybe pop by, then. I'll give you a ring first.'

'Have you got my number?'

'I have. I saw it in the phone book, if it's still the same.'

Maggie looked a little puzzled; if it hadn't been so dark she could have sworn that Andy was blushing.

He grinned a little awkwardly. 'I looked it up a couple of months ago, when you first said you might like a loan of the drill.'

Ah. Before he overheard the Niall phone call. Before the unfortunate clifftop threesome. She understood. Now Maggie was blushing. She smiled. 'OK. I look forward to hearing from you.'

'Look after yourself, then. I'll be seeing you.'

They climbed into their separate vehicles and drove almost in tandem for eleven miles. Maggie felt a sense of loss as she saw Andy indicate left and turn off into Pittenweem. He was a lovely man; for a moment she almost wished that he was coming back home with her.

Chapter Seventeen

Maggie, her brain swirling with images of the night's music and the unexpected meeting with Andy, had only just got to sleep when she was woken abruptly by shouting and a loud battering on her front door. Startled by the noise, she clambered out of bed, sleepily pulled on her dressing-gown, went to the window and opened it.

'Who is it?' She peered into the icy darkness.

'It's me. Gilbert. Gilbert Menstrie. It's my mother ...' The man sounded panic-stricken. 'She's had a fall. Please could you help me?'

'OK. I'll be down in a minute, just wait a tick.'

Puzzled that Gilbert should have chosen her to be a good Samaritan, Maggie switched on a light, noted that it was almost half past two, hurriedly pulled on trousers, socks and sweater, and stumbled downstairs. She grabbed her coat and opened the door to the blinking Gilbert, who like herself had pyjamas on under his clothes. His sparse hair was wild and his specs askew.

'I'm coming. Tell me what happened while I pull my boots on.'

'I was asleep, and Mother went to bed early as she usually does but I woke to hear her call and when I went into her bedroom she was on the floor, gasping. She's an awful colour – I think it might be a heart attack ...'

'Have you rung for an ambulance?'

'No. She's terrified of hospitals . . . I didn't know what to do.' As he climbed the steps to his front door, Maggie, aware of the stars and a high tide swirling only a few feet away from them, followed him, shivering.

'She's in here,' Gilbert gestured to a room at the end of the drab hallway. Mrs Menstrie, a bulky-bodied woman, lay on the floor near her bed, her walking stick and a spilt tumbler of water beside her. Maggie winced, trying not to look at the set of false teeth which grinned up at her from the carpet. The old woman, breathing heavily, was a blueish colour, and there was a messy cut on her forehead where she must have hit the bedside table.

'I can't lift her by myself.' Gilbert sounded frantic. 'I'm always telling her to call me if she needs anything in the night, but she's very independent.'

'Maybe we should just make her comfortable on the floor,' suggested Maggie. She didn't feel at all confident that she and Gilbert would manage to heave his massive mother back on to the old-fashioned high bed, where Gilbert had almost certainly been conceived, though it was almost impossible to imagine that Mrs Menstrie would ever have allowed such intimacy. 'I'll try and sort her out with pillows and covers, but I think you must call an ambulance.'

'She'll be livid with me if I do,' wailed Gilbert.

'You'll never forgive yourself if you don't.'

He nodded unhappily, and went back into the hall. As Maggie inserted a pillow under Mrs Menstrie's unconscious head and covered her with a big green satin quilt, she was aware of Gilbert, stuttering on the phone. The room was freezing, but there was an aged two-bar heater with a tattered flex in the corner which she plugged into the wall. Only one of the bars seemed to work, and a smell of singeing dust arose as the heat came on, but it was better than nothing.

Gilbert came back in. 'They'll be here as soon as they can, but it might take half an hour. We've to keep her warm and not give her anything to eat or drink meanwhile.'

'The electric blanket was wet from the water spill,' said Maggie, 'so I've turned it off.'

'I'm always telling her not to go to sleep with it on,' groaned Gilbert. 'It's lucky she wasn't electrocuted.'

Maggie tried to mop Mrs Menstrie's head with a cloth she'd moistened in the wash-hand basin in the corner. The wound had stopped bleeding and the old woman's forehead was clammy. Glancing at Gilbert, Maggie saw the man was in an awful state. She touched his arm. 'Look, Gilbert, why don't you sit by your Mum and I'll go and make a cup of tea, and maybe fill a hot water bottle if you have one.'

'There's one under the sink.'

'It might help. She's very cold. The shock, I suppose.'

Gilbert nodded bleakly. 'I know . . . She's freezing, and she made a dreadful clunk when she fell; I keep hearing it in my head.'

It was a relief to go into the kitchen, which was spartan in its formica cleanliness. The bedroom smelt of old age.

Maggie found teabags and located the electric kettle. There was milk in the immaculate fridge, sugar on the table and various packets of biscuits in a big tin on the sideboard, which she put on a tray. Gilbert would probably like some.

He was kneeling on the floor, holding his mother's hand when she came back.

'I'm always telling her to call me if she needs help or a cup of tea, or to go to the toilet in the night, but she's awfy wilful.'

His mother moaned and her eyes fluttered. Gilbert's eyes looked huge and moist behind his thick lenses as he leant over her.

'It's all right, Mum. The ambulance is on its way. I'm right here beside you. Don't you worry. And Maggie from next door is here to help.'

There was an answering grunt and Mrs Menstrie's eyes opened fully. 'I'm not going to any hospital,' she croaked. 'Not on your nellie.'

Gilbert wailed. 'Just you stay quiet, Mum. They'll be here in a minute.'

Mrs Menstrie moaned horribly and her hands waved about momentarily. 'It's my side, oooh . . . I feel terrible dizzy.'

Awkward as a cormorant drying its wings, Gilbert tried to hold her, but she groaned so loudly and told him to stop fussing that he retreated and patted her arm helplessly instead.

Maggie handed him a mug with a picture of the old kirk on it. 'Here, Gilbert. Have some tea. D'you take sugar?'

Gilbert nodded, sniffed. 'Three please.'

His mother was suddenly so still that Maggie wondered for a moment if she was dead, but then the old woman spoke again.

'What's she doing here?' she croaked.

Maggie flinched, and eyed Gilbert as he sipped his drink with trembling hands.

'I told you, Mother, she's here to help. Maggie's being very kind.'

'I never liked yon woman, nor her foreign mother before her. She was always awfy wild . . . they were an unholy family . . . a bad influence . . .' A deep moan followed.

Unexpectedly, Maggie felt an almost overwhelming desire to giggle. Pictures from her childhood with Mrs Menstrie gazing beadily out at her and her brothers from her kitchen spy-hole, scolding Donnie and Alistair, shouting at Astrid. It had been a war between Mrs Menstrie and Maggie's family since ever she could remember.

The phone rang. Gilbert looked even more flustered.

'Shall I answer it?' asked Maggie.

He shook his head and lurched up clumsily, letting his mother's head fall. Maggie moved over and knelt by her childhood enemy and held her, stroking her hand and soothing her brow.

'They'll be here to help you soon, they'll make you comfortable. Don't worry, Mrs Menstrie.'

Gilbert's mother moaned and nodded. 'I don't know why ye're being so kind to me. I'm worried about Gilbert though, he's in an awfy state and there's nobody to look after him but me. You know he lost his father.'

This was agonising. Mrs Menstrie was crying now; Maggie found a tissue and mopped the old woman's face.

'He never even saw his father – I was only six months gone when his destroyer was blown up.'

'I'm so sorry . . .' murmured Maggie and stroked the old woman's bulky shoulder and arm as best she could through her faded blue candlewick dressing-gown. 'So very sorry. I didn't know that.'

To be honest, she'd always vaguely imagined that Mr Menstrie had fled his wife because she was so outrageously bad-tempered and vile. And nosey to boot.

'Your man died as well, poor soul,' Mrs Menstrie suddenly wheezed.

Maggie almost choked. 'Yes, he did.'

'Heart attack, eh?'

Maggie nodded, and tried to keep calm as Gilbert came back into the room.

'They'll be here in a minute. They went down the wrong road, but they're just up at the Braehead.' He knelt down and took his mother's hand. 'How are you doing, Mother?'

Her eyes were shut again and she was in obvious pain. 'I'll be OK, son. Dinnae worry, I'm sorry to be such a nuisance . . .' She seemed to faint away as the doorbell rang.

The paramedics fixed up a drip and with some difficulty levered his mother on to a wheelchair. Gilbert watched them, looking appalled.

'I'll need to go with her, but how will I get back? I can't take the car, I don't want to travel separately . . .'

'You go with her in the ambulance,' said Maggie decisively. 'I'll follow in my car, and bring you home when she's been attended to.'

Gilbert stood looking lost. 'What will I need to take?' he muttered.

'Hat, coat, gloves?'

He frowned. Nodded, patted his chest. He was still in his dressing-gown and pyjamas. 'I'll need to put some more clothes on. And my wallet . . . I might need money.'

'Just go and change, Gilbert. They'll be sure to wait for you.'

Maggie watched as Mrs Menstrie was wheeled through the hallway. She was wheezing and not a good colour. 'Where's my son?' she murmured. 'I told him I didn't want him making a fuss. I'd much rather stay at home.'

'He's just getting ready to come with you,' Maggie told her. 'And I'll follow on with my car.'

Eyes closed, Mrs Menstrie nodded breathlessly. Then she opened them and grasped Maggie's hand.

'It's been an awfy responsibility, ye ken,' she wheezed. 'Bringing him up without a father. I was right sorry for you when your man died. He was a very kind man. You chose a fine man even if ye were a wild girl.'

Her son reappeared. He was dressed, but his pyjamas were still sticking out below his trousers. Not a bonny sight. He pulled on his coat, his dreary grey muffler and woolly hat and nodded to Maggie.

'I'm sorry to have bothered you like this, but I just came for help with thinking.'

Maggie was wide awake now, bemused and unexpectedly moved by Mrs Menstrie's sudden softening. 'No problem,' she reassured him. 'After all, what are neighbours for? I'll get what I need and see you at the hospital.'

He nodded bleakly and bit his lip. Maggie watched as he climbed anxiously into the ambulance. One of the paramedics had fixed up a drip and was taking Mrs Menstrie's pulse. The old woman seemed quite out of it.

'She'll be fine, you just sit there beside her,' said the ambulance woman to the shocked Gilbert, and stood up to slam the doors shut.

Four hours later, Maggie drove back to Inverie with

Gilbert. His mother had been made comfortable and was sedated. The doctors had advised him to go home and get some sleep, and ring the ward sister after eleven. It was still dark when they got out of the car. Only one or two houses had lights on.

'I'm going back to bed for a few hours,' said Maggie. 'And I think you should do the same. You surely won't go into work today, will you?'

Gilbert shook his head, miserable. 'Thanks very much for your help. I'm very grateful.' He started to hold out his hand as if to shake hers, then changed his mind. 'I've been meaning to ask you,' he said suddenly, 'about the French lad.'

Maggie frowned. It struck her, not for the first time, how repellant Gilbert was in every sense.

'Sophie's boyfriend? What about him?'

'I just happened to notice that he didn't seem quite himself a couple of months ago, and your daughter was obviously anxious. Was everything all right?'

Maggie paused. The unforseen plethora of intimacies she'd experienced all in a few hours felt suddenly intrusive. 'He's fine,' she snapped. 'Absolutely fine. They're both very well, thank you.'

'Good,' mumbled Gilbert. 'I was a wee bit worried . . . so was my mother.'

Nosey old besom.

Maggie put her key in the front door. 'I'll see you, Gilbert. I hope your mother's OK. Let me know how she is.'

'I will. I certainly will,' said Gilbert and gave a feeble half-masted wave as Maggie went in, and shut the door behind her, relieved to be home and warm.

The clatter of the letterbox woke her from deep sleep three hours later and she stumbled into the kitchen to make tea to wake herself up. There was a small parcel from Denmark, addressed in Karin's handwriting, and she was surprised to see that there was another letter from Niall –

also, like the earlier one, mysteriously postmarked St Andrews.

She opened the parcel first and was thrilled to unwrap a perfect rounded fossil, with an accompanying photo of Karin and Sven sharing a glass of wine and smiling out of the picture. They were obviously enjoying their life in Scandinavia. '*This stone sea-urchin made us think of you,*' said the card which was signed by them both. '*We look forward to looking for treasures on the beach with you when we visit in the spring.*'

Tea wasn't enough for how she felt, so Maggie stood up and made herself a huge mug of coffee before reading Niall's missive, which was a first for him. He never wrote, apart from almost incomprehensible postcards from connubial foreign holidays, but this one was very different. So different that she required an extra piece of toast and marmalade to cope with the emotion it released.

> *Beloved Maggie,* wrote Niall.
> *I am sure it will amuse you to know that I am still imprisoned here by my politically incorrect ailment, which incidentally hurts like hell, and life is exceptionally dire and tedious as the gorgon sister-in-law who has arrived from Benbecula is in spectacularly ghastly fettle. As you have no doubt noticed, I have been forced to smuggle my communications to you via a fellow conspirator in St Andrews for fear of discovery back at the ranch.*
>
> *I miss you so much, your humour, your delightful body and the laughs we have. I can think of nobody who has ever given me such easy joy. I was incredibly fed up to miss the Marra concert with you, and have been in a vile mood for lack of leavening by your beloved self. I know we meet only rarely, but my dearest girl, those short visits are oases in my somewhat dreary life. I want you to know that I pine for you, and long for a good natter, and to share wine,*

good food and lovemaking with you as soon as the body permits. It is precious to me, what we have. You are precious to me and please never forget that. So much is shared between us and it seems to me that there is such a complete understanding between us that much can comfortably remain unsaid. If we had met even ten years earlier, we would almost certainly have run away together.

My love to you, Maggie, my love. We will meet soon, I promise.

Kisses everywhere and all the other things you like.

Yours, Niall.

PS: I have to add that this is written stone-cold sober. The GP has banned even the tiniest dram as being harmful to my condition. XXX

Maggie could hardly see to make her second mug of coffee. She poured in the milk and held Karin and Sven's smooth fossil against her cheek as she read Niall's missive for the second time. That it was so entirely unexpected, and so affectionate, hit her hard. She was still feeling very emotional when the phone rang.

'It's Gilbert.' He was obviously choked. 'The hospital just phoned ...' He spluttered into silence.

'Oh Gilbert, how's she doing?'

'My mother ... she's gone. She passed away half an hour ago from a massive heart attack. And I was sleeping in my bed. I should have been with her. I'll never forgive myself.'

'You mustn't say that. You did everything you could. You've spent your whole life with her and been a wonderful son. I'm very sorry, Gilbert.'

She tried to think of something kind to say, but Mrs Menstrie with her bad temper and nosiness had been such a ghastly old witch in her childhood that for a moment she couldn't. She remembered her mother, Astrid, predicting that Gilbert was destined to remain for ever tied to his mother's apron strings. 'She'll never let him go,' Astrid would say. 'Poor Gilbert, there's no escape for him. He's forced to be her husband, her lover, her friend, her everything. He'll never be free till his mother dies, and he'll be lost when she does.'

'Your mother was a very strong character; I'm sure you'll miss her, but she had a good long innings,' Maggie stammered at last, feeling pretty feeble.

'She was ninety in August.'

'That's a wonderful age to have reached.'

'I suppose it is . . . was. I just thought I'd better tell you. You were very helpful last night.'

'Can I do anything to help now?'

He shook his head. 'I'll manage, thanks.'

Maggie relaxed. She put the phone down and looked at the time. It was still only half past nine. She looked at Niall's letter again and put it back in its envelope. A love letter from Niall was something she'd never even imagined and she felt quite weak with the sensations of the last few hours. Maybe she would just go back to bed for a little and try to recover her equilibrium.

As she tried to rest, she remembered what Niall had written. It was certainly romantic and had stirred her deeply, but she was aware that it wasn't actually true. If they'd really met ten years earlier than they did, Fergal would still have been alive and Niall's son would only just have died, so there was no way that she and Niall would have allowed themselves to fall for each other. It was a romantic thought, all the same. Or was it, she wondered as she drifted into sleep, simply a charming and elegant cop-out on his behalf?

Chapter Eighteen

Down by the harbour, in the window of the local post-office, a black-bordered notice announced that the funeral of Euphemia Menstrie was to be held on Thursday morning in the parish church of Inverie. Maggie wasn't keen to go; it felt almost dishonest to attend the interment of her childhood enemy, but as Gilbert had dropped a note through the door written in green biro and slanting capitals, which informed her of the time of the funeral and said he hoped she would be able to attend, she felt obliged to make the neighbourly gesture. She hadn't been brought up as a churchgoer and had married an atheist, so visits to the old kirk for reasons other than aesthetic were rare, though she'd always enjoyed the singing.

From her front window she could see the hearse drive slowly past, followed by a surprisingly large crowd of black-clad guests and villagers walking very slowly. Many of them were old and leaned on a friend or a stick; Mrs Menstrie's passing had produced a sizeable and dignified following. Hurriedly, Maggie put on black shoes and coat and joined the congregation. Gilbert, pale, dignified, and all in black, nodded to her. Maggie slipped into a back pew and was delighted to find herself next to Andy Johnstone.

He smiled. 'Hi there. I thought I might call in afterwards. I've got that drill for you in the car.'

'How come you're here anyway?' she whispered.

My Dad and Gilbert's were at the school together and they went into the navy at the same time; they were great pals as lads. My Dad came out in one piece, but Gilbert's didn't.'

'Ah . . .' Maggie nodded. She couldn't really imagine it but felt she had to ask. 'And . . . are you and Gilbert pals?'

'No, not really. We know each other. I'm older than him, but I remember him from school and we always say hello, but we're not close or anything like that. How about you? Did you know the old lady well?'

'Only as a next-door neighbour who terrified us as kids. I used to have nightmares about her.'

'I can imagine. Effie always had a reputation for her bad temper, but she probably had her reasons.'

They stopped whispering as the organist started to play and the congregation fell silent as the minister entered and began to speak of the life of our dear departed sister Euphemia Jemima Helen Agnes Menstrie – née Mackinnon. It was tragic, and the minister, originally a historian, made the point that it was the story of the twentieth century as it turned out to be for thousands of working-class women. The family came originally from Skye, but Euphemia Mackinnon, the fourth of eight children, was born in Glasgow in 1911. Two of her older sisters died in infancy of diptheria and her twin brother died of scarlet fever when she was four, which tragedy happened within weeks of the death of her father, Isaac Lachlan Mackinnon, who was killed whilst serving in the trenches of the First World War, aged only thirty-four. Her oldest brother, Robert James, volunteered to be a soldier towards the end of the 1914–1918 war when he was still only a boy – he lied about his age, like many others – and was killed three weeks later on his seventeenth birthday, just before Armistice Day. After this, her mother's health gradually fell apart and Euphemia, from a very tender age, took on the role of caring for the remaining three children and her now invalid mother until her mother's early death and the children's safe passage to adulthood.

It was a terrible tale. The monster transformed to heroine. And it grew worse: after she had spent her childhood as a surrogate mother to her siblings and nurse to her own mother, Gilbert's mother had gone into service in a big house in Blairgowrie. Here, nearing thirty, love had at last entered her life when she'd met and married Allan Menstrie, the head gardener, an ex-fisherman from Inverie. The young couple returned to live with Allan's ageing parents in their house opposite the old kirk in Inverie and had happily settled there, when the pregnant Euphemia was forced to watch her man go off to war. Allan Menstrie was serving on a destroyer doing Atlantic convoy duty when it was blown up in March 1941, three months before the birth of his one and only son, Gilbert.

All that loss. How could anyone be normal and easygoing with a history like that? No wonder Mrs Menstrie had always seen the dark side: like the Witch of Inverie she was forever warning them of dangers when they played on the beach or calling Gilbert in so he was never allowed to take risks, or run wild on the beach with the other village children or with Maggie's family. Presumably she'd turned into a kill-joy because all her own personal joys had been killed off one by one. If one thought about it, the poor woman had never really had a childhood, so it was probably bitterly painful for her to view the freedom allowed to Maggie's generation. As for Gilbert, what sort of a childhood was it for him with a seven times bereaved mother and grandparents who were already dead and buried by the time he started primary school?

Maggie felt shame for a lifetime's venomous thinking and for all the times she and her brothers had imitated or teased Gilbert. But he'd still grown up as a man not easy to like, and knowing the reasons for his unattractiveness didn't really help to extinguish her basic distaste for him.

The congregation sang 'The Lord is my Shepherd' and minutes later, they went outside and stood in silence and watched as Euphemia Jemima Helen Agnes Menstrie née Mackinnon's heavy coffin was lowered into the wet earth. Gilbert, red-eyed, shovelled in the first spadeful as the purple-nosed minister (it was freezing and starting to hail) blessed his mother for the last time. A lone seagull shrieked from the church tower and Maggie saw a tall gaunt-looking man who must surely be Mrs Menstrie's one surviving brother, gaze blankly down into the grave.

At last Maggie and Andy found themselves in the warmth of the cottage, where Andy hung up his jacket and scarf and shook his head. 'My God, what a sad bloody story. What some folk have to put up with. You and I know only too well that it's bad enough losing just one person. It's no wonder the poor soul was half off her head.'

'No.' Maggie handed him a mug and put shortbread on a plate.

'Not for me, thanks. I think I've lost my appetite for the moment. I'm glad of the coffee, though. I don't know about you, but I'm frozen stiff.'

'What did Mrs Menstrie live on after her husband was blown up?'

Andy shrugged. 'She used to take in washing and do ironing and a wee bit of mending. I know she was always busy with something; it must have been hard, though. Her father-in-law – Gilbert's grandfather – had emphysema from being gassed in the First World War so he wasn't able to work for years.'

'What was he like?'

'He was a lovely man. I met him once walking along the cliff path when I was about twelve, and he stopped for a chat, but he obviously really needed to talk for he suddenly told me how of all the lads he'd been in the primary school with only about four or five survived the Great War. He was crying when he told me, like he could see them all there right in front of him. "All deid, all deid..." I think he said there had been twenty-one of them and seventeen of them were lost; most of the lads he was at school with were killed at Gallipoli. Our children haven't a clue how lucky they are that there's no major war for them to go to.'

They drank their coffee in silence, then Andy sighed. 'I'd better go and fetch that drill for you or I'll be driving off with it.'

'OK.' Maggie looked at her watch. 'It's nearly lunchtime; would you like a bowl of soup? I made some yesterday.'

Andy grinned. 'That sounds very civilised. And I just happen to have stocked up in Safeways this morning and have a bottle of wine in the car. I don't know about you but I could really do with a drink.'

'It usually makes me go to sleep in the middle of the day, but I must confess it sounds tempting.'

'Great.' Andy stood up and pulled on his jacket, and went out, slamming the door.

Maggie felt unaccountably nervous as she lit the cooker and warmed up the soup. She was trembling, nervous and excited at the same time, like a bloody teenager, and couldn't find either the cheese or the breadboard, which were both exactly where they were usually kept. It was ridiculous.

Andy was back in a couple of minutes, brushing sleet from his hair. He came in carrying the drill box and bits and a bottle of red wine. 'It's hellish out there. What a day to be buried.'

'I don't suppose it matters too much by the time you're in the box.'

He chuckled. 'I suppose not. Now where's your bottle opener?'

She set out two glasses and he pulled the cork and filled them quickly. Smiling at the gurgle, they clinked glasses.

'This is very basic,' said Maggie, ladling out soup.

'It smells fantastic. What is it?'

'Home-made lentil soup.'

'One of my favourites. Lord, I'm starving.'

Warmed by food and wine, they both relaxed.

'Is Gilbert having a meet-up at the house now?' asked Andy.

'He's just taking one or two old folk to lunch at the Harbour View Hotel. He didn't want to have to organise anything himself.'

'Fair enough. The poor man won't know what's hit him. I don't think he's ever been away from his mother for more than a night or so.'

'Maybe he'll surprise us all and take up salsa dancing or start to play the trombone.'

'He might. It'll be interesting to see. Or he might just take to the drink. A lot of people do.' Andy quaffed his glass. 'I nearly did when my wife died. Everything just seemed so damned pointless.'

'I was a bit the same. It feels comforting at the time; I guess it numbs your pain.'

'Aye. I can still find a bottle of whisky too bloody tempting at times, specially in the winter.' He finished the soup and stood up. 'That was absolutely fantastic, but I'd better show you how to use this drill before I have any more wine.'

'OK. I'll just clear this stuff away.'

Andy was looking at the photos on the dresser. 'I think I recognise most of these people from the May Island trip. That's your daughter, isn't it?'

'Yes, that's Sophie with her Frenchman, Michel.'

'And it's them that's having your first grandchild?'

'Yes – only three and a half months to go.'

'You must be looking forward to it.'

'Very much.'

'I'm telling you,' Andy said earnestly. 'Grandweans are great. A real bonus. It's like winning the lottery and you didn't know you had a ticket; it's brilliant, and you can always hand them back if they get difficult. It's a magic arrangement. You'll love it.'

'I can't wait.'

'This is the drill,' said Andy, when the table was clear. 'And maybe you should show me some of the things you want drilled out, and I've brought a flat bit of wood to work on.'

Maggie brought a couple of boxes of fossils, stones and sea-worn metal and they sat together at the table.

'Some of these are amazing. Did you really find them all on the beach?'

Maggie nodded. 'I did, but I haven't found much recently, there's far too much seaweed covering everything.'

'OK then. Now let's try and drill out this piece for you. Just you show me exactly what you want me to do.'

They leaned together over the drill and the stone, which already had a small hole through it but which was too small for the waxed thread Maggie wanted to string it on. Andy rolled up his sleeves, and Maggie, highly aware of his muscular forearms furred with blond hair, pointed out where she wanted the hole to be enlarged and he drilled it out in a moment.

'That's perfect.' Pleased, she examined it.

'Give me more.'

He did several, and one fossil cracked in the drilling. 'I'm sorry about that, but it'll happen sometimes, different strengths in the layers of stone, or maybe I should have tried a smaller drill.'

Two hours later, there was a small pile of newly drilled objects.

'This is wonderful,' said Maggie. 'I'll really be able to get going now. I feel inspired. I've been so unproductive for the last couple of months.'

'Maybe you were just lying fallow. Don't castigate yourself. You need to lie fallow sometimes.'

When he rolled his sleeves down and buttoned up his shirt cuffs she felt an almost painful sense of deprivation. He left after a cup of tea, saying that she could hang on to the drill for as long as she wanted. He had a slightly better one at home that he was using on a model boat he was repairing for the Fisheries Museum in Anstruther.

'Like you, I've been awfully lazy recently. I just can't get myself going and by the time I get started, the day's half over. It must be old age.'

He left, saying he'd be in touch, and Maggie went back into her cottage from waving him off. On the way home, Andy found himself wondering if she was still seeing the West Highlandman with the fancy shirt, and was surprised at how illogically annoyed he felt at the thought of the married Niall. It wasn't right, messing about with a woman like Maggie; she deserved respect.

Maggie had a leisurely bath and finished off the lunchtime wine. As she lay there in the warm, listening to Nina Simone, she tried not to keep remembering Andy's chuckle, his hypnotically tactile forearms and the way the back of his neck looked when he was bent over, concentrating on drilling out shells and stones. Strong, but vulnerable – and definitely fanciable. She smiled as she acknowledged to herself how tempted she'd been to reach out to him.

Chapter Nineteen

In Denmark, in Sven's wooden house, which lay surrounded by tall oak trees overlooking the fiord, Karin and Sven, both clad in old dungarees, were kneeling on the floor. Sven was sawing a pale wooden floorboard, and Karin laying boards, slotting them together rhythmically, one by one.

'It's such a practical system. I think we could actually get it done by tonight,' said Karin.

'I'm sure we could. I've only got four or five more to trim.'

'Do you think the youngsters will be impressed when they come on Sunday?'

'They'd better be. At the New Year party last month Malin told me that she's been nagging Magnus to do something with their sitting-room floor for five years. I think she's quite jealous.'

'Maybe she'll commission us to do theirs?'

Sven chuckled. '"Octogenarian Enterprises". Shall I give up going to the lab?'

'I sometimes wish you would.'

'We'll see. If the grant money comes through, that will be enough to fund three more years' work, and I could afford to delegate almost everything. I'd just need to keep an eye on it all, but I am taking two whole months off in May and June to go to Scotland.'

'Our Scottish honeymoon – less than three months to go. It'll be so lovely to see everybody. We'll be there for Michel and Sophie's baby.'

Sven suddenly stopped sawing, his face serious. 'Do you miss your life there terribly? Are you sorry you came here?'

She put down the special tool for clicking the boards together, and looked at him. 'Not for one minute.' She held out her hand. 'I'm so happy here with you. I can't believe we've been so lucky.'

Sven kept her hand, and they sat for a minute. 'By rights we should be in the old age home or in one of those burial mounds overlooking the *Limfiord*. Instead, we are exhausting our aged bodies with manual labour. Perhaps we're mad?'

'Maybe we are.' Karin sighed, stretched and winced. 'I am just a little tired, and rather sore. How about you?'

'I'm wrecked. We've been at it since breakfast. Let's stop for today and have a schnapps and eat something simple. We'll easily finish it tomorrow.' He stood up wearily and she stood beside him. Reached up to tidy his tousled white mane of hair.

'I love you,' they murmured to each other, and arm in arm, walked slowly to the kitchen where Sven climbed out of his dungarees and filled two glasses with Akvavit as Karin turned on the CD player and began to heat up some soup to the strains of a Bach cello concerto.

Almost three weeks after Gilbert's mother's funeral, towards the end of February, Maggie, bathed and already in her nightie, was poised for an early night when the phone rang. These days she was always a little anxious in case it was Sophie in an unhappy state – Michel still had the occasional black mood, which alarmed Sophie – but it wasn't her.

'Hi there. It's Andy.' (Only Andy knew that he'd needed a dram for the courage to phone her.) 'How're you doing?'

'I'm fine. I've been drilling away, I made three new necklaces today.'

'I ... er ... wondered ... I've er ... got some tickets for a fiddle concert at the weekend. One of the players was a winner in the Gaelic *Mod* last year and I think that red-headed laddie we heard before is playing as well, so it should be good.'

'It sounds great, I'd love to come.' Maggie grinned to herself.

'I'll pick you up at five-thirty on Saturday, then, and maybe we can have a bite to eat before it. The concert's in Dundee.'

Automatically independent, Maggie protested that he didn't need to pick her up. 'I'll come to you. Save you the bother.'

There was a pause. 'I'd like to give you a lift,' said Andy firmly. 'It's only five minutes extra. It'll be my pleasure. I'll bring you home again too – unless you can think of a better plan.' (At this point, if anyone had been watching, they'd have seen Andy grimace terribly, and bang his fore-head with the flat of his hand.)

Maggie put the phone down and hugged herself. He'd rung at last, just like he said he would. She'd feared he might be too shy. She knew that she wouldn't be able to get to sleep for ages now, so she made herself a hot drink, went to the wardrobe and started sorting out her clothes. It was time a few of them went to the charity shop in St Andrews. Before she went to bed, she looked at herself in the mirror and held her hair in various ways. It needed attention, that was for sure. Renewed colour, perhaps. She hated the double chins – her jowls, she called them – but if she held her head high and pulled her tummy in, she didn't look too bad for somebody who'd only a couple of years to go before qualifying for a bus pass. She felt optimistic, extra alive. Young almost, but not hungry for sex as she once had, thank goodness.

*

As he emerged from the train station in Oban, Niall Maclean felt like a dog let off the leash, and infinitely grateful that Katy and her sister had taken bloody Jocky with them. He'd never really liked the wee dog, who was definitely becoming increasingly yappy as he got older. The relief of being well and able to walk without the agony of the gout and the prospect of five whole days to himself was positively intoxicating. Maybe he should have a dram to celebrate. He walked towards his favourite pub which overlooked the harbour and had a quick nip, which suddenly inspired him with a desire to go and see Maggie. After he'd written his emotional letter to her a couple of weeks back, he'd actually managed to ring her when his female keepers had gone out shopping. Maggie had sounded lonely and depressed, and upset about a funeral she'd been to – Niall reckoned it must have been the old bat who was always spying out of her kitchen window and even had a driving mirror fitted to the side of the house so she knew exactly who was doing what.

How fabulous it would be to arrive unannounced and surprise Maggie and for once be able to spend more than one night together. Suddenly he couldn't wait. He put down his empty glass and nodded to the barmaid. 'See you, Sheena, I'm off.'

'See you, Niall. Watch it now, you want to keep the weight off your feet. Don't overdo things.'

In the high street he stopped at the florist's and bought an enormous bouquet of white and pink flowers – lilies and things, he wasn't really sure what – but beautiful and shockingly expensive. Maggie would love them, he knew. He reckoned they'd keep cool in the boot of the car; he'd be at Inverie by late afternoon if he popped home now to pick up a few bits. Perhaps it would be a good idea to book the Lobster Pot restaurant for tonight; they'd both enjoy that. And tomorrow they could shop together for the next couple of days. Booze, though, that was important. A good bubbly for when he arrived – a Taittinger perhaps – he grinned at the image of Maggie's delight – and maybe two good bottles of red. There had been some beautiful Hermitage in Oban Fine Wines last time he was in. With luck they might still have a few bottles left.

An hour later, Niall hummed as he drove. It was a bright day for the time of year and the roads weren't icy, so he made good time. When he was outside Aberfeldy he wondered if he ought to give Maggie a ring to warn her that he was coming, but the mobile battery was flat. It was a pity, but he didn't really see the need to stop and find a phone box; it would take away the surprise element. She was forever saying that the whole point of living at Inverie was the peaceful life she lived. 'I hardly ever go anywhere except to shop in St Andrews,' she was always telling him. 'The odd concert or film maybe, but that's about it.'

In Pittenweem it was growing dark when Andy went out into his garden and searched for anything that might be blossoming. He liked the way Maggie always had little vases of fresh flowers in the cottage, usually plucked on her walks along the coastal path, and he hoped his small posy of hellebore – he'd grown several kinds, in varying subtle greeny whites and purply pinks – would please her. He found a few snowdrops too, and some early primroses. The result looked so good when he put the flowers in a piece of tinfoil that he felt quite proud of himself. Then he felt worried; might she take it amiss and get scared off if he arrived with flowers? 'Beware of men bearing gifts,' his mother used to say. 'They usually want something from you.'

He grinned to himself. She was probably right.

Urged by her sister-in-law, who had gently suggested that she was looking a little wild and woolly, Maggie had gone to the hairdresser's. She arrived home in time for a quick cup of tea and a change of clothes before Andy was due to arrive, and had just tried on a new blue jersey when there was a great knocking at the door. It surely couldn't be Andy half an hour early? Puzzled, she went to answer it and as she reached the bottom of the stairs there was a loud barking as though from a massive dog, which made her freeze.

My God, it's Niall, she realised in dismay. The barking at her door was a joke long shared between them.

Cautiously, she opened the door and beheld her married lover, beaming, his arms full of flowers and bottles.

'Niall! Good heavens! What on earth are you doing here?'

'I have come to see you, my love.' He moved to embrace her, 'To give you these and to surprise you. And I'm all yours for four days if you'd like that.'

'Why on earth didn't you phone me?'

'I tried, but my mobile wasn't working and I thought you'd rather appreciate being taken by storm and lured out for a meal at the lovely seafood restaurant. I've booked us for eight so we can walk there and back and drink as much as we like.'

Struck dumb, Maggie watched aghast as he marched past her into the sitting-room and unburdened himself on the table.

'Come here,' he commanded, and came to her with open arms. 'Give us a hug, woman. God, I've missed you.'

He clutched her and it was all she could do not to return his embrace. Part of her longed to be enfolded, to let go and have a four-day Niall oblivion; she could hardly think of anything nicer, but she forced herself to draw back.

'Niall, this is very bad timing. I'm sorry, but you'll have to go.'

'What?' He was laughing.

'I mean it. I'm going out to a concert tonight and I'm being picked up in less than half an hour.'

'I don't mind. Can't I can come too? Or I'll just stay here, I'll get some fish and chips and we'll go out to eat tomorrow night.'

'Niall. You don't understand. I'm asking you to go. I

don't want you here. Not today or tomorrow.'

He appeared nonplussed.

'My love, what's the problem? I'm sorry if you're annoyed by my unheralded arrival, but surely that's an excusable mistake? I'll fit in with whatever plans you have. For once we've got more than an eighteen-hour furlough.'

'No,' said Maggie. 'That is actually the point. It's usually never more than an overnight, and it's always on your terms.'

He looked completely bewildered. 'But, my love, I'm married . . .'

'I know you're bloody married!' said Maggie. 'That is entirely the point. And despite your lovely letter . . .'

'Which I thought had surely meant something to you,' groaned Naill in disbelief.

'Yes, it did. It meant a lot to me; it was beautiful, it moved me deeply, but it also did me the favour of opening my eyes to the fact that you'll never leave Katy, nor have I ever expected you to, and that is right and proper and as it should be. You couldn't leave Katy after the tragedy you've shared.'

'But, Maggie, I love you. Don't you realise that?' Niall was almost crying.

'Niall. I love you too in a way; I know that we do really feel deeply for each other, but it's doing me no good. It's bad for me. I need more than you're able to give.'

'But I give you all that I can, Maggie.'

'Well, it's not enough! If I had gout or had a hip replacement, would you come and look after me?'

'I'd come and visit you, cheer you up . . . grope you . . .' he made to do exactly that and it was hard to push him away – he'd always been a damned fine groper.

'Forget it, Niall. I need somebody who's there for me; I want somebody to really love and care for me and me alone. I deserve it. And I want some dignity in my life.'

'My love, I've always said that I wished you'd find somebody . . .'

'Yes, you have and it always hurt to hear you say it. And I know that my chances are slight, but at least I won't be hanging on in there hoping for the occasional visit from you to remind me what it is to feel human again.'

Shaking his head, Niall drew away from her, frowning. 'I thought you'd be delighted to see me. I have missed you indescribably.' He banged his chest dramatically. 'Not seeing you HURTS me.'

'And not seeing you has hurt me like hell off and on over the years, but I've had enough of going nowhere, of hitting the bloody brick wall of your marriage. Can't you understand? It's over!' she shouted.

'Maggie, this is not reasonable. Can we agree to meet tomorrow? You go out and do what you have to do. I'll stay in the hotel and come and see you tomorrow. How about that?'

'You don't get it, do you?'

He looked puzzled, worried, angry, in turn, and shook his head.

Suddenly Maggie took both of his hands. 'Niall. If as you say, you love me, you have got to let me go. To free me. It's been lovely, passionate, funny, loving, but it's over. I can't put my life on hold just because it suits you to arrive.' She glanced at her watch. 'And my God, it's almost half past five. Please will you go now.'

'Can't I see you tomorrow?'

'No.'

'When then?'

'Not for months. Please can we give it a break, at least six months or something.'

'This is crazy,' said Niall, suddenly becoming really angry. 'You're an illogical besom. I don't believe that you don't want me.' He came close to her so she could inhale him, and the feel and familiar smell of him was like some sweet anaesthetic, ready to disempower her, but she pulled away fiercely.

'Niall. Please . . . understand that I want you to go. Now. I mean it. I want you to go away and stay away and leave me alone. I'm sorry, my love, but that's the truth.'

He stared at her as though she'd clobbered him and shook his head bewilderedly. Then he turned, frowning. 'OK. If that's what you want. I will bloody go.'

Without looking at her, he made for the door.

'Please ... Take the flowers with you.' Maggie thrust the glorious bouquet towards him. 'They're absolutely beautiful, but I'd rather you took them away.'

'What am I supposed to do with them? They were for you, Maggie. I want you to have them.'

She was crying. 'Please. Take them and go. I'll only cry every time I look at them if you leave them here.' She held them out again. 'And the champagne. Here.' She handed him the bottle. 'Niall, I'm sorry, and I don't for a minute regret what we have had together.'

'Big deal,' muttered Niall; he was trying hard not to cry as well. 'Give them to me then. I'll bin them.'

He took the flowers and stood for a moment, then decisively, he leaned forward to kiss her and for a moment they hugged each other and suddenly he was gone; the door slammed behind him, and she was left breathless.

Andy was a little late; the dog had eaten a decayed seagull on the beach and been sick on the kitchen floor just before he set off and he'd had to clear it up. As he turned left out of Pittenweem, he almost bumped into a grey Mercedes driven by a big blond man who looked familiar; then Andy remembered that it was that man that he'd met with Maggie, the married one. He frowned; he'd been hoping from what Maggie had said that he was off the scene. It was dark when he parked in the car park above Maggie's place but he recognised Gilbert Menstrie in the light of the street-lamp. He was bending over a rubbish bin. Amused and curious, Andy walked towards him. 'Hello there, Gilbert. What are you up to?'

Startled, Gilbert stood up and tried to hide a huge bunch of flowers behind his back.

'Oh ... I er ...' he stuttered, obviously embarrassed at being found in flagrante with a rubbish bin.

Andy realised immediately that Gilbert had changed his image. What hair he did have was cropped short, no longer dragged across his bald patch in slimy lines, and he looked unshaven. Could he actually be growing a beard?

'Surely you're not throwing those flowers away, are you?' he asked. 'They look awfully expensive.'

'No. Not at all. I've just found them. Somebody had stuffed them in the bin. I thought I'd better rescue them.'

Andy came closer. 'They're lovely. Lilies eh? At this time of year they must have cost a bomb. Why d'you think they were thrown away?'

Gilbert shrugged. 'Maybe somebody came too late for a funeral.'

'Surely if they'd come late they'd have put them on the grave or in the kirk anyway.'

'Aye, maybe. Anyway, I'll take them. I know somebody who'd really like them.'

'You do, do you? I'm glad to hear it.' Andy grinned and looked at him teasingly. 'Are you courting, Gilbert?'

Gilbert, embarrassed, nodded furtively. 'I am actually seeing somebody ... er ... well ... I must be getting a move on. Good to see you, thanks for coming to my mother's service.'

'You're welcome. She was an unforgettable character, your Mum.'

'Aye, I suppose she was. It's still a shock, getting used to it.'

'You're looking well, Gilbert; I like the hairstyle. And the leather jacket. Very nice.'

'Well, be seeing you ...' Almost tripping over his own legs and then the bouquet, Gilbert fled downhill to his house by the sea.

When Maggie opened the door, Andy saw immediately that she was upset, but she looked very pretty. Shyly, he presented her with his own little bunch of home-grown flowers and watched as she put them in a vase and filled it with water.

She set them on the table beside two bottles of what looked like rather good wine.

'Been partying?' he asked.

Maggie flushed. 'They were an unexpected present.'

'Nice friends you must have.'

Maggie smiled a little oddly and fetching her coat and handbag followed him out to the car.

'Thank you for your flowers,' she said as they walked up the hill. 'They're really lovely. I miss flowers at this time of year.'

Andy chuckled. 'Then you should have been out here five minutes ago. I just met Gilbert scrabbling in the rubbish bin. Somebody had thrown away a huge bunch of expensive lilies, completely fresh. It was really strange.'

Maggie started to laugh, a painful, almost hysterical laugh.

'What's the joke?' asked Andy, opening the car.

She was laughing too much to answer properly, and as they climbed in and he closed the doors he wondered for an uneasy moment if she'd ever stop.

'I'm sorry,' said Maggie at last. 'I just couldn't help myself. There's a story behind those flowers which I'll maybe tell you one day, but not now, because it isn't really very funny.'

Andy frowned, grunted. Wished he knew what on earth she meant. Thought about Mr Purple Shirt. Tried not to.

'Have you seen Gilbert's new hairstyle?' he asked at last.

'I have. He looked almost presentable. And yesterday I saw him shopping in St Andrews with a woman who used to work in Boots. He was wearing a bright yellow sweater and a trendy jacket. All his life I've only ever seen him in grey or navy blue – and black for the funeral.'

Andy laughed. 'Good on him. He's got years and years of catching up to do. What was she like, the woman?'

'Peroxide blonde, about forty-five, wears specs. Quite a good-looking woman – wears very bright colours.'

'I think that might be Alison Hardcastle, Pete Hardcastle's widow. She's a nice woman. No kids. It also explains the yellow sweater. D'you know, I don't think Gilbert's ever gone out with a girl.'

'She'll have a lot to teach him if he's still a virgin.'

'Could be fun though; maybe he'll be a good learner.'

'I hope she's a model railway fan,' said Maggie.

They looked at each other for a moment and burst out laughing, and when Andy, still chuckling, put on a Country and Western CD, Maggie, cocooned in the warm, leaned back with a sigh, and decided to enjoy herself.

Chapter Twenty

'He's asked for another whisky,' whispered the freckled waitress. 'I don't know what to do. He's already had two, plus two bottles of wine – and an aperitif.'

The manageress of the Lobster Pot restaurant frowned. 'Is he the one that had banoffi pudding as well as trifle?'

The waitress nodded. 'And soup, a starter and a main course with an extra plate of chips. He must be busting. He's been here for almost five hours.'

'It's nearly midnight. There's nobody here but him, they've all gone. I'm going to ask him to leave.'

'He's been muttering to himself ever since he arrived,' said the waitress. 'He's in an awful state.'

'Give me the bill. I'll handle it. You clear up, Suzie.'

'Thanks, Hazel. I didnae fancy that.'

The manageress walked briskly over to where Niall sat alone, staring into his glass, oblivious to the view of twinkling harbour lights and moonlit sea beyond.

'Your bill, sir.'

'Oh . . .'

He looked very flushed, but not a bad-looking chap all the same – if you happened to like that sort of thing.

'I asked the waitress for another whisky.'

'I'm very sorry, but we're closed.'

Niall frowned. 'Oh. Well, I'll just take a bottle of malt away with me.'

'Sorry, but the bar's closed.'

Niall, half-specs askew, had a go at reading the bill upside-down, but couldn't make much sense of it.

'Try it this way, sir,' said the manageress gently, turning it round.

'Oh Lord, I'm sorry. Now what does it all come to? Certainly not cheap but all delicious. Here's my card, and by the way, are you open tomorrow?'

'We're not open on Sundays or Mondays.'

'That's a shame, but we might make it for Tuesday ...' Frowning; he counted his fingers. 'Saturday, Sunday, Monday, Tuesday ... yes indeed, I expect I'll still be here. She'll change her mind. It's a woman's prerogative to change her mind at least six times a day, did you know that?'

'No, sir, I didn't.' Briskly, the young woman put his card through the machine and handed it to him to sign.

'Where do I sign?' He was standing now, pretty unsteadily and she watched a little anxiously as he painstakingly wrote his name and added ten percent.

'Thanks very much, sir.'

'Thank you. You're a very unusual-looking young woman; do you come from round here?'

'I do.'

'Are you married?'

She laughed. 'No, I'm not.'

'What do you do now?'

'What do you mean?'

'I mean now. Do you go home, have a drink, go dancing? After all, it is Saturday night.'

'I go home and go to sleep.'

'Not alone, I hope? That would be a criminal waste of a beautiful, intelligent and attractive girl. Now, why don't you come with me up to my hotel. They've got a late licence. Please come and join me for a drink, I think you're a real wee stunner.' He was clutching her arm now, a little too tightly.

The woman pulled away, flushing. 'No thanks. I'll just go and fetch your coat.' She moved off quickly and looked at the waitress. 'Tell Jim to get in here quick!' she hissed as the girl brought Niall his long tweed overcoat.

The three of them watched with relief as he staggered out, firmly guided by Jim, the muscular tattooed chef of the establishment.

'I hope the silly beggar gets back to his hotel OK and doesn't fall in the harbour,' he murmured as he bolted the door behind him.

'I don't care if he does,' said the manageress. 'He's a dirty old man. If my Sharon knew he'd made a pass at me she'd chop his willy off; she's very possessive.'

On the way back from the concert, Maggie woke and was immediately pleasantly aware of Andy close beside her in the driving seat.

'Are you OK?' he asked softly.

She stretched. 'I'm sorry, I must have fallen asleep. How rude. Where are we?'

'Just turning off the St Andrews road; we'll have you home in twenty minutes.'

'That was a good evening.'

'It was great. The music was grand, wasn't it?'

'Fantastic. Sad, happy, funny. "The Lament for the Second Wife" . . . that certainly got to me.'

'I was greeting away with the best of them. And that "Lament for Whisky", what an amazing tune, eh? Is that on the CD?'

'Yes, they both are. I checked.'

'I'm glad you've cheered up a bit; you were in an awful state when I arrived this evening.'

'Was it that obvious?'

'It was to me. I felt sorry for you, but I could see you didn't want to talk. Are you OK, now?'

She nodded. 'Yes. I'm fine, thanks. I feel really relaxed.'

'Your upset didn't by any chance happen to have something to do with that big bunch of flowers, did it?'

Maggie groaned. 'Don't remind me.'

'They looked lovely; no expense spared.' Andy was smiling a little.

'You know my West Highlandman, as you once described him?'

'I do. I thought maybe I saw him drive past on the way in.'

'Ah . . . well . . . yes, you probably did. As a matter of fact, I'd just sent him packing and it wasn't very easy.'

'Ah . . .' Andy didn't say anything for a minute or two, then he asked gently, 'Do you mean he wouldn't go quietly? Or you're not sure if you really wanted him to go?'

Maggie, too, took a while to answer. The thought of Niall was still highly confusing. 'I don't know. He just arrived completely out of the blue and expected me to be there – I was supposed to drop everything and put my life on hold for as long as he chose to stay – with no warning at all.'

'You know I told you I'd had a relationship with a married woman?'

She nodded.

'I had a terrible time trying to stop that affair. She didn't believe I meant it, kept on phoning me at all times of day and night and it always seemed to be when my daughters or my grandweans were there. It was hellish. It felt undignified, somehow. I was nearly forced to go ex-directory.'

'It sounds awful.'

'It was, but I kept making it worse, because we'd meet and fall into bed and it would all start up again and in the end I knew that for my own sanity I had to end it. I'm no good at duplicity. Some people can hack it, but I actually liked being one of a pair. I miss being married.'

Maggie sighed. 'What I miss is the feeling that you come first for somebody, no matter what. If you don't have that special person in your life, you feel peripheral, no matter how kind or loving your family and friends are.'

'Aye. Too true. Anyway, it sounds to me in this case like you're doing the right thing for you, but I do understand that it's not simple.'

Maggie nodded. 'I'm just wondering where he is: if he went away or is waiting for me to come home. I couldn't face another scene. Not tonight, I really couldn't.'

There was a long silence.

'He'd not be violent, would he?'

'Oh, God no, but he might be pissed and very silly.'

'That's not so bad, then.' He looked sideways at her, trying not to grin. 'You're welcome to come and stay the night with me.' He took his hand off the wheel and rested it on hers for a long moment.

She looked at it dumbly, not knowing quite what she was feeling, except that its friendly warmth was very pleasant.

'I mean it,' said Andy shyly. 'I've got a spare room you could sleep in.'

Maggie felt very confused. 'I don't know what to do. He was pretty upset and talking about coming round tomorrow morning.'

'What did you say?'

'I told him a definite no, but he wasn't really listening. I expect he thought I was bluffing.'

Andy drove on slowly in silence for a mile or so, and they both murmured in pleasure when a fox flared across the road, orange in the headlights.

'I'll tell you what,' said Andy at last. 'How does this strike you? Why don't you come back to my place for coffee or tea or wine or whisky or whatever you fancy. You've never been to my house and you can have a wee think when you're there. I'll take you home after that if that's what you want.'

Maggie swallowed. 'OK. That sounds really nice. I'd like that.'

'You're no frightened of a strange man?'

'You're not that strange. I've known you since I was eight.'

They both laughed and he held her hand again, this time for much longer, until he had to change down again, and after he'd done that he took an even firmer hold of her.

'I like you, Maggie,' said Andy suddenly. 'I like you a lot. And I fancy you. I've honestly not stopped thinking about you since the day Gilbert's mother was buried.'

Maggie swallowed. 'Well . . . I must confess that I was very pleased when you rang at last.'

Andy chortled. 'I was scared stiff you might say no. To tell you the truth, I needed a drink before ringing you.'

'Well, I'm glad that you did summon up the courage.'

'I'm afraid that I'm going to have to halt here for a minute,' he said suddenly, and pulling into a lay-by he stopped the car engine and turned off the lights. 'There's something I've been wanting to do ever since I came to pick you up.'

Five minutes later they pulled apart, breathless, and gradually became aware of the moonlit landscape surrounding them.

'What a beautiful night,' said Andy. He turned to Maggie. 'I knew you'd be a good kisser,' he said softly. 'Now, are we heading for my place or yours?'

Maggie paused. She had nothing to lose. 'Yours,' she said. 'I'll come and have a cup of tea and decide what to do.'

'This is my house here,' said Andy a few minutes later, and parked the car by the kerbside in Pittenweem's main street.

As Maggie climbed out, she noticed an antique shooting brake sitting across the road under the orange street light. 'I think that's Gilbert Menstrie's car,' she said. 'But it's long past his bedtime. I wonder what on earth it's doing here?'

Andy was smiling. 'Strange that you should ask, but Alison Hardcastle only lives a few doors up from me. Good for him, eh?'

In Alison Hardcastle's house, Gilbert and Alison too had only just arrived back from a night out in Dundee.

'Here,' she said, hanging up their coats and hats. 'You make the fire a wee bit livelier, and I'll pour us a drink.'

He frowned. 'I'd better not. I've still got to drive home.'

'You're not going anywhere in a hurry, surely?' She smiled at him in that way that made him go all shy and excited at the same time.

He blushed, shrugging awkwardly.

'Here,' she came very close to him and he closed his eyes as she helped him off with his jacket. 'You see to the fire, then sit down and relax for heaven's sake. Enjoy yourself – you're not working tomorrow.'

He dealt with the fire, poked it and riddled the ashes and put on another couple of logs. Felt pleased when it flamed up, and held his hands out to it.

When she came back into the room, she was wearing a red robe of shiny red stuff and carrying the flowers he'd given her in a huge vase. She had let down her long blonde hair and its tendrils glinted in the firelight.

'These are just amazing.' She smiled at him. 'I've never ever had such a fantastic big bouquet.'

He was blushing again. 'Well . . . I just saw them and immediately thought of you.'

He watched as she set them carefully on a table.

'They must have cost a fortune. I'd better put a mat under them or it'll spoil the varnish. Could you pass me one from the left-hand drawer in the dresser, please?'

He slid the mat, which had a picture of a puffin on it, under the vase, and she nodded, pleased.

'Lovely. Now, drinks: would you like a malt?'

He hesitated yet again. 'It might be wiser to have a cup of tea.'

'You don't have to be anywhere at any special time, do you?'

He shook his head and she touched his arm delicately.

'Stay a while, please. I'd really like you to.'

'I've nothing to go home for now,' he said. 'Absolutely nothing. It feels very strange sometimes.'

'Of course it does. You're just not used to it yet. Here, come and sit and take a weight off your bottom.'

He almost smiled. 'Mother used to say that.'

'My granny used to say it all the time. There now, here's your dram, and why don't you take those shoes off and make yourself properly comfortable?'

Like a man in a dream, Gilbert sat and suddenly found Alison kneeling at his feet, competently sliding off his brown slip-ons. As he stared amazed at her ebullient pink cleavage, he felt himself harden and crouched to hide it from her.

'Right,' she laid his shoes neatly beside the sofa and lifted his legs up on to the seat so that he lay almost recumbent, but still bent in the middle.

'And loosen your tie. Please . . . just let's relax and take things easy. There you go, does that not feel a lot better?'

Wordless, he slid a cushion gingerly across his trouser front and nodded. He could feel the sweat on his forehead when she handed him a large whisky.

'You sit back and enjoy that. I'll be back in a minute.'

He could hear water gushing in the toilet. Alison was humming to herself, a peaceful, tuneful hum. He leaned back on the sofa, relieved to find himself subsiding, and tentatively tasted the whisky, which was marvellous. Marvellous, capital 'M'.

She came back and stood in front of him.

'Look,' she said smiling. 'I've put your present on. How does it look?'

He stared at her, the friendly blue eyes (she'd taken off her specs), the yellow hair and the crimson silky robe. She was wearing his mother's necklace, a silver chain with a small Iona cross at her neck.

'It suits you. You look absolutely beautiful.' Gilbert scrambled awkwardly to his feet.

'I want to give you a wee thank-you kiss for my lovely

presents.' She came towards him and he felt himself held, clasped warmly to her scarlet bosom. Her lips searched for his, and he almost stumbled.

'Why don't you take your glasses off as well?' she murmured. 'Then everything'll be a lot easier.'

He did as he was told, and fumbling, laid them on the mantelpiece. As he did this he noticed for the first time that her feet were bare and her toenails painted scarlet.

Gilbert had never realised how all-consuming yet tender a kiss could be; nor how long it could last. He was shy at first, but when her tongue amazed him with little adventurous and unexpected darts, he did the same back. It was like a wee game, a quick dart to the left and a feel round the molars at the top then a retreat, then a long tingly sort of rest, like a boat sitting becalmed, then there would be an unexpected enlivening from the opposite side and his whole body seemed to thrum with the adventure. He groaned with pleasure, and almost without realising it, felt his hand reach out to grasp her breast.

In response, she moaned, murmured that it was lovely and rolled her body against him. Reeling with excitement, he felt her fingers reach for his other hand and firmly place it under her robe on top of her second, naked breast. He could feel her nipple against his fingers, swollen, as big as a loganberry. Experimentally, he rolled it between his fingers and when she groaned, loudly this time, he froze.

'Oh . . . Lord. I'm sorry . . . I didn't mean to hurt you.'

She chuckled. 'You didn't. It was lovely, please don't stop, but why don't we go and lie down?'

'Lie down?' It was almost a yelp.

'Yes,' she stepped back from him and smiled. 'You and me. It's about time we did, we've both been thinking about it for long enough, haven't we?'

'I . . . er . . . Well, yes, I suppose that I have . . .'

She stroked his face. 'Come on, dearie, we are consenting adults after all. Let's go through to the bedroom, but maybe you'd like a wee wash first?'

'I ... er ...' Somewhere during the long kiss, Gilbert seemed to have lost the power of speech.

'Don't worry, I'll still be here, waiting for you.' She pulled her hair back off her face and suddenly looked much younger than her forty-eight years. 'You know, I'm really glad you got that haircut, it does suit you, and I think you'll look very distinguished with a beard, or ...' she cocked her head and appraised him, 'you could just leave it short and have that designer stubble. It looks really trendy.'

'Trendy? Me?' Gilbert was amazed. 'I think I'll have another whisky. I'm not used to all this.'

She handed him the bottle and he refilled both glasses. He drank his in a long gulp, then stared down at the fire, his brow furrowed. 'You know, Alison, I'm not very er ... I ... er ... very experienced at all this. I think maybe I should be getting home ...'

She set down her glass and came to him. Laid her hands on his narrow chest, stroked his cheek.

'Don't even think about it, Gilbert. You're just feeling nervous, which is quite natural. It's all quite natural, and there's plenty of time to learn and there's nothing better in the world to learn about, I'm not impatient. I think you're a dear man and just you relax and take your time. I laid a clean towel out on the towel rail for you.'

'I ...' He was looking panic-stricken.

Alison gave him an almost motherly kiss. 'Off you go and have your wash; I'll be here waiting for you – or ...' She smiled. 'Maybe you'd like me to come and help you?'

Gilbert gasped. 'Oh, no, thanks, I'll manage fine, thanks very much. I'll see you ... I'll be back in a minute ...' Blushing violently, but beginning to feel very excited again, he put down his empty whisky glass, kissed her on the lips, smiled eagerly at her, and fled abruptly to the sanctuary of Alison's pink-mirrored bathroom to prepare himself for imminent defloration.

Niall looked up at the moon and the stars, which were

whirling around, spiralling, rocking, like the stars in van Gogh's *Starry Night* painting. He'd managed to stagger up the hill from the restaurant, bouncing off the wall once or twice on the way, his coat flapping, and now he was standing at the top, staring down towards Maggie's house and the old church. Even the silhouette of the old kirk itself appeared to him to be rocking. God, he felt awful. He could see Maggie's old Renault standing in its usual place, parked in front of her cottage, but there were no lights on inside the house, so he presumed that she must have come home and gone to bed when he was eating. Remembering the food reminded him uncomfortably of the two puddings he had consumed.

He banged hard on Maggie's door, but there was no answer. He banged again and looked up to her bedroom window and shouted her name loudly a couple of times, but there was still no response. A light when on in the neighbouring cottage and somebody looked out of the window.

'Can I help you?' a woman called.

'No thanks, Wilma. It's Niall Maclean here. I'm just looking for Maggie.'

'I don't think she's there; her car's been there all evening. I saw her going out much earlier. I don't think she's back yet.'

'Thanks, sorry to disturb you,' Niall called and hung on to the door post to balance himself. He was finding it extremely hard to keep himself upright – his lack of physical balance reminded him of sailing in the Western Isles. Wilma, unimpressed, didn't answer but slammed her window shut and pulled the curtain.

'Bloody hell. Where is the woman? I need her. I want her.' Frowning, Niall moved away and pulling his coat and tartan scarf tighter, made his way clumsily down the hill to the stone steps which led up to the church. It was terribly cold, but he thought he might just sit there on the bench in the moonlight for a wee while in the hope of surprising Maggie. Unfortunately the bench made him feel just as seasick and an all too vivid memory of bananas and toffee surged before him as he lumbered up the steps, clutching at the balustrade, trying not to trip over.

In Andy's spare room, Maggie, was finding sleep impossible. She lay there, wondering what she was doing in this uninspiring bedroom with its old-fashioned curtains and bedcover, and pervasive smell of mothballs, none of which she found very arousing. She peered at her luminous watch dial and, seeing that it was almost half past three, sat up and put the light on. It had been pleasant, exciting even, the kissing in the car, but now she was feeling alarmed. Worried that Andy seemed a bit too keen, and unsure of what she really wanted. If they did now sleep together, where would it lead? He was decent, clean, healthy, funny – and most of all, he was kind and practical. So why was she holding back? A younger person would almost certainly just go for it anyway, try it for a while, see if they were compatible. But sexual compatibility wasn't the only thing that Maggie yearned for. She longed for cultural compatibility too. Could she ever be happy with a man who was content to live in such a house? She eyed the heavily embossed, creamy floral wallpaper thoughtfully. It was old-fashioned and just plain boring. She sighed. Perhaps it was the dead wife's taste? She frowned, annoyed with herself that she couldn't help finding it alien.

Andy had shown her where everything was in the kitchen and said to help herself if she needed anything. She was longing for a cup of tea, and didn't think she would get to sleep any other way. It was a chilly night, so she took her jersey and pulled it on over the men's pyjamas that he'd thoughtfully provided her with.

She crept quietly down the staircase and felt her way along the hall wall, her feet cold on the flagstones, until she found the kitchen light. When she saw the rather dully furnished room again, she felt the same disappointment that she had at the first sight of it. She hadn't really anticipated how Andy's house or Andy's décor might be, but when they turned out to be very ordinary – lacking anything that appealed to Maggie visually in terms of colour or texture – she was shocked by her own sense of disappointment. It was all very clean: neutral colours – cream walls and woodwork, nothing to fault – but it lacked any aesthetic sense. The furniture was ordinary yellow pine, ugly but practical, folksy in style. The armchairs and sofa were floral, the pictures almost non-existent, except for some cheap seaside prints. Even the bookshelf was a let-down: yes, there was the book of Scottish poetry she'd seen before, the gift from his daughter, but it appeared to be a one-off: the rest were paperbacks – war stories, kidnaps, action dramas – the sort of thing that Maggie never read, plus a few history textbooks. The nicest thing in the house that she'd seen so far was a black and white photo of a fair-haired young man in dungarees, standing proudly in front of a half-built fishing boat. She'd stopped to look at it wonderingly.

'Is that you as a lad?'

'That's me when I was working at the boatbuilding. Fifteen or sixteen, I was.'

'It's a lovely picture. I can sort of remember how you looked. I thought you were wonderful, then. You were my childhood hero.'

'Well, I'm pleased to hear it. And I think you're wonderful now,' Andy had said, and kissed her lightly on the cheek.

And then he'd said that he thought he had another photo from that time which might interest her. She'd watched as he opened a cupboard and brought out an old biscuit tin.

'I'm pretty sure it's in here.' Andy was searching through a bundle of old papers. 'Yes, here it is.' And he handed her a small black and white photo.

Maggie peered at it and saw two young lads, the smaller one wearing glasses with a cheeky smile, both with piano accordians.

'Oh my goodness. It's Alistair, my brother, and that's you again, at the harbour. That's amazing.'

'Aye. Somebody must have taken it at one of the dances on the pier. You can have that if you like.'

'Thank you. Maybe I'll send it out to him in Australia.'

'Could you not sleep either?'

Maggie almost dropped the scottie dog mug she was about to fill.

'I'm sorry, I didn't mean to give you a fright,' apologised Andy.

Her heart thumping, she turned to look at him, and was pleasantly surprised by how good he looked – rumpled, clad also in pyjamas and wearing a tartan dressing-gown – definitely appetising. And he had lovely feet.

'I just can't get off. D'you want some tea as well?'

'Please. Have you been awake since you went to bed?'

Maggie nodded.

'Me too.' Andy sat down at the table, watched as she made tea for both of them, and took the 'Best Granddad in the World' mug she handed him. 'Thanks.'

'It's a lovely comfy bed . . .' Maggie offered.

'So's mine, but it's cold and lonely.' He smiled a little, looking at her. 'How about you?'

She could feel herself blush. 'I was warm enough . . . I just had a racing brain.'

'Are you worrying about your West Highlander?'

'A bit,' she admitted reluctantly, 'but I truly don't want to see him. I just hope he's gone away.'

'He must be keen.'

'Yes and no. He's keen, but on his terms.'

Andy sighed. 'Aye, I know. It's a dead-end: it doesn't go anywhere.'

She frowned, looked for a long time at the wood grain of the table. Suddenly she became aware that Andy was standing right beside her. In moments, he was holding her, hugging, lightly stroking her arms, head and face, tentatively kissing her; and she, half-embarrassed by her negative thoughts about his interior decoration, desperately trying not to think of Niall, but hungry for some basic human warmth, allowed herself to be hugged, and found herself gradually returning the kisses. It had been lovely back in the darkness and warmth of the car, and now, as she shut her eyes and concentrated on the sensations of their touching bodies, it was starting to be very pleasant all over again.

'Maggie,' he said softly and stroked her shoulder, 'Please will you come to bed with me? We could just cuddle each other, if that's all you want.'

Maggie froze. 'Sometimes I think I don't know what I want.'

'Well, I know what I'd like, but I don't mind waiting.' He drew back and touched her cheek with the back of his hand. 'A friendly cuddle would be just grand. We could surely both do with one.'

She looked at him, his hopeful blue eyes, his strong hands which fondled her so gently. He was good-looking, likeable, unattached, she repeated to herself. And he smelled very nice. She sighed, 'OK. But please can we just cuddle? I don't feel ready for more – and I do really need to sleep.'

Andy chuckled. 'So do I. I've not slept a wink. I think we'll manage some sleep between us – I'm very well behaved really – I'm actually quite shy, believe it or not. Come on, Maggie girl. Come away to my nice big bed.'

They'd both been asleep, half-entwined, for several hours, when Maggie woke. It was almost half past seven. She stretched, closed her eyes and dozed, pleasantly aware of Andy's arm holding her and the rise and fall of his sweet-smelling breath. She was relieved that he didn't snore, and thank goodness this bed didn't smell of moth-balls, she thought as she melted back to sleep.

Later, half-awake, there was cuddling, which led to the gentlest of kissings, on shoulder, chest and breast – shared butterfly kisses – which grew more passionate as she felt him harden against her thigh.

'Are you sure you want this?' he whispered.

And she nodded and closed her eyes, blindly caressing his face and surprisingly hairless chest (both Fergal and Niall had been very furry) and finally, firmly grasping his warm, hard, cock.

He moved up and on to her, and moist, she opened for him.

'I've been wanting to do this for an awful long time. Ever since we met up on the boat on your uncle's birthday,' whispered Andy, as she guided him into her.

It was good. So good. Like losing yourself in a warm sea, moving up and down, up and down, oh so good, so good – he was touching her so delicately. He knew exactly where to go. Letting go, Maggie groaned, a long, low gasp of relief and pleasure. 'Aah . . . I'm nearly there,' Andy panted as he ran the breathless race with her. The dog barked twice when each of them came, and they both chuckled.

'You're quite right, son, it's worth barking about,' said Andy and Dougie barked again, and they both collapsed in giggles and Maggie got a violent cramp and very soon Andy needed to climb of out of bed to go for a pee.

Sophie, her pregnant tummy pressed against the steering wheel, wondered why her mother hadn't answered the phone this morning. Surely she wouldn't have gone out as early as this? She'd left Maggie a message saying that she expected to arrive before ten, instead of eleven o'clock as predicted. Michel had caught an earlier train to London and she'd come straight on from taking him to the station. She was looking forward to spending time in Inverie, to walking on the beach even if it was freezing, and to lazing for a couple of days. In less than two months she was due to give birth. As she drove, Sophie envisaged the child who would come, lying in the cradle she and Michel had found for It-him-her, and felt in turn excited, frightened and awestruck.

Maggie's car was outside the cottage when she arrived, and the door on the latch, but her mother wasn't there and

Sophie was surprised to find that the kettle was cold. Obviously Maggie hadn't yet breakfasted, but there was no note on the table and the only message on the answerphone was Sophie's own. Puzzled, she presumed her mother must still be asleep, so she made herself a drink and turned on the hot water. The Sunday paper lay unopened on the hall floor, so she settled down to read it while she drank her tea and waited for Maggie to emerge. She was deep into an article on breast-feeding, which amazed her by saying that some women could breast-feed without the stimulus of a pregnancy, when she heard a deep roar like some huge wild animal from upstairs. Sophie, leaped up, spilling her tea, and for an awful moment wondered if she might go into a premature labour. The roar, followed by loud grunts and groans, turned into a cry of 'Oh God, my head.'

The voice was male, so it obviously wasn't Maggie. Petrified, with a quickly grabbed potato-masher in hand for protection, Sophie bravely mounted the stairs on tiptoe.

'Maggie! Are you there, woman?' shouted the unknown creature, and as the intrepid Sophie crested the stairs, she was confronted by the sight of Niall, who looked terrible, hair and tie askew, one shoe off and the other shoe on, standing in the doorway of her mother's bedroom.

Sophie lowered her culinary weapon and gazed at him in astonishment.

'Niall? What on earth are you doing here?'

'I was looking for Maggie. The door was unlocked, I was absolutely frozen, so I came in to wait for her and must have fallen asleep. Lord, I feel terrible ... please excuse me ...' with which he suddenly pitched sideways and disappeared into the bathroom where he made more terrible noises, which made Sophie too feel quite ill.

'I'll not come in with you now,' said Andy as he stopped the car. 'I've to be in St Andrews in half an hour, but I'll ring you tonight.'

'You know my daughter's here for a couple of days?'

'I do, but maybe we can have a meal after that ...' he paused. 'That's if ... er ... you want to meet up again so soon?'

Maggie put her hand on his arm and held it there. 'I definitely do,' she said.

'D'you not mean you definitely did?' Andy teased and leaned across to kiss her.

Maggie pulled away. It was a bit too public here.

'I'd better go.'

Andy nodded. 'Me too. I'll call you later.'

'That was lovely, by the way,' said Maggie. 'All of it.'

She felt strangely reluctant to climb out into the cold morning, unwilling to leave Andy's comforting presence.

'It was lovely. I look forward to the next time, Maggie.'

She watched him drive off, and was a little embarrassed to see her neighbour Wilma walking past; she'd obviously been drinking in the sight of the fond farewell.

'A bit better today, isn't it?' commented Wilma, squinting at the weather. 'I see you've got visitors.'

'Much better,' agreed Maggie and noted with delight that Sophie's car was already parked outside the house. She was singing as she walked down the road to her own front door.

Chapter Twenty-One

At the cottage door, Maggie and Sophie hugged. Sophie was blooming.

'Hi, Ma, where on earth were you? I was getting worried.'

'I . . . er stayed the night with a friend – we were at a concert and I'd had a drink and didn't feel like coming home.' Maggie, hanging up her coat, had no desire to confess where she had been.

'But what about Niall?'

'What about him?'

'Why was he here and you there?'

'How did you know he was here?'

Sophie looked puzzled. 'Because I've seen him.'

Maggie paused. 'Where did you see him?'

'He's upstairs.'

'What?'

'He was asleep in your bed and now he's in the bathroom and I don't think he's feeling too well.'

'The bugger!'

Sophie nodded, her eyes big with questions.

Suddenly weak at the knees, Maggie sat down. 'I need a coffee,' she said faintly.

'I'll make it.' Sophie went to fill the kettle and turned it on. Maggie frowning, was staring into space.

'What's going on, Ma?'

'How did Niall get in?'

'He said the door was on the latch.'

'Oh ... I suppose I did leave in a bit of a state.' She looked at Sophie. 'I told him to go away, that I didn't want to see him.'

'Honest? You really told him to go – truly out of your life – go?'

Maggie nodded unhappily.

'I'm impressed, Mother. Very impressed. So he has absolutely no right to be here?'

There were noises from above. The women eyed each other as they listened to the sounds of Niall emerging from the bathroom, groaning, followed by silence.

'I'm pretty sure he has a hangover,' said Sophie helpfully. 'He looked really rough, to put it mildly.'

She filled the cafetière and carefully poured out coffee. 'Here,' she handed Maggie a steaming mug. 'What are you going to do, Ma?'

'I am going to drink my coffee and have a shower,' said Maggie.

At which point Niall walked in. He wasn't looking too bad, Sophie noted. He'd wetted his hair and scrubbed up quite well.

He stood in the door, contrite, hands held in prayerful mode. 'Maggie, my dear, I've come to beg your forgiveness. I'm aware that I've disgraced myself, but as your door was open and I'd fallen by the wayside and almost passed out with the cold, I really wasn't fit to stagger any further ... Please forgive me, and please ... aah ...' Suddenly, he sniffed, inhaling deeply. 'Is there any of that coffee going spare?'

'Here, have this.' Sophie handed him her own mug.

'Thank you, sweetheart, but is that not the one you were drinking?'

Sophie grinned. 'It gives me heartburn, though I keep on trying. I can see that your need's greater than mine.'

Niall smiled, indicating her bump. 'When's the babby due?'

'About seven weeks.'

'Marvellous; you're looking fabulous, my dear. Oh Lord, I need to sit down.'

Maggie, numb, watched as her lover of ten years sat down and shut his eyes. 'I haven't felt as bad as this for several decades,' he confessed. 'Even breathing hurts my head.'

Maggie stood up, 'I'd like you to go, please, Niall. Now. You can get coffee in the village. I'm going for a bath,' she said firmly, and strode out of the room.

Niall turned to Sophie with a wry smile. 'Oh my Lord, am I in the doldrums now. Your mother's definitely not amused.'

'You can hardly blame her.'

'Perhaps not.' Niall sighed. 'But I was so looking forward to seeing her properly, to actually spending real time with her.'

'But she didn't even know you were coming.'

'I know. I'm an idiot. A bloody lovesick fool.'

'I think I'll go up and see her,' murmured Sophie, embarrassed. 'Perhaps you'd better go.'

Niall sighed. 'I will, as soon as I've drunk this coffee. And please, d'you mind if I grab a piece of this?' He waved a piece of bread at her, and she rolled her eyes, shrugged and left him to it.

'Ma?' Sophie tapped on the bathroom door.

'It's open,' called Maggie. 'The lock's broken.'

Sophie entered and found her mother naked, enshrouded by steam.

'Is he still here?' hissed Maggie.

'I think he's making toast.'

'Oh God.'

'I'll go for a walk, Ma. Give you two a bit of space to yourselves.'

'The problem is, I don't think he's anywhere near fit to drive.'

'He said something about his things being at the Harbour Hotel.'

'OK. Then I'll take him there and say goodbye.'
'Ma?'
'Yes?' It was snipped.
'He's awfully sweet . . .'
Maggie groaned. 'He always was. That was the problem.'
'Right, I'm off. See you later.' Sophie went out, then put her head back round the door. 'Ma?'
'What is it?' Maggie wasn't pleased.
'Where were you last night?'
'With a friend.'
'Who?'
'Mind your own business! What is this interrogation?'
'Just curious, Mother. Sorree . . .'
Maggie immersed herself in shower water. If only Niall would disappear and leave her to get on with things.
With Andy? It had been pleasant, friendly, funny. Afterwards, when the violent cramp in her calf had subsided, and he'd been for his pee, Andy had cuddled her and said, 'Well, at least we're no deid yet.' Then he'd gently disentangled from her and gone to make them both a cup of tea, which they'd peaceably drunk together in bed. In a way, that had been the nicest bit of the whole episode.
She felt bewilderingly un-together. It was as though part of her were still back in Pittenweem, snugly ensconced with Andy – his apparent lack of visual taste notwithstanding. But she kept remembering Niall's unexpectedly moving letter, and his last few visits, most of which had been a joy. It was all horribly perplexing. She climbed out of the shower and had just wrapped herself in the huge green towel she'd bought in anticipation of the leather-jacketed Murdo's visit last summer, when she was shocked into reality by a knocking on the bathroom door.
'What do you want?' she called.
'It's me.' The door swung open and Niall stood there. She really must get that lock fixed.

'Would you like some breakfast?'

'No. I wouldn't. Please go away.'

'Maggie. I am truly sorry for getting in your hair. It was idiotic of me, I can see that now – You are, by the way, looking terrific, my love – Am I forgiven?'

'Niall!' She was yelling now. Pushing him backwards so that he crashed against the chest of drawers on the landing. And her towel fell off.

'Ouch! That bloody hurt! God, you really do look great!' His balance regained, he made to come towards her, open-armed.

'Please, get off me, Niall. Now please will you go downstairs and leave me in peace to get dressed. I'll come down when I'm ready.' Scarlet, she tried to regain some dignity by rewrapping herself in the towel.

Niall walked backwards, appealing. 'Maggie – I really want to talk to you sensibly. I've been thinking a lot about things, ever since I wrote you that letter . . .'

'Later, Niall. Now please will you leave me to put my clothes on.' Maggie stormed into her bedroom where she saw her unmade bed with Niall's unusually scrofulous coat sprawled across the duvet. She threw the coat downstairs after him, and had just finished dressing and drying her hair when there was a tap on the front door.

Maggie went down to open it and found the elderly Wilma from next door, standing there.

'I'm sorry to bother you, Maggie, but could I borrow a bucket?'

'Of course,' said Maggie and went into the kitchen where Niall silently handed her a blue plastic pail.

'Thanks very much,' said Wilma. 'The reason I need it is that somebody's been sick on the church steps and there's a service at eleven.'

'That's terrible.' Maggie tried not to meet Niall's eyes. 'There are some very irresponsible people about, aren't there?'

'Aye, it's disgusting,' said Wilma, shaking her head.

The phone rang and Niall, who was nearest, automatically answered it.

'Yes, she's right here,' he said, frowning, and handed it to Maggie.

'Hi there,' it was Andy. 'Who was that?'

Maggie closed her eyes. 'It was Niall.'

'Oh.'

'He let himself in when I was away.'

'Are you all right?'

She sighed. 'More or less.'

'Do you need any help?'

'I don't think so, thanks.'

'Well, I'll speak to you later,' Andy's voice was awkward, abrupt.

'I'll phone you tonight,' promised Maggie, mortified, and put down the phone.

'What the fuck did you have to do that for?' she shouted.

'Do what?' Niall stared at her, and watched appalled as her face contorted.

'Pick up MY phone in MY house without asking!'

'Oh God, Maggie, I'm sorry. I . . . it was automatic, hungover, thoughtless . . . I am so very sorry. Who was he anyway?'

Maggie stopped breathing for a long count as Niall watched anxiously. Then suddenly the smoke alarm started to bleep, but its ear-splitting screech was no louder than Maggie's inner ragings. In moments the living-room was full of smoke.

'Something's burning!' yelled Maggie in dismay. 'What the hell's going on?'

Niall heaved across to the cooker and withdrew two flaming pieces of toast. 'It's these,' he said forlornly. 'I'm sorry – I forgot about them . . . I'll open the window.'

'You can't open the window,' snapped Maggie. 'I've taped it up for the winter. And now, I'm going to take you back to your hotel. You've done enough damage for one day.'

Niall didn't speak at all when they were in the car. He sat holding his coat, looking rather dignified and – despite not having shaved – handsome.

Outside the hotel he turned to her. 'Please, Maggie. I know that the last few hours have been farcical and I deeply regret that, but I really have been thinking. I care about you; I love you. I miss you. I'd like to be with you, and I'm prepared to ask Katy for a divorce. That's what I've really decided.'

'*Send in the clowns* ...' a voice in Maggie's head sang. How did it go? '*You on the ground, me in mid air* ...'

'Maggie.' Niall's big hand was resting on hers, stroking her fingers. 'I know that I'm disgustingly hungover, that I've made a fool of myself several times over, that I've almost set your house on fire and have probably frightened off a boyfriend – the last of which I have to confess I don't really regret – but I do love you. I think we'd be a great team, and your children quite like me. It's dawned on me at long last that it's madness for us not to be together.'

Maggie stared out of the car window at the harbour. She couldn't see very well, there seemed to be rain all over the windscreen, but dimly, she could see Sophie walking towards them. She was wearing a big striped woollen hat and carrying a bag of shopping. Maggie sniffed.

'I'm going to drive on a little, I can't talk to Sophie right now.'

'Fair enough,' grunted Niall and hung on as the tyres screeched and Maggie, breathing deeply, did a sudden left up and away from the harbour as Sophie, amazed, turned to watch.

'Would you like this?' asked Niall, handing her a paper hankie. Maggie nodded, wiped and sniffed.

'If you stop the car, I could get out and propose to you on bended knee. I did come prepared with flowers and champagne but you rejected them both. The champagne's in my hotel bedroom; we could go there if you like.'

'We're not going anywhere,' said Maggie bringing the

car to a halt at the end of a road which led to the sea. 'But we'll stop here for a minute, then I'll take you to the hotel. I just didn't want to smile for Sophie just then.'

Niall tried to put his arm round her but she shrugged him off, offended within herself at how pleasantly familiar it felt.

They sat in silence for a while, looking out at the black rocks and the grey water and sky.

'How long have you been married to Katy?' she asked at last.

'Thirty-two years.'

'You can't just shove thirty-two years in the bin, Niall, not with what you and Katy have shared. What would she do?'

He wanted to answer that Katy would knit and bake cakes and kiss Jocky's snout, but remained silent.

Then he remembered Katy as a girl. She'd been working in the hotel on Iona when they first met, and he'd had a summer job on the ferry. An island girl, freckled, red-headed, pale-faced and shy, he'd found her irresistible. He grunted. Sighed. Scanned the years in a swirl.

They stared across the Firth of Forth, counted seagulls, boats, waves.

'Were you happy once?'

A deep sigh. 'I suppose we were quite, briefly. And sometimes it's OK now. It's comfortable. But it's you I love, Maggie.'

'My Scandinavian mother used to say that there were many kinds of love, that in Gaelic there were thirteen different words for it.'

Niall was astonished. 'I didn't know your mother spoke Gaelic.'

Maggie shook her head. 'She didn't.'

They were silent and he took her hand again, and this time she allowed him to hold her. At last Niall sighed.

'I'm too late, aren't I?'

'By about nine years, yes.'

'Is this other bloke going to be any good to you?'

'I don't know yet.'

'You're sleeping with him, aren't you?'

Maggie frowned. How did he know that?

'You don't get that glow from a night out with the girls, Maggie; I know you, my love, and you know, I hope, that I do really love you, probably in more than thirteen ways.'

She nodded.

'We've had some good times, haven't we, Maggie?'

She nodded again. 'I'm very fond of you, Niall, you know that without asking.'

'But . . .?'

'But it's too late for me. I've forced myself to not care for you too deeply. It hurt too much at the beginning. I've been too lonely for too long to trust you now.'

'I was looking forward to proposing to you on bended knee.'

'Let's just say goodbye,' she managed to say with difficulty. 'I think that's better.'

As they sat together in silence, she hoped that Andy wasn't going to suddenly appear, walking the dog along the shoreline towards them, then she remembered with relief that he'd gone to St Andrews.

Niall stared out of the window, blinking.

'"*Ae fond kiss and then we sever.*
Had we never met and pairtit
We had ne'er been broken hearted,"' he said at last. 'Burns knew all about love and pain.'

Niall was always the jolly one, the elegant clown. Maggie had only seen him cry once before, when he spoke of his son's death in the murky waters of Loch Awe.

This time he wept soundlessly for what seemed like ages.

Suddenly he took his hand away from hers, opened the car door and took his muddy coat from the back seat.

'I'm getting out now, Maggie. I think I'll have a wee walk by myself before I go back to the hotel to collect my things, so I'll say goodbye.'

She looked at him as he nodded to her almost curtly, raised a hand in farewell, and, dignified, turned and set off for the village.

She sat there for a while and turned on Radio 3. Extraordinarily, Schubert's Quintet in C was playing. Schubert knew a thing or two about love and pain as well. She wondered if he and Burns had ever met. She must look up their dates.

When she got back to the cottage, Sophie had made lunch and was playing Bob Marley's 'No Woman No Cry'.

'D'you still want this played at your funeral, Ma?' she asked smiling. Then, when she saw Maggie's expression, she came to give her mother a long, warm hug, so tight that Maggie could have sworn she felt the baby's kickings.

Sophie was tactful, didn't probe too much. She just asked if Niall had really gone and hugged her again when Maggie nodded yes.

'I think you're doing the right thing, Ma,' Sophie told her earnestly. 'Even if it hurts.'

Maggie wiped her eyes. 'He asked me to marry him.'

'But he's already married, isn't he? Has he left Katy?'

Maggie shook her head.

'Has he instigated divorce proceedings?'

'I don't think so.'

'D'you really think he meant it?'

'Kind of, but he hasn't sorted anything out. I fear it's just a romantic notion that he'd be happier with me.'

'He probably would be.'

Maggie shrugged. 'I don't know.'

'But you do kind of love him, don't you?'

Maggie sighed. She didn't want to think about it right now.

'Poor guy, I feel quite sorry for him. I really like Niall.'

'Yes,' said Maggie sadly. 'He's a lovely man.'

'Where is he now?'

'At the Harbour View Hotel, I guess, sleeping it off.'

'Ma, do you want some lunch? I'm starving.'

'No thanks.' Maggie stood up. She looked exhausted. 'I think I need to lie down as well. I didn't sleep very well last night.'

'I might go down to the café for a bowl of soup.'

'OK. I'll see you later.' Heavy hearted, Maggie turned to go. She'd reached the bedroom and was climbing into bed when there was a knocking on the door. She froze. Surely Niall hadn't come back? She heard Sophie answer it and realised that it was her neighbour Wilma again, eighty-five years old, bright-eyed and always curious as to what was going on. What now? Maggie wondered and went to listen.

'I'm awfy sorry to bother you again so soon, but I thought you'd like to know, I think that Gilbert Menstrie must be going a bit mental.'

'Why?' Intrigued, Maggie started to come down the stairs.

'Well, he's out there in a white boiler suit and he's painting his front door flourescent pink. I'm sure the planning department will complain.'

Maggie was bemused. 'But he *is* the planning department.'

Sophie grinned from behind Wilma. 'I've just seen it. It really is hideous, Ma. You must go and have a look.'

'I will,' said Maggie. 'Later.'

'The thing that I'm wondering now,' said Wilma, 'is, d'you think it was Gilbert that was sick on the church steps? Maybe he's been out drowning his sorrows since Effie died.'

Sophie and Maggie's eyes met. Sophie was trying not to giggle.

'I'm sure not,' said Maggie. 'Gilbert has far too much respect to behave like that, he's a church elder, after all.'

'Well, I don't know. You should see his front door. It's an absolute eyesore.'

'I'll see it later. I'm off for a lie down, please excuse me.' Maggie retreated to her bedroom, sank into the tumbled duvet which still smelt of Niall. In moments she was sound asleep, dreaming of Andy and Niall. In her dream both men were kilted, enormously tall and shouting at each other. Then Andy turned up alone; he was sitting on a raft made from Gilbert's flourescent pink front door, paddling through a storm.

'I've come for you,' he said. 'We're going to the Isle of May.' Maggie was swimming, floundering, but Andy pulled her aboard and she felt safe. But when he'd navigated them through the storm and they were about to land on the rocky island, there was Niall, huge and one-eyed liked Polyphemus, wearing a tattered kit, throwing great chunks of rock of them, shouting 'No way! No way can you come here! I'll never let you land!'

Then along came a seal, whirling like a porpoise, doing joyful somersaults and the seal turned into Fergal, her dead husband, and he stared at her from the sea with his big dark eyes and called, 'Why have you been so long, darling? I've been waiting for you here!' and he dived into the depths of the waves and Maggie woke up weeping because she was afraid to follow him.

Chapter Twenty-Two

Patrick stared glumly at the palm fronds which waved above him and across to the pale sand where Jennifer Earlsferry shrieked with her grandsons. Nobody would believe that he wasn't enjoying his Caribbean trip: the food was marvellous, the drinks – exotic cocktails mostly, made with fresh fruit juice and coconut milk laced with huge amounts of rum – were pleasant and plentiful enough, though he still preferred a straight malt; he was glad he'd bought a big bottle at the airport, and the sun had shone almost without a break. Nor had there been any of those famous hurricanes predicted, and the bedrooms were pleasantly designed, airy and comfortable, with private bathrooms and balconies. There was nothing he could fault really, other than the discomforts of his gammy ankle and dicky hip, both of which ached relentlessly and stopped him from uninhibitedly enjoying a swim or going fishing or walking.

The real problem was that he'd had enough, in fact much more than enough, of Jennifer.

William and Fanny had been wise before the event. 'D'you really know her well enough?' they'd asked. 'D'you really like her son and his wife? You always said they were uncultured snobs . . .' And so they were. Rich, spoilt snobs. He was missing his own family and friends. What he would give for a visit from any of his children or grandchildren or from Maggie's lot. He could relax with them, have a laugh and time wouldn't hang so heavy.

Jennifer, oh Lord, here she was now, galumphing towards him, waving a bloody great shell at him; she looked like a sea-monster with that snorkel and the designer-draped swimming costume all covered with giant crudely drawn poppies. Her other costume was even worse, it was a hideous acid yellow which set Patrick's cultural teeth on edge.

Maybe he could feign sleep and avoid her for a while, but dammit, no, she'd caught his eye and was shrieking something to him.

'Patrick, do come for a paddle, or come into the pool. You know the doctor said swimming was good for your leg.'

'Later, perhaps.' He heaved himself upright – a painfully slow operation – and grasped his walking stick. 'I was just off for a little power nap . . .' he smiled his most charming smile and she tinkled in reply.

'You and your power naps – you are so sweet!'

He grimaced. 'Sweet' was not a word he found particularly apposite, but he said nothing, only grunted that he'd see her later.

'D'you want an arm to lean on, my dear?'

'Not at all, thanks. I'm doing fine.'

'Yes, you are, you really are.' She watched him, her expression a little anxious as her six-year-old granddaughter, very fair with huge slanting eyes, came up to her and stood watching Patrick's retreating back.

'Poor old Uncle Paddy, he's a little bit off-colour today.'

'What does off-colour mean?'

'Oh . . . a little tired . . . fed up, perhaps.'

'Grumpy, you mean?'

Jennifer hugged the small girl. 'Oh no, darling, Not grumpy, that's a bit cruel to say. He's got a sore leg and wants a wee lie down.'

'Please can I have an ice cream?'

'Of course you can, darling. Let's go and see what we can find in that huge fridge in the kitchen.'

In his room, Patrick stared gloomily out through flowering bushes and banana palms to the turquoise sea, where he watched a couple of black fishermen pulling in their nets. It was lovely here, but so was the view from his own sitting room and he was missing that. And Karin. Did she ever regret her choice, he wondered. Did she long for the unexpected beauties of the East Neuk, and did she miss her family and old friends like himself? He'd thought about her often since coming here with these alien people.

Not far from him, Jennifer's two oldest grandsons, who'd just left Eton, were having a smoke with one of the kitchen boys. The three of them were laughing hysterically. Glumly, Patrick cleaned out his pipe.

Harry, his favourite of the two, in fact the only person he really liked at all in the house-party of twelve, waved to him and Patrick, smiling, flourished his pipe at him.

Harry took something from the black lad and came running over to him.

'Hello there, sir.'

'For heaven's sake call me Patrick or Paddy. Not sir on any account.'

Harry grinned. 'OK. I just wondered if you'd like to try some of this *ganja* in your pipe? Or have a puff of one of our joints?'

Patrick's eyebrows rose up until they almost disappeared.

'Does your mother or grandmother know what you two are up to?'

The boy shrugged. 'Not really. Mum's tried, but it always makes her sick. Dad forbids it; he prefers getting drunk.'

'So I've noticed,' said Patrick dryly.

'It's very pure stuff, si ... I mean Patrick ... I just thought that it might cheer you up a bit. I know a man in Cupar who takes it for his MS, and it's the only thing that really helps him with the pain.'

Patrick frowned. 'I did try it years ago,' he confessed, 'when my son liked that sort of thing, and I had a controlled go with mescalin in the States in 1951. It was fascinating – I have to admit I rather enjoyed it.'

Harry cocked his head. 'Shall we come over with some? You could try just a little.'

Patrick eyed the lie of the land. None of the rest of the house-party were within sight.

'Why not?' he said, and much cheered, limped out on to the verandah, where with difficulty and a bit of help from Harry, who'd gestured to the other two lads to join them, he eased his long, aching body into a handsome rattan chair with a leg rest.

'I haven't told her yet. Of course I will – I just didn't get the chance, there was too much going on.'

Maggie still half asleep, came into the sitting-room as Sophie crooned kisses into the phone and whispered, 'Goodbye, darling, speak to you tomorrow . . .'

'What haven't you told me yet?'

Sophie was shocked at how white and strained her mother looked. 'Are you OK, Ma?'

'I'm fine; I was dreaming. I haven't quite come to. I need a cup of tea.'

'Sure you don't want a whisky?' Sophie was grinning.

'No thanks. Why? Is what you haven't told me that serious?'

'No. You just look whacked. Has Niall been getting to you?'

'I'm fine,' said Maggie tersely. 'Tell me what you were talking about.'

'I'll make tea first. You sit. I got some biscuits, and, incidentally, I think Niall's still in the village. He drives a grey Mercedes doesn't he?'

Maggie sighed, nodded. 'He's probably still asleep, judging by the state of him.'

'Here.' Sophie handed her a mug of tea and Maggie sipped. 'Aaah . . . life returns. So, get on with it.'

'Well, it's good news really, or I hope you'll think so . . . it er . . . just seems like bad timing to tell you today after the upset with Niall . . .'

Maggie stared at her daughter and saw how happy she was. 'You've decided to get married, haven't you?' she asked suddenly.

'How on earth did you know?'

'Some people do it before they're seven months pregnant,' said Maggie dryly and they both laughed.

'You're the first person to know; we haven't told anyone.'

Maggie rose to hug her. The bump was beginning to make the action a little awkward. 'That's great, darling. When?'

'Well, we want to do it after the baby, just in case we make all the arrangements and it arrives early or there's a problem. And we want to be married here in Inverie.'

'In the cottage?'

'No, it's far too teeny. In the old kirk, if the minister will let us and if he has any spaces left for this summer. And Mark'll be back from Australia in time for the baby, so we'll all be here . . .' She paused and their eyes met.

Except for Fergal, Sophie's dead dad. Neither of them actually said it, but each knew from the other's face that the thought was there for an instant.

'I've actually got a date to see the minister this evening at half past seven,' said Sophie at last. 'He says he'll need to meet Michel as well before he decides if it's OK. Michel's coming over next week.'

'Doesn't it matter that you aren't churchgoers – and nor were any of your four parents?' (Michel's parents were a lapsed Catholic and a Jewish rationalist.)

'That's what I need to find out, if he's persuadable.'

'We should have some champagne,' declared Maggie. 'To celebrate.'

Sophie shook her head. 'Not for me, Ma. It would just make me sick. Can we wait till Michel comes next week?'

'Of course. How is he anyway? Has he really been completely OK since his episode last summer?'

'Pretty good. We're being very careful he doesn't overwork, but at least I'm not walking on eggs any more. He does get the odd blip, but he's down to a tiny dose of the pills now, and will soon come off them, and his therapy seems to be going OK; I went with him a couple of times, which was very hard work, really harrowing, but helpful, and that'll finish in a couple of weeks. But best of all, Ma, it's lovely to see him so happy about work and excited about the baby.'

Maggie tried to concentrate. 'Where d'you want the wedding reception?'

'Maybe in the village hall; it's not expensive and it's got tables and chairs, a kitchen and a stage so we could have a ceilidh with all our musician friends.'

She looked at Maggie. 'What I'd really like, is for William to make our wedding rings. D'you think it would cost a fortune?'

'I've no idea. Ask him.'

'I'm so excited, Ma. About everything.'

'Me too, darling. It's really great news. I'm very happy for you both.'

'D'you think I could phone William now and tell him? He was so good to us when Michel went funny. He really helped me to hold things together.'

'Of course. Go ahead.'

Maggie watched Sophie's delight as she told William and heard her shout of amazement when he said that the rings would be his wedding present.

'But you can't . . .' said Sophie. 'We want to commission them, please.'

Obviously William was saying that if he wasn't allowed to make them a gift, there wouldn't be any rings.

'Well, maybe . . .' muttered Sophie. She was clutching her big tum and giggling. 'OK, we'll come to supper on Friday and argue about it then; that'll be smashing.'

'Maggie too!' Maggie heard William shout through the phone, and was glad. Worriedly, she remembered that she'd promised Andy that she'd ring him, but with Sophie's surprise news, and an unspoken, completely unexpected, but vividly present grief for her dead husband, plus the fact that she couldn't stop being aware that Niall was still in the village, she didn't feel ready to. Perhaps she'd try later when Sophie went out again or took a bath. Right now she simply didn't have space in her head to analyse how she was feeling about Andy.

'He wants to talk to you,' Sophie handed over the phone.

William's voice was warm with pleasure. 'Wonderful news! Did you have to twist their arms?'

'No. I was taken completely by surprise.'

He chuckled. 'You old bohemian, you. By the way, I spoke to Karin today: she hadn't heard from Dad for several weeks and wondered if he was OK. I must say she sounded rather icy when I told her he'd swanned off to the Caribbean with her old enemy La Earlsferry.'

'Poor old Patrick. When are Karin and Sven coming over?'

'In good time for the baby, Karin said, and now of course there'll be the wedding. She sounded euphoric at the thought of seeing everybody.'

Andy looked at the time. It was already nearly eight o'clock and he'd said he'd go round to give his son-in-law a hand with lifting up an old carpet. Maybe he'd better phone Maggie, although she'd said she'd ring him. He just wanted to hear her voice, to feel sure that last night had really happened and could maybe lead somewhere.

He debated for a moment, but when he dialled her number it was engaged. He frowned as he remembered Niall. Five minutes later she was still talking, so he gave up, called Dougie and went into out into the chill of the March night feeling upset and insecure.

Niall woke in his hotel bedroom and peered at his watch. It was half past eight, and for a moment he wasn't sure if it was night or day. But when he turned the radio on and heard the Today programme, he realised that he'd slept solidly for almost eighteen hours. He certainly felt a lot better than he had yesterday morning; he grimaced when he remembered his farewell with Maggie and looked wryly at the bottle of champagne he'd taken from the cottage, sitting unopened on the dressing table. He slowly stretched, showered and shaved, and telephoned for some coffee and toast to be brought to his room.

'There was a phone message for you late last night, Mr Maclean. Did you get it?' asked the woman on the desk. Niall's heart leapt. Maybe Maggie had relented, would agree to meet him for lunch or come for a walk and talk more fully about things.

'No, I didn't. What was the message?'

'It was Mrs Maclean's sister from Glasgow. Your wife isn't well. Please can you phone them.'

Niall froze. 'When did it come?'

'Late last night. We did try to summon you, but there was no answer from your room.'

'OK. Give me the number please.'

The toast and coffee arrived and Niall ate and drank as he dialled. To find him here, Katy or her sister must have called Maggie. As he dialled, he remembered that his mobile wasn't charged. He'd forgotten to plug it in when he fell into bed; they'd probably tried the mobile first and then tried Maggie. For once he hadn't even told Katy that he was coming here. Damn it, what on earth could be the trouble?

Katy's sister sounded very flustered and he could hear bloody Jocky yapping in the background. Her words all came out in a breathless rush: 'It's dreadful . . . poor Katy just suddenly collapsed with severe chest pains after being in the cinema . . . then she was sick and we took a taxi to the hospital. The casualty doctor – who was just a wee slip of a girl – decided to keep her in overnight and she's to see the cardiologist this afternoon – they seem pretty worried, and Katy's still got to undergo a few tests. And for sure, the train journey back to Oban will be far too much for her, so it'll be better if you can come and see what's what with the doctors and take her home if she's allowed to go – It's really dreadful – She keeps asking for you, Niall.'

Niall's heart was thumping. 'Of course I'll come. Let me see now, I'll leave this place in half an hour or so and head straight for Glasgow. All going well I should be with you by mid to late morning.'

He sighed as he put down the phone. He was surprised by how upset he felt. Upset, guilty and somehow responsible. Poor Katy, she hadn't ever had any heart trouble that he'd been aware of, but her mother had had angina and her eldest sister suffered from severe high blood pressure. And what about Maggie? He'd planned to try again, to see her and persuade her that his proposal was serious. But how could he now? He sank his face in his hands and sighed gustily. He must quickly pack and set off. First things first; Maggie would just have to wait.

He stood for a minute, gathering his thoughts, and stared gloomily at the bottle of champagne. Tattinger Brut. Nothing but the best for Niall. He thought of leaving it with a note for Maggie, but then her other bloke might drink it, and he definitely didn't fancy that.

Sighing, he quickly packed his small travel bag, then with great solemnity he picked up the bottle and removed the foil, and pointing it at the far wall, eased out the cork. 'Point taken, Maggie. Maybe I was just kidding myself,' he murmured sadly as he watched the bubbles surge to the top and climax dramatically.

Sighing, he then slowly and deliberately poured the champagne down the sink and watched as the last of it frothed, swirled and disappeared.

'Down the bloody plughole, that's where it goes,' he groaned. 'OK, Katy girl. I'll be with you soon and I'll take care of you and the bloody dog.' Picking up his suitcase and coat, he checked that the room was clear before closing the door behind him.

'Barbados is five hours behind us, so it's ten-thirty in the morning there. I'm going to ring the old man and see how he's doing.'

'Give him my love,' called Fanny. I'll catch up with you later. Bye . . .' and the door slammed.

William put on half-specs and dialled carefully and listened to the ringing tone. Eventually a small girl answered and said, 'Hello, who are you?'

'Hello there . . .' began William but then he heard a shriek, followed by a slap and screaming and a woman's voice saying loudly, 'No, you may not! Give it to me this instant!'

'Having trouble?' enquired William at last.

'Oh dear. I am so sorry. Who's calling, please?'

'It's William Maitland here, Patrick's son. Is that Jennifer?'

'Oh William dear, yes it is, sorry about that, my granddaughter's feeling the sun, I fear. How are you?'

'Very well. I was just wondering how my father was coping with his new exotic lifestyle.'

'Oh . . .' Jennifer Earlsferry's tinkle of laughter seemed to have frozen in mid tink. 'Yes . . . er . . . well, he's fine, er . . . absolutely fine.'

'I wondered how his legs were doing? Is he managing to move around OK?'

'Yes.' This time the voice was definite, somewhat chilly. 'I'd say he was managing very well. I'll just go and fetch him. Do hold on.'

William could hear the phone being put down and the small voice came again and said 'Hello? Who are you?'

'I'm William,' said William. 'Patrick's son.'

'Are you Patrick's boy?'

'I am yes, but I'm quite a big boy.'

'Are you his Daddy?'

'No, he's my Daddy.'

'My Granny says Paddy's vewy, vewy iwwesponsible.'

'Does she now?' William eyebrows went high up his forehead. 'Now why does she say that?'

'She says he's a bad affluence on the boys and should ought to know better than to . . .'

William, highly amused, longed to continue the conversation, but Jennifer's screech broke across the girl's treble.

'I told you, Antonia. I specifically told you not to pick up the phone. That was VERY NAUGHTY!'

'Hello, William?' William heard his father's voice.

'Hello there, Pops, how are you doing?'

'Bloody woman,' grunted Patrick. 'Thank God she's taken the child off so I can talk in peace. She's quite awful; I might throttle her one of these days if I have too many rum cocktails. She bosses everybody about, can't mind her own business.'

'Why, what have you done?'

'What do you mean what have I done?' It was a fairly belligerent roar. A sure sign with Patrick of a guilty conscience.

'A little bird told me that you'd been a naughty boy.'

Patrick suddenly chuckled. 'Which little bird? Antonia, was it? Now she's all right; I can talk to her and the other youngsters, it's the adults who are the problem.'

'Tell me more, Pa.'

'I've thoroughly blotted my copy book, but the blotting of it has improved my life here no end.'

Intrigued, William, waited for more.

'I've been caught taking drugs with the boys.'

'What sort of drugs?'

'Just a little cannabis, for heaven's sake. Very good, pure stuff, as it happens. We had a delightful time but Lady J discovered us because we were laughing rather a lot and now we're all in the dog house. She's grounded the boys, but I'm grounded anyway because I'm so lame, so she can't really punish me, and she's more or less sent me to Coventry, which is frankly a great blessing.' He was roaring with laughter; so was William.

'How's your ankle doing?'

'To be honest, it's been bloody awful, but this *ganja* stuff really diminishes the pain. It's true what they say about it. I tell you, William, when I come home I am going to campaign to legalise cannabis. I mean it. I feel positively messianic about it and stuff Lady bloody J!'

'Well don't overdo it or get arrested, please.'

'Don't worry, I won't. We're leaving in a couple of days, anyway. I'll stick to the whisky till we leave.'

Andy looked hopefully at his answerphone when he got back from his son-in-law's, but nobody had called. He felt very let down. Maggie had promised, after all, that she'd phone tonight. Fed up, he made himself a cup of tea and went gloomily to bed.

In the morning, after a couple of hours he was feeling very fraught. He wanted her to call him, yet found it impossible to simply pick up the phone and ring her. What if she wasn't easy and friendly, or if that Niall man was still around? What if the other night was just a one-night stand? He didn't think he could face the disappointment, but he was going mad waiting. In the end, he decided to take himself off to Dundee for the day. There was a new film which sounded interesting. He'd been going to suggest such an outing to Maggie but he couldn't hang around all day in the hope that she might actually call him. Better to be busy and let her do the wondering, if she did decide to phone.

In Denmark, Karin and Sven were looking at travel brochures.

'I think we should do it,' said Sven. 'I've never been to the Faroes or to Shetland. It's expensive, but it should be a wonderful trip, and we can stop off here and there on the way and have a look at the places where we berth. Then we can drive down to Fife through Sutherland – which I've never seen – maybe even have lunch in St Andrews at the little place where we decided to marry.'

'But it's such a lot of money . . .'

'Let's do it,' said Sven, hugging Karin. 'We've got the money, and very soon we really will be too old to do such a journey, and we'll probably see lots of whales, porpoises and dolphins. I think it'll be lovely.'

Sophie's two-day stay proved to be very intense. Between them, she and Maggie organised the guest list for the wedding, which included a couple of painful arguments as to which friends and relatives were to be invited.

'It is me that's getting married, Ma,' Sophie would point out, and Maggie felt unable to point out that it was her money that would be paying for much of it (Michel's parents, Sophie assured her, would go halfers with her). The minister, who'd been friendly to Sophie but wanted to meet Michel as soon as possible, had offered them a date for the wedding – his one vacancy – in late June.

'If the baby's on time it will be six weeks old.'

'And if it's late, as they so often are, it'll be barely a month old and you may well be exhausted, so how will you cope with a wedding as well?'

Sophie beamed. 'I'll be all adrenalised and benignly overflowing with breast milk – and you'll help, won't you?'

'Presumably there'll be a big French contingent?'

'Huuuge . . .' Sophie made the word itself enormous. 'So we must go to the tourist office and find details of hotels and B and B's for them all.'

Then there were baby items: they went to Dundee on a search for these, and Maggie bought a bath and a pram, and muslin squares and babygros and little hats and gloves and socks and creams and cotton wool and cuddly blankets and changing-mats. The lists of requirements for both wedding and baby seemed infinite; Maggie felt quite dizzy at the prospect of a grandchild. She was uneasily aware that she hadn't phoned or heard from Andy, but with Sophie's continued presence, it just felt impossible. There was also the Fergal *Doppelgänger* effect, as she called it to herself. The family intimacy and the emotions evoked in her by the imminence of the two events made Fergal's memory very solid – painfully so, in many instances. An expression of Sophie's, or even the way her toes looked, would sometimes remind her so vividly of her husband, that several times she felt very vulnerable. She tried to hide it; she was determined to present a positive image to her beautifully ripening daughter. '*I am the grown-up in this situation*,' she would chant to herself like a mantra whenever she felt even a little bit feeble.

At last Sophie left, her car filled with all the new baby gear they'd managed to find in Dundee.

'Bye, Ma. You've been great. Michel and I will both be back very soon for him to see the minister. Take care. Try not to get miserable.'

Their last ten minutes reduced them both to total giggles: as they loaded the car, Gilbert Menstrie astonished them by walking past wearing an extraordinary sweater in pink, lemon yellow and turquoise diagonal stripes. He looked as though he was growing a beard and was even wearing new specs – quite trendy ones, sideways ovals. It was so unlike the Gilbert they were used to, that both Sophie and Maggie were forced to run inside to hide their shocked laughter.

'What d'you think has made him go for all this bright colour?' asked Sophie. 'It's pretty amazing.'

'It's either love or madness, and they of course can be indistinguishable,' Maggie clutched her side. 'I've got a stitch from laughing. Poor Gilbert, but at least he looks cheerful. That was a very chatty "Good morning, when's the baby coming?" wasn't it?'

After Sophie had driven off, Maggie made coffee and sat quietly, gratefully absorbing the sudden silence. It was four days since she'd last seen Andy. She must phone him.

Her heart was thumping. 'Andy? Hi, it's Maggie.'

'Oh, hello there.' He sounded distant, abrupt.

'I'm really sorry that I haven't rung, but I've just had Sophie staying, and it's been a bit like living in an earthquake because she's decided to get married almost immediately after having the baby, and I honestly haven't stopped for a breather till now.'

'Don't apologise.' He sounded like a total stranger.

She frowned to herself; he was bound to be hurt because she'd promised to phone him and hadn't.

'You know Niall was here?' she said at last.

'Aye. I spoke to him.'

'Well, he came in uninvited. I was furious and told him to go. And he has truly gone. I've said I won't see him again.'

There was silence at the other end.

'Andy?'

'Yes?'

'Please . . . can we meet? Soon? Would you like to come to supper one night?'

He was obviously hugely offended. 'I'm quite busy at the moment,' he said gruffly.

'Andy, please let's meet; we had a lovely time together, a really lovely time. I hope we'll have more like that. I'm truly sorry I didn't ring when I said I would.'

More silence. Maggie could feel her heart counting out the seconds.

'OK,' said Andy at last. 'What are you doing later on?'

She grinned at the phone. 'Maybe eating supper with you?'

'I don't know,' said Andy slowly. 'I've got things to do.'

'I'd really like to see you . . .'

A long agonising pause.

'Please . . .' said Maggie and felt herself redden.

'Well, as it happens,' said Andy at last, 'my daughter's just made a Bolognese sauce for me, and I was going to freeze some of it, but I could bring it round and save you cooking. You're probably worn out from everything that's been going on. I've got some spaghetti I could bring as well. Would you like that?'

'Sounds wonderful. I'll make a salad.'

'What time then?'

'Seven?'

'Grand. I'll see you then.'

Maggie put down the phone. She was relieved. Glad too that she didn't have to cook. It meant that she had time to go up to Karin's house; she hadn't seen to airing it or watering the plants in the conservatory for a few days.

In Karin's studio she gazed down at the glittering sea and imagined seeing her aunt re-installed here for an entire month. It would be lovely, and then there would be the baby, and the wedding. And Andy . . . How on earth would she manage it all? It would be chaos, but hopefully, enjoyable chaos. Obviously she wouldn't be making many necklaces or driftwood sculptures in the next few weeks.

Chapter Twenty-Three

A week or so later, Maggie was woken by Dougie's frantic barking.

'There must be somebody at the door,' she muttered, climbing out of bed and pulling on her dressing-gown. 'It's only half past eight, the postie doesn't come before nine.'

'Don't stay away too long.' Andy reached for her as she went past. 'It's chilly here without you.'

There was shouting outside. And singing. Puzzled, still half-asleep, Maggie opened the door and peered out.

'*Bonjour* Ma-outlaw-soon-to-be-in-law!' sang Michel. 'But my God, where did this dog come from? We are so sorry to surprise you, but we have good coffee and a lot of *pain au chocolat* for you, so we hope we are forgiven.'

Speechless, Maggie smiled a little bewilderedly as Dougie, very excited, danced up and down alongside the grinning Michel and Sophie.

'Sorry, Ma. We should have rung, but Michel only spoke very late last night to the minister and he's going off on holiday tomorrow. It was either today or a three-week wait for Michel to see him, so we just decided to come straight over.'

'Right,' Maggie nodded, grabbed Dougie by the collar.

'What a lovely dog, whose is he?'

'Er ...' Maggie pulled her robe tighter. 'He's ... he belongs to a friend.'

Sophie looked at her. 'Ma ... have you got somebody here?'

Maggie blushed and the three of them eyed each other as they listened to the lavatory flushing.

'Is it permitted to come in?' asked Michel gently. 'Would you prefer that we go to the studio?'

Maggie laughed a little nervously. 'I feel like a naughty teenager caught in the act.'

'Good for you, Maggie.' Michel bowed elegantly. 'I am glad you have some company. Now, shall we be tactful and leave you?'

'No, hang on a minute, I'll go up and have a word.' Maggie fled upstairs, where she found Andy starting to get dressed.

'D'you want me to go, or to hide under the bed?' he asked quizzically.

'I think you should come down and have breakfast. It's Sophie and Michel – both, I have to warn you, in excitable mode.'

'Fine by me.'

'I'll just tell them to put the kettle on, then I'll have a quick shower and dress.'

'OK, but come here a minute, there's something I want to tell you.' Andy reached out and slid his hands inside her dressing-gown. 'You're a fabulous woman,' he whispered. 'I could get used to this.'

It was the second time this week they'd spent the night together at Maggie's house and last night they'd talked till late, and their modest act of lovemaking had been very agreeable. Cramps and all.

Maggie returned his embrace and Dougie, who'd followed her back upstairs, barked excitedly. 'You too, Dougie boy, we love you too,' murmured Andy and pulled away. 'You'd better go down and tell them that it's OK to stay.'

'What a fab man, Ma, where did you meet him?' said Sophie later, when Andy had breakfasted with them and taken the dog out for a walk with Michel.

'On the May Island trip. He was the skipper.'

Sophie smiled in recognition, 'Of course, he's Kenny's uncle – I've only just realised . . .' She looked sternly at her mother. 'I hope he's unattached.'

'He's a widower.'

'Good. Glad to hear it.'

Later that morning, Michel and Sophie returned from their meeting with the minister.

'It's all OK,' said Michel, beaming. 'He has agreed to marry us heathens.'

'How did you persuade him?' asked Maggie.

'I sang to him,' said Michel proudly. 'And he was converted.'

'He really did sing to him,' said Sophie, her eyes sparkling, 'and you could tell that he was really moved. But he did say at one point, that we must remember that it was his job to read out the Lord's word in the church, so we have to have some actual hymns or psalms and a bible reading.'

'I suppose we did present him with rather a full programme, with Robert Burns, Rimbaud, Shakespeare and Voltaire, plus all sorts of strange music. Poor man, he really did turn a little bit purple when he said that bit about it being a Christian ceremony, but he was very *sympatique* and amused that we were having the baby first.'

'Speaking of the baby, Ma. Did I tell you I've decided to have a water birth?'

'In the hospital?'

'No. I'm definitely having a home birth: I'm going to hire the birthing pool from a woman who lives out towards Portobello. We've to pick it up a couple of weeks before the due date so that we can practise using it and have it at the ready.'

'Do you actually intend to have the baby underwater?' asked Maggie, puzzled.

'No, it's just meant to be very soothing and natural. You fill the bath with warm water and lie in it during contractions, it's meant to be very comforting.'

Her mother nodded. 'Well, you live and learn. Maybe you'll have a mermaid.'

There had been no word from Niall for at least a month. Maggie didn't know if his wife or he were dead or alive. It felt weird to think that the Niall door was truly closed, but she kept assuring herself that it was better that way. Sometimes, unbidden, a memory of him would come, of him laughing, barking at the front door or happily opening a bottle. They'd had a lot of fun, illicit though it had been. She hadn't spoken to Andy about Katy. It somehow hadn't seemed relevant. She was startled when Niall's letter, postmarked Oban, arrived several weeks after she'd given him his final marching orders.

Dearest Maggie, it read.

I feel that I must write to tell you how things are at this end. I had meant to make one last effort to talk to you again on my last unfortunate visit to Inverie, but fate intervened. Katy has suffered a stroke and is not at all well and will obviously take months to recover – if she ever does fully recover, which is doubtful. At present we are both at home and I am her carer and she does physio several times a week and various helpers come in daily to give me a little respite.

The timing was strange. When I thought that I had at last found the strength to leave my marriage, this happened. But in an odd way I don't regret it. Katy is both grateful and loving to me; I think she was all too aware that I had left her emotionally and that was deeply painful for her. Perhaps this is a punishment of sorts for my infidelity. I don't know, but it makes sense of being married, of being there for somebody. I still wish that in other circumstances I could have been that person for you. We do all need a helpmate, a partner. Life is too hard otherwise.

I think of you often. Ours was a sporadic sort of paradise, mea culpa, but for me our meetings were always full of joy and I miss you. I will probably always miss you and I only wish that things could have been otherwise.

Forgive me, my love, if in aught I have offended. I know that you will soon be a grandmother and knowing you, I expect you will be a full-hearted one. Enjoy it and be happy.

Yours always, Niall.

Maggie was sitting at the kitchen table with the letter in her hand when a phone call from Sophie – now eight and a half months pregnant – brought her up short.

'Hi, Ma, could you possibly come this afternoon to help me to collect the birthing pool? Michel's got an unexpected problem with his synthesiser, and just can't do it.'

In her ignorance, Maggie agreed immediately to help her daughter. Naively, she had imagined the birth bath to be a slightly enlarged but deflated plastic paddling pool which would fit easily into the car boot, but when she and the now massively bulging Sophie climbed the four flights of stairs to the supplier's flat – which was set in a far corner of a council estate north-east of Edinburgh – she blanched at the roomful of bulky objects confronting them.

To start with, there was a heavy pump, a heater, metres of hose for the inning and outing of water, and numerous rigid pieces of plastic which slotted puzzlingly together to make the containing wall for the pool itself. The latter, which looked like a huge collapsed blue tent, proved – even when deflated – to be alarmingly unwieldy.

Besides having four young children, who were all much in evidence, Kylie – the talkative young woman in charge – was doing a double degree in mathematics and psychology on top of the obviously flourishing pool rental business. She was useful so far as information on assembly went, but it was quite obvious that helping to heave the various components down four flights of stairs and into the car was not to be part of the service.

It was at this moment that the mantle of granniedom really fell upon the startled Maggie for the first time, simultaneously almost stifling her in its ambivalent embrace; her heart sank as it dawned on her that Sophie was so heavily pregnant that some of the tubes and perhaps the instruction sheets were all she could be allowed to carry.

Maggie attempted to hide her dismay by bravely muttering something like 'Better get on with it,' and stoically heaving the billowing ectoplasm of thick blue plastic pool on to her back, staggered out of the flat. As she made her way slowly towards the lift, a passing neighbour clung somewhat nervously to the wall. Cloaked in the pool, Maggie supposed she must look like a huge liquefying, giant aqua-blue turtle of a certain age. There was no room in the minute lift for more than one person and at most a quarter part of the birthing pool kit, so she heaved in as many of the pool components as she could, and entered the appallingly smelly cubicle by herself.

'I pray,' she growled indignantly to Sophie, 'that the architect of this lift will spend his – it was obviously designed by a man – time in hell living in just such a tiny space. It isn't big enough for a pregnant or even moderately large person with shopping; it couldn't accommodate a pram, a wheelchair, a coffin or a stretcher. It's utterly inhuman . . .' Her words were cut off abruptly as the doors slammed automatically, unstoppably shut.

She'd done three loads into the lift and down to the ground floor, carefully balancing each one to avoid noxious puddles, and was trying to emerge, when to her horror the whole mechanism juddered, gave a hideous gasp and the door threatened to rend her in two. She only escaped injury with difficulty. Later, as she limped to the car to load up, she became uneasily aware of a suspicious-looking couple of neighbours sizing up the unguarded accumulation of pool parts she'd stacked on the ground-floor landing. She remembered uncomfortably that Kylie had told them that only a couple of months earlier, an anonymous person (presumably a neighbour), had literally kicked to death a shiny new bicycle which was parked outside her front door.

The entire loading process took five trips. Breathless, Maggie had at last settled down in the car ready to drive back to Sophie and Michel's flat, when she realised with dismay that she'd left her handbag behind. She'd been doing her very best to behave well, but now feared she might explode. Amazingly, the young multigravada, like a good fairy, suddenly appeared unexpectedly. Exuding female spirituality, she beamed as she handed the lost bag through the car window.

On the way home, as Maggie backed the car down a one-way system in a forlorn effort to match the street map with the reality of No Entry and No Right Turn signs, Sophie shook her head in disbelief. 'My God, that Kylie is a truly awe-inspiring role model.'

But Maggie's maternal task was not yet fulfilled. They still had to find their way back to Sophie and Michel's flat, where she almost alone must unload, deliver and perhaps even assemble the birthing pool.

'Is there any chance that Michel might be home in time to help?' she asked hopefully.

Sophie phoned him on her mobile, but to Maggie's disappointment, he didn't expect to get home till long after midnight.

Maggie had never thought of owning a hip-flask, but today she really wished she had one. As they crawled through hideous rush-hour paralysis, she glanced a little anxiously at her daughter. Sophie, patting her bulge, smiled. 'It feels like a football match in here tonight.'

She looked beautiful but exhausted. Maggie sighed. She wasn't looking forward to the unloading, bearing in mind that their goal was a third-floor flat with no lift.

'I need cakes,' announced Sophie suddenly, and at once a surge of cheerful camaraderie engulfed them both.

Maggie knew there were home-made Greek cakes to be found in a shop en route to the flat. Much cheered, she grinned as a miraculously enlivened Sophie vaulted the double yellow lines towards the shop.

When they arrived, the expectant granny was left to unload the car and heave the pieces of pool up the stone spiral tenement stairs to the third-floor flat. It sounded easy, only she didn't manage to park nearby, so it was an uncomfortably long haul each time from car to stairwell.

'Hell, I'm getting too old for this,' muttered Maggie breathlessly, as she heaved. At last, wearily clasping a last armful of plastic tubing, she staggered into the flat and closed the door behind her.

'Would you like a drink, Ma?' asked Sophie, smiling, offering her a glass.

Exhausted, Maggie dumped the tubing, disrobed herself from the deflated pool, which was still draped round her shoulders, and managed a breathless nod.

'I tell you, cakes never tasted better, nor that first gulp of wine than they did that night,' she said later to Andy, as they lay side by side in his big double bed and she made him roar with laughter with her tale of woe.

'Heavens, woman, why on earth didn't you ask me to help? It would have been a pleasure. Why are you so blooming independent?'

Maggie shrugged. 'I don't know. I suppose I'm just used to doing things by myself.'

He turned her to him and looked searchingly into her eyes. 'You're daft. That's what I'm here for, to help you if you need me. Please remember that. It's OK not inviting me to the wedding; I know it's far too early days with us for that, but I'm always happy to help you with anything practical. You really must remember that. I'm here for you, Maggie.'

He was a good man. So helpful. Maggie sighed to herself. It was a pity she didn't love him, not yet at least.

Discreetly pretending to do his accounts, the second-hand bookseller in the St Andrews shop eyed his only two customers as they sat together leafing through folios of old Scottish prints. The woman looked familiar, but he couldn't quite place her. They were an amazingly good-looking pair, though they must have knocked up a good few decades between them. The bookseller thought for a moment that Zeus and Hera might have looked like that if the Greek gods had ever grown old, but the celestial home of this particular couple was more likely to be a northern Valhalla than a Mediterranean Mount Olympus.

'These are really fine,' said Sven. 'It's very difficult to choose.'

'We want to find two,' said Karin. 'We're looking for a print of Inverie if possible – one of the old kirk – and maybe a May Island picture.'

She held up a dramatic image of puffins and a seal and high sheer crags behind. 'This is wonderful. What date is this one?'

'Yes, that's the Isle of May,' The man peered at the print using a monocular lens as well as his half-specs. '1810, it's a good one. A David Masterton. He specialised in sea birds and islands like Staffa and Lunga, the May and the Bass Rock.'

'Here's an excellent one of the church and Maggie's cottage.' Sven held up an etching with a view taken from the shore.

'I like that one myself. I had it on my mantelpiece for a while.'

'We're looking for a print to celebrate our anniversary,' announced Sven, smiling.

'That's nice,' said the bookseller. He appraised them. 'Is it a big one? A golden one?' he asked shyly.

'For us it's a golden one, but not a fifty years *jubilaeum*; in fact it's exactly a year to the day since we decided to be married.'

The older man's answer was certainly unexpected, and the bookseller felt a little embarrassed to have made such a presumption. 'My goodness, I'm impressed,' he stammered.

Karin nodded. 'And the Inverie print's a wedding present for my great-niece, Sophie Lawrence, her mother lives in this cottage here.' She pointed to the print.

'Ah, Lawrence . . . Inverie. Is her mother called Maggie, by any chance?'

'Do you know Maggie?'

'I've – er – had dealings with her. I sent one or two things on to her recently.'

He remembered Niall's letter for Maggie that he'd posted. He couldn't get Niall out of his mind today – not since this morning's phone call. The bookseller remembered the young Katy so well; he'd been working on Iona too, when they first met, and he'd really fancied her. A stroke. It didn't bear thinking about: Katy must only be a couple of years younger than himself.

At last Sven and Karin stood up.

'We'll take these two.' Sven handed over the two prints. 'Could you wrap them separately, please?'

They watched as he worked neatly with paper and sellotape.

'Which is which, now?' asked Karin. 'I've got mixed up already.'

'This one's the Masterton one,' he held it out.

'I'd like just to write which is which so we don't give the wrong one. May I borrow your pen?'

'Of course.'

He watched as Karin firmly and clearly wrote 'Sophie

and Michel' on the brown paper.

'Thank you. Now we'll definitely remember. I have to write down everything that I want to remember these days.' She laughed.

What a charmer, the bookseller thought. A real lovely woman, no matter what age she was.

'And now.' Sven signed the receipt and put his plastic card back into his wallet. 'We have one more question for you. We are looking for a particular place where they sell juice.'

The man mistook his accent. 'Youth?' he grinned. 'The elixir, you mean?'

Sven laughed loudly. 'No, I don't mean that, though I'm sure we could do with some elixir of youth. I meant *juice*,' he pronounced it very slowly and distinctly this time, making sure to emphasise the 'j' and not turn it into a 'y'. 'It's a small café, but we can't remember exactly where it is. When we were here last they were selling freshly made juice, and it was there that we resolved to be married one year ago.'

'You must mean the juice bar. That's just down the road. Go out of the shop and turn right and cross over. On a day like this they've usually got some tables and chairs on the pavement outside.'

'I'm sure that's the one,' said Sven, grinning. 'Come,' he held out his arm to Karin. 'Let's go.'

In Inverie everybody was getting ready for the big arrival. Maggie was outside in the garden picking a bunch of pink and yellow flowers when Sophie and Michel arrived. Michel jumped out and hugged her. 'Hi, Maggie, how are you?' He gave her a loud kiss and stood back to admire her flowers.

'I'm good. Excited about everything – seeing Sven and Karin, and your new person. I'm really glad you thought it OK to come.'

'Sophie was a little worried, but I can get her home quickly if anything starts.'

'Did you speak to the midwife?'

'Yes. She said no problem, just come back immediately if she goes into labour.'

'First babies usually take a good few hours.'

Michel nodded. 'Maybe it is necessary to put the kettle on,' he said seriously.

'Why?'

'Surely you know that you need lots of boiling water when people give birth? Just in case, I mean . . .' He widened his eyes. 'Be prepared, Ma-out-law.'

Sophie came to hug her mother and smelled the flowers. 'Mmm . . . lovely bouquet, Ma. Are they for me?'

Maggie laughed. 'No, they're for Karin.'

'What time'll they be here?'

'Sven just rang. They're in St Andrews doing some shopping. They plan to arrive here mid-afternoon.'

'Great. Can we have lunch soon? I'm starving.'

Michel was rootling in the car boot. He emerged with a big cooking pot and a cloth over his arm like a waiter.

'*Mesdames*, your luncheon awaits. Today we have a special presentation of *bouillabaisse écossaise*.'

'Cullen skink by another name,' said Sophie. 'It's his speciality. I can't stop eating it, it's fantastic.'

'OK. Let's eat.'

'I've ordered my dress,' said Sophie, scoffing soup. 'My pal Lydia's going to make it from patchwork pieces of silk and velvet, mostly tartan with a few cream and white insets in different textures.'

'Remember that you'll probably be breast-feeding.'

'You might be pregnant again, you never know,' said Michel cheerfully.

Sophie thumped him with her spoon. 'No fear. If we have another, you're having it. It's your turn.'

'For you, darling, I'll do anything . . .'

Maggie watched, moved by their obvious delight in each other as they cocked their heads together and sang in tandem, '*I'll do anything for you, dear . . . Anything . . .*' Michel singing falsetto.

They were a joy to behold: Maggie felt happiness surge up inside her. How good life was, how generous. And then the phone rang.

'Inverie 323,' said Maggie.

'May I speak to Maggie Lawrence, please.'

'Speaking.'

'Er ... good afternoon. This is Ian Mackenzie, of St Andrews Rare Books, speaking.'

Maggie was puzzled. 'Yes, what can I do for you?' As she spoke, she watched Michel fondle Sophie's huge tummy and listen to it, smiling.

'I'm a friend of Niall Maclean's, he rang me this morning and asked me to call you.'

Maggie frowned. 'Why?'

'It's about his wife, er ... Katy ...'

Maggie froze. 'What's happened?'

'I'm afraid she had a massive stroke and died last Tuesday night. Niall just felt that perhaps you ought to know. He's pretty distraught. The funeral's in Oban, tomorrow afternoon.'

Sophie, emerging from Michel's embrace, saw her mother's face suddenly blanch and rose up to go to her as Maggie, shaking, put down the phone.

'What is it, Ma?'

Maggie paused. 'It was a friend of Niall's – someone I don't know at all.' She sat down weakly. 'Niall's wife is dead.'

'Katy the Knitter?'

'Yes.' For a wild moment Maggie had an image of Katy in a hideously coloured fairisle bikini, lying in her coffin, staring up accusingly at her.

'God. Out of the blue?'

'No, she had a stroke when he was here last month.'

'Oh, God, yes ... the phone call ... I'm sorry, Ma, I should have remembered to ask.'

'You had enough to think about. I didn't know anyway, not till a day or two ago. I haven't spoken to Niall since he left.'

Michel, his eyes serious, ladled out more soup, and touched her back softly with his other hand.

'I wonder why Niall don't let you know himself?'

Maggie shrugged. 'I dunno. I told him to go, after all. We said our goodbyes. We all do strange things at times like that.'

'How will this affect you, Ma? What about . . .?'

Michel gestured to her not to ask the whole question.

Maggie felt numb. 'Poor Niall. He'll be very shocked.'

'Has he any family?'

'No kids. Brothers and sisters galore.'

She tried to eat the soup she'd asked for, but her oesophagus had gone on strike.

'I can't manage this. I'm sorry.' She pushed away her plate. 'It's absolutely delicious, thanks, Michel.'

'Ouch . . .' Sophie was frowning. 'I think I'm maybe having a contraction.'

'This is the place.' Sven stopped outside the juice bar. 'You sit outside, and I'll go and look.'

'If they still do the one with ginger called an "IQ", I'll have one of those, and a sandwich.'

He went in and came out with a newspaper for Karin. 'Here, while you're waiting.'

'Thanks.' Karin leafed through the paper and read a couple of book reviews, then she closed her eyes and basked in the sun. They'd been travelling from Denmark for three days now, with two days on and off the ferry and a good five hours' drive from Scrabster. She was tired, but it had been worth it. The journey had been spectacular.

Sven came back and sat beside her. 'They all looked so good I couldn't make up my mind. I'm having a "Booster".'

They watched as a young blond man in a T-shirt served their drinks and three vast sandwiches.

'We'll never eat all that,' said Karin. 'They're huge.'

'Speak for yourself,' said Sven. 'I'm extremely hungry. Let's cut them all in half.'

Karin tasted her drink. 'Delicious. Just as I remember it.'

Sven toasted her. 'To us, my love. To another wonderful year. It has been the happiest year I can ever remember.'

She clinked glasses. 'For me too. It has been wonderful. We are so very luck . . .'

He didn't let her say it, but put his finger to his lips and shook his head, smiling in gentle admonition.

'You're right. I won't tempt fate, but it has been fantastic, hasn't it?'

'*Fantastisk.*' He said it in Danish, and they beamed at each other.

In Karin's house, Michel helped Maggie to make up Karin and Sven's bed.

'He must have such problems with his height,' said Michel. 'He's much longer than a normal bed, isn't he?'

Maggie nodded. Between them, they smoothed out the indigo blue duvet.

'That looks great,' said Michel. 'Everything in Karin's house is so good to look at and yet it's all very simple.'

Maggie nodded. 'I've always found her visual sense inspirational.'

They went out of the bedroom. 'Was Sophie resting when you left her just now?' asked Maggie.

'Yes. She said she'd have a little sleep before everyone arrives. She's been having these contractions for several days now – they're called Braxton Hicks. But until they are really severe we mustn't become too alarmed.'

'Been doing your homework, have you?'

'I certainly have. We were taken round the torture chamber last week; they showed us all the forceps and horrible instruments they might have to use. It made me glad she was having the baby at home.'

'I bet it made you glad it wasn't you that was having it?'

'Oh my God, Maggie, I don't want Sophie to suffer. I couldn't bear it.'

'I know, but it's probably good to know the dark side, just in case.'

'I guess so. I'm just scared of seeing her in pain and I suppose to be honest, I'm scared of the whole thing.'

'Everybody is before their first child.'

'Really?'

'Yes, really. I remember looking at the empty Moses basket before Sophie was born and finding it completely surreal that it was up to me to fill it with a baby.'

Michel nodded. 'I'm frightened but I'm also very excited.'

'Cooeee!' A call came from the front door. 'Can we come in?'

'Great! It's Kerstin and Catriona.' Maggie opened the door and there were hugs all round.

'I've brought a quiche,' said Kerstin, 'and Catriona's baked a cake for Mum and Sven.'

'Lovely. We're just about to lay out everything on the table. Put the quiche in the fridge for just now.'

'What lovely flowers – it all looks so festive.'

'It's a party, they'll be so happy to see everybody. They sound in great fettle, don't they?'

There was knocking on the door, shouts of hello, and in came Donnie and Morag – Donnie carrying a cooked salmon. 'Where shall I put this?'

'Here.' Maggie showed him. Her brother had trimmed his moustache and put on his tartan trews for the occasion. It was a wonder he hadn't put on full military regalia, she thought, and tried to hide her smile.

'I've just spoken to Sophie,' said Morag. 'She's just on her way up.'

Sophie arrived, yawning. 'Hi, everybody. Aren't they here yet?'

Donnie looked at his watch. 'No, they're taking their time. They've probably met up with somebody and Karin will be talking non-stop, catching up on the East Neuk gossip.'

'Shall we have a cup of tea while we're waiting?' asked Maggie.

'Good idea.' Morag reached for the kettle.

'Can we start on my cake?' asked Catriona.

'No. Let's keep it for Grandma and Sven.'

'Are you all right, Sophie?' asked Donnie, looking down at his niece, who was frowning, eyes shut.

She waited a moment before looking up at him. 'I think so. It's just every so often, my tummy goes tight.'

'When's it officially due?'

'Last Tuesday.'

'Och, my three were all late,' said Morag.

'So were my two,' said Maggie.

'And mine,' said Kerstin. 'First babies tend to be, but don't worry, Sophie, we'll keep a good eye on you.'

Morag poured tea.

'I wish they'd come,' said Catriona.

'I wish my baby would come as well, it's a week overdue,' moaned Sophie in a little girl's voice and everybody laughed.

'Me too, I'm fed up waiting.' Michel sighed, sipped his tea. 'But Karin and Sven – are they not very late now?'

'They are, but you know Karin, she's never punctual for anything. They could be ages yet. It's so nice, why don't we go outside?' suggested Kerstin, opening the back door.

They all went out to the garden, except for Michel, who stayed to talk to Maggie, who was at the sink.

'Maggie,' he said softly. 'Are you OK?'

'Of course,' she said brightly. 'Why shouldn't I be?'

'I mean . . . the phone call, about Niall's wife. You must feel strange?'

Maggie plugged in the kettle and turned it on. 'To be

honest, Michel, I don't know what I feel. It's too complicated to express simply. Part of me feels utterly detached, that it's simply not my business, yet another part of me is very disturbed indeed.'

'And ... your new man? He – seemed very nice ...'

'He is nice,' snapped Maggie. 'Very nice. So is Niall nice and I actually don't know what I should feel or what I do feel. It's just too complicated. Knowing Niall, he's probably found himself a twenty-five-year-old in the interim.' She shook her head. 'Anyway, that's not what I want to be thinking about, thanks very much. There's more than enough going on here what with your baby about to appear, your wedding to organise and us all waiting for the travellers to return.'

'Now then,' said Sven in the driving seat. 'When do we turn off to the right?'

'At the top of the hill after this next roundabout where you bear left.' Karin sighed happily. 'Oh, it's so good to be back. I love the views from this road, fields and sea – It's beautiful all the way to Inverie.'

'It is, and the weather's so fine. Lucky us. We aren't too late, are we?'

'Only half an hour or so. I don't think we need to phone them again.'

Sven negotiated the roundabout and drove up the hill. 'Is this the turning coming up now?'

Karin checked, looked out to the right. 'Yes, you're OK behind on this side.'

'And OK ahead. We'll be there in fifteen minutes.' Sven patted her leg, and smiled as he indicated and manoeuvred the big Volvo.

As the vehicle completed the right-hand turn Karin screamed. 'No!' and Sven shouted 'Oh my God, what ar ...'

Directly came a screech of brakes, and a huge percussion of metal and glass exploded across the road, followed immediately by a chorus of a hundred tattered crows which errupted violently – jagged and squawking – from the wayside trees.

Then silence.

Chapter Twenty-Four

There was a knock on the door, and Maggie turned to Michel, her eyes shining. 'That'll be them! Go out and tell everybody.'

Out in the garden, the others, sprawled on chairs and grass, were laughing so loudly that they hadn't heard the knock.

Beaming, Maggie opened the door to greet her darling aunt, only to be confronted by a hangdog Gilbert Menstrie.

He was wearing a navy-blue T-shirt with a collar, which, coupled with his new specs, made him for once look almost presentable.

'I'm sorry to disturb you, Maggie, but the police were looking for your aunt's place, so I brought them up here.'

'It's all right, thank you, sir, I'll deal with this.' A very young, fair-haired policeman came forward and looked at Maggie. 'Is this Karin Maitland's house?'

'Yes – only she's Karin Jacobsen now. Why? Where are they?'

'Are you a relative?'

'I'm her niece, but her daughter's here.'

'Can I speak to her, please?'

'Of course. What's the problem?'

The young man coloured. 'I need to speak to a close relative.' He coughed uncomfortably. 'There's been an accident, I'm afraid.'

Ice-cold, Maggie watched her body go through the motion of summoning Kerstin away from the laughter. She was aware of herself, whispering to Kerstin as discreetly as possible that she was wanted outside.

Kerstin was immediately alert. 'What is it?'

'There is a policeman at the door who wants to talk to you.'

'Oh my God.' She took Maggie's arm. 'Come with me, please.'

The policeman was very embarrassed. 'Are you the daughter of a Karin Maitland or . . . Jacobsen?'

'Yes, I am. I'm Dr Kerstin Fairlie. What is it, what's happened?'

'I'm very sorry but I have to inform you that there's been a terrible accident – between a green Volvo with Danish numberplates and a Bedford van.'

'What's happened to them?'

'It was a head-on collision. It must have been instantaneous – I'm afraid that the driver and the passenger of the Volvo were both killed.'

Kerstin gasped. Paralysed, Maggie became aware that Kerstin was gripping her tightly. 'How did you know it was them?' she somehow managed to ask.

'We need somebody to identify the bodies, but we found two passports and one of them had this address on it and the name of the lady . . . who . . . er . . . might be your mother. I'm terribly sorry, I really am.'

Donnie joined them. 'What's going on?'

They told him. Maggie watched in a sort of slow motion as her brother's eyes suddenly spurted almost horizontal tears.

'Oh, hell, no,' he moaned. 'That's too bloody cruel.'

Kerstin gasped, and Donnie held her as they both wept and Maggie and Morag held out their arms to Catriona, who howled like a wild creature at the shocking news, and Sophie and Michel stared in disbelief.

When Donnie and Kerstin had set off for the hospital

morgue, Michel and Sophie tried to comfort the weeping Catriona.

'Maybe they've made a mistake?' she sobbed.

'Maybe, maybe they have,' soothed Michel, and he and Sophie took her by the hand for a walk along the shore, where the three of them sat and stared out to sea trying to understand what had happened.

'I wanted to show her the pottery things I've been making,' wailed Catriona suddenly. 'I made a bowl specially for her – and the cake . . .'

'I wanted her to be here when our baby is born,' sobbed Sophie.

'Maybe she'll be there. Maybe she's watching us now,' said Michel quietly. 'She was a truly fantastic lady. Beautiful, kind, unusual. And she was brave enough to love and marry at that crazy age when most people are past any sort of real living. In a way it's wonderful that neither of them will ever have to watch the other grow really old or become invalids and die. They've bypassed that misery.'

'But we're miserable and we wish they were still here,' protested Catriona.

'They're still here in our love and our memories,' Michel soothed. 'And in you, Catriona. A whole quarter part of you has been created from Karin's genes, just think of that privilege. You're very lucky to be her granddaughter.'

'But I want her here! I don't want her to be dead!' shouted Catriona and Sophie, agonised, rocked her like a baby.

Back at Karin's house, Maggie and Morag clung to each other, remembering the times they'd spent with Karin – the arguments, the fun, the picnics and holidays.

'At least they had that wonderful final love flight. They really did love each other, those two, as passionately as younger people do,' said Morag.

Maggie couldn't speak, and Morag hugged her.

'Karin was the last of our old ones,' said Maggie at last,

when they were both calmer. 'It's us for the front line now.'

Donnie and Kerstin came back after a couple of hours. Donnie's expression was grim and Kerstin's face very pale.

'What happened?' asked Michel.

'They obviously hadn't a chance,' said Donnie tersely, his arm round Kerstin's shoulder. 'It was a head-on collision like they said, at the turn-off before Boarhills. They were hit by a van full of American tourists driving on the wrong side of the road.

Kerstin handed Sophie a flat package. 'This is for you two. It was in the boot, it's got your names on it. I think you should open it.'

Sophie unwrapped it and found the etching of Inverie with the rocks, the sea and the church and her mother's cottage.

'It's beautiful,' murmured Michel, choked. 'Do you think it was a wedding present?'

Kerstin nodded. 'I'm sure it was. Are you OK, Sophie?'

Sophie, abstracted, frowned, muttered. 'Only just. It's beginning to feel quite sore.'

'These were lying unharmed in the boot,' said Donnie and showed them two bottles of red wine. He smiled sadly. 'Crozes Hermitages, a very good vintage. Sven did like his wine.'

Maggie wiped her eyes. 'So did Karin, very much.'

Somehow the evening came. Kerstin made phone calls to tell her brother and sister the news and her husband Graham arrived a couple of hours later with a red-eyed Callum, who'd grown tall in the last year and now had a deep bass voice. They ate the food they'd prepared for the welcome party. They even laughed, and at Donnie's suggestion, they opened and drank the good red wine.

At one point, Catriona, quiet on the sofa, looked up at her mother and asked. 'How is it that we can laugh when we're so sad?'

'It's life, and even in the middle of death we have life

and feel a need to celebrate being alive,' said her mother, hugging her. Then she looked at Sophie, who was obviously not comfortable.

'Michel,' she asked. 'How many hours does it take to fill that birthing pool of yours?'

He shrugged. 'About four hours till it's really full.'

Kerstin nodded, her eyes serious. 'Well, if you'd like my professional opinion, I think you'd better ask a neighbour to turn on that tap and get Sophie home as soon as possible.'

Chapter Twenty-Five

Andy frowned at the telephone; once again it was just ringing and ringing. It was odd. He presumed that Maggie must have listened to his messages but she still hadn't got back to him. Maybe she was up at her aunt's house or had gone over to see Michel and Sophie – he knew that the baby was due soon. He tried her mobile, but it was turned off, which was also strange; he was fed up that he couldn't even leave her a message.

The dog pawed his leg.

'What is it, Dougie? You want a walk, son? Of course you do; maybe we'll just take a wee dander over to Inverie and find out what's going on.'

In Inverie, in Karin's house, the shocked family was still trying to come to terms with what had happened. Maggie and Kerstin were in the kitchen making hot drinks for everybody when Kerstin suddenly froze, a mug of hot tea in either hand.

'My God,' she said. 'Patrick. We'll have to tell him. We'll have to tell him tonight. He's expecting to come here for lunch tomorrow.'

'Of course. I'd completely forgotten about him. He'll be shattered; we'd better phone William and tell him too.'

'I'd phone him . . .' said Kerstin, then she paused. 'But we can't just phone Patrick . . .'

'I'll do it,' said Maggie. 'You need to be here with the kids. It won't take more than half an hour; I'll take my mobile in case there's news from Sophie and Michel.'

She was shaking as she drove to Elie; her throat and chest felt congested with grief and when she imagined telling Patrick the news she imagined herself his executioner.

Patrick had obviously been resting when he came at last to answer the door. His face was creased from sleep and he walked slowly with a walking stick. He beamed with delight when he saw it was her.

'Maggie, my dear, what a delightful surprise. Come in, come in, I was just about to have a dram, I hope you'll join me.'

'I . . . I have something awful to tell you, Patrick . . .' she stammered.

He had turned from her and was shuffling towards a large sideboard.

'Here now, my dear.' He pointed to a bottle. 'If you'd be kind enough to bring that through with a couple of those glasses, we'll go and sit out there.'

Obediently, Maggie carried the bottle and glasses and followed him out to the conservatory, which overlooked the garden and the big sandy bay. It was starting to grow dark, and there was sublime sunset which made everything glow slightly orange.

'There we are.' Patrick eased himself into a large wooden armchair and sighed with relief. 'Now my dear, if you will be mother, we can relax.'

Biting her lip, Maggie filled both glasses and handed him one.

He smiled and sipped blissfully. 'Thank you. That's what we both need by the look of you. *Slainte*. Are you all right, Maggie? You are terribly pale.'

'Patrick. I've got some terrible news to tell you.'

He looked concerned. 'Not Sophie surely? Is the baby all right?'

'Sophie's fine, she went home because she seemed to be starting labour, it's not her. It's Karin.'

He stiffened, looked at her piercingly. 'What?'

'She . . . and Sven . . . it . . . they have both been killed in a car crash.'

'Oh my Lord. When?'

'This afternoon, they were on their way out to Inverie. It was instantaneous.'

He sat as though paralysed for almost a minute. 'I . . . I was expecting to see them tomorrow. Oh my Lord.'

Maggie felt as though she had shot him. She put her hand out to his and he allowed her to grip it for a while, then he looked up and reached for his whisky and emptied the glass.

'No wonder you were looking pale. Give us a refill, there's a good lass.'

She reached for the bottle and poured another two fingers of whisky which he took and sipped thoughtfully, shaking his head.

'Death always takes you by surprise, even when people are obviously dying or ancient like myself. It's always a shock, the sudden silence, the cutting of so many ties of love and friendship.'

Maggie nodded. He seemed to be taking it very well so far, but then she saw that he was crying.

'She was such a fine woman.' He took out a huge hanky and wiped his eyes, then he looked at Maggie.

'I was madly in love with her you know, for years.' He smiled bleakly.

'I know you were, and she loved you too, for a long time.'

'I believe she did, but sadly, not for long enough.'

'Patrick, can I get you anything, phone anyone for you?'

'No, my dear, I expect you'll need to get back home and be on the qui vive for Sophie. The giving and the taking of life, eh? All at more or less the same time. It can be very confusing.' He smiled properly now and pointed to the sunset, which was fiercely dramatic. 'Look at that; sometimes you'd think nature was commenting on our tiny lives. Isn't that splendid?'

It was beautiful. They watched the changing colours and fading light in silence. Then Maggie stood up to go, and as she turned, she noticed half a dozen earthenware flowerpots, each one with a delicate spidery leaved plant growing in it.

'Patrick . . . are these what I think they are?'

He nodded benignly, 'Just a little horticultural experiment, to see if *ganja* can grow in the East Neuk. They're doing rather well, don't you think?'

She nodded. 'Very well, but don't invite the local policeman in for a cup of tea or we'll be visiting you in Barlinnie.'

She bent to embrace the old man and said she would let herself out.

Alone, Patrick sat for a while and finished his whisky, then he stood up and took his walking stick, turned it upside-down and whacked the handle violently across his chair, shouting a wordless curse as he did. Surprisingly, the stick didn't break. Glaring, Patrick looked at it and laid it down on the table with the handle near him, then he slumped back into his chair and started to weep, with terrible, tearing groans which were heard by nobody but a couple of late-flying seagulls.

Sophie, naked, was lying back immersed in the huge blue bath. 'I keep thinking about Karin,' she sobbed.

Michel, in the pool behind her, held her to him. 'I bet you Karin is somewhere watching, cheering you on.'

'Oohh . . . Here's another one . . . Aaaaah . . .' her face closed up, tight with concentration as she breathed deeply, trying to ride the pain. 'Can you do my back again, please?' she gasped at last.

'Sure.' Obediently, Michel rubbed in a soft butterfly motion over her sacrum.

Sophie was tired, panting a little. 'Michel, maybe you should phone Ma.'

'You want her to come? It's two in the morning.'

'Leave her . . . ouch . . . aahh . . . Here's another one . . .' She breathed again, slow pantings. Then, breathless, 'Yes. Just leave her a message if there's no answer. I'd like her to be here soon.'

'You're doing great, Sophie,' the midwife, black and plump, knelt beside her. 'Can I just have a wee listen, please?'

'Sure.'

The midwife listened and smiled. 'That's fine. Your baby's doing away OK. It'll not be long now.'

'It seems awfully long,' complained Sophie, 'and you say I'm only half-dilated.'

'I know it seems long, but it's all quite normal for a first baby; don't worry, it really will soon be over. You'll have a baby some time this morning.'

Maggie, her throat raw from weeping and talking, after seeing Patrick, helping Karin's daughter to phone relatives in Denmark and the UK, comforting, bewailing, and trying somehow to realise the full implications of the double tragedy, had only just got off to sleep when she heard Michel's voice on the answerphone. She almost fell out of bed in her hurry to pick up the receiver.

'Hello? Any news?'

'Well . . . she's definitely having a baby.'

'Is she properly in labour – it's not a false start, is it?'

'No. It's for real. Her waters broke as soon as we got home.'

'How is it?

'Hard work. The midwife says everything's normal but it's obviously very sore. She's asking for you, Maggie. Will you come?'

'Of course.'

'Are you OK?' His voice was concerned.

'What do you mean am I OK? You're the father-to-be. Are you OK?'

'No, I mean all this life and so much death in one day business. It's too much to bear, to understand. Sophie keeps crying for Karin. I don't know how to comfort her.'

'I know, dearie, but thank goodness they both went at the same time. Imagine if . . .'

'Michel!' Maggie could hear her daughter's yell.

'Bye, Michel. I'll see you as soon as I can.' Maggie reached for her clothes.

The dawn chorus had started, and Michel, bare-chested and bare-footed, was clad in shorts when he opened the door. He led Maggie into the sitting-room, which was dominated by the vast birthing pool. Sophie, naked, huge, was on all fours like a dog, on a sheet stretched out on the floor, attended to by a midwife wearing green.

'Hi, Ma,' muttered Sophie between pants.

'This is all very *ER* . . .' muttered Maggie feebly, eyeing the sangria-coloured water of the obviously well-used aqua blue bath.

Michel went over to Sophie, who sat up exhausted and leaned back against him to rest. They looked fantastically beautiful entwined together, pale, sculptural.

The midwife nodded to Maggie as Maggie slid into a chair, clutching her camera.

'You're eight centimetres, you're doing just fine,' the midwife told Sophie after peering at her and measuring intently.

Michel and Sophie had asked if Maggie would photograph the birth and she'd just opened up the camera case and adjusted the lens when all hell broke loose.

Sophie was pushing, yelling, panting, the midwife was saying 'OK now, push, push, good girl, that's it . . . PUSH!'

A pause followed the push, and Sophie, her face damp, eyes shut, lay back looking half-dead, with Michel, anxious, soothing her, giving her sips of water, softly pulling back her hair.

Then, a minute later, she pushed and yelled and pushed harder and shouted louder, and they all shouted.

'Yes! We can see the baby's head, yes, gently now. OK, push, yes, good girl, well done, Sophie! Big, big push!'

There was quite a lot of blood coming from her daughter, the neutral artist observer part of Maggie noticed as she clicked the shutter. And yelling.

'Yes, you can, you can do it!' they shouted, and yes, she did and could and Maggie took pictures like an automaton and Michel shouted with excitement and the midwife encouraged and pushed and gentled and pulled and helped and eased, and suddenly, amazingly, out slithered a scarlet baby with a huge blue corkscrew of an umbilicus and the baby opened its newborn mouth wide and proclaimed to the world that he'd arrived and they all gasped and shouted with joy and saw that it was a BOY!

Maggie could hardly see, she was so moved, but kept on taking pictures till she had to change the film.

The midwife, neat and efficient, praised, showed Michel how to cut the cord and tidied up the new mother and her baby, wiping with white cotton, smoothing, soothing. Then she lifted the baby and wrapped him in a white shawl and handed him to Sophie, who showed him to Michel then put him to her breast which he nuzzled and latched on to almost at once, and the pair of them gazed in wonder, anointing him with their mingled tears.

'He's beautiful,' Michel stammered. 'He looks so tranquil but tough too, really strong.'

After a while, the midwife said that she needed to measure and weigh the child and they watched as she did.

'Eight pounds six – a really good size, and twenty-two inches long. He's going to be a big, tall boy. He's lovely. Perfect, well done, Sophie.'

'I'm so thirsty,' said Sophie, lying back, relieved, pale and huge-eyed. 'Please can I have a cup of tea?'

'I'll make it,' Maggie got up and made a pot and served everybody.

The little boy had been dressed now by the midwife in spotless white garments and a tiny, white pixie hat. Michel was holding him, staring down at his face, smiling, shaking his head in amazement. Then he looked up at Maggie.

'This is a present for you to share with us, *Grand'mère*. Would you like an armful?' And carefully, lovingly, he laid his newborn son in her arms.

'This is your Maggie,' he told the child. 'And I know that you are going to love her very much.' And he kissed the baby's nose, and hugged Maggie and went to hold his wife-to-be and they all cried and drank their tea.

It was the strangest month of her life, Maggie often thought afterwards, when it was all over. There was the news of Niall's wife, followed almost instantly by the awful accident, then the drama of the birth and the double funeral of Karin and Sven, culminating – in what seemed like moments – in Michel and Sophie's wedding. And through it all her budding relationship with Andy, which had very little space in the tangle of events. Everything happened one on top of the other, and they were all such big dramas that there never seemed to be enough time to catch up, or to digest what she was feeling about any one of the incidents.

Karin's and Sven's funerals were held together in a crematorium in Kirkcaldy, where a woman minister not known to any of them – tall and thin, with piercing blue eyes and granny specs – gave a surprisingly articulate and moving service. She described the double death as being like Icarus's marvellous flight towards the sun, which had ended so unexpectedly with his fall into oblivion.

'But these two made their inspirational flight,' the

woman said in a clear, strong voice. 'And they knew happiness together and had the courage to take the immensely brave step of marrying and committing to each other, even at their great ages and even when it entailed, for one of them, leaving behind so many of her family and the friends whom she loved and who so deeply loved her. Let us be joyful for the two of them, for the great happiness that they shared, for the examples of love and courage they showed to us and for the fact that they were fortunate enough to have ended their lives at the very same moment, heartbreaking though that moment has proved to be for those who survive.'

Twenty-two of Sven's family members came over for the funeral. They were all ages, many of them tall like Sven. After the service, Maggie spoke to his eldest son, who looked very like him, and was if anything a centimetre or two taller than his father.

'We have been talking,' he said, 'about the two pots of ashes. We are not happy to separate the two of them now. Kerstin and her brother and sister have suggested that we bring them to Inverie if we may, and spread them on the outgoing tide near a big rock . . . she told me the name, but I don't remember it.'

'Partan Rock,' said Maggie. 'It means Crab Rock. Yes, that's a fine idea. I can tell you from my diary when the high tide comes in the next day or so.'

'We discussed taking them both back to Denmark and putting the ashes into the sea at Skaagen.'

'The place where the two seas collide?' asked Maggie. 'Sven told us about that.'

'The Baltic and the North sea,' Sven's son nodded. 'My mother's ashes were thrown into the sea there,' he smiled sadly. 'But we thought it was perhaps better that Sven's and Karin's ashes were put together into the Scottish sea, so near where they fell in love, and where they died.'

Maggie nodded. 'It sounds like a good plan. I don't

think they did anything with my uncle's – Karin's first husband's – ashes,' she explained. 'Nor did we with my parents – they were just cremated and that was it. Very unimaginative.'

Chapter Twenty-Six

After the ashes had been strewn on the waters, watched by a small group of relatives, several cormorants, seagulls and a lone shag, the Scottish contingent said goodbye to the Scandinavians, and in what seemed like a blink came the wedding. The sun shone for the first time in weeks ('Lucky ye've got a window in the weather,' said Maggie's neighbour, Wilma) and relatives and friends came from France, Australia, London, Denmark and Scotland.

Sophie's brother Mark arrived home two days before the wedding. He'd grown tall and strong and spoke loudly, like a real Australian. Maggie was amazed by her new son, who'd been a gentler, shyer soul before his trip to the Antipodes. He'd even been at last to visit his Uncle Alistair, whom nobody had seen for over forty years.

'What's he like?' asked Maggie, remembering her big brother's red hair, broken specs, and always manic energy.

'He's great, eccentric, hairy. Look.' Mark pulled out a stack of photographs, and Maggie and Donnie, amazed, saw a tall old man, with a huge straggly red beard, grinning shyly out at them. His face was battered, but it was undeniably Alistair.

'He's a sweet, funny guy,' said Mark. '"Happy as a pig in shit", he kept telling me. He stopped drinking twelve years ago when he heard Grandma was dying, but nowadays he grows – and smokes – lots of dope.'

Just like his Uncle Patrick, thought Maggie with a half-smile. 'We did invite him to the wedding,' she said. 'I'd have loved him to come.'

'He did think about it, but he hardly ever leaves his place. It's a sort of paradise, really. He lives in an old, rusty Dormobile that's embedded in the earth in the middle of the bush, and there are wallabies, goannas and turkeys all round.'

Maggie gazed, fascinated, at the pictures. 'What does he do all day?'

'He listens to his Walkman a lot – Mozart and Bach mostly – and he plays chess to championship level with his computer. He seems really happy in his own hermit-like way.'

'Does he still play the accordian?'

'A little bit. Occasionally he has sing-songs with his neighbours and sings the filthiest version of "The Ball of Kirriemuir" I've ever heard.'

'He used to sing that in the garden here and infuriate Gilbert Menstrie and his mother. They once even called the police.'

'So much for the best Scottish public schooling,' Mark grinned and looked quizzically at his uncle, and Donnie groaned. 'Yes, it was meant to be the best, but poor old Alistair never really fitted in. He always wanted to escape and refused to become part of that class system. He was nearly expelled more than once.'

'Well, I'm glad he still plays the accordian,' said Maggie.

'He sent you this,' said Mark, and handed over a small, flat parcel.

It was an Aboriginal image of two creatures; one was a fish of sorts and the other looked like a crab; they were painted on bark, not touristy, a real artist's image.

'It's absolutely beautiful,' said Maggie, much moved. 'I love it.'

'It was painted by an alcoholic Aboriginal friend of his,

who died young. Alistair found it on the local dump after the man died, and saved it. He thought you'd like it because he remembered that you always loved to draw and paint.'

Michel, kilted, and fantastically handsome, wept all the way through the wedding service - huge tears which plopped on to his shirt - dappling the dark green fabric - which fastened at the neck with criss-cross leather thonging. When planning the wedding Sophie had found it hard to decide as to whether her mother, William or Donnie should give her away. In the end she had chosen her Uncle Donnie when he promised to wear his most exotic military regalia for her - the full dress kit, with kilt, scarlet jacket, silver buttons, white spats and epaulettes. Sophie looked delicious in a patchwork of tartan satins and silks, and carried a bouquet of lilies and pink roses, and Donnie looked proud and magnificent and even waxed his moustache for the occasion. (Very high camp, his sister thought privately.)

Maggie and Michel's mother - petite and very giggly - decorated the church with enormous bouquets of red poppies and cow parsley. Donnie had made up a dish of pickled herring and donated a couple of salmon he'd caught and cooked, and six-week-old Alistair (who'd been named not in honour of Maggie's and Donnie's brother, but simply because his parents liked the name) behaved impeccably and neither soiled himself nor wept during the actual ceremony.

The musical friends played violin and cello and one of them played a trumpet, and afterwards, a tall, sensitive-looking young man, a Breton piper, who doubled later as a hilarious best man, led the wedding procession out of the church into the sunshine. Later, in Donnie and Morag's garden, where the guests were entranced by the glittering sea and the wheeling gulls, Maggie gave a speech: 'It was only a few feet from where she's standing now, that today's bride - aged three - came to me with something clutched tightly in her hand, and asked with great seriousness, "Can you kiss worms?"'

One of the older French aunts had near-hysterics at this, but at last Maggie was able to continue: 'And I told her yes, you could, but suggested that perhaps she might find other things that were nicer to kiss . . .' She paused, enjoying the laughter, then came the serious bit.

'Many of you here will remember Fergal, Sophie's father. Strangely, today would have been his sixtieth birthday, and as a family we know how much he would have liked to be here to celebrate with us this continuation and affirmation of life. We all miss him terribly – as we do my mother, whose garden this once was – and Sophie's Great-aunt Karin, and her husband, Sven, who died so recently and so tragically.'

At the end of her speech, Maggie raised her glass. 'To Michel and Sophie – and young Alistair: let's wish them my Aunt Karin's favourite blessing – Love, Luck and Laughter – may they have lots of all three.'

William, distinguished in a pale brown linen suit, also gave a speech, describing to a rapt audience how he'd known the bride since she was born, and had once found her – when she'd gone missing for over an hour, aged four – sitting concentrating in a hen-house, 'laying an egg for Mummy's tea', which led him to declare how exceedingly relieved and pleased he was that the baby Alistair had not in the end turned out to be a flamingo as many of those present had feared he might.

Patrick was present, sad but benign, enjoying the champagne, and much cossetted by family and friends. (Jennifer Earlsferry was not on the guest list.) Later, when she recollected the whole proceedings, Maggie surprised herself by declaring it to be one of the happiest days of her life – despite everything.

A week after the wedding, almost everybody had disappeared. The bridal pair and offspring had departed for a breast-feeding honeymoon in Provence, and the guests had all gone home, except for Maggie's London friend, Felicity, who was staying on for another couple of days before starting rehearsals for a new play.

Felicity was an early riser. 'There's a letter from France for you,' she called, and Maggie, coming down to breakfast, thinking it too early to hear from the honeymooners, froze when she saw that the letter was from Niall.

Felicity, making coffee, peered at her. 'Are you all right, Maggie? You've suddenly gone completely white.'

Maggie nodded. Opened the letter, and read it in silence, watched quizzically by her friend.

> *Maggie, my beloved,* Maggie imagined Niall's voice as she read.
>
> *I heard the terrible news of your aunt's (and her new husband's) accident from my contact in St Andrews – and the good news Sophie and Michel's wedding – and I saw the birth announcement in a* Scotsman *sent by a friend. I felt so sorry and then almost immediately so glad for you, that I felt compelled to write.*
>
> *I am living for the moment near Cahors in the Lot, with my brother and wife, helping them to do up an old farmhouse. I felt very strange to suddenly be on my own – for even though I had often wished that I wasn't with Katy, her death was a terrible shock. It has made me realise how complicated we are, with our needs, and our desires, which so often seem to conflict.*
>
> *I'm working hard here, digging, heaving, sawing. I haven't quite got a six-pack, but the belly is shrinking and I am feeling well physically. I think of you constantly, wondering how you are, and how you have survived all the conflicting emotions of the last couple of months. And of course I wonder if you are attached, and have at last found that somebody I know you long for – and need.*

I am now a single man again, truly unattached. Shocked to be so, and I sometimes feel quite desolate at the thought of a life alone.

I know that I made an absolute idiot of myself last time we met, but I wonder if you might have it in you to tell me how you are, if only for old times' sake.

I would love you to come down here and stay here for a while. It is a most lovely place, with a river to swim in and very good local markets. My brother and wife will be away for most of September and I plan to stay on by myself, doing a bit of work on the house when I feel so inclined, and I'll probably spend the winter here.

I wish I could hug you, to tell you how sad I am about your aunt, and how glad to hear that you have a grandson, and to tell you how often I think of you.

Am I allowed to say that I miss you? That I hope for my sake that you are not attached, and that you might come down here to spend some time with me. We both have the rest of our lives ahead of us and maybe we could spend them, or some of them, together.

Please answer me soon. Write or phone.

My love. Niall XX

PS: I gave away the dog to Katy's sister.

'Are you all right?'

Maggie blinked. Felicity was peering at her.

'Sort of.' She nodded. 'I don't really want to talk about it right now.'

Later, she took Felicity to the London train, and as they waited on the platform Felicity had a farewell cigarette and eyed her friend thoughtfully.

'That was so lovely. Are you going to be OK with everybody gone away?'

'I'll be fine. I'll see you soon, anyway.'

'Will you?' Felicity looked dubious. 'I rather get the feeling that we've lost you to your homeland.'

‘I’ll have to come south to sort out the house, one way or another, I’m definitely going to sell it.’

‘Humph. It certainly doesn’t sound like you’re coming back south for good.’

Maggie shrugged. ‘I don’t know. I really don’t know, too much has happened too quickly.’ She was blushing.

Felicity looked keenly at her, blew meditative smoke rings. ‘Why, I do believe you’ve maybe found yourself a lover, honey chile,’ she drawled.

Maggie tried to look non-committal.

‘You have, haven’t you? Is it the leather-jacketed one?’

‘No!’ Maggie yelped, and shook her head violently, giggling as she remembered Monologuing Murdo and his Asphyxiating After-shave.

Felicity obviously wasn’t going to let go. ‘Or is it still that same old married one? I always liked the sound of him.’

Maggie frowned. ‘Well, actually, the letter that came this morning was from Niall.’

‘The married man?’ Felicity persisted. ‘The one who used to bark like a dog?’

Maggie laughed. ‘Yes and no.’

Felicity was puzzled. ‘What do you mean?’

‘Yes, he did bark like a dog, and no, he’s not married any more.’

‘Is he divorced?’

‘His wife died.’

‘Oh. My goodness, that could change things, couldn’t it?’

Maggie shrugged. ‘I don’t know. His wife only died a few weeks ago.’

‘Did she now? You didn’t tell me. And . . .?’ Felicity’s actress eyes were large with questions.

‘And nothing. I knew she’d died, but didn’t know how or where he was until this morning. Anyway, I’d already sent him packing.’

‘Oh, kitten, what a shame . . . what a waste. He was rather good news, wasn’t he?’

'He's gone to France for the winter.'

Felicity chuckled. 'Everybody seems to have gone to France.'

Or to have died, thought Maggie. She looked up. 'Here's your train. It's only twelve minutes late; that must be a record.'

Felicity threw away her cigarette, climbed into her carriage and spoke through the open window. 'But . . . I rather think there's more going on. There is, isn't there? I can tell.'

Maggie tried not to smile. 'Maybe.'

'Well, I hope whatever it is doesn't keep you up here. We need you down there . . . oops . . . we're off. Goodbye! Thanks so much, it was fantastic. A wonderful wedding! But remember my vote's with the barker! Go to France and see him – you must! You owe it to yourself.'

Maggie waved till her friend was out of sight, and walked slowly up and over the railway steps to where her car was parked.

Back in Inverie, she cleaned the strangely empty house and put on a load of washing. In the afternoon, she decided to go for a walk along the beach. She hadn't climbed her big exercise rock for ages, so she put on her purple shorts (which seemed somehow to have shrunk), and did so enthusiastically, enjoying using her body.

Later, she wandered along the rocky foreshore, pensive. She still often thought tearfully of Karin, but only minutes later she'd find herself smiling as she remembered the beautiful new child.

'I'm a grandmother,' she told herself, amazed.

A couple of hours later, weary, as she lay on the warm shingle, her head on a boulder, soothed by the sunshine and the surge of the sea, she reread Niall's letter intently. After a while, her eyes thoughtful, she put it away in her bag. She was almost asleep when she felt the coolness of a shadow falling across her.

'Hi, there. I had a funny feeling I might find you here.'

It was Andy. He looked a little shy, but Maggie felt quite pleased to see him, even though he was wearing her least favourite blue sports shirt. They hadn't met for almost three weeks.

'Am I disturbing you?'

'No.' Maggie sat up. 'It's a lovely surprise. Sit beside me. I was having my first quiet moment in ages. It's just strange with everything finished and everyone gone home. After weeks of being adrenalised, suddenly I don't know what to do with myself.'

'Not quite everybody has gone,' said Andy, sitting down beside her. 'We're still here.'

He turned to her. 'I was wondering if you'd like some wine?'

Maggie grinned. 'What? Have you got some with you?'

'It just so happens that I have.' From a small rucksack, Andy produced two glasses and a bottle of claret which he proceeded to open.

'How excellent.'

'I just thought you might fancy a wee drink. You've had quite a dramatic time, haven't you?'

'I'm sorry I've hardly seen you.'

'It's OK. We've spoken once or twice. I know you've been totally preoccupied with family happenings, but I've been missing you – and I must confess, your body. Anyway, how was the wedding?'

'Exhausting, satisfying. Marvellous.'

He sat down beside her and poured two brimming glasses of burgundy and handed her one. 'Did you find any stars in your stones today?'

Maggie savoured the wine. 'Mmmmh . . . perfect. I'm not sure – Maybe . . .' she murmured.

'Where? I thought this wasn't a good beach for fossils.'

'Right here, perhaps – but I don't really know yet . . .' She looked at him and sipped her wine, smiling enigmatically.

Andy grinned. 'Well, at least I'm not three hundred

million years old, not yet anyway, you daft besom *slainte*.'

They sat together amicably, watching the incoming tide, and chuckled at Dougie, who was barking at the waves, running in and out of the water.

'How is it to be a granny, by the way?' asked Andy after a while.

Maggie smiled. 'Just as you said it would be – like winning the lottery and you never knew you had a ticket. Anyway, how did you know to find me here? It's not a beach I usually hunt on.'

'Alison – Gilbert Menstrie's new woman – told me. She seems to be well installed, watching from the kitchen window just like old Effie used to, even down to using the car mirror to see who's coming down the road. She knew exactly where you were.'

He refilled her glass. 'I'm glad you were here, by the way,' he said quietly. 'I've been thinking about you a lot. Wondering what's what.'

'How d'you mean?'

'Well. Your London place, the tenants; I know they're due to leave. Have you decided what you're going to do? You've had your year in the East Neuk. Are you going to go back south and take up your London life again, or what?' He looked at her intently. 'I confess I'm anxious to know.'

Maggie drained her glass. 'No, I'm not. I'm going to sell up and stay here. I want to be near my grandson.'

'And is that the only reason?' asked Andy after an almost palpable silence.

Maggie frowned as she thought about it, aware of his yearning for her answer to at least include him.

'No,' she said at last, and smiled up at him quizzically. 'It's not. There are lots of reasons.'

'Ah, well,' said Andy. 'I have to say I'm relieved that you've decided to stay.' He took a good hold of her hand. It felt warm and friendly, and almost without thinking she gripped him back.

‘Now.’ He looked at her searchingly. ‘I have a proposal for you.’

‘What?’ Surely he wasn’t suddenly going to get heavy?’ Maggie suddenly felt extremely anxious.

‘Don’t look so worried,’ Andy smiled. ‘It’s only a proposal for tonight.’

She still felt uneasy, chilly even. ‘And what might that be?’ she asked nervously.

‘Well, how about some fish and chips and a night in, in Inverie or Pittenweem, whichever you prefer? How does that grab you?’

She smiled in relief. ‘That sounds really good to me.’

‘We can just take it a day at a time, Maggie.’

She paused. ‘I don’t understand . . .’

‘I think you do.’ He let go of her hand and looked at her. ‘What I mean is we can just spend time together sometimes, till we see how we feel. It’s early days . . . I know we don’t really know each other properly yet. There’s no need to rush things.’

‘OK.’ she nodded. ‘I’ve got to go down to London soon to clear out the house and put it on the market. My tenants leave next week, that’ll take me a wee while.’

‘Would you like me to come down and help?’

It was hard to imagine Andy transplanted to London. Somehow he didn’t fit – although she knew he’d be extremely useful.

She paused, swirling with ambivalence. ‘Can I think about it? It’s a very kind offer.’

‘Sure.’ Andy showed the palms of his hands like a man saying *pax*.

‘And then I have to go to France . . .’ She was truly surprised to hear herself saying it. She took a deep breath. ‘For at least a couple of weeks . . . I’ve got some unfinished business to attend to.’

Andy frowned, then he stood up and held out his hand to help her to her feet. Still frowning, he very deliberately put the cork back in the wine bottle and gazed at it for a long moment before stashing it away in his bag. Then he looked at her with great seriousness.

'I expect that I'll still be here waiting for you, Maggie,' he said. 'But just remember that I can't wait for ever.'

She sighed and nodded solemnly. 'I understand,' she said quietly and their eyes locked.

'OK, then . . .' He took her arm. 'Let's at least enjoy today. I don't know about you, but I'm starving. Shall we make a move and go and get those fish and chips?'

And as they walked towards the village together, Maggie, who suddenly felt an overwhelming surge of optimism and excitement at the thought of meeting with Niall in France, wondered how on earth she was going to tell this dear, decent man, that she wanted to sleep alone in her own bed tonight.